The Penguin Book of Comics

A slight history devised by George Perry and Alan Aldridge

Penguin Books

Penguin Books Ltd, Harmondsworth, Middlesex, England
Penguin Books Inc., 3300 Clipper Mill Road, Baltimore, Md 21211, U.S.A.
Penguin Books Australia Ltd, Ringwood, Victoria, Australia

First published 1967

Made and printed in Great Britain by
Jarrold & Sons Ltd, Norwich
Set in Monotype Times

Contents

The Comics -What can they give us?

The Comics – What Can They Give Us? *Pictures as communication – the Bayeux tapestry – Hogarth – the comic strip, its form, its conventions, its style – who reads them – the strips as a mirror of our times, as entertainment, as a form of narrative art – the vision of Rodolphe Töpffer – use of the imagination.*

We think in pictures; we dream in pictures. A child can recognize and interpret a visual image long before he has reached the stage where he can learn to read. Prehistoric man could draw several millennia before he could write. Vision ignores the barriers of language; a picture needs no translator's explanation to Eskimoes or Swahilis.

In this present age of intense visual communication, when the television screen dominates broadcasting and the Nikon 35-mm camera rules the picture-magazine pages, there is a tendency to think of the conjunction of illustration and the printed word as a fairly recent phenomenon. Such an impression appears to be confirmed by a search through the old files of some English newspapers. Before the invention of the half-tone block, and in many cases long after, the pages seem to present a grey acreage of arid type, unrelieved by any graphic design. Until recent years it was the policy of a number of 'quality' newspapers to publish editorial pictures very rarely, such vulgarities being left to the advertisers and the gutter journals. Such was the hangover of a Victorian tradition of literacy which decreed pictures to be unrespectable – a form of neo-Puritanism. Pictures were too easy. They did not demand the same intellectual effort as words to make their communication. They encouraged mental laziness which could in time lead to more serious moral collapse. With their passion for compartmentalizing, the middle-class Victorians let the *Illustrated London News* take care of the week's news pictures and *Punch* the humorous ones.

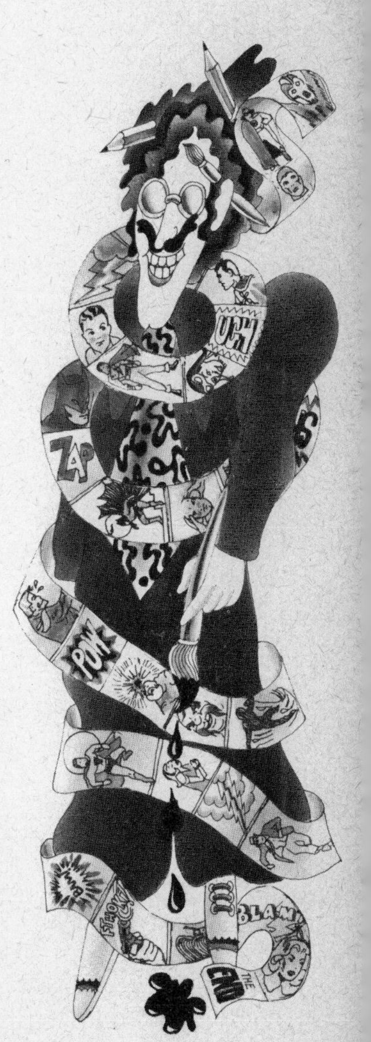

Yet graphic illustration has a long history. The earliest known images created by man, scrawled in Palaeolithic times on the walls of caves in the Dordogne, show in the fluid force of their line an awareness, in simple, stylized drawing, of the power to communicate a religious or a magical idea. A dead Egyptian was not properly equipped for his passage to the after-life without an elaborate scroll depicting the supposed perils of his journey being placed in the tomb alongside his body. As decoration, illustration has been an element of design throughout all mankind's civilizations. The exploits of Hercules would be shown on Greek artefacts and the Romans honoured their heroes by raising arches and columns adorned with episodes from their military careers. The Middle Ages did the same for the Battle of Hastings with the Bayeux tapestry, a remarkable narrative in comic-strip form, made centuries before the *genre* had been properly invented.

The great watershed of cartoon and caricature, which was to lead in time to the modern comic, occurred in the eighteenth century, the age of Hogarth and, later, Thomas Rowlandson. William Hogarth brought the novel, a new literary form then rampant in England, and the theatre together in painting. His great satires, painted in series – 'A Harlot's Progress', 'Marriage à la Mode', 'A Rake's Progress', 'Industry and Idleness' – founded the narrative sequence style in art. Engravings of these were hawked to an eager public, and pirated by unscrupulous copiers anxious to take advantage of Hogarth's popular reputation.

The modern comic strip is a visual communication medium of equal influence. The products of American syndication are seen by more than 200 million people in sixty countries every day. Why should it be so popular? Obviously the function of the newspaper strip is entertainment – a diversion from news, features, and advertisements. It is an added dimension to the coverage of the newspaper carrying it. American newspapers take strips for granted: only the *New York Times* and the *Wall Street Journal* do without them. There are 160 weekly strips in colour available for the special Sunday supplements and more than 250 daily strips produced by the syndicates.

A comic strip can take many forms. Fundamentally, however, it must consist of a sequence of narrative pictures featuring a regular cast of cartoon characters. A daily newspaper strip has three or four of these in frames, either forming a complete incident – the 'gag strip' – with a joke in the last frame, or as an episode in a continuing serial. The American Sunday page can inflate the day's episode to a dozen panels, or provide a complete gag sequence.

The comic book, from which newspapers tend to dissociate themselves, is a magazine with a page size of ten inches by seven; it features one or more complete stories told in strip form throughout its pages. The British children's comic, a form of publication unknown in America, is a periodical containing an assortment of gag strips, serial strips, stories and other matter. With few exceptions there is no interchange between newspaper strips, comic books, and children's comics. Comic-strip forms are also used in advertising and in magazines featuring cartoon humour such as *Punch* and the *New Yorker*.

For the most part strips attempt to fulfil no high-flown social purpose, any more than gossip columns do. They are pure light relief, using fantasy, adventure, slapstick, or satire to create a dramatic, usually comic, effect. A strip can comment satirically on serious problems as does Walt Kelly's Pogo, but editorializing is not generally condoned by the syndicates or their clients.

For this reason, perhaps, the strips are often accused of being mindless and superficial. Their role is usually an equivocal one since they are called upon to attract readers of all ages and educational standards; this formidable limitation is accepted by the strip artists as one of the disciplines of their medium. Some, Walt Kelly and Al Capp in particular, are able to surmount this obstacle by providing a double layer of interest: superficially the Pogo strip is about a lot of Disneyesque animals living in a Georgia swamp, but Walt Kelly's constant

readers are well aware that it is an allegorical portrayal of the shortfalls of American society.

The strips use certain conventions of technique which have evolved throughout their history. Dialogue within the frames is usually contained in balloons issuing from the mouths of the characters. Thoughts as opposed to speech are denoted by a series of diminishing bubbles linking the balloon with the thinking character. Balloons are not new. They were used extensively in the cartoons of Rowlandson and Gillray at the beginning of the nineteenth century, and have even been traced in woodcuts as far back as the fourteenth century. Shouting is shown by large lettering within the balloon. Movement is indicated by 'speed lines' emanating from the moving object to indicate the space it has just left. Impact is expressed by a whole vocabulary of onomatopoeic words such as *Wham!*, *Pow!*, *Zap!*, each followed by a mandatory exclamation point, and usually enclosed within a starburst. Sleep is indicated by *Z-Z-Z-Z-Z* and swearing by *©*!&?*!*. Worry is suggested by drops of perspiration visibly pouring from the character concerned, surprise by the unaided lifting of his hat a foot in the air.

In composition, strips often use cinematic techniques. Situations will be established in long-shot; the following frames will then move into mid-shot and close-up. Sudden switches of scene or reverse angles echo film cutting. In adventure strips particularly, such as Milton Caniff's Steve Canyon, changes of viewpoint are used to keep the visual pace brisk. Certain devices belong entirely to the strip cartoon; in the cinema they would fail. Location can be established by dialogue coming from a house on the horizon, alternating with close-ups of the characters doing the talking. Sudden switching of the action into silhouette, a trick practised by Doré in *L'Histoire de la Sainte Russie*, published in 1854, can increase the dramatic effect. Sometimes the background is completely eliminated so that the characters compel full attention.

The drawing style of a strip can vary from the photographic realism of Apartment 3-G to the high cartoon style of Schulz's Peanuts, whose tiny-bodied children are equipped with large heads and huge mouths. The strip reader will readily accept a face so briefly stylized as Dick Tracy's with its pointed, meat-chopper chin and barely-outlined mouth. Within the few square inches of newsprint that a strip occupies the artist must, in order to move the narrative forward, create a multiplicity of effects. Thus there is a special shorthand, a language of ellipsis, to convey as much information as possible to the reader in as little space.

America must not be considered as the sole progenitor of the modern strip. Although well over 2,000 have been syndicated from that country in the course of the history of strip cartoons, many other countries have developed their own. Ginger Meggs is an Australian institution of nearly fifty years' standing. Moomin, from Scandinavia, is syndicated throughout the world. Astérix, the warrior of Ancient Gaul, is France's most popular cartoon character. And Britain has developed many excellent newspaper strips, as well as a flourishing juvenile comic industry.

In America more than a hundred million people read the strips every day.

Washington bureaucrats, Chicago businessmen, Minnesota farmers, Harvard undergraduates, Westchester housewives – all will be familiar with the current plights of Li'l Abner, Little Orphan Annie, Joe Palooka, Dick Tracy, and the rest. The strips, like television programmes, reach a little into the consciousness of the big nation. If it is to achieve mass readership the strip must know no class barriers. The syndicates insist that it stays within defined limits of taste so that it can be sold to a wide non-specialized list of newspapers. Its language must be subtle enough to satisfy the intelligent, yet simple enough to be followed by the semi-literate. The mass of its readers will fall in between, *l'homme moyen sensuel*, the amorphous middle-of-the-road public mass revered by Madison Avenue and politicians in election years.

Consequently, the American strip concerns itself with American life on a mundane rather than an heroic level. The domestic suburbia of Blondie, Hi and Lois, the Berries, Dennis the Menace, the small-town torments of Juliet Jones, Mary Worth, Rex Morgan, Judge Parker, the city crime detection of Kerry Drake, the love of children in Peanuts, Dondi, Henry, Nancy, and all the strips featuring American kids – these are the common themes. Oddly enough, even the most far-fetched fantasy and adventure strips are rooted solidly in a normal American background. The criminals and crimes in Dick Tracy may be wildly exaggerated; his police work is sound and orthodox and his domestic problems have included a long and heart-breaking betrothal with Tess Trueheart. Steve Canyon's travels and entanglements may be heavily exotic; the Air Force settings are real. The Flintstones act out a perfect duplication of the life of Blondie and Dagwood in prehistoric times. Even those strips which can get away with an element of didacticism within their fantasy start from a clearly defined base. Al Capp's Dogpatch and Walt Kelly's Okefenokee Swamp are instantly recognized by many Americans as prototypes of their own society.

But however basic the concept, the mode of expression is in constant evolution. The strips must change – to keep their readership, to stay in tune with the fashions, to reflect the preoccupations of their time. The American strip has in seventy years, about the same length of time as the cinema, evolved through several phases. Its 'silent' period ended early in the twenties when the experiments and excitements of the pioneer days gave way to an acceptance of the new medium in the form in which it still exists. Strips of the twenties were full of the New Woman, shocking her stuffy elders with rolled stockings and office romances; in the thirties, escapism from the Depression trauma brought forth the adventures in steamy jungles or on alien planets; with the war came neo-realism, believable situations and straightforward representational artwork. The fifties and sixties have brought a vogue for allegorical satire and surrealistic gags, the wry jokes of the psychiatrist's couch.

The strips have propagated a special morality – with success. The Second World War provided an opportunity for the villains to be specified. The G.I.s in action on Omaha Beach carried comic books of Superman conquering the Axis in their rucksacks. The newspaper strips preach an ethos of conformism, of the safety and comfort of marriage, children, and the home. The life of Blondie and Dagwood, for all its frenetic disasters, is fundamentally secure and decent. Sexual excesses are taboo in the newspaper strips, and violence is rarely realistic. The heroes are not mavericks; they always stand for community values and the upholding of the commonweal. It is the wrongdoers who are the individualists, the self-seeking social enemies, corruptedly satisfying their own desires before those of their fellows. The newspaper strip industry bears its responsibilities to the family readership with high seriousness.

Alongside the new strips of each age stalk the successes of the past, some of which can survive to advanced middle age or even beyond, as in the case of The Katzenjammer Kids, now in its seventieth year. Some characters like Major Hoople of Our Boarding House and Jiggs of Bringing Up Father possess their own anachronistic humour. They are the coelacanths of the Great Society, recalling an American type vanished with the twenties. Other old stagers like Little Orphan Annie and Gasoline Alley owe their longevity to their continual adaptation to the changing American dream – or nightmare. Annie, once pitted against the New Deal, then fifth columnists, then the Communist menace threatening American values, now hits out at long-haired delinquents and radical intellectuals with the same zeal that has always made her the Joan of Arc of the American Right. Gasoline Alley has merely aged its characters naturally with the years so that Skeezix Wallet, who went through high school in the thirties and the Army in the forties, is now well entrenched in paunchy middle age, unwillingly possessed of the attitudes his children regard as square.

The strips are therefore a lively and usually accurate mirror of the times we live in; the world they show may be watered down or exaggerated, but it is portrayed with a firm grip on the taste of the moment. The strips themselves can influence fashions: expressions like 'heebie-jeebies', 'goon', and 'twerp' derive from them; so too do films, plays, musicals, ballets, radio and television programmes. Even popular events may result: Sadie Hawkins Day is taken from Li'l Abner and at one time was celebrated at 500 schools and colleges. The strips have also influenced serious art, particularly in the works of the pop artists Lichtenstein and Warhol; they have influenced the cinema, most notably in France; they have actively propagated the American way of life throughout the world. Before the war Mussolini banned American strips from Italian newspapers; yet even a Fascist dictator had to yield to the public clamour for Popeye.

The strips are ephemera. But this is an age when higher premiums are beginning to be placed on the ephemeral arts. They more honestly represent their time than the work which is deliberately created to last, and which will perhaps be scorned by succeeding generations – like Victorian genre paintings, for example. But it would be absurd to pretend that the strip is high art. It is not, any more than the front-page lead in a newspaper is great literature. It is commercial art, turned out with due regard to the pressures of space, time, and taste. Some examples will be poor, others magnificent of their kind. But their interest to the social historian is considerable.

What sort of evaluation can be made of the strips? Readership surveys have frequently revealed that they are the most read features in many newspapers.

Yet many readers suffer feelings of guilt and shame if forced to admit that they read them. Is this a hangover in the racial subconscious of the Victorian equation of pictures with illiteracy and ignorance, a combination of snobbery and Puritanism? Some psychologists and educators have tried to blame many social ills on the pernicious effects of comics on the developing imaginations of children. The vociferous pressures of certain voices in the early fifties nearly brought the American comic-book industry to its knees. Yet the newspaper strips take trouble to avoid bad taste and for the most part seem innocuous. They are unselfconsciously trivial and it would be unfashionable to admit too much enthusiasm for a joke situation requiring only a few seconds attention. The strips are not meant to be serious, even if they portray tragic events. Cartoonists have often come across in dialogue with their readers the type of person who takes the whole thing seriously enough to write a letter of sympathy when a character in a strip dies. But for most people the strip is a miniature, encapsulated form of entertainment, available at times when films or television would be impractical. To be ashamed of taking advantage of such opportunities would seem to be irrational and unnecessary.

In aesthetic terms the strips' achievement is the development of a form of narrative art using its own unique conventions and techniques. Perhaps the most outstanding early visionary of the possibilities of the strip was a Swiss schoolmaster called Rodolphe Töpffer, who lived from 1799 to 1846. Töpffer devised a series of illustrated novels, consisting of a series of drawings divided by frames, with a continuing narrative enclosed in a panel at the foot of each. The range of Töpffer's imagination was astonishing, embracing space travel, violent and surrealistic fantasy, and dreams. He was encouraged by Goethe to publish his work and his story of M. Cryptogramme appeared in the Paris magazine *L'Illustration* in 1845.

Töpffer, the son of a painter, was thwarted by poor eyesight from pursuing his father's calling; but he was able to give a great deal of thought to graphic technique, some of which was crystallized in his essay on physiognomics also published in 1845. Töpffer described two means of story-telling – the novel, with its words, and the picture story, with its illustrations in the manner of Hogarth. He went on to make a comment which is remarkable for the acuteness of its prophecy, and for its current validity.

'The picture story,' he wrote, 'to which the criticism of art pays no attention and which rarely worries the learned, has always exercised a great appeal. More, indeed, than literature itself, for besides the fact that there are more people who look than can read, it appeals particularly to children and the masses, the sections of the public that are particularly easily perverted and which it would be particularly desirable to raise. With its dual advantage of greater conciseness and greater relative clarity, the picture story, all things being equal, should squeeze out the other because it would address itself with greater liveliness to a greater number of minds, and also because in any contest he who uses such a direct method will have the advantage over those who talk in chapters.' He was talking about comics before they had even been discovered.

Professor E.H.Gombrich has pointed out that Töpffer's outstanding discovery was that it was possible for the artist – the cartoonist or caricaturist – to evolve a pictorial language without reference to nature, that an abbreviated style can rely on the onlooker to fill in the gaps with his imagination.

On such a simple premise the art of the strip cartoon has been based.

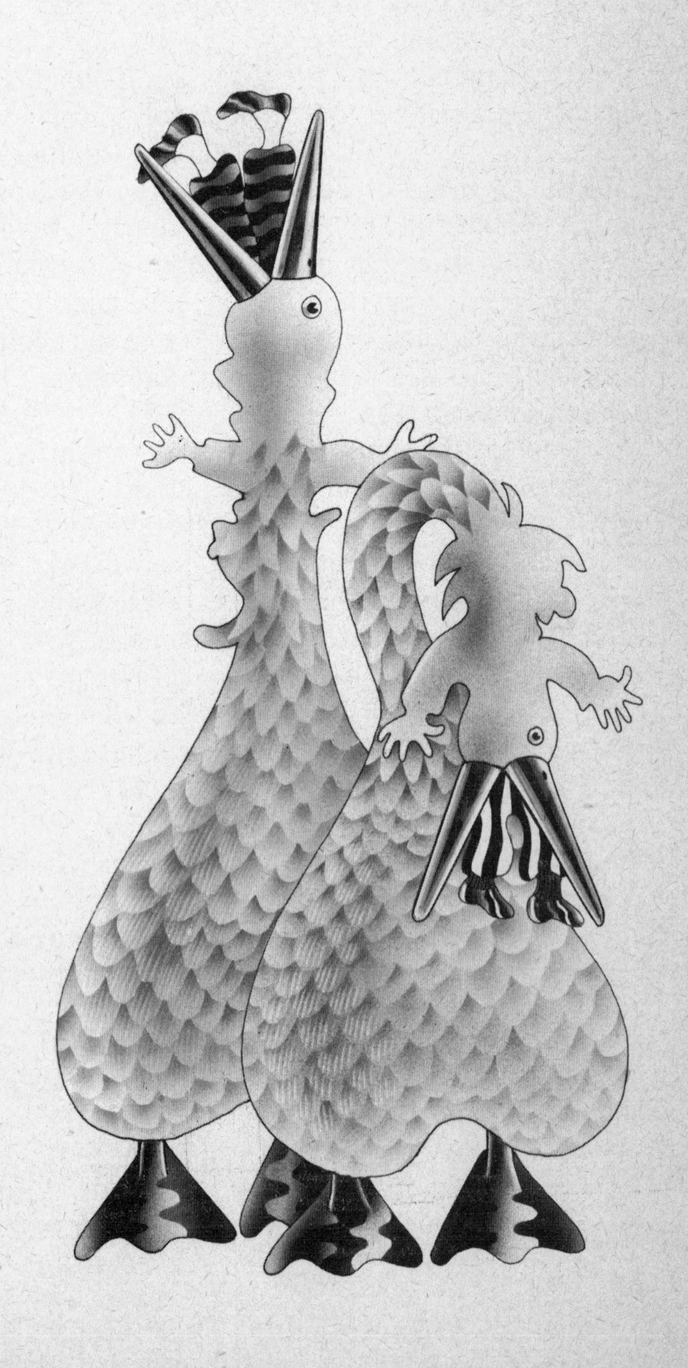

Picture Section

Magic art: the first known pictures by man are perhaps 30,000 years old and their purpose is still conjectural. But it seems that the two main uses of pictures – as record and as 'art' – must have been defined fairly early in prehistory. Art in this case is synonymous with magic. Early man is thought to have used art to invoke his deities; the custom persists to our own times and may be one reason why the use of art for entertainment has been feared by authority in so many civilizations.
The great cultures of the Mediterranean basin developed pictorial art to elaborate and often sophisticated levels; its character was still religious and commemorative, although the narrative element becomes more marked. And man himself gradually becomes as important a subject as his gods.

Sacred beast: a Palaeolithic cave painting of reindeer grazing from Font-de-Gaume, France (*above right*). The purpose of such paintings, some of which may be 30,000 years old, was probably religious: the men of the tribe would pray before these images of the animal god before going out to kill its living counterpart for food. The bold sweeping strokes, the strong sense of pattern shown in the treatment of the horns, and the lifelike representation, indicate that our ancestors' artistic talents were far from primitive.

Comic man: a pot-bellied, hook-nosed caricature found at Tassili n'Ajjer in Africa; perhaps an example of man's first graffiti (*below right*). Although most discoveries of Stone Age paintings have so far been made in Europe – Spain, the Pyrenees, the Dordogne – the cave paintings of Tassili are a rich and remarkable exception. Dating from about 4000 B.C., they record traces of a people who perished when the desert finally conquered their green country of rivers and grassland.

Victory celebration: a great Sumerian king feasting to celebrate peace after a battle (*far right, above*). This early example of art as narrative decoration is from the 'Standard' of Ur, a mosaic-adorned box nearly two feet in length, dating from between 4000 and 2000 B.C. when the Sumerian civilization flourished in southern Mesopotamia. Shown here is the 'peace' side, depicting the leader and his men, musicians entertaining them, and animals and produce being brought as offerings for the feast. The other, or 'war', side showed the battle order, with infantry and chariots.

Eternal judgement: a scene from an Egyptian papyrus of the New Kingdom, about 1000 B.C. (*far right, below*). The aristocratic culture of Ancient Egypt was extremely elaborate and formal. Funerary art was rich and many examples survive. Illustrated is part of a 'book of the dead', a kind of passport to heaven without which no person of importance was buried; this one charts the progress of the soul of the scribe Ani. Anubis, the jackal-headed funeral god, weighs the heart of Ani against the feather of divine justice; a hybrid monster waits to devour it if it is found wanting.

Satirical intent: an irreverent example of Egyptian art in strip form (*overleaf, above left*) dating from about the same period as the papyrus of Ani. Similar drawings have been found on *ostraca* (pot or limestone fragments) near the Tombs of the Kings; it is thought that workmen passed them round for a laugh. This very rare example on papyrus is obviously more sophisticated; its intention is perhaps to ridicule the Egyptian convention of showing gods as animals by showing animals behaving like men. The mouse on a chair (*middle right of the lower strip*) is a caricature of a well-known subject for tomb paintings – the lady of fashion attended by her servants.

First supermen: a Greek vase of about 500 B.C. (*overleaf, below left*). Below its rim a frieze of demi-gods and men fight a running battle portrayed with a brilliant vigour, counterpointing the placidity of the stylized leaf and flower forms on the neck and handles. The action frieze – the one on the Parthenon is the most famous – is a significant contribution to narrative art; it is enhanced by the glittering pantheon of Greek gods and heroes and by the Greek admiration for the human form. This example records the fabled exploits of Hercules – the first popular superhero.

Longest strip: a detail from the Column of Trajan (*overleaf, far right*). The Romans had a notable talent for the commemoration on a heroic scale of mortal men; this is one of their most spectacular surviving monuments. Erected by the Emperor Trajan early in the second century A.D., it is in the form of a continuous relief which winds up the column in a strip more than 600 feet long. The various military triumphs of his reign which are portrayed offer many fascinating details of the Roman skill in warfare. The section illustrated shows a party of Dacians, on the north-eastern frontier of the Roman Empire, attacking a fortified strongpoint resolutely held by legionaries.

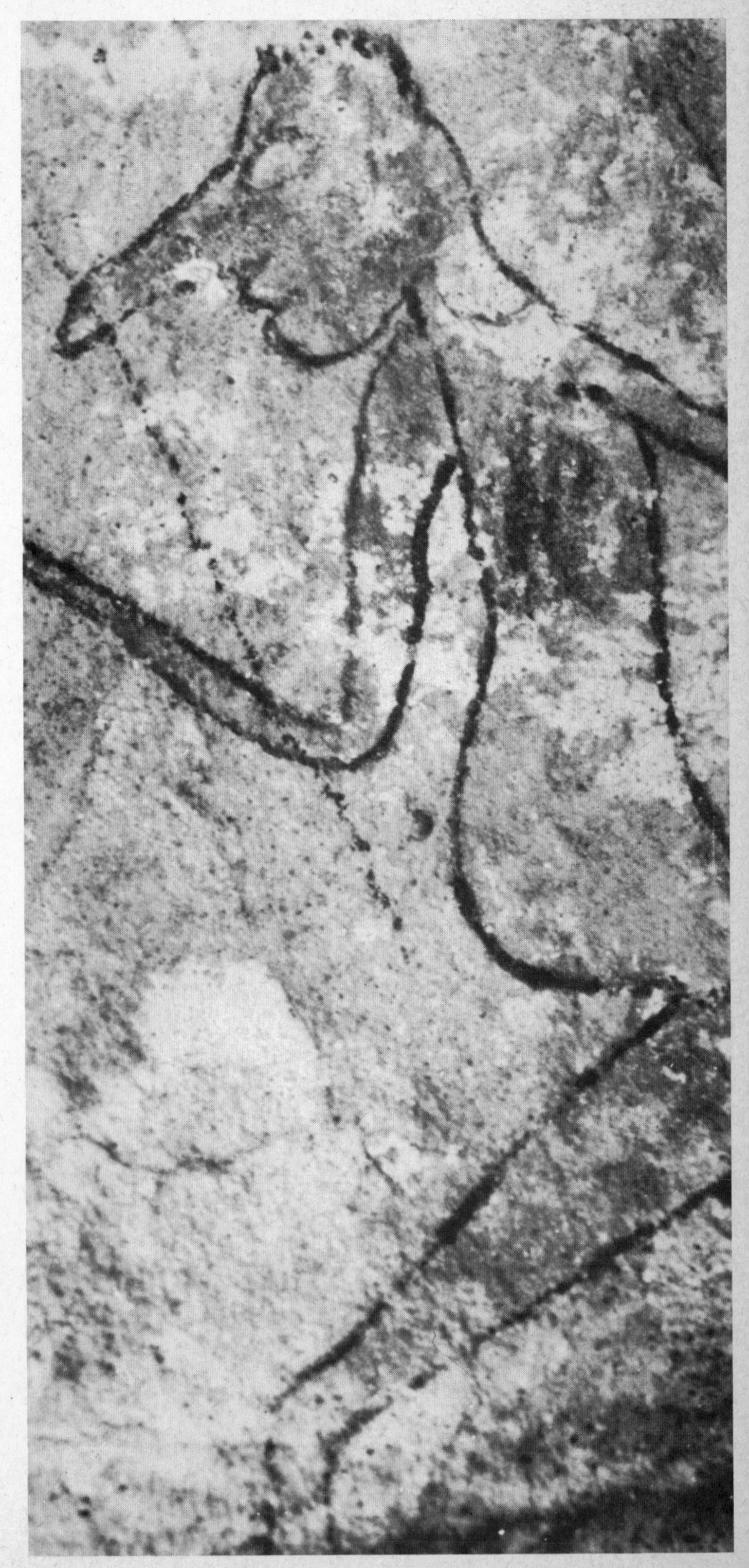

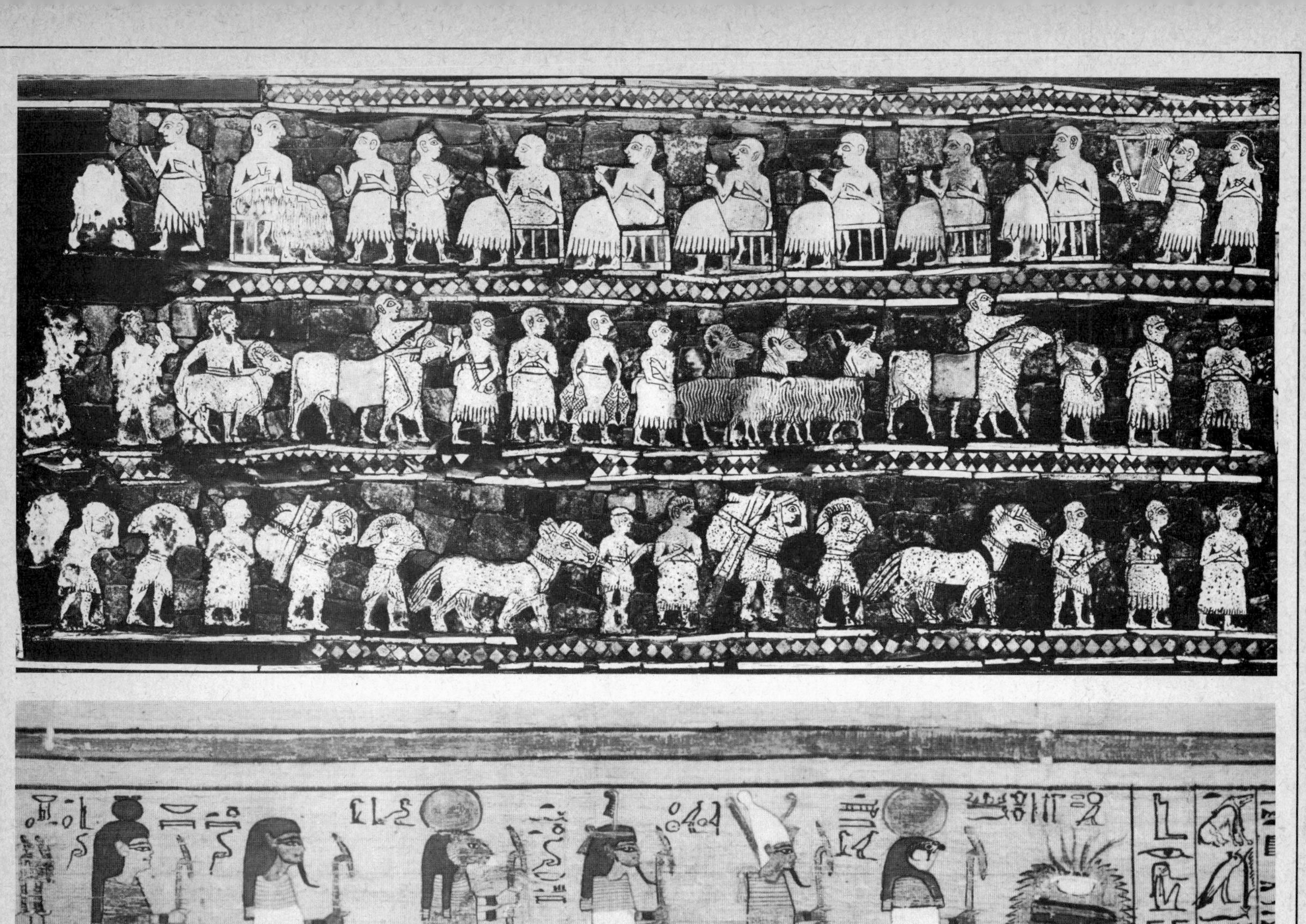

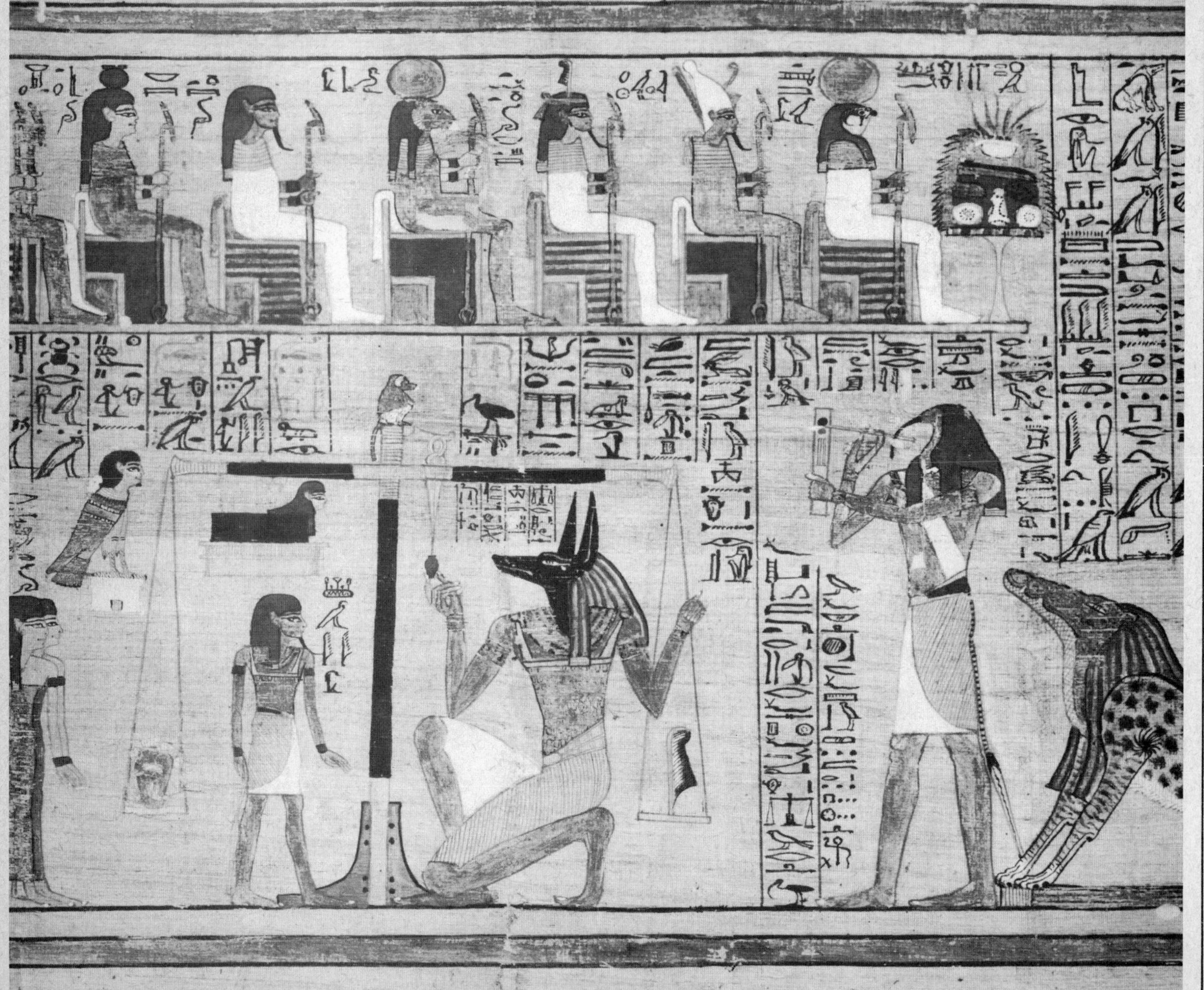

SAMS. 23. I
10016

SAMS. 23. II
10016.2

Graphic survival: from the fall of the Roman Empire to the period around the Norman Conquest, European history grows dim. Much of the Continent was in the grip of barbarians; it was the Eastern world which kept the light of culture burning.

From China via the Muslim world paper came westward to challenge vellum. The art of illumination, of which the earliest known example is a fragmentary copy on vellum of Homer's *Iliad*, evolved through the book decoration of the second and third centuries, particularly the Byzantine copies of the Gospels. The earliest books, one-off jobs known as *incunabula*, competed with the illuminated manuscripts produced by patient and often imaginative artists in the great monastic houses of Europe.

In the mid-fifteenth century, a printer of Mainz called Gutenberg, anticipating the surging demand for knowledge engendered by the Renaissance, built the first printing-press using movable metal type. The illustrative tradition of the monks was carried into the new medium: pictures would take their place with the printed word in what is probably the biggest single landmark in the history of communication.

Pictorial invasion: the Bayeux tapestry was woven in England within ten years of the Battle of Hastings on the orders of Odo, Bishop of Bayeux, Earl of Kent and half-brother to

William the Conqueror. It is one of the greatest artistic achievements of the Middle Ages; it is also one of the most remarkable precursors of the strip cartoon. Strictly speaking a hanging rather than a tapestry, it narrates in an embroidered strip, 230 feet long and 20 inches wide, the Norman invasion of the Anglo-Saxon kingdom of Harold, seen (*below left*) on his throne; in the upper border is Halley's comet, then regarded as a portent of impending catastrophe. Harold's coronation, a violation of his oath to the Norman duke, is the justification for William to mount his invasion. For the most part, a decorative border top and bottom is used to display various beasts and occasional bits of side action. The main narrative is in more or less conventional comic-strip form, with simple legends in Latin describing the events. The lower illustration shows a ship sailing across the English Channel to Normandy bearing news of the crowning. The three illustrations on the right show the invasion, redrawn from the original to indicate the detail more clearly. In the top strip the invasion fleet is under construction and finished boats are dragged to the water. The middle strip shows the army's supplies, weapons, armour, barrels of wine carried to the fleet, and William leading his officers to the point of embarkation. The bottom strip illustrates the actual sea-crossing, the ships laden with Norman troops in battle order, a signal lantern at the masthead of William's flagship.

Enriching words: a beautifully drawn and coloured example of illumination, from the early fifteenth century (*below left*). It is a page from an edition of Dante's *Divine Comedy* prepared by an unknown Italian artist for Alphonse V, King of Aragon. Like a modern comic strip it contains three phases of action, but unseparated by frames. On the left Dante and Virgil are threatened by a young centaur. In the centre, having passed him, they encounter Chiron who orders Nessus to accompany them. On the right, Nessus carries Dante and Virgil off on his back; they pass a boiling lake of blood in which the heads of tyrants such as Attila afford the centaurs an opportunity for target practice with their bows and arrows.

Mysterious doodles: a page from the notebooks of Leonardo da Vinci (*below right*). A ceaseless explorer of new ideas, Leonardo (1452–1519) was the greatest pictorial innovator of the Renaissance. The exploded technical drawing, the cut-away, the detailed graphic analysis of anatomical or biological construction, were all perfected by him. Towards the end of his life he drew on several pages of his notebooks what appeared to be strips of picture writing. These strangely linked words and pictures are more than senile doodles; they are without doubt an attempt to discover and understand a new means of displaying knowledge. Had Leonardo begun earlier, perhaps his mysterious jottings might have developed into the comic strip itself.

Early printing: Schedel's *Liber Chronicarum*, published in Nuremberg in 1493 by Anton Koberger, the busiest printer of his day (*right*). Thirty years before Gutenberg, wooden book-blocks, or xylographs, were used in primitive presses. With the invention of movable metal type, the woodcut became a new art medium, inseparable from printed illustration until the introduction of metal blocks in the 1890s. Early printers imitated the illuminated manuscript in their designs, deploying the blocks in and out of the text to achieve continuity. The *Liber Chronicarum* contained 1,809 illustrations; the characters shown are, once again, from the *Iliad*. As with many early books, the illustrations were hand-coloured in a special limited edition.

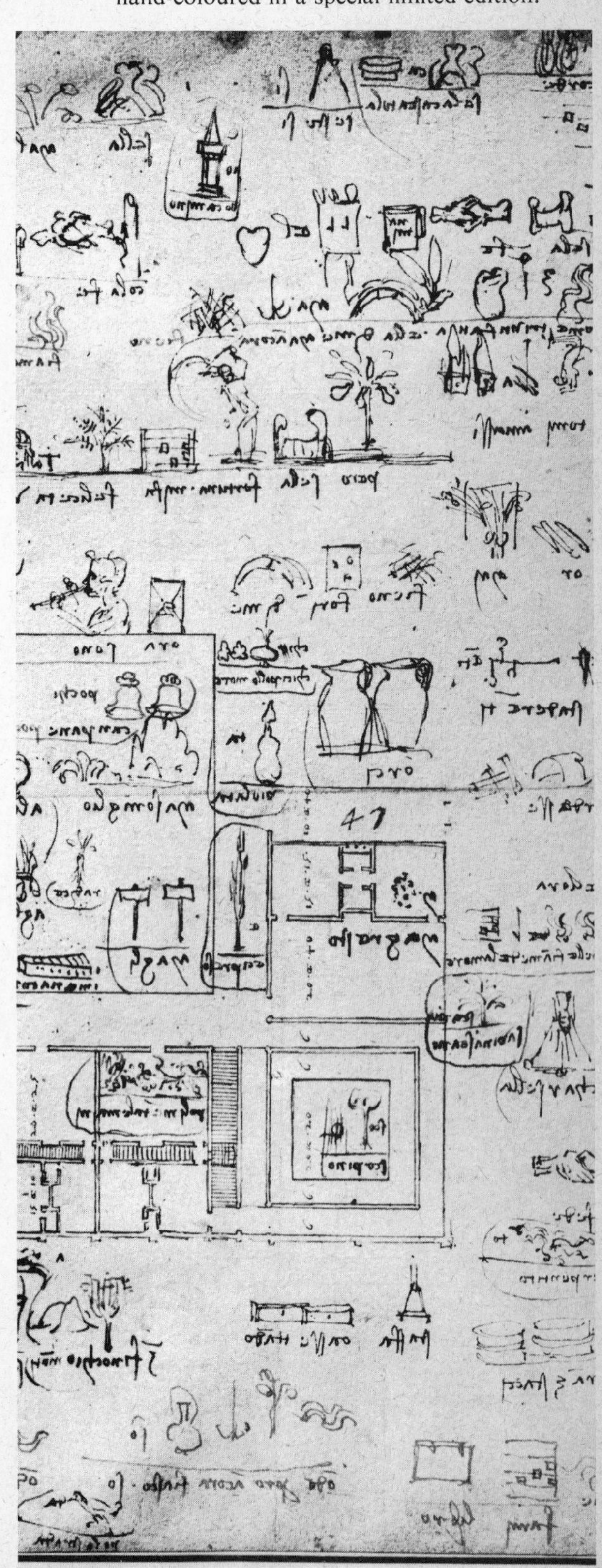

TRoyanum bellū decēnale primo Esebon siue Abesson iudicis anno (teste eusebio) surrexit. quo tpe sequētes claruerūt. Troya eñi quā Ilion tros regis troyanoꝝ filius amplissimā instaurauit mille ꝛ quingentis passibus a mari remota erat: vbi oīm rerum vbertas erat: Ipsa quippe que decēnalem grecorum obsidionem passa fuit: et ab eis tandē deletā.

Hercules

HErcules ille cū Iasone troyā vastauit que statim a priamo fuit reedificata. Idez hercules agonē olimpiacuz cōstituit et bella multa cōfecit quē dicūt duodecim insignes et inhumanos pfecisse labores.

Hector

ISte hector fuit pmogenitus priami ex hecuba vxore incōpabilis fortitudinis et strēnuitatis. Iō ob maximū eiꝰ militie fulgorem apud troyanos maxio ī precio habitus est. Nā ob incredibilē eiꝰ prudētiā atq; fortitudinē nō solū parētes: sed et patriā nobilitate atq; glia splēdidā fecit. hic ex Andromacha ꝯiuge plres genuit filios. E qbꝰ fracꝰ vnꝰ fuit A q (vt ait vincētiꝰ hystorial' burgūdꝰ) frāci originē habuere.

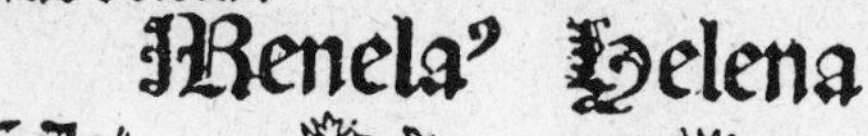

Menelaꝰ Helena

HElena fuit vxor menelai regis ꝛ a paride filio priami rapitur. ꝛ ad troyā pducitur. ppter qđ troyanū bellū exortuz Ipsam tñ post troye excidium Greci menelao reddiderūt. q gaudēs nauim cū illa cōscendit patriam petiturꝰ: sed tēpestatibꝰ acti in egiptū ad polibuz regez deuenere. Indeq; discedentes octo ānis errātes (vt testis est eusebiꝰ) tandez in patriam redierunt.

Paris

PAris qui et Alexāder dictꝰ est eiusdē hectoris frater: ex priamo ꝛ hecuba natꝰ: sb specie legatiōis cū. xx. naibꝰ in greciā mittitur Et a menelao hospicio suscipit. Cuiꝰ cū aspexisset vxorez illaz. absente marito tandē cū oibus regijs thezauris abstulit et Troyam pduxit. Ex qua rapina bellum decēnale grecoꝝ aduersus troyanos susceptū est. Hic cū troyanis vrbem obsidentibꝰ multa strēnue gessisset: A pirrho achillis filio occisus fuit.

Agamenon

AGamenon fuit frater regis Menelai dux totiꝰ exercitus grecoꝝ. cōtra troyā bellauit. q tandem traditorie et turpissime capit. fuitq; Atrei regis filiꝰ. ab omni exercitu imperator designatus. ad bellū pergens Clitemestram coniugez ex qua multos susceperat filios reliquit. Et apud troyam multos passus labores. ꝛ simultates principum pro quibus ab imperio depositus ꝛ illi palamedes suffectꝰ est. Quē cum vlixes occidisset ipse maiori gloria imperium reassumpsit. Tandez Troya capta et diruta cum ingenti preda et cassandra priami filia in patriam redditurus naues conscendit Uerum ꝛ ipse tempestate actus. p annū fernic errauit.

Isti duo de Troya fugientes duo regna constituūt: longe tamē post.

Franco

FRanco quidē ex hectore filiꝰ priami nepos a quo francoꝝ nomē tractū est. a troya fugatꝰ postea tota Asia puagata in danubij ripis tande puenit. Ibi cū aliq;diu cōsedisset. deinde locum querēs a cōmuni hominū societate seiunctū: ad thanai fluentia ꝛ paludes meotidas secessit. vbi Sicambriā condidit vrbem.

Turcus

TUrcus filiꝰ Troili filij regis Priami. A q ppl'm ab eo descendentē. quidem turcos denoīari dicūt. Alij eoꝝ originē ex Scythia referunt.

THE EXPLANATION.

BEhold Here, in This Piece, the Plague, the Fate
Of a Seditious Schism in Church, and State:
Its Rise, and Progress; with the dire Event
Of a Blind Zeal, and a Pack'd Parliament.
It was This Medly that Confounded All;
This damn'd Concert of Folly and Cabal,
That Ruin'd us: For ye must know, that Fools
Are but State-Engines; Politicians Tools
Ground to an Edg, to Hack, and Hew it out;
Till by dull Sots Knaves Ends are brought about.
Think on't, my Masters; and if e're ye see
This Game play'd o're again, then Think of Me.

You'l say This Print's a Satyr, Against Whom?
Those that Crown'd Holy Charles with Martyrdom.
By the same rule the Scripture you'l Traduce,
For saying Christ was Crucifi'd by th' Jews:
Nay, and their Treasons too agreed in This;
By Pharisees Betray'd, and with a Kiss:
Conscience, the Cry; Emanuel was the Word;
The Cause, the Gospel; but the Plea, the Sword.

[A] Now lay your Ear close to That Nest of Heads.
Look, don't ye see a Streaming Ray, that sheds
A Light from the Cabal down to the Table;
To inspire, and Push on an Enthusiast Rabble?
In That Box sits a Junto in Debate.
Upon their Soveraigns, and Three Kingdoms Fate:
They're Hot, and Loud enough. Attend 'um pray'e,
From point to point; and tell us what they say.

Is it Resolv'd then that the King must Down?
Not for a World; we'l only take his Crown:
He shall have Caps, and Knees still; and the Fame
Of a fair Title, and Imperial Name:
But for the Sword; the Power of War, and Peace;
Life, and Death; and such Fooleries as These;
We'l beg These Boons our selves: And Then, in Course,
What cannot be Obtein'd by Prayer. we'l Force.
It Rests, now, only; by what Arts, and Friends,
Methods, and Instruments, to gain These Ends.

First, make the People Sure; and That must be
By Pleas for Conscience, Common Liberty:
By which Means, we secure a Popu'lar Voyce
For Knights, and Burgesses, in the Next Choyce.
If we can get an Act, Then, to Sit on
Till we Dissolve our Selves, the work's Half-done.

In the mean while, the Pulpits, and the Presses
Must ring of Popery, Grievances, Addresses,
Plots of all Sorts, Invasions, Massacres,
Troops under Ground, Plague-Plaisters, Cavaliers:
Till, Mad with Spite, and Jealousie, the Nation
Cry out, as One Man, for a Reformation.

Having thus gain'd the Rabble; it must be our
Next Part, the Common-Council to Secure:
And Then; let King, Law, Church, and Court-Cabal,
Unite, and do their Worst; we'l Stand 'um All.
Our Design's This; to Change the Government;
Set up our Selves; and do't by'a Parliament.
And This t' effect, needs only Resolution;
We'l leave the Tumults to do Execution.
The Popish Lords must Out, Bishops must Down;
Strafford must Dye; and Then, have at the Crown.
We will not leave the King, One Minister;
The House, One Member; but what We Prefer:
No nor the Church, One Levite; Down they go:
We, and the 'Prentices will have it so.

(Done:
[B] This was scarce sooner Said, then the thing
For up starts Little Isaac, in the Room
Of Loyal Gourney, with a Sword in's hand;
The Ensign of his New-usurpt Command:
Out of his Mouth, a Label, to be True
To the Design of the Caballing Crew:
[C] His Holiness at's Elbow; Heart'ning on,
A Motly Schism; Half-Pope, Half-Puritan;
Who, while they talk of Union, Bawl at Rome;
Revolt, and set up Popery at Home.

(see
[D] Now, bring your Eye down to the Board; and
Th' Agreement of that Blest Fraternity:
Cov'nanters All; and by That Holy Band
Sworn En'mies to th' Establisht Law o'th' Land.
These are the Men that Plague all Parliaments,
For the Impossible Expedients
Of making Protestant Dissenters, One,
By Acts of Grace, or Comprehension:
When, by their very Principles, each other
Thinks himself Bound to Persecute his Brother.
They never Did, they never Can Unite
In any one Poynt, but t' o'rethrow the Right:
Nor is't at all th' Intent of Their Debate
To fix Religion, but t' embroyl the State;
Ill Accidents, and Humours to improve,
Under the fair Pretexts of Peace, and Love;
To serve the Turn of an Usurping Power.
But read their Minutes, and They'l tell ye More.

[E] Take a view, next, of the Petitioners.
But why, (you'l say) like Beasts to th' Ark, in Pairs?
Not to expose the Quaker, and the Maid,
(By Lust to those Brutalities betray'd)
As if those two Sects more addicted stood
To Mares, and Whelps, then other Flesh and Blood:
No, But they're coupl'd Here, only to tell
The Harmony of their Reforming Zeal.

[F] Now wash your Eyes, and see their Secretarius
Of Uncouth Visage; Manners most Nefarious,
Plac'd betwixt Pot and Pipe, with Pen and Paper;
To shew that he can Scribble, Tope, and Vapour:
Beside him, (craving Blessing) a Sweet Babby;
(Save it!) the very Image of the Daddy!
He deals in Sonnets, Articles, takes Notes,
Frames Histories, Impeachments, enters Votes,
Draws Narratives, (for **Four Pound**) very well;
But then, 'tis **Forty more**, to Pass the Seal.
Beside his Faculty, at a Dry Bob,
That brings him many a comfortable Job.

(Rout
[G] Mark, Now, Those Club-men; That Tumultuous
Crown, Bible, Magna Charta, under Foot!
Those Banners, Trophies; and the Execrable
Rage, and Transports of an Incensed Rabble!
Here, the Three States in Chains; and There, the Head
Of a Good King, by Rebels murthered.
And all this while, the Creatures of Those Knaves,
That blew the Coal, themselves, the greatest Slaves.
What Devil could make Men Mad, to This Degree?
Only mistaken Zeal, and Jealousie.
Liberty, Conscience, Popery, the Pretence;
Rapine, Blood, Sacrilege, the Consequence.

[H] Let's Cross the way, Now, to the Doctors Side.
'Tis a good, pretty Girl, that holds his Head! (on;
What's his Disease, Sweet-Heart? Nay, That's a Questi-
His Stomach's Foul, perhaps, 'tis Ill Digestion;
But 'tis a mercy, 't comes so finely away:
Here's Canons, Surplices, Apocrypha!
Look what a Lump there lies of Common-Prayer.
Ay, but the Cross in Baptism, that lies There:
O, how he Reacht; and still, as I provok'd him, (him!
He'd Heave for Life; 'twas Ten to One't had Choakt
Nay verily; This Stuff, in Holder-forth,
May be as much as a mans Life is worth.

How Do ye Sir? Why somewhat more at Ease,
Since I've Discharg'd these Legal Crudities.
But if your Stomach be so'extremely Nice;
What Course do'ye take? O, I have Good Advice:
All the Dissenting Protestant-Divines;
There's not a man in the whole Club, but Joyns.
This Pect'ral, you must know, keeps me alive;
Sequester'd Livings are Preservative!
But for the Soveraign Remedy of all,
The Only, never-failing Cordial;
There 'tis upon That Shelf: That Composition
Th' Assembly Took, it self, in my Condition.
The Tears of Widows, Orphans Hearts, and Blood
They made their daily Drink, their daily Food:
Behold our Christian Cannibal's Oblation,
To auspicate their Moloch Reformation.

[I] Well! But what means This Excremental Swarm
Of Human Insects? How they Fret, and Storm;
Grin at the Vomit; and yet for all this Pother;
At the same Time, ly teizing one another.
Alas! 'Tis too, too true. you've Hit my Grief:
And there's no Help, no Help for't; no Relief.
While They joyn'd Hands with Us, against the Crown,
And Church; How sweetly the Lords work went on!
But when we came to plant our Directory,
'Bless me, what Freaks they play'd! you know the Story.
Oh! of themselves, they're e'en a Vip'rous Brood;
Begot in Discord, and brought up with Blood.
'Twas We that gave 'um Life, Credit, and Name:
Till the Ungrateful Brats devour'd their Dam.

What could ye look for else? For 'tis Dominion,
That you do all contend for, not Opinion.
If you'l have any Government; then say,
Which Party shall Command, and which Obey.
Power is the thing ye both Affect, and Hate.
Every one would, ye Cannot, All be Great:
This is, in short, the Sum of the Contest;
Still He that's Up, 's an Eye-sore to the Rest.
Presbytery breeds Worms: This Maggot-Fry
Is but the Spawn of Lawless Liberty.
License, is like a Sea-Breach to your Grounds;
Suffer but One Flaw, the whole Country Drowns.

LONDON: Printed by Mary Clark, for Henry Breme, at the Gun in St. Paul's Church-yard. 1680: 15: Aprill:

Religious propaganda: a broadsheet published in 1680 (*left*), a century before *The Times* was to make its first appearance. It dealt with the dangers of dissensionist cabals in post-Restoration England and the 'seditious schism between Church and State'. In the foreground lies the broken bust of Charles I, the monarch executed thirty-one years earlier. The narrative is a warning that such martyrdom could occur again. The engraved illustration makes liberal use of balloons to signify speech.

The public prints: from the sixteenth to the eighteenth century printing proliferated. But books were not for the masses; literacy trailed a long way behind the production of raw material to feed men's minds. Long before books were available to any but the educated few, there was a way of communicating to the masses.

The broadsheet informed the masses of the topics of the day. Subject-matter ranged from the ravages of the Plague to religious propaganda, from political scandal to popular songs. To aid comprehension all were liberally illustrated with woodcuts. At first they were hawked near printing shops or in the streets.

As early as the fourteenth century speech balloons and labels were used; later the frame technique was introduced – an example exists of 1603. Add to this the critical, mocking, and entertainment intent of the public prints – and the basic elements of the strip cartoon are already discernible.

Political satire: published in 1741, 'The Motion' (*below*) comments on a parliamentary movement to remove Sir Robert Walpole from office on account of various malpractices, including bribery and a disregard for liberty. The scene is Whitehall, with Inigo Jones's Banqueting Hall in the background; Walpole's opponents are lampooned in the cut. The joke, with its tedious puns and disguised names (e.g. Little-Toney for Lyttelton) is to modern eyes laboured and feeble. But the print was very much to the taste of the public of its time: it was advertised by several newspapers including the *Daily Gazetteer* and the *Daily Post* and was in fact an enthusiastic response to a similar one put out by Walpole's opponents.

I.

WHO be dat de Box do ſit on?
'Tis *John*, the Hero of *North-Britain*,
Who out of Place, does Place-men ſpit on,
Doodle, &c.

II.

Between his Legs de Spaniel Curr ſee,
Tho' now he growle at *Bob* ſo fiercé,
Yet he fawn'd on him once in *Doggerel* Verſé,
Doodle, &c.

III.

And who be dat *Poſtilion* there,
Who drive o'er all and no Man ſpare?
'Tis *Ph—l—p E—le* — of here and there,
Doodle, &c.

IV.

But pray who in de Coaché ſit-a?
'Tis honeſt *J—nny C—t—ritta*,
Who vant in place again to get-a,
Doodle, &c.

V.

Who's dat behind? 'tis *Dicky Cobby*,
Who firſt wou'd have hang'd, and then try'd *Bobby*.
Ah, was not that a pretty Jobb-e?
Doodle, &c.

VI.

Who's dat who ride aſtride de Poney,
So long, ſo lank, ſo lean, and bony?
O he be de great Orator *Little-Toney*,
Doodle,. &c.

VII.

Cloſe by ſtands *Billy* of all *Bob's* Foes,
De wittieſt far in Verſe, and Proſe;
How he lead de Puppies by de Noſe?
Doodle, &c.

VIII.

Who's he dat lift up both his Handes?
O that's his Wiſdom Squire *S———s*,
O de Place-Bill drop! O de Army ſtandes!
Doodle, &c.

IX.

What Parſon's he dat bow ſo civil?
O dat's de Biſhop who ſplit the Devil,
And made a Devil and a half, and half a Devil,
Doodle, &c.

X.

So, Sirs, me have ſhewn you all de *Hero's*,
Who put you together by the Ear-os,
And frighten you ſo with groundleſs Fear-os,
Doodle, &c.

Printed for T. Cooper, at the *Globe* in *Pater-noſter-Row*, 1741.

Publiſh'd according to Act of Parliament.

Price Three-Pence.

Hogarth's achievement: the English painter William Hogarth (1697–1764) combined theatrical and literary forms in several narrative series of large canvases which were translated into popular engravings. 'A Harlot's Progress', his most successful in public terms, was set to music and used as a motif for the decoration of teapots and fans. Satirical in tone, his works were copious in background detail and formed a perceptive indictment of the hypocrisies of elegant drawing-rooms and an insight into the horrific slums of eighteenth-century London. The illustrations at left are the last two of the eight which tell the story 'The Rake's Progress'. The upper one shows the feckless heir in a debtor's prison, his fortune gambled away, with not enough money to buy even a pot of beer. The lower shows him in the notorious madhouse, Bedlam – his final degradation, surrounded by lunatics and his weeping mistress, and observed by ladies of fashion who found madness a diverting spectacle for an afternoon's amusement. Hogarth was victimized by plagiarists who pirated his works with total unscrupulousness. This, coupled with the unpopularity he earned from his satires in eminent circles, left him bitter and broken-spirited.

Strip technique: an excellent example of the prototype strip cartoon by Thomas Rowlandson (*below*). As well as captions, balloons and a fully-developed frame format, this waggish account of the uneasy coalition between Charles James Fox and Lord North after Fox's Commons victory in 1782 contains 'thinks' balloons and a plethora of 'in jokes'. In frame three, for example, the Badger (North) is shown dreaming of the gallows – a fate often threatened by the Opposition during his Ministry; frame six contains punning references to three well-known newspaper editors of the time. This print probably aided the fashion for 'strips' which became a craze between 1784 and 1794; here, strip usually means one long pictorial narrative sequence. Rowlandson himself produced *The School for Scandal*, the story of an elopement, not to be confused with the play by Richard Brinsley Sheridan, in strip form.

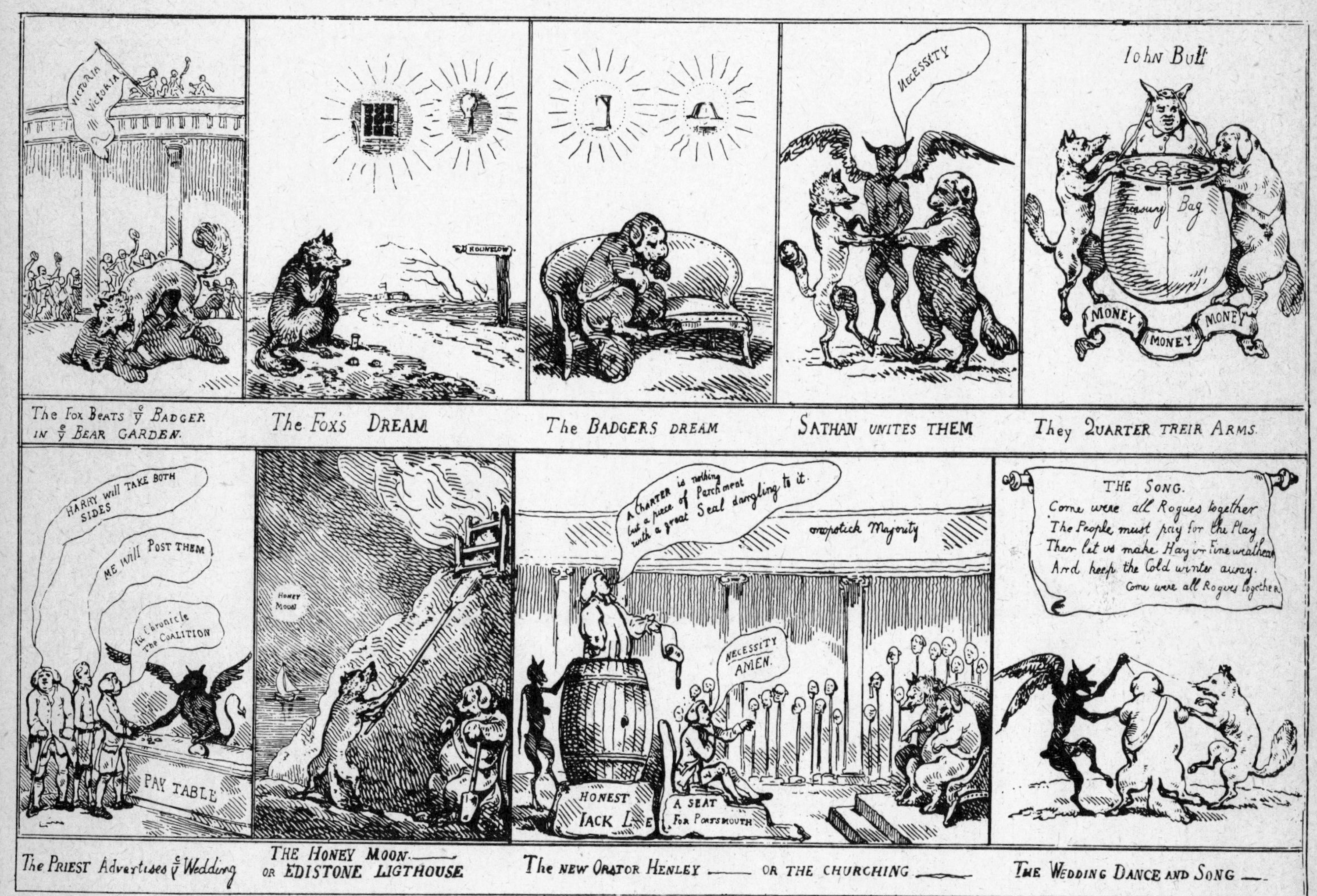

The cartoon explosion: the great age of political cartooning lies between the end of the eighteenth century and the middle years of the nineteenth century. In this period the *genre* developed in two separate directions: the political cartoon, extended into our own time by the work of David Low, Vicky and Herblock, and the satirical strip.

Each was often practised simultaneously by the most famous artists of the time – Thomas Rowlandson (1757–1827), whose Dr Syntax was the first regular cartoon character, James Gillray (1757–1815), renowned for the biting savagery of his style, and George Cruikshank (1792–1878), whose father Isaac was one of the foremost cartoonists of the Napoleonic era. Rowlandson and Gillray particularly were responsible for bringing the balloon, the device used to indicate spoken dialogue within a drawing, into regular use.

Cartoon criticism: a Gillray of 1802 (*below*). This cartoon is a mature example: its deceptively understated style reveals many subtle touches. It represents a protest against the government's conciliatory attitude to Bonaparte's repeated aggression, and disappointment that, in spite of the great play made of the commercial benefits of peace, trade was nevertheless unforthcoming. With its full-blown Britannia and Ministers dressed as old nursemaids (*from left to right*, Hawkesbury, Fox, and Addington) it would transplant easily into the modern idiom – as comment, say, on the Common Market negotiations.

Magazine satire: the issue of *Maclean's Monthly Sheet of Caricatures* for 1 July 1832 (*right*) satirizes both Radicals and Whigs, who saw the Reform Bill as a 'permanent and final measure'. The top picture shows (*left to right*) O'Connell, Attwood, Hume, and Burdett; the soliloquizer (*lower left*) is Grey and the Ambassador (*lower right*) is Durham. Other items of this popular cartoon magazine and its many imitators would usually include illustrated puns, fashionable dress, *mores* and pastimes, social comment, and parodies of song-titles or well-advertised products.

The NURSERY; _ with Britannia reposing in PEACE.

Vol. 3rd
July 1st 1832.

Mc. LEAN'S MONTHLY SHEET OF CARICATURES. No. 31.
OR THE LOOKING GLASS,

Price 3s Plain.
6s Cold.

PUBLISHED ON THE FIRST OF EVERY MONTH.

STRANGE SYMPTOMS AS TO THE FINAL NATURE OF THE LATE BILL.

A SOLILOQUY.

AN EXCELLENT REPUBLICAN KING.

AN AMBASSADOR
ABOUT TO VISIT THE COURT OF PETERSBOURG.

Mr Jabot ne peut dormir que d'un œil.

Mr Jabot rêve des Airs de masourke

Mr Jabot rêve des choses enivrantes

Mr Jabot rêve des hauts faits en présence d'une femme adorable.

Au milieu du détroit, le paquebot saute, et le Télescope est lancé à une hauteur prodigieuse.

L'astronome Apogée, savant Ginvernais, qui se promène à l'oeil nu dans son jardin aperçoit le nouveau corps céleste.

Les vingt huit observateurs salariés qu'il emploie à regarder le ciel jour et nuit l'aperçoivent pareillement.

51.

European pioneers: a Swiss schoolmaster, Rodolphe Töpffer (1799–1846) made illustrated novels for his pupils. Under the encouragement of Goethe, some of his work was published at the end of his life. The upper illustration (*left*) is from *M. Jabon*, a satire on romantic courtship. The sequence shows the hero in a fitful sleep (one eye open), dreaming of charming his beloved with deeds of valour. The lower is from *Le Docteur Festus*, a satire on Faust, the search for knowledge, and the foolishness of savants. Involuntary early space travellers are hurled into the air on a giant telescope, to the astonishment of an astronomer and his twenty-eight paid observers. Töpffer's weak eyesight was responsible for his elliptical drawing style which anticipates modern cartoon technique.

Of the many English humorous magazines in the 1840s only one remains – *Punch*. Started in 1841 by Henry Mayhew, Mark Lemon and Joseph Stirling Coyne, it was in its early days radical in tone. Richard Doyle, whose cover design was to last for well over a century, drew the comic adventures of three companions, Brown, Jones and Robinson. After a row with *Punch* over their anti-Papal attitudes he left, and published *Brown, Jones & Robinson* (*below*) in book form in 1854. The extract shows the start of a Jerome K. Jerome-ish jaunt to Europe.

THEY ARE AT THE DOUANE, WAITING FOR THE OFFICIALS TO SEARCH THE LUGGAGE.

ROBINSON AND JONES (ALARMED BY EXPRESSION OF BROWN'S COUNTENANCE).—"WHAT'S THE MATTER NOW?"
BROWN (IN A VOICE OF AGONY).—"I'VE LEFT THE KEY OF MY BAG AT HOME!"

LONDON.

THE MAIL TRAIN TO DOVER. BROWN, JONES, AND ROBINSON, STARTING ON THEIR TRAVELS.

COLOGNE.

THE ARRIVAL AT COLOGNE.

TRAVELLERS PASSING THEIR EXAMINATION. IN THE FOREGROUND IS JONES'S PORTMANTEAU UNDERGOING THE "ORDEAL BY TOUCH."

OSTEND.

AFTER A ROUGH PASSAGE, BROWN, JONES, AND ROBINSON ARE HERE SEEN LANDED AT OSTEND, SURROUNDED, AND A LITTLE BEWILDERED, BY THE NATIVES, WHO OVERWHELM THEM WITH ATTENTIONS—SEIZE THE LUGGAGE, THRUST CARDS INTO THEIR HANDS, DRAG THEM IN SEVERAL DIRECTIONS AT ONCE, ALL TALKING TOGETHER (WHICH PREVENTED THEIR DIRECTIONS BEING SO CLEAR AS THEY OTHERWISE WOULD HAVE BEEN)—AND, FINALLY, ALL EXPECTING MONEY

MANNER AND CUSTOM OF THE PEOPLE, AS SEEN FROM THE RAILWAY BY BROWN, AND MADE A NOTE OF.

Epic vision: in 1854, while he was in his early twenties, the French artist Gustave Doré (1832–83) published in Paris his magnificent work, *L'Histoire de la Sainte Russie*. It was an epic series of violent drawings in continuity form, outlining a cartoon version of Russian history. The blood flowed through 477 pictures spanning the centuries. Doré anticipated many of the techniques of the modern comic strip – the sudden plunging of action into silhouette, the use of speed lines to simulate movement, the juxtaposition of close-up and long-shot. The pages on right are from a German edition of the work published during the First World War. The sequence shows in vivid graphic terms a barbarian invasion and its consequences.

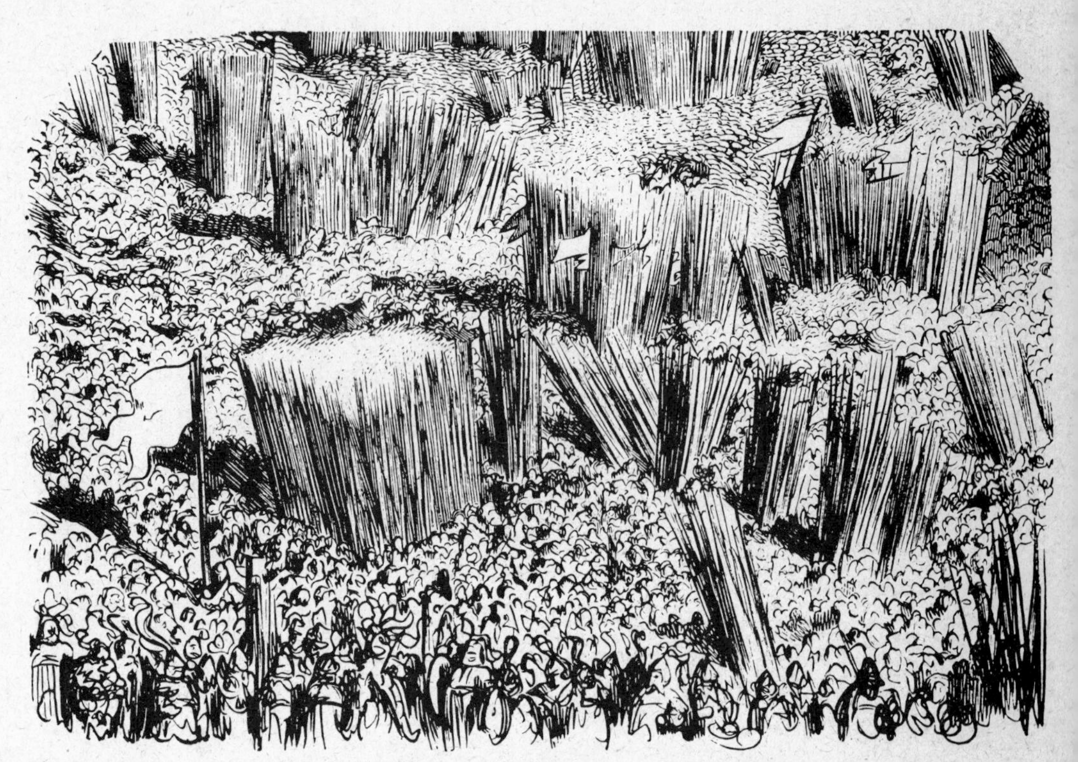

Die asiatischen Barbaren überschwemmen das heilige Rußland.

Das Land ist so erfüllt von ihren Horden, daß sie sich selbst im Wege stehen.

Sie kommen weder vorwärts noch rückwärts und müssen den Pfeilhagel der Verteidiger hilflos über sich ergehen lassen.

Nun steigen die tapferen Russen von ihren Wällen und quetschen die Barbaren zu Mus.

Die Millionen toter Mongolen verpesten die Luft derart, daß die Russen zu den verächtlichen Mitteln der Reinlichkeit und Desinfektion ihre Zuflucht nehmen.

Die Folge dieser grauenhaften Zustände ist eine Hungersnot. Die Bojaren beraten beim leckern Schmaus, was man dagegen tun könne.

Zar Iwan, dem vor Tisch Klagen des hungernden Volkes zu Ohren gekommen waren, wirkt in angeregter Laune auf seine Ratgeber ein.

Am andern Tage setzt Iwan seine tatkräftigen Bemühungen um die Zufriedenheit des Volkes fort, indem er seine Minister öffentlich kitzeln läßt.

Dann richtet er die Frage an sein Volk: „Seid ihr nun befriedigt?"

Das Volk, von jenem Schauspiel ergötzt und gerührt, erklärt, daß es zum Dank gesonnen sei, gegen die Feinde des Vaterlandes zu ziehen. Auf den Einwurf des Herrschers: „Wir haben ja gar keine Feinde!" erwidern sie: „Aber wir müssen welche haben – unsere patriotische Begeisterung ist so groß, daß wir sie gegen irgend jemand betätigen müssen."

Victorian diversions: newspapers in Victorian England were usually barren of illustrative matter and the two examples of graphic design here help to explain why pictures in print had a less-than-respectable reputation. Below is the cover of a 'penny dreadful', the Victorians' equivalent of horror comics. They featured the deeds of a regular character – in this case the terrifying and grotesque Spring-Heel'd Jack who enjoyed something of the notoriety later to be assumed by the real-life bogy-man Jack the Ripper. A sensational cover drawing was always required, for publishers were already well aware of the value of point-of-sale display in raising circulation. The *Illustrated Police News* (*right*) had a bogus air of respectability, mocking the sober *Illustrated London News* in style. It was, however, a magnificent opportunity for the presentation of scandal and sensation, put across with the Victorian penchant for retribution and punishment indulged to the full. Unlike its distinguished contemporary, the *ILN*, the artists and wood engravers employed were poor exponents of their craft. The inconsistent perspective of the execution scene would suggest that a different hand was responsible for the background. Often such illustrations were totally inaccurate and it was not unusual for the same woodblock to be used more than once for different subjects. In this example the joins in the woodblocks engraved to make the large illustration are clearly visible.

NO. 2 GRATIS WITH NO. 1. ONE PENNY.
SPRING-HEEL'D JACK,
THE TERROR OF LONDON.
SPRING-HEEL'D JACK'S DARING LEAP.
Spring-Heeled Jack will, in type, perform over again his midnight freaks and daring adventures.
WITH ILLUSTRATIONS EVERY WEEK OF HIS DOINGS.
NEWSAGENTS' PUBLISHING COMPANY, 147, FLEET STREET, LONDON, E.C.

THE ILLUSTRATED

POLICE NEWS.

LAW-COURTS AND WEEKLY RECORD.

No. 202.] [Registered for Transmission Abroad] LONDON, SATURDAY, DECEMBER 28th. 1867 [Office–275, Strand. London] [PRICE ONE PENNY

THE EXECUTION OF FREDRICK BAKER FOR THE MURDER AT ALTON.

THE NIGHT BEFORE THE EXECUTION. PORTRAIT OF CALCRAFT. BAKER ASCENDING THE STEPS OF THE SCAFFOLD.

Comic threshold: Alfred Harmsworth started *Comic Cuts* and *Chips* in 1890 with the intention of diverting readership from publications such as these. The lively 'penny bloods' were the staple reading fare of errand-boys. An exciting cover masked stories of ingenious complexity within, delivered in print so tiny that only young eyes were possessed of the stamina necessary to decode it. By 1890 the wild American West was already a favourite subject for English readers. Lightning Charlie seems to have an unusually polished mode of speech for a Texan gunman. The penny bloods' vernacular was dented but not swept underground by the Harmsworth invasion. In time they became the story comics, such as *Rover*, *Wizard*, *Champion* and, most famous of all, *Magnet* and *Gem*, existing in harmony alongside their strip-carrying companions.

No. 23. Vol. I. Edited by VANE ST. JOHN. One Penny.

"CRIKEY," HE SAID, HOARSELY, "WHERE AM DAT HAT?"

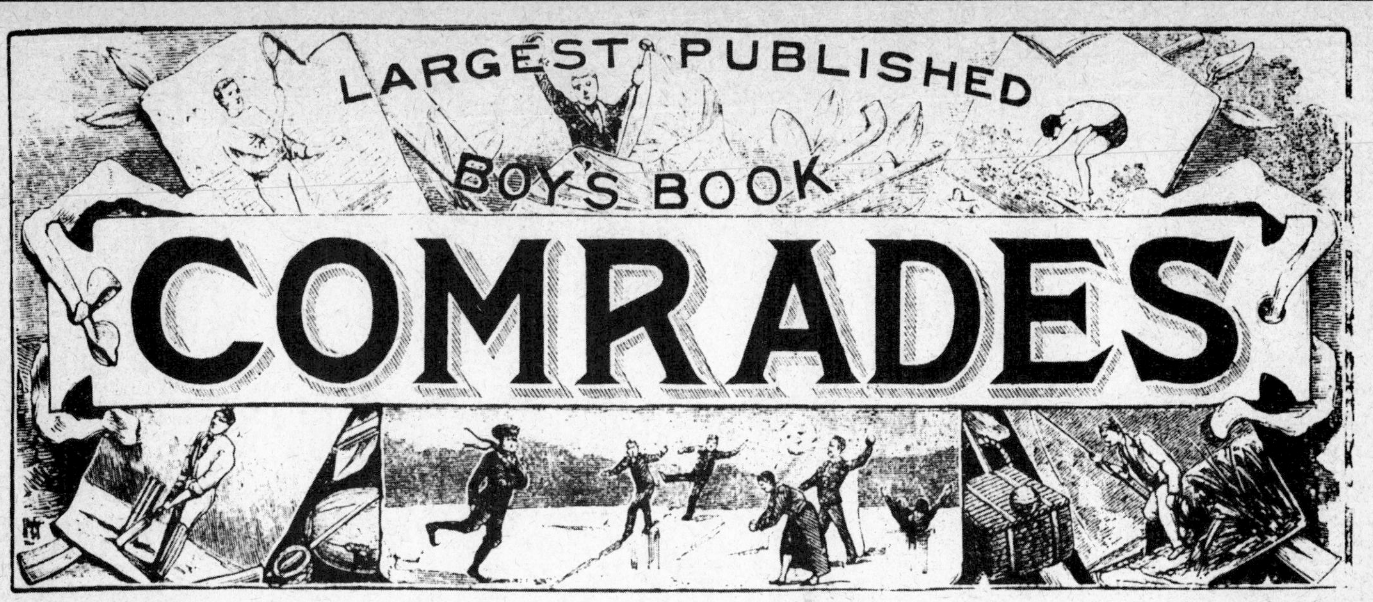

No. 26. Vol. III.] *Edited by* CHARLES SHUREY. [Price One Penny

"WHAT DO YOU MEAN BY THIS INTRUSION?" CHARLIE ASKED.

Moritz! what fate led you and Max,
To cut holes in the miller's sacks?

See! peasant Meck is coming round
To lift his maltsacks from the ground;

Scarce has he got one on his back,
When out the corn runs from the sack.

The rustic cries in wondering plight –
'Why! bless my soul, the bag grows light.'

Ah! now he spies with gladdened face,
Our Max and Moritz' hiding place;

Quick, pops them into his great bags,
Just like two bundles of old rags,

Savage genius: in the 1860s Wilhelm Busch in Germany began producing his *bilderbogen*, a kind of children's library of cartoon characters. The most famous were Max and Moritz, two spiteful small boys whose main preoccupation was the teasing of adults. The German graphic tradition of cruelty was a prominent element of Busch's work. In this incident, the unfortunate pair, as punishment for a silly prank, are ground into mash and fed to the geese. Busch's output was leisurely, yet Max and Moritz held on to the German imagination for many years. Towards the end of the nineteenth century the American newspaper magnate, William Randolph Hearst, on a trip to Europe, had his eye caught by Busch's work and took several of the *bilderbogen* back to New York. Max and Moritz appealed to him and he commanded Rudolph Dirks to create a new strip based on them, with episodes tailored to American tastes. That is how Hans and Fritz, the Katzenjammer Kids, who still appear, originated. It is Wilhelm Busch who brings us to the modern American strip.

And Max and Moritz both feel ill,
For Meck is going to the mill.

'Hi! master miller, come this way!
Grind this for me without delay!'

The miller says – 'come give it here',
And down the funnel shoots the pair.

Rick-rickserackey! rickserack!
Round goes the mill with measured crack;

And here you can the urchins see,
Ground down as fine, as fine can be.

And all the pieces quickly were
Devoured by the poultry there.

Britain -the Comic Cuts tradition

Britain – the Comic Cuts Tradition.

Ally Sloper's Half-Holiday, *the first true modern comic – the Harmsworth revolution – Weary Willie and Tired Tim – the comics' golden age – Tiger Tim – visual style of* Film Fun *– the Dundee invasion – fadeout for the old comics, birth of the new – American take-over – incentive for improvement.*

The British comic strip has developed quite differently from its American counterpart. The changes in direction were already pronounced as long ago as the last years of the nineteenth century. In America the impetus for the publication of strips has always come from major newspaper companies. The comic supplement in colour has been a familiar feature of the week-end newspaper scene for about seventy years. The British newspaper Press, however, was slow to start carrying strips, the *Daily Mirror* leading the way in the twenties. Even today the number of daily strips appearing in Britain is a fraction of those in American newspapers. On the other hand many children's papers devoted partly or entirely to strips have been produced in Britain, whereas the juvenile comic, published on its own rather than as a newspaper supplement, is generally unknown in America.

The first regular comic in the modern sense is probably *Ally Sloper's Half-Holiday*, the first number of which appeared on 3 May 1884. It was published in London by the Dalziel Brothers and was to continue with minor interruptions until 1923. Its claim to be the first comic rests on the fact that it was based on a regular character. A seedy proletarian loafer, Ally Sloper delighted in swigging gin and pouring scorn on his fellows. The paper was crude and hard-biting, aimed initially at a young adult readership. Its broad humour and its contempt for stuffed shirts and pomposity were directed towards the new literate masses emerging as the first effects of the 1870 Education Act.

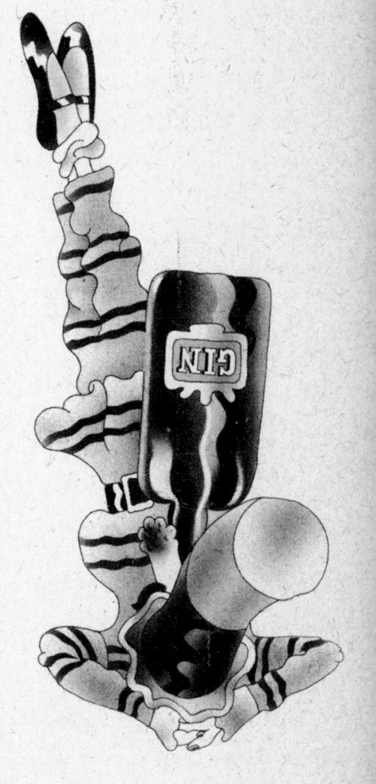

The paper's early frontispieces featuring the detestable Ally were drawn by W.G.Baxter, an American who had moved to England in childhood; like a character from one of the popular moralizing novels of the time, he ultimately died in poverty from drink. He was succeeded by W.Fletcher Thomas who went on to draw the character for many years.

The year 1890 saw the birth of two great comic papers which were to enjoy sixty-three years of life. These were *Comic Cuts* and *Chips*. Both came from the Amalgamated Press and were the inspiration of its twenty-five-year-old proprietor, Alfred Harmsworth, who had just inherited the company. Later, as Lord Northcliffe, he was to be one of the most influential and controversial Press tycoons to walk the Fleet Street stage.

Harmsworth's objects were twofold. First, he wanted to break into a market dominated by the penny dreadful, with its sensational serials and crude drawings. But his publication was to be priced at a halfpenny – and later A.A.Milne was to say that Harmsworth 'killed the penny dreadful with the ha'penny dreadfuller'.

Second, he wanted to give his modestly successful publication, *Answers*, a boost to beat its competitor, George Newnes's *Tit-Bits*, which had a much better circulation. The plan was to induce readers to buy *Answers* after their appetites had been whetted in *Comic Cuts*. Houghton Townley, an *Answers* editor, was seconded and ordered to get the new paper ready in four days. The first number sold 118,864 copies; within a few weeks it had reached a steady and unpredicted 300,000, which was 120,000 more than *Answers*.

The early issues of *Comic Cuts* owed much to *Ally Sloper's Half-Holiday* in format, consisting of innumerable cartoons interspersed with jokes. The strips that appeared were usually those gags which could not be told in a single picture. In England line blocks were then known as 'cuts', the term still used in America, for the age of woodcut illustration had only recently passed. Hence the comic's name, which puzzled its ultimate generation of readers.

Chips, or to give it its formal title, *Illustrated Chips*, was announced ten weeks after *Comic Cuts*. It had a central character, Mr Chips; like its stablemate it was priced at a halfpenny. By the creation of these two papers, Harmsworth not only effectively blocked competition by competing with himself, but pioneered a format which persisted for decades.

Chips introduced its famous characters Weary Willie and Tired Tim (initially Weary Waddles and Tired Timmy) in 1896. These two survived until the paper's own demise in 1953 when they were appointed to join an eccentric millionaire as his companions for all eternity. The pair of tramps were the creation of an artist called Tom Browne. He had left school at eleven to make ends meet for his impoverished family; after the huge success of his two rogues he never went without work. Other comics demanded tramps too, and preferably from his pen: at one time Browne was drawing seven different sets of six-frame strips. When *The Wonder* started in 1898 he created offspring for the team, Little Willie and Tiny Tim. He died in 1910, worn out at thirty-eight, and his mainstream strip in *Chips* was carried on by a succession of other artists.

Harmsworth's comics proved themselves commercially, and although the content was generally unexceptional the dressing was attractive – so much so that *Comic Cuts* was advertised as 'the poor man's *Punch*'. *Punch*, unamused, sent a solicitor's letter.

Although a great deal of American material was lifted and adapted for the two Harmsworth papers, mainly because there had been too little time to build up a resident pool of artists and writers, it was now that the British and American comic strips began to go in different directions.

Comic Cuts and *Chips* were able to establish the comic *genre* in British publishing much more effectively than the earlier *Ally Sloper's Half-Holiday*, for they brought to the humorous paper the weight of mass circulation. Their combined totals were more than half a million. More comics followed in the nineties, some from Amalgamated Press themselves, such as *The Wonder* and *Funny*

Wonder, some from rival houses – *Larks* from Dalziels, *Comic Life* from Henderson's, *Jolly Bits* from Charles Fox, *Halfpenny Comic* from Newnes, and countless others.

One of the most interesting of the rivals was *Dan Leno's Comic Journal*, which first appeared early in 1898 and ran for just under two years. Here the central figure was not fictitious but the much-loved knockabout music-hall comedian, who supposedly addressed his public in the role of editor. On the front cover there was always a big cartoon of the cockney Leno, often shown as destitute after the failure of one of his own racing tips. This is among the earliest examples of a personality being used in such a way to sponsor a paper.

If there is a golden age of the English comic it is the period from the turn of the century until late in the First World War. It ended when paper shortages and government restrictions had forced many publications either to merge or to close; those that remained had to reduce their size and print on poorer paper. Already by far the largest publisher was Northcliffe's Amalgamated Press, an empire which was to grow as lesser companies were taken over.

The leaders of the field were still *Comic Cuts* and *Chips*, now joined by *Butterfly*, *Puck*, *Merry and Bright*, and the short-lived *Firefly* introduced in 1915. The format in nearly all of them was the same: on the front a single strip usually in six frames; then a couple of pages of stories, serials and regular series – *Comic Cuts* for example had Martin Steel, Detective and his twelve Lady Assistants; a centre spread followed, packed tight with strips running both vertically and horizontally, single-cartoons and jokes; then another two pages of stories and finally a couple of regular strips or drawings on the back page. There was usually a signed column (grossly mispelled) from the 'office boy', giving a strong hint of the intended readership.

Colour was not used for *Chips*, *Comic Cuts* and *Butterfly*, although the last was printed on coloured paper. But some comics, particularly *Puck* and *Chuckles* from the Amalgamated Press and *Lot-O-Fun* and *Comic Life* from James Henderson, had their covers and occasional other pages printed in colour, sometimes of such good quality that they remain bright today. Technically, the front page of *Chuckles* was particularly remarkable, the artist of Breezy Ben and Dismal Dutchy being a master of the subtle overlay of half-tone colours to produce Benday stipple effects. At Christmas it was customary to double price and pages and bring out a 'bumper number'.

The pattern in comics for a younger age group was formed with the publication of *Rainbow* in 1914. On its polychromatic cover were the Bruin Boys, a creation of J.S. Baker who first drew them in 1910 for Arthur Mee's *Children's Encyclopaedia*. Baker also created Tiger Tim who was to be featured in several papers and turned out to be one of the most popular characters ever to appear in British children's comics. *Tiger Tim's Weekly*, with the constant Bruin Boys on the cover, began in 1920; and in 1925, when *Playbox* started, the Bruin Girls, led by Tim's sister Tiger Tilly, appeared. Tiger Tim's most famous artist was H.S. Foxwell, who took over from Baker less than a year after *Rainbow* started. These comics with their brilliant covers, decoration-crammed borders, and big type set a classic style which persisted, in spite of several major casualties in the course of the Second World War, until the mid-fifties.

In the twenties an outstanding new comic appeared. This was *Film Fun*; it also had a companion paper, *Kinema Comic*, which lasted until 1932. There had already been several comics featuring strips based on real celebrities, such as *Funny Wonder* with Charlie Chaplin on its front page. *Film Fun*, however, featured real comedians in all its strips. The first issue had Harold Lloyd on the cover; inside were to be found Fatty Arbuckle, Larry Semon, Baby Marie Osborne, Mack Swain, Ben Turpin, Slim Summerville, and others. Printed in black and white, the drawing possessed a firmness of line and sharpness of detail not matched by its competitors.

By the thirties *Film Fun*'s visual style had settled in and the pictures were drawn much smaller with no loss of clarity, giving the paper a very packed value-for-money appearance. It was then that George William Wakefield began drawing Laurel and Hardy on the front and back cover, a finely detailed strip with curiously conventionalized backgrounds. This was a world where the heroes would be rewarded with fancy dinners: while they waited in mouth-watering apprehension, knives and forks at the ready, waiters appeared bearing mountainous silver platters of – mashed potatoes with protruding sausages! When Wakefield retired, his son continued to draw the strip.

In the years immediately before the Second World War the Dundee firm of D.C.Thomson launched three comics, *Dandy*, *Beano*, and *Magic*. The first two still survive. They represented a new type of comic, powerful in gag humour and slapstick, with a stubborn toughness and scorn for the higher virtues. The cartoon heroes in *Film Fun* had to turn out to be good-natured at heart if only to keep within the libel laws. But no such scruples could possibly affect the cow-pie eating, steer-tossing tough guy Desperate Dan in *Dandy*, or the authority-hating Lord Snooty of *Beano*. Schoolteachers, policemen, officials of any kind were usually figures of ridicule to be thwarted at every opportunity. This, in itself, was not a new phenomenon, but the Thomson papers pushed the situations much further than the older comics, and provided a satisfying escapist dream to appeal to children. Occasionally authority turned the tables. When this happened savage punishments were meted out with exaggerated ferocity.

Alongside this robust Scottish invasion the older comics looked positively effete. Amalgamated Press began to compete, bringing out *Radio Fun*, a tougher, cruder paper than *Film Fun*, though it used real comedians for its strips in the same way, and *Knockout*, which with characters like Stonehenge Kit, the Ancient Brit and Deed-a-Day Danny came closer to the D.C.Thomson product than any of their other papers.

Until *Dandy* there had been a convention of accompanying the strips even though they carried dialogue balloons, with a few lines of typeset copy under each frame. The purpose of this was obscure since the pictures contained all the information necessary to understand the strip and few children could have bothered to read the text. Perhaps it provided a sop to the attackers of comics who alleged that excessive comic-reading encouraged illiteracy. Thomson eliminated captions from all except their adventure strips, and *Radio Fun* and *Knockout* followed the same practice. Yet *Chips* continued printing text under the pictures until its dying day in 1953.

The Second World War was unfortunately hard on the comics. As in the first war, many famous titles vanished or were combined with younger publications. Paper shortages restricted circulations and salvage drives reduced the number of back issues. The war children swapped their comics from hand to hand until they were in shreds.

After the war, in 1950, Hulton Press, publishers of the national picture magazine *Picture Post*, entered the comic field with a gravure publication. It was not the first; *Mickey Mouse Weekly*, started in 1936, used the same process. Hulton's publication, *Eagle*, was aimed at raising general standards with the then expensive selling price of threepence and was launched with a large advertising campaign aimed at parents. In spite of the big drum-banging at the time, today the early *Eagle* looks surprisingly old-fashioned and not noticeably well drawn. Nevertheless, the venture was successful enough to encourage Hulton to produce companion papers, *Girl*, *Robin*, and *Swift*.

The fortunes of the Hulton Press declined in the mid-fifties with the death of *Picture Post* and today *Eagle* survives, in a different dress, under the Odhams imprint. But others have disappeared. As television began to draw children's interests in other directions the old comics faded away and the 1950s and early 1960s saw the deaths of *Chips*, *Comic Cuts*, *Film Fun*, *Knockout*, *Radio Fun*, and many others, including more modern runners in the field like *Girl*. Amalgamated Press became Fleetway Press, like Odhams a division of the giant International Publishing Corporation, and remains the largest publisher of comics in Britain. Under the direction of Alf Wallace, Odhams have also produced British versions of the successful American Marvel Comics, first as features in *Smash!* and *Wham!* and from February 1967 in an exclusive paper called *Fantastic*. D.C. Thomson keep *Dandy* and *Beano* running supported by *Beezer*, *Bimbo*, *Rover/Wizard*, *Victor*, *Topper*, *Hotspur* and a number of romantic picture-strip papers aimed at the seventeen to twenty-one female market.

The market for children's comics is probably half what it was in the mid-fifties but it is still substantial. Many current publications are based on successful TV series, such as *Thunderbirds* and Hanna-Barbera cartoons like *The Flintstones* and *Yogi Bear*. There is also an active section of the business devoted to the quasi-educational field, the sectional encyclopaedia-style magazines like *Look and Learn*, *Knowledge*, and others.

There is, in Britain, a great gulf between children's strips and those designed for adults. The absence of British-style children's comics in America has given the strips there a greater universality in readership. American parents, on the whole, are more familiar with their children's reading matter than British ones. British comics are at a disadvantage. They lack the incentives for improvement that an audience broader-based in age and intelligence could provide.

Comic Section

England's first comic: there had been humorous cartoon papers for at least fifty years before the arrival of *Ally Sloper's Half-Holiday*. Few had staying power; the exception was *Punch*, founded in 1841. But *Punch*, by 1884, had settled down to the comfortable, faintly radical, middle-class position it still occupies. The fictional Ally Sloper was totally vulgar – an insolent layabout who might have emerged from Dickensian back-alleys. He was usually featured in a special frontispiece – adding his groatsworth to the topics of the moment. In this case he is commenting on the unsuccessful and notorious Victorian lawsuit of the Tichborne claimant. The comic paper was a *mélange* of jokes and little drawings, packed into every inch of the page. Many of the cartoons were thumbnail size. They were influenced by the work of Priestman Atkinson in *Punch*, whose 'Dumb Crambo' visual puns were a surprisingly hilarious feature of the Late Victorian scene (*below*). Rudimentary strip sequences were already appearing in *Ally Sloper's Half-Holiday* (*overleaf*). This is a back page of a holiday issue, and a moderately serious study of the joys of Herne Bay was not considered out of place. *Ally Sloper's Half-Holiday* was a paper for young men, clerks and counterhands – the new generation of white-collar workers. Alfred Harmsworth, later Lord Northcliffe, had the same audience in mind when he started *Comic Cuts* in 1890. Priced at ½*d.* it undercut the popular 'penny bloods', the story magazines which always featured a spectacular cover and masses of close, grey text within. *Comic Cuts* was less vulgar than *Ally Sloper's Half-Holiday* and its layout was as unscientific. But with its companion paper, *Chips*, launched the same year, it achieved a phenomenal circulation of half a million, and eclipsed the competition. The comic had truly arrived.

DUMB CRAMBO JUNIOR'S EDITION OF THE BRITISH POETS.
FISHM
"Chaw, Sir!"
Shakes Peer.
Dried 'Un.
Crabbe and Shelley.
Scott and Moore.

Ally Sloper's Half Holiday

BEING A SELECTION, SIDE-SPLITTING, SENTIMENTAL, AND SERIOUS, FOR THE BENEFIT OF OLD BOYS, YOUNG BOYS, ODD BOYS GENERALLY, AND EVEN GIRLS.

No. 15.] SATURDAY, AUGUST 9, 1884. [ONE PENNY.

THE CLAIMANT.

The "*Daily News*" says, "*On his regaining his liberty, the Claimant will appeal to the public for support.*"
SLOPER says, "*Why don't they let the poor man out at once, so that he may have the benefit of the Seaside season.*"

THE MISTAKE: A Running Tale.

SCENE—*Amateur Athletic Sports.* Knobbs (*Spots*) and Bobbs (*Stripes*), the only two entered for the half-mile race.

Bobb's pa, who is present, is very short-sighted.

And thinking that Bobbs, Junior, is *Spots*, wildly encourages Knobbs, so much so that he wins.

Knobbs. "Sir, though you are an entire stranger to me, I must thank you; for it is wholly through your encouragement that I won the race." (Oh!)

TO BATHERS.

SLOPER *has much pleasure in presenting to his Lady Readers some designs for Bathing Costumes by his daughter.*

1. The "Olivia" Goldsmith.

2. The Jane Shore.

3. The Normandy

4. La Russe.

5. The Harlequin.

6. The Folly.

7. The Serpolette.

8. The Floral.

AGONY of UNCLE BENJAMIN!

FRIGHTFUL PROPOSITION!
INFAMY OF HIGGINS!
UNPARALLELED ATROCITY!
UNHEARD OF DEPRAVITY!
A TALE OF TERROR!
HORROR! HORROR! HORROR!
BLOOD, AND BLOOD ONLY!

THINGS have reached a hideous pitch.

• • • • •

What is next to come? Goodness only knows.

• • • • •

Bill Higgins is at present pondering on Uncle Benjamin's doom. He

BY THE SAD SEA WAVES.

A Sea Gull.

An Old Crab.

A Limp-et.

ON THE BEACH AT HERNE BAY.

A SHOCKING AFFAIR.

1. Young Sprouts, who suffers from extreme debility, especially in the head, consults Dr. Twister, the Eminent Galvanist.

2. He suggests the use of the machine.

3. It is very simple, says Twister. Just catch hold of these two handles while I charge the battery.

4. Oh!

5. Oh! Oh—o—o!!

6. Oh—o—o—o! Ah!—ha—ha! Whew!! (General dislocation of Sprouts. Bits swept up afterwards with a hearth-broom.)

A Sandy Little Cove.

THE SECRET OUT.

1. *She.* "Now that we are alone, Ronaldo, there is something I wish no longer to keep secret from you."
He. "'Tis strange, Sophronia, that I also have a secret which I wish now to unfold."

2. *She.* Pray calm yourself, and know, Ronaldo, that I wear a wig! "
He. "Control your emotion, and learn, dearest Sophronia, that these locks are not my own!"

3. Mutual relief thus finds vent.

ONE HALFPENNY **PICTURES, PRIZES, JOKES.** ONE HALFPENNY.

Comic Cuts.

½d. ½d.

No. 1. Vol. 1.] ONE HALFPENNY WEEKLY. [May 17, 1890.

THE STRONG MAN FRAUD; OR, THE 1000-LB. AIR-BALL.

"You women don't know how to hang pictures—takes a man to do it!"

"I think I'll put it here, or—a little farther over."

"A trifle farther yet—this is the spot; now just hand me a hook and some string, and I'll have this picture up in a jiffy. I tell you, I understand hanging pictures right down to the——

—ground!"

THE LATEST BOTANICAL DISCOVERY.

THE BLOOMING IDIOT
(*Genus Cigarettus*).

THE JOYS OF THE SUBURBANITE.

This style of breakfast is known as the Suburban 8.13 A.M.

BY HOOK AND CROOK.

"O, you may laugh, but it's a great deal better way than the old-fashioned chain round his neck."

WHY TIMPKINS IS GOING TO MOVE AGAIN.

Timpkins said (last September) "I've moved to Chingford. Awfully jolly place; fine fresh country air; splendid walk to the station and back: making a man of me." His friends said nothing; they were picturing Timpkins in the winter.

Timpkins's splendid walk in October.

And in December.

Start of a fifty-seven-year career: in 1896 Tom Browne created a pair of tramps and they appeared on the front page of the 16 May issue of *Chips* – a position that was to be exclusively theirs until 1953 when the paper died. For the first few weeks they were Weary Waddles and Tired Timmy. They became Weary Willie and Tired Tim, sobriquets for indigence and blissful idleness.

Cockney comic: *Dan Leno's Comic Journal* (*overleaf*) of 1898 was one of the first papers to be built on the fame of a celebrity, in this case a prominent music-hall comedian at the height of his career. The paper lasted little more than two years. In 1901 Leno had a serious mental illness and died three years later at the age of forty-three.

General's daughter: The *Jester* was more a story paper than a comic, but it ran cartoons on some of its pages. The example is from the Christmas issue of 1913, doubled in size and price as was the custom.

Bumper number: the front and back pages of *Puck* show a typical Edwardian bumper number. At Christmas and New Year the title lettering of a comic always bore a massive weight of snow and icicles. *Puck* was one of the first comics to be printed in full colour.

Solid centre: the centre spread of *Chuckles* is a good example of the solid, packed layout of a comic in the golden age. Such displays, with strips running both horizontally and vertically, gave a value-for-money appearance, appreciated by young readers, if an art editor's nightmare. In twenty-two years of existence, *Comic Cuts* had developed into a standard comic with regular cartoon characters. A ticket-of-leave man was an ex-convict on a form of parole. Jokes about 'niggers' were not taboo in 1912. The Mulberry Flatites, the dwellers in a curious mobile apartment block, thwarted an attempted German invasion two years before the Great War.

½D ILLUSTRATED CHIPS ½D

No. 298. Vol. XII. (New Series.) [Entered at Stationers' Hall.] PRICE ONE HALFPENNY. [Transmission Abroad at Book Rates.] May 16, 1896.

INNOCENTS ON THE RIVER.

1. Weary Waddles: "I say, Timmy, a great idea has hit me in the head. If we catch that horse we can make him tow us in this boat."

2. Tired Timmy: "That's a noble scheme. You do the fancy work, and catch the animal."

3. W. W. "How's this? Ye'd take me for a Dragooner in the Queen's Bodyguard, wouldn't ye?"

4. T. T. "Ah! this reminds me of the old days at Oxford. Have you the luncheon-basket, Willie?"

5. W. W. "Great Pip! Bridge ahoy! Hi! Whoa—
T. T. whoa, you brute!"

6. And then they got out and walked.

FORCE OF HABIT.

1. There was no mistake about it; he was badly henpecked. He had a bald top, and his wife used to relieve her feelings by rapping it with her knuckles.

2. And so used to this did he become that, when his wife went away to the seaside, he quite lost his appetite—

3. Until he invented a little machine like this. Then his relish for food returned. It was quite like old times again.

THOUGHT IT WAS MAGIC; HADN'T SEEN A LIFT BEFORE.

1. Farmer Groats: "Bring me a glass of cider, will you?" Waiter. "Yessir!"

2. Calls down the lift to bar: "Send up one cider, quick, please."

3. Farmer Groats: "I just seed you open that cupboard door, and there was nothin' there. Now you open it again, and there's a glass of cider. If you tell me how you work it, so as I can do it at home, I'll give you a shillin'!"

WORKING IT OUT.

Lazy Larry: "Watcher doin', Willie?"
Weary Willie: "Oh, just wipin' out a little debt I owe."

HELLO! I'VE BEEN WAITING FOR YOU. PAY YOUR HALFPENNY AND LET'S BE OFF.

DAN LENO'S COMIC JOURNAL ½

No. I. Vol. I.
WEEK ENDING
February 26, 1898.

"ONE TOUCH OF LENO MAKES THE WHOLE WORLD GRIN."

EVERY TUESDAY.

A PEEP AT THE EDITORIAL DEN.

My dear friends,—Greeting. I am informed by everyone I know that the funniest thing I have ever done is to become editor of a funny paper. Well, that's just how it ought to be; otherwise the pains I have taken in getting out my first number would have been used to better advantage for glazing purposes. You can read all about my staff—whose portraits appear above—inside. The telegrams of congratulation from the Emperor of Germany and other crowned heads of Europe on the appearance of my Comic Journal have been crowded out to make room for the Police News. They will be published next week; so till next Tuesday, ta, ta, and be good.

Herewith my hand and quill, Yours ever, Dan Leno

They Weren't Dis-turban Him.

1. "I can't say I feel quite comfortable in this European get up," thought the Rajah of Bundlepore. "No, I don't like these top hats at all," said he. And just then a lad shied a big snowball—

2. Which roosted on his new silk hat, an in another second the other lad let him have one on the other side, making him look like this. "Ah! That's more like it!" chuckled the Rajah. "I feel more like an Oriental now. Good!"

SMILER & SMIRK, Ltd., Mirth Merchants.

1. "This looks like being a merry Christmas for us, Smiler, me old marvel," quoth Smirk, as they stood idly by the jolly old post office, watching Uncle Bernard posting a big jack-in-the-box to his dear little nephew Willie. For, of a truth, our pals were sad of heart, being short of the old £ s. d. Ugh! Fancy being hard up! Ugh! U-G-H! Ugh! Well, still they stood there.

2. And anon there came a pampered menial—the head footman at the Marquis de Mystitte's, with little Albert, the page, and they proceeded to post sundry choice chickens and plum puddings, all marked with the coronet. And Smiler stifled a sob as he remarked to Smirk, "O-o, Smirky, old son! Had we but one of those birds, with a pudding to match, how happy could we be!" "Ah, boy!" replied Smirk.

3. Then, having nothing particular to do for the next year or two, they idly sauntered over to the post office. "Ha! What have we here?" said Smirk. And he pulled at the label which hung out of the letter-box. And then a wondrous thing happened. A merry marvel, forsooth! "What luck!" you'll say in a tick, gentle reader. Well, we must tell you what happened. You'd never guess.

4. Why, when Smirk pulled that string it opened the lid of the jack-in-the-box that Uncle Bernard had posted, and that sent a whole collection of choice birds, plum puddings, sweeties, and all sorts of good things flying out, and Smiler and Smirk filled their pockets prompt-o, and hopped it back to their apartments, and did tuck in well and truly till they could tuck in no more. Oho! Oho! "A right Merry Christmas, all!"

THE ADVENTURES OF JESSIE JOLLY, THE GENERAL'S DAUGHTER.

1. "These poor little kiddies don't seem to be having much of a time of it," thought Jessie, when she spotted the little hard-up ones gazing with eager eyes at the toyshop window on Christmas Eve. So what do you think she did?

2. Why, she got one of those balloons that look like plum puddings when blown out, and filled it with Christmas toys of all sorts and kinds and shapes and sizes. Then she tripped across the road. "Come in, kiddies, and have some fun!" she cried.

3. And down they all sat to a jolly fine dinner. And when the pudding was brought in, Jessie said, "Now, then, sit tight while I cut this pudding!" As she put the knife across it. BANG! And out fell all the toys—

4. Much to the delight of the kiddies. And they weren't disappointed about the real pudding, either, for May, the maid, arrived with the real eatable article itself. And a jolly good time they had, too. "Merry Christmas, Miss Jessie!" was the shout.

A MONSTER BUDGET OF CHRISTMAS FUN!

No. 229. Vol. IX EVERY FRIDAY. DECEMBER 12th, 1908.

CHRISTMAS DAY ON BOARD THE "GADABOUT."

1. 'Twas Christmas Eve, and aboard H.M.S. *Gadabout* all was joy. Did I say all? Well, all excepting in the case of Gertie, the pet mule, who had, alas! been left out in the cold. And it was cold, too—cold enough to turn a custard into ice cream. "Well, well," moaned the mule, "Christmas may be a nice warm-hearted time for most people—but so far as I am concerned it's an absolute frost.

2. "Nobody asks me to have a nice, juicy cut off the turkey and a slice of plum pudding, or drinks my health, or puts presents in my stocking. No; Santa Claus never drops in *via* the funnel specially to see me." And, with a tear bedimming her soft, Rickett's blue eye, the pretty creature turned sadly away from the merry scene. 'Twas then that another and more stirring sight caught her eagle optic.

3. "Hullo! who might you be?" she gurgled, as she caught sight of a strange, fearsome-looking frontispiece peering over the ship's side. "If they haven't invited me to the party I'm sure they haven't invited anybody with a face like yours. Get out of it!" And the pirate (for such he was) got out—and so did his friends, as fast as they came aboard—plonkety, plonk, plonk! "That's funny!" said the pirate chief.

4. But he didn't think it the least bit funny when presently he clambered up the ladder to see the cause of the trouble, and found Gertie waiting to give him a helping hand—we should say mouth—aboard. And just as the pretty pet took a firm grip of him abaft the beam, the alarm was raised and the ship's crew turned out to repel boarders. "All's well," smiled Gertie; "here's the last of them."

5. Yes, there was no mistake about it, the merry mule had saved the ship, and, dear us, what a fuss they did make of her! Talk about a merry Xmas—well, there, children, look at the animated picture and let it tell its own tale.

PROF.
RADIUM
HAS SUCH A
HAPPY XMAS
WITH THE BOYS
(TEE HEE)

1. Christmas is here again! All together, hip-hip! And Uncle Radium, the man who knows All About Everything, is down to stay with his two nephews. Yes, Radium knows the lot. Who said so? Why, Radium, of course, and *he* knows. And the boys were delighted, because they wished to learn something, and when boys wish that, look out. Isn't that so, ma? Anyway, they made a nice dummy figure with heavy leaden boots to keep its feet down, and they filled its head with gas, and put skates on it, and away they tore to the lake to gather meaty bits of information for Uncle Professor Radium. Ah, woe, woe!

2. And there they found him large as life, wearing scientific smoked-glass to "obviate the glare of the snow." Brainy man. "Oh, uncle," said they, "we've got a Scotch school friend with us, Sandy McLauder, for Chrissmus, and he wants to know if you'll teach him skating. He wants to learn the theoretical and practical side of it, having a geometry head, and being a prize-winner, and he's nuts on your books, and would feel obliged if you would give him a likkle help." "Why, of course, sir," said Radium. "How do you do? I shall be delighted. Any friend of my nephews is a friend of mine. Come along.

3. "I should have thought," said Radium, as they clasped hands and whizzed off, aided by a twenty-eight pound push from the kids, "I should have thought, my lad, that, being Scotch, you would have already acquired a considerable proficiency in skating. Your people do a great deal of it. They skate in large numbers over the border, where they sell their skates in case they went back in their sleep. Strike out my boy! Left. Right. Might I ask are you any relative of Henry Lauder's? He interests me greatly. Now push out with the left. Don't be afraid. Right out.

4. But, alas and alack! Poor young Sandy McLauder lost his legs somewhere under Rade's, with a nasty side-slip, and over went the show! "Bless my chronometer!" gasped Radium, as his nose gave a beautiful metallic C sharp on the ice. "How did that happen? A loose strap, I suppose. I *do* hope the Scotch youth escaped injury. I would never forgive myself if——

5. "Too terrible. It's too terrible! His legs have broken off. The keen frost has—wait a moment and I will put on my other glasses—Help! My surmise was all too correct. His bones were brittle with the frost, and now—— Horrible! How shall I break it to his parents? Where is his body? (What-ho the body, with the heavy boots off and the gas head lifting things.) "I must at least return that to——"

6. "Come on, uncle dear," yelled the boys. "Dinner bell's gone and we mustn't keep the turkey waiting, must we?" "T-t-tell me, boys," panted Radium; "t-tell me, can you see anything floating over there?" "Nothin' at all, uncle, 'cept a couple of sparrers." "Not your friend, Sandy McLauder?" gasped Rade. "Then my brainy grey matter is confusticated, and my convolutions are a conglomeration of confounded complexity. Help!" And the amount of ma's Xmas cordial it took to get him round would make you laugh till your hat split. Here's to you all!

Printed for the Proprietors by the London Colour Printing Company, Ltd., and published at 25, Bouverie Street, London, E.C. Subscription, 7s. per annum. December 12th, 1908.
Registered for transmission to Canada at magazine postage rates.

BRIBERY AND CORE-UPTION!

Gent: "That's a nice apple, my lad. What are you going to do with it?" Lad: "Take it to teacher!" Gent: "Ah, that's kind of you. Is it his birthday?" Lad: "No; but I'm about an hour late to-day!"

GREAT SNAKES!

1. "Heavens!" groaned the ham and beef dealer. "Here's old Screwem, the landlord, come for his rent, and I can't raise it nohow! I ham in a predicament I've never been in beef-ore!"

2. But by skilfully arranging a few stray sausages to look like a ferocious snake he scared that landlord so that—

3. His screams rent the air, and that was about the only rent that *was* raised. True? Why serpently!

MUSTARD KEEN AND HIS TERRIBLE TERRIER

1. Mr. Editor, my cheeriest old chum, sir,—I must confess that I was done. I was keeping watch in an empty house when the heat overcame me, and, sir, believe me, I snoozed. And when I came to, or three—

2. I found my wrists tightly bound. "You'll find it difficult to a-wrist me like that!" Slacker Sam—who had perpetrated the deed upon me—was chuckling humorously. "How to escape?" I silently quothed.

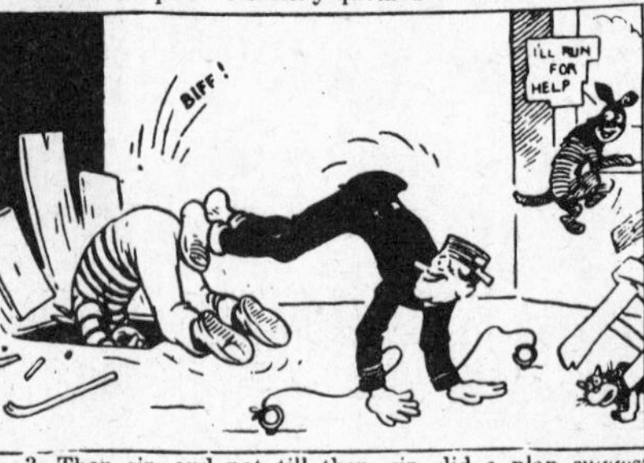

3. Then sir, and not till then, sir, did a plan suggest itself. While Slacker Sam—with his head buried in a hole in the floor—presented the soles of his boots to me, I up and smote him with my own trotter-cases—

4. With the startling effect that he almost and suddenly disappeared from view. "There's your man!" I chortled—when P.-c. Beetlecrusher and attendants appeared—"with his head buried in buried treasure!" Smart capture! Pat, pat!—Thine, MUSTARD KEEN.

LITTLE TOMMY TREDD

1. "The boss says I can go when I've cleaned the bo groaned the page-boy; "but there are so many, I shall miss boy scouts' parade! What's to be done?"

3. And while he chuckled it he was busy fixing the bootbr to the propeller. "I am doing this sole-ly for your bene he said, treddling terrifically.

O. K. POKAY SQU

1. "Ha, ha! Watch me closely peoples!" chuckled Tricky Teddy. "If I don't make somebody look very foolish with this bad coin, I'll give up trying to be funny for ever!"

2. And he the corner w is about to twigged the

PUT A DIFFER

1. "Well, I don't know," gurgled Useless Eustace. "I must fill in time somehow, so I don't see why I shouldn't pack this trunk and stay here for the week-end!" With which witty remark—

2. He cli and a few m merchant, c posters ri breathe," y

HIS NON-SCENTS!

"I want a cake of soap, please." "Yessir! Scented or unscented?" "Oh, you needn't trouble. I'll take it with me!"

FELT "BOUND" TO.

"Johnny, where are your school-books?" "Well, you see dad, when notices appeared that books were wanted for the soldiers, I sent mine!"

SOLD AGAIN!

First Clown: "Most things that are bought go to the buyer!"
Second Clown: "Yes, all except coal—that goes to the cellar!"

THE NIGGER

1. "Oh, dear me! and mai word!" gushed the knut on the cliff, "here's a common nigger fellow asleep. Just watch me spring a humorous surprise on him—what? Oh, do watch me!"

2. And he p on to the nig's that a little har that hat was a

HIS TOY AEROPLANE.

Then little Tommy Treddles flew to the rescue with his toy lane. "You look as gloomy as if all the 'shine' had gone of your life!" he chuckled.

And in almost less than no time that huge heap of hoof-ings was shining brightly. "Thanks!" whuffled the old boy picture. "Here's a shining sixpence for you!" Loud cheers!

PRACTICAL JOKER!

coin right on
l O. K. Pokay
urned it, and

3. "Got it!" he chortled as he stooped to capture the coin. And down came his board hard on Teddy's hatpeg. "Wow! I'll never practical joke again!" sobbed Tricky Ted.

LEXION ON IT!

w tree-trunk,
dds, the soap
ed one of his
"I can't
e—

3. And he pushed his headpiece through the paper for air. "Oo-er!" shrieked Sudds. "My poster's come to life. Oh, what a nor-ful face! I'll give up soap-boiling and go in for growing green gooseberries, I will!"

BOXO THE MUSCULAR MARVEL

1. "Now then, what d'ye mean by playing nap during business hours?" yelled Boxo, who'd got a job as foreman in a cask factory, to two labourers whom he'd caught napping.

2. "You're both sacked!" he went on angrily. "I never knew such double-barrelled loafing. Get out, and I'll do the job myself!" And a moment later he was hoisting the casks with great easiness.

3. And so busy was he that he didn't notice that those two bad labourers had prepared a weighty surprise for him. "Ho, ho!" they ho-ed. "He'll lift that cask full of water. Oh, yes! We *don't* think!"

4. But they didn't know Boxo. He hoisted that cask as easily as if it had been empty, and the water emptied itself over the labourers. "That'll do you good!" he chuckled. "You were too full of dry humour!"

MIGHT NOT OC-CUR TO HIM!

First Tramp: "Don't be afraid, Bill! Don't you know that proverb, 'Barking dogs never bite'?"
Second Tramp: "Yes; but do you think the dog knows it?"

SERGEANT SHRAPNEL THE CYCLIST SCOUT.

1. "You won't catch Sergeant Shrapnel being robbed of his bike!" chuckled that worthy, as he fixed the box of caps to the front wheel.

2. Then he went inside the shop, and a nasty sneak-thief person immediately mounted the sergeant's bike and very nearly made off.

3. But not quite! Nunno! For the box of caps went off first and put the lid on the manœuvre. "Well, that caps it!" groaned the thief. And Shrapnel exploded with laughter!

LOOK BLACK!

ble very heartily
pose you'll think
the knut. But

3. So that when the knut threw the stone the hat returned the compliment and the stone at the same time. "I thought I heard somebody say they'd 'spring' a surprise on me!" snorted the nig.

GETTING ROUND HIM.

Tailor (to very stout customer): "Would you mind holding the tape just here, sir? I'll be round in a minute or two!"

CRUSHING!

Tragedian: "Ah, laddie, I remember once playing 'Macbeth,' and it took the audience two hours to get out of the building after!" Friend: "Was he lame?"

FALSE AIRS!

"Miss Banger says she can make the piano talk when she plays!" "Well, if it spoke, it would say, 'Woman, you have played me false'!"

31-7-15

COMIC CUTS ½D. | **BEGIN TO-DAY.** **"QUEER STREET!"** **Our Thrilling New Story-Drama.**

EVERYBODY'S BUYING IT!
LOTS OF FUN FOR EVERYONE.

Comic Cuts. ½d.

One Hundred Laughs for a Halfpenny.

No. 1172. [Registered.] PRICE ONE HALFPENNY. October 26, 1912.

THE SIDE-SPLITTING ADVENTURES OF TOM, THE TICKET-OF-LEAVE MAN.

1. Dear Mister Editor,—You know how passionately fond I am of little children, and how it wrings my heart to see them cry? I don't mind the sound so much, but the sight is awful! The other morning, for instance, I came across a small face with a large hole in it, and I asked it what was the matter. "They won't let me play cherry-bobs!" was the rejoinder.

2. Now, there was a terrible state of affairs for you, Mister Editor! And you call this a free country! Oh, the hollowness of it all! Well, it was no use going to a solicitor; for, after all, the young ruffians had the law on their side—the cherry-bob apparatus really did belong to them. So I took the plaintiff and introduced him to some caterpillars that I knew.

3. "We'll settle this unpleasant business out of court, young feller!" says I to my client. Then we persuaded the caterpillars to accompany us to a lonely spot, and requested them to do as they were told, and not to answer us back, or our reply would certainly be a crushing one. Luckily, they were very well-behaved caterpillars—quiet with children, and all that. So when I'd chalked some numbers on the fence, they took up their positions as above.

4. Then it suddenly occurred to me that I deserved a holiday. It was a beautiful day for a stroll in the park, so in I went; and after I'd had a drink at the fountain (just one cupful, Mister Editor, as you know I'm very moderate), I thought I should like to have a look at the ducks. So I took a short cut across the grass, softly whistling that old refrain, "Everybody's Doing It!" when a harsh voice interrupted me. 'Twas P.-c. Fairyfoot.

5. Oh, he was in a nasty temper! "How dare you walk on the nice clean grass without first wiping your boots!" he yelled.

6. Then he started to track me down. "The footprints come to an end here!" he blithered. "I shall have to borrow an aeroplane!"

7. The crook of his walking-stick was just over his neck. "This is just about my drop!" I tootled, as I jumped on to it.

8. It was an (n)eck-cellent notion, and worked like a charm. "Au revoir!" I chirped.

TOM, THE TICKET-OF-LEAVE MAN.

ALL THE STARS APPEAR (AND DISAPPEAR) AT THE "COMIC CUTS" COLONY HIPPODROME.

The new COMIC CUTS Colony Hippodrome opened for the first (and last) time on Monday. There was a very good attendance considering, and the gallery was packed. It wouldn't have held any more without collapsing. The first "turn" was a white-eyed nigger who played on for about three hours without stopping. There's no knowing when he would have stopped if Stripes, the tiger, hadn't suddenly popped on to the stage by one of the early doors and carried the minstrel off. Judging by the satisfied smile on the animal's face afterwards, it is pretty evident that this "turn" "went down" very well indeed.

THE MULBERRY FLATITES REPEL THE GERMAN INVASION!

1. The Mulberry Flatites took their famous edifice up on the East Coast the other day, and while there they did a good stroke of business with the local bill-poster in letting him stick a Grenadier cigarette bill on their wall. As Oofbird, Esq., explained to him, it was a splendid position for a poster, for it could be seen by all the passing fishing-smacks and winkle-trawlers in the North Sea. The old boy agreed, and paid a nice little sum for the privilege. "That's it!" piped Joey, the parrot. "The poster can stick to our flats, and we will stick to the money!"

2. But that same evening, just as the Mulberryites were about to retire, a strange noise was heard outside. Frowsy Freddie said it was someone sawing wood; but Bachelorboy, who once worked in a sausage factory, at once recognised it as a German whisper. "Great pip!" he cried. "England is being invaded! Where are the police? Where are the Boy Scouts? Where are——" "Shut up!" exclaimed Frowsy Freddie. "I know what we'll do. Let's paint the flats to look like a sentry-box." So while Oofbird got busy with the paint-brush, the others carved out that picture of the Grenadier.

3. And when those bold invaders got to the top of the cliff our friends were waiting for them with their soldier picture. "Great Limberger!" they yelled, as they tumbled back again. "There's a great big sentry up there! Wow! Back to das boats!" "Yes, you'd better get back," tootled Freddie, "before our soldier lets moonlight into some of you!" "Bye-bye!" warbled Miss Olemaid. "Don't you dare come again until you're invited!" And they're not likely to either. Three cheers for the Mulberry Flatites. They've saved England, Home, and Peckham! Well done!

Printed and published weekly by the Proprietors at 25, Bouverie Street, London, England. Published in Australasia by GORDON & GOTCH, Melbourne, Sydney, Adelaide, and Brisbane and Wellington, N.Z.; in South Africa by the CENTRAL NEWS AGENCY, LTD., Capetown, Johannesburg, and Branches. Subscription, 4s. 4d. per annum. Registered for transmission to Canada at magazine postal rates. Saturday, September 28, 1912.

In glorious colour: *Chuckles*, which started in 1914, was one of the best of the coloured comics. The artists and engravers were adept at securing complex overlay patterns instanced here in Breezy Ben's trousers and the texture of the sea in the fourth frame.

Paper tiger: *Rainbow*, which also started in 1914, was a brightly coloured paper for a slightly younger age group. It introduced the Bruin Boys to a wider public. Their leader, the perennially popular Tiger Tim, had first been seen in Arthur Mee's *Children's Encyclopaedia*. The artist was J. S. Baker.

Lusty colour: *Comic Life* was a coloured comic produced by Henderson's, a small company which like so many others was eventually taken over by the giant Amalgamated Press. In appearance it was more vigorous, without the surface gloss of the big firm's products.

Personality cult: *Funny Wonder* was a black and white comic and possessed a valuable property, Charlie Chaplin, as a strip on its front page. Other comics imitated, using Chaplin's brother, or even pseudo-Chaplins copying his *persona*. The *Firefly* also presented a front-page personality, the eccentric music-hall comedian T. E. Dunville. The war forced a merger of this paper with the *Butterfly*, which originated from the same Amalgamated Press stable.

No. 1 GRAND NEW COLOURED COMIC PAPER!

No. 1. Vol. 1. PRICE ONE HALFPENNY. January 10, 1914.

SHIP AHOY! BREEZY BEN FROM THE BRINY AND DISMAL DUTCHY ARRIVE!

1. "Hip-pip-pip-hoo-RAY! I feel like doing the hornpipe, I do!" piped Breezy Ben as, after many weary and dry months and weeks ploughing the Zuyder Zee, he once again gleefully inhaled the dear old ozone from the glue-factories of his native village, Wapping. Dismal Dutchy had also been ploughing the Zuyder Zee, and, judging by the furrows in his classic features, his face must have got ploughed in mistake one day. But Ben and Dutchy want to get ashore.

2. Ah, here they are landed on the wharf, having first ingeniously disguised their pets of the livestock persuasion as a bundle of washing, a basket of lunch, and a bag of carpenter's tools separately and respectively, to get them through the Customs. But that Customs official fellow wasn't having any, not he. "Come here with that luggage!" he roared draughtily. "Avast there!" cried Ben. "Slack off steam! The idea of heaving our kit about in that rude way!"

3. And then, paragorically speaking, the band began to play. "Wow!" yelled that smart Customs chap, as the pieces of luggage started to tango round the warehouse. "What is it—or am I seeing things? I'll swear I've had nothing to drink since I had milk with me porridge at breakfast. Oh, lor'!" "Hear them noises?" murmured Breezy Ben to Dismal Dutchy. "Someone has hevidently blunderbussed! as me father's pal, Horatio Nelson, said as he put his darkened telescope to his right ear."

4. "Ach! But mine poor tripehound Snitzel! Wot inchoyments can I haf mitout him? I am filled mit der egsasberations right oop from der basement to der roof, aind't it?" "Cheer up, matey," chirrupped Ben, "but don't smile all at once, or you might break your frontispiece, so's I'd have to putty up the cracks. Still, I'll whistle for your dog, 'cause them lubberly Customs officials seem to have more luggage than they can handle without putting in overtime."

5. Just then the door of the shed burst open. "Hi, hi!" bellowed the Customs man to our merchants. "Take 'em away! There's a heavy duty on furs and feathers, but I pass this lot. Wow!" "Thankee kindly, sir," tootled Breezy Ben. "We intended to have had the poor animals shaved, but we'd left our fourpence in the bank. Howsomever, if you've *quite* finished examining the luggage, we'll have it." "Here, vot's dot queer fellow-looking man taking mine dog avay for?" asked Dutchy.

6. Well, our pals got their belongings all right, and jolly glad were those officials to see the last of them. But why those smoles on the faces of the assembled populace? It is because they've just got No. 1 of CHUCKLES. And, our word, didn't they give Breezy and Dismal a rousing reception! Next week they—ah, but that's tellings! Anyway, we'll tell you in confidence that they indulge in the franticest, side-splittingest antics on record, so mind you're all in time.

No. 1. A SPLENDID TOY MODEL GIVEN FREE WITH THIS NUMBER. 1D.

No. 1. Vol. 1. PRICE ONE PENNY. February 14, 1914.

THE JOLLY ADVENTURES OF THE BRUIN BOYS.—THEIR SNOW-MAN HAS A WARM TIME.

1. There was a great surprise awaiting the boys at Mrs. Bruin's Boarding School when they awoke the other morning. "Look!" cried Tiger Tim excitedly. "It has been snowing in the night! Isn't it grand!" "I wish we could go out," grumbled Willie Ostrich. "It will all have melted away by the time we've finished our lessons."

2. "I know!" exclaimed Tim. "Let's dress and go up on the roof before Mrs. Bruin gets up! We can have some fine fun up there." The other boys thought it a jolly fine idea too, and in less than half a minute they were climbing through the roof door. "Come along boys!" piped Joey, the parrot. "Who'll take me on for a snowball fight?"

3. But Tiger Tim had a better idea than that. "Let's make a snow-man," he said. "He'll look fine sitting up here on the chimney!" So they all set to work, and this is the beauty they made. "Now, that's what I call a real work of art!" cried Jumbo, as Tim put on the finishing-touch. "Well done, sir! You ought to get a medal for that!" "Bravo, Tim!" chimed in Joey. "That's the coolest piece of work I've seen for a long time!"

4. But while all this was going on Mrs. Bruin was busy down in the kitchen below, preparing breakfast for her pupils, and as soon as the fire began to burn up, down the chimney came a great heap of snow—plomp!—which put the fire out. "Goodness me!" she exclaimed, with a start. "I've never known it to snow such large flakes as this before! What ever can be the cause of it all?"

5. And she promptly went up on to the roof to find out. Meanwhile, the naughty boys were wondering what had become of their snow-man. "He needn't have left us in such a hurry," cried Georgie Giraffe, who was looking down the chimney for him. "He has done the disappearing trick, if you ask me!" "I wish I could do the same," groaned Jumbo, who just then spotted their teacher. "Oh dear! We're in for it now, I can see!"

6. And Jumbo had guessed quite right, for Mrs. Bruin pretty quickly had them downstairs again, and they had to put up with a cold breakfast. "Isn't she cool to us this morning!" remarked Jacko. "Yes, and so is everything else," agreed Fido. "Cold tea, eh! Bur-r-h!" Anyway, Mrs. Bruin made up for it by giving them all a good dinner, because they promised to be good in future. Do you think they will be? We shall see next week!

COMIC LIFE ½d. "PETER FLINT AND THE SERPENT DOG" A GREAT DETECTIVE SERIAL THIS WEEK.

No. 7.—GORDON HIGHLANDERS. (See Inside.)

James Henderson & Sons, Ltd.

February 13, 1915.

Our Tramps Drop a Lifte to the Germ-hun Gunners.

1. Our fat tramps were roused from their beauty sleep the other morning, by a tug at Tom's leg that nearly shook their shanty down. The general wanted his car out, and here they were, still snoozing.

2. It was one of those mornings that freeze your eyebrows, and the old car was thoroughly chilled. They patted her and punched her, but she wouldn't start. They gave her gargle of hot water—then Butterball thought of a mustard plaster.

3. The mustard plaster round her radiator started her like magic. "Odds cough-drops! You've done something now, boys! Hang on, while I keep her from going to the moon!" roared the general.

"I must get across the valley, and exchange a word with my friend Colonel Buster before the Huns are awake!" "Hullo! there's some in the road below!" gasped Tall Thomas.

5. "We must change 'em, that's all!" roared the general. "Why, we're going up in the air!" "It's the snow on the wheels!" laughed Butterball. "Fine!" It's lifted us over 'em, but let's try to rope in their gun!"

6. Having passed clean over the Huns, the general pulled up. Our fat tramps had neatly looped up the machine-gun as they passed, so the enemy were helpless, and responded to the general's order of "Hands up!"

1/2D. THE FUNNY WONDER. 1/2D.

"THE GOLDEN FANG!" Grand Detective Serial. Turn to Page 2.

You cannot go wrong if you follow CHARLIE'S footsteps!

VOL. II.—No. 98.] EVERY TUESDAY. [WEEK ENDING FEBRUARY 5, 1916.

CHARLIE CHAPLIN, The Scream of the Earth (*The Famous Essanay Comedian*).

1. Dear Everybody,—What ho! I had a strange stroke of luck t'other nice double-width mornin', the noo. As I passed a pedlar who was peddling pigs that do the squeak when unblown, my stick caught one of said pigs—and lo! it came along o' your old pal. In the dim distance I heard a merry chant: "His boots are cracking for want of blacking!"

2. Well, old dears, I ambled on into the park, and after some exploration I discovered a joint of extreme age with a nurse. "Oho!" I said. "Oho!" *Some* nurse my bright and breezy ones. Phwpsts! I was struck surprised on the spot, and no error. Talk about Beauty and the Beast—wow-wow! So I wagged the old curl-case like steam.

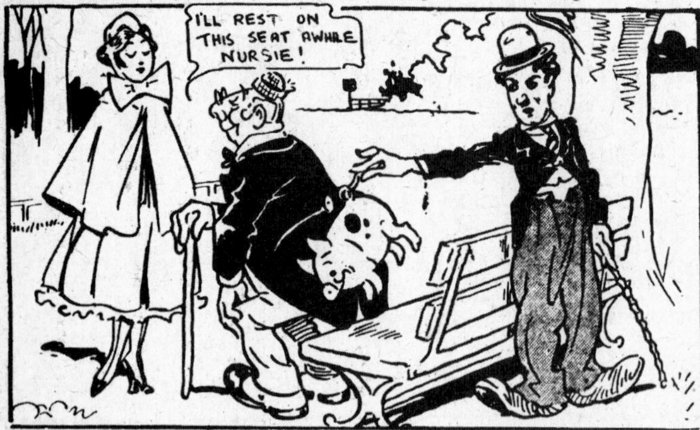

3. But about that pig. I simply hung that piglet on one of the buttons of his jolly old cutaway coat, as he proceeded to take his ease, if you please. "Whps!" said I: "this way for the surprise packet, Iago!" So down sits the old sportsman, with light-hearted chat going. Oh, *what* a nurse, laddies! *What* a nurse!

4. Well, down sits old Herbert Sidney well on the pig, which did its bit well and truly, my bonny boys. "Week!" says the pig. "Weekeek!" And good old Gustavus Adolphus says: "What the song of the cuckoo is this? What's this row?" says he. Absolutely amazed, he was, good fellows all. Mystyfidio, completely. How I *did* laugh behind the acacia!

5. So he says "Phwpsts! 'Tis the song of the Banshee! I'll look into this," he says. So he has a look. Two looks, for luck, in fact. And he remarks: "This place is no good for *my* complaint. It's haunted!" he says: "I will away! I will avaunt! I will leg it off unto my specialist!" And the nurselet occupied the seat.

6. Well? Well, well! Very nice, too, says you. Hear, hear! While old Alonzo was breaking all the records on the map, 'twas your old pal for the cheery chat and the courtly caper. Me, a winner every time. My dear old boys and girls, I do get luck in lumps, and no error. How's your father? See you next week! Your one and only CHARLIE CHAPLIN.

No. 95.] PRICE ONE HALFPENNY. [December 9, 1916.

T. E. DUNVILLE, THE ELONGATED LUMP OF COMEDY.

1. It's getting worse and worse, my friends! It is really! You remember how last week I had all the furniture yanked out of my flat? Well, now I've lost my flat. At least, the flat lost me. You see, I hadn't paid up very regularly, and the landlord let the place over my head to some overfed, large-sized sort of man. "Op-pit!" cried he, when I put in an appearance t'other day. "This is my flat now, so you needn't worry about it any more!"

2. There I was, shot out in the cold streets! "B-u-rr!" It was parky! My spirits were not improved either by having a look in at the window of what was my dinky little home! There was that beefy-merchant busily preparing a great gorge for himself of sausages, potatoes, and hot milk! It really was too bad to see that lovely warm fire and me shivering like a leaf! "Something must be did!" I gurgled, as I cast my eye around.

3. Now, just outside the wall where I knew the fireplace was situated I spotted a big, powerful motor-car. There was also a strong length of rope lying near and out of a job. I thoughtfully adopted this, and attacked it first to the back axle of that motor-car. The other end I securely tied to a hook in the brick wall of my late flat. You notice the artist of the above has been very careful to show you that the fireplace is just the other side of that wall with the hook in it.

4. Now you begin to see the cunning wheeze, don't you, my friends? As soon as that motor-car started off it tightened that rope and pulled on the hook. I told you it was a powerful car, didn't I? Well, just notice what it's done to the wall—pulled all the middle of it out, hasn't it? I expect you're all wondering the reason I did this, aren't you? Or have you looked at No. 6 picture out of turn? Anyway, if you will kindly pass along—

5. You will now see the whole nutty notion. With half the wall gone it was easy to get at fatty's little feed that he had prepared for himself. You see, I had a good tuck in and a nice warm in front of that roaring fire, which made me feel ever so much better. Even all the little dogs of the neighbourhood couldn't help laughing at my cute little wheeze.

6. Well, once all the grub was gone, there seemed nothing more to wait for, especially since the fire was soon blown out by the cold, frosty air that came in through the hole in the wall. So off I waddled, leaving the old chap to enjoy the draft! Tootle-oo! More next week.

Some Butterflies have wings of gold, and some have wings of flame.
This "Butterfly" has none at all, BUT IT GETS THERE just the same.

No. 86 (New Series). [Entered at Stationers' Hall.] WAR-TIME PRICE THREE-HALFPENCE. [Transmission Abroad at Book Rates.] November 23, 1918.

BUTTERFLY BILL KEEPS THE BALL ROLLING THIS WEEK.

1. Dear Mr. Editor and Readers,—I had a great surprise one day last week. Yes, I met my old friend Jerry Hogan. Now, when I knew Jerry he was a bricklayer's confidential clerk, and I never knew anyone who could beat him at carrying the hod. But from the look of him he'd struck it rich since then. His missus seemed to be a bit haughty—

2. But he whispered, "Meet me at Binks', Bill! You know, the old place!" And a bit later on I met him at the renowned balloon factory. "Oh, Bill," he murmured, "being rich is not what it's cracked up to be! I married money, and I'm earning it! Got to go to a fancy-dress ball to-night, when I'd far rather play cards at Sullivan's!"

3. "Don't let that worry you, old sport!" said I. "I'd do anything for an old pal! Gimme a couple of Bradburys and I'll go in your place! I like fancy-dress balls!" And Jerry bit it. "Come on," he chortled, "and get into the clobber! It'll be worth a lot to have a decent evening for once!" And he fixed me up so that I looked a dandy.

4. And then I trotted off to the Duchess of Dinkums, where the ball was to be held. And the old dear was quite pleased to see me. "How de do, Mr. Hogan?" she said, thinking I was Jerry. "'Ow's yourself, mum?" says I. "Hope the dear dook has got over the jimjams!"

5. Then I went into the ball, and oh, Mr. Editor and dear readers, I did have a time! My! I haven't enjoyed myself so much since I saw a horse bite a policeman. The fuss the girls made of me reminded me of the time when I was a prize in a raffle.

6. Yes, it was a time to dream about, and I can assure you, sir, Lady Marshmallow, the Turkish delight, and your right hon. humble made a great sensation among the dancers. Some of them didn't seem to like it very much, but Marshy and I got on a treato.

7. Then, just as I was taking Maudie Minx, the Cinema Queen, into supper, blessed if a jolly old flunky didn't come up and say that Lord Blobbs wanted to see me at home at once. Of course, I knew it was Jerry they wanted, so I told him there was nothing doing.

8. And I went into supper with Maudie. We were just making the best of a bit of a war-time snack when a pusson entered. 'Twas Mrs. Hogan. As soon as she saw me she yelled out: "That is not my Jeremiah! 'Tis an impostor!"

9. And the end of it all was that I got the boot—several boots, in fact, and me dream of joy was over and did with. Still, I got a bit of my own back, for I went to Sullivan's, and told Jerry what I thought of his swell friends.—Yours ever, Butterfly Bill.

Casualties of war: during the last year of the First World War the paper shortage became really acute. The halfpenny comics soared in price to three-halfpence and several were closed down altogether. The *Butterfly* and *Firefly* merged, later became a fatal casualty of the Second World War in 1940. The mini-skirted (for 1918) Maisie the Messenger Girl on the *Butterfly*'s back page was awarded with one of the new pound notes, called a Bradbury after the Bank of England cashier's signature on it.

Silent movies: *Film Fun* and *Kinema Comic*, first published in 1920, based all their comic strips on real film comedians. The first issues featured Harold Lloyd, Larry Semon, Ben Turpin, Chester Conklin, and Baby Marie Osborne. Among the regularly appearing stories were Fatty Arbuckle's Schooldays. The Ben Turpin–Charlie Lynn strip on the front and back cover illustrates some of the comic's special quirks. Although the two film comedians worked exclusively in California their strip setting is deliberately English. Sudden wealth was invariably shown by instant transformations of dress and the additions of diamonds in extraordinary places. The artist George Wakefield had his own particular idiosyncrasies, one of which was always to include a small dog at some point among the spectators. Although *Kinema Comic* was relatively short-lived *Film Fun* continued until the early sixties. It established a pattern for the black-and-white comic with its front and back cover strip and inside strips alternating with text stories. The artwork was invariably of a high standard.

8 THE BUTTERFLY and FIREFLY.—Every Tuesday.—War-time Price, 1½d.

1. "Ah! dirty work on the cross-roads," thought Percy the pavement spoiler, as he twigged two individuals gazing at some jam tarts and puffs in a cookery establishment. "We'll pinch that lot to-night!" quoth one.

2. But Percy wasn't going to stand that. Nunno! He straightaway went in the shop, took the pastries away, and drew their likenesses on the window-pane. "This ought to draw 'em!" said Percy to the manager.

3. And it did. For that night, when the cats were warbling tenderly on the tiles, those two persons stole up. "My! what a fine lot! Stand by with the bag, Bill," murmured one, as he opened the jolly old window.

4. But, alas and alack! those jam tarts had changed to a full-grown gentleman in blue, who collared those two bad feller-me-lads, and took them where there weren't any tartlets to steal. Bravo, Percy!

The Adventures of Beatrix Buttercup.

1. Dear Boys and Girls,—Do you know, dears, I've not done the camera-breaking stunt for donkeys' years, and when I saw Philpot Bottles t'other day, I asked him to take my photo. "You'd break the plate!" he said.

2. But, as you know, dearies, when I make up my mind to do anything, I do it. Yes! I put a jolly old mirror on the end of a broom, and held it in front of Philpot's camera—

3. Just as he was about to pull the trigger of the camera. Consequently, he snapshotted my beautiful features reflected in the mirror. But when he saw what he had taken—my! wasn't he in a rage!

4. Yes, he threw the photo at me and toddled off, declaring he would have vengeance. Ha, ha! "Thanks!" I cried, as I caught the photo. You see, I didn't break the camera, after all, eh?—Beatrix Buttercup.

1. Oh, dear, Tommy's luck looked as if it was right out this time. Yes, a nasty thief fellow had taken a liking to Tommy's sample air-balloons, and he gave chase, too, over a ford.

2. But the thief-fellow had not counted on Tommy's great brain, for our hero took out one of the sample balloons from his case, and blew it out with all his puff. And—well—you twig the stepping-stones don't you?

3. Our artful friend threw the balloon in the wetness between two jolly old stepping-stones. But observe Tommy's follower. "Now for it!" he shouts.

4. My, yes! He did have it, too! For he spotted Thomas and ran over the stones, but when he came to the balloon it slipped under him, and gave him a large-sized drenching. He won't chase Tommy again. Nunno!

1. Dear Butterflies,—T'other day I was delivering a lady's handbag when a nasty, thief-fellow stopped me. "Snice bag!" he said, and I knew by the stick he held behind him that he wanted to relieve me of it.

2. But a notion struck me. Yes, dears. This is how it happened. "Hold it open while I examine the contents!" growled the feller-me-lad. "Yes, sir!" I said meekly. Then—

3. He poked his nose well into the bag. And what did I do? Why, I jerked it upwards and caught it round his neck. Then I pulled the strings. My! he was waxy when he found he was my prisoner. But—

4. He was worse when I marched him off to the home for little thieflets, where he was welcomed. And the inspector fellow gave me a Bradbury for my trouble. Nice of him, wasn't it?—Yours, Maisie.

No. 1 of Our Companion Paper The "KINEMA COMIC." Now on Sale! | O.

No. 15. Vol. 1. (Every Tuesday.) April 24, 1920.

Ben Turpin AND Charlie Lynn

HEROES OF THE

Paramount Mack Sennett Comedies

This week's Film:—"A-TENT-TION TO BUSINESS."

1. Ho, what a crowd! All the funny old FILM FUN favourites off to the briny for a spell. And they just filled up a carriage nicely, thank you. All the whole shoot of them. And, of course, everybody cried: "No earthly! No room in there! All the FILM FUN filberts have it! They win!" So they popped off and got in anywhere they could. Guard's van, cattle trucks, or any old where. And that was that.

2. REEL II. AT THE OTHER END.—Ho, what artful young chaps are Ben and Charlie! Wouldst believe it? They'd got a lot of air balloons, and painted the faces of all the favourites on them, and held them up against the windows of the carriage! No wonder that the lads at the other end were wild! "Diddled!" they cried. "Done! Packed like sardines, and these nuts have done it on the cush!"

3. But merrily laughed Ben and Charlie as they legged it off out of the station with the air balloons, bearing the faces of Ambrose, and Baby Marie Osborne, and Fatty Arbuckle, and all the stars, on those balloons. And merrily they cried: "Aha! Tra-la-la! We diddled 'em!" But little they knew that the other young chaps were up and doing! No!

4. But one of those hearty roysterers had borrowed a hat pin from the lady who purveyed part-worn buns in the refreshment-room, and he slipped up and punctured the old balloons, much to the dismayment of Ben and Charlie. "Pop! Pop!" went the balloons, to the loud and hearty chorus of "Ha, ha's!" from the villagers up stage. (Continued on page 20).

Ben Turpin and Charlie Lynn

Heroes of the Paramount Mack Sennett Comedies

(Continued from page 1.)

5. And yet they stuck it like the fiery Roman on the bridge in the brave days of old. Old Ben got a drum and Charlie got a cornet, and they started to perform the "Sock Seller's Serenade," from that splendid opera, "Willie's Whiskers." But these same lads of the village hurled carrots and eggs at them.

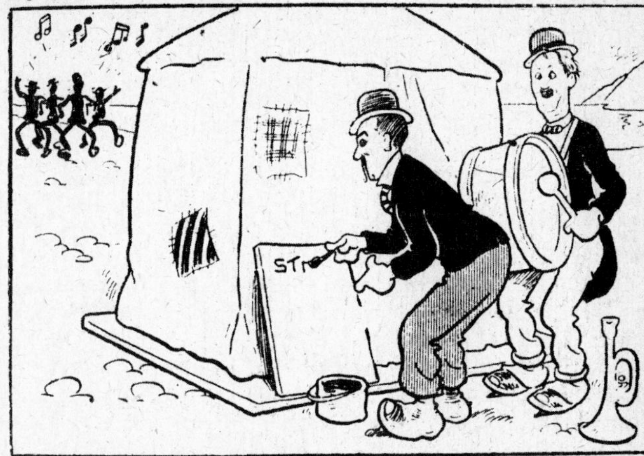

6. And the cry of the hearty filberts was: "We've got 'em! Now we'll show 'em what's how! Tum-ti-dum-ti-tiddley-um!" And much mirthful music they made. But old Ben and Charlie had got going, y'see. They found an old bathing tent, and Charlie started to paint an announcement on a lump of board.

7. Ho, it goes a treato! Old Charlie's board attracted the lads of the village to the tent, and they bunked in with the speed of the young policeman after a rabbit pie. Meanwhile, Ben was painting a rum old face on the near side of the tent. Very good, then. Ve-ry nice, too!

8. Well, when the interior of said tent was packed with these persons, Ben and Charlie pulled the string tighto, and as old Ben had finished his funny face on the canvas, a vastly diverting how-d'ye-do the old outfit presented. My word! You would have laughed if you'd been there!

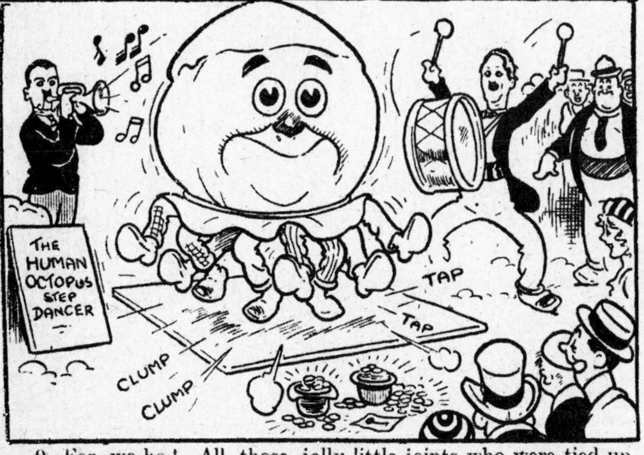

9. For, wo-ho! All those jolly little joints who were tied up in the tent started to kick their heels, and kick up a row, and do the jump. Which was just what our old pals wanted. "Yoi!" they cried. "Walk up and see the human octopus step-dancer! Yi-ho!" And didn't the populace pop up! Well, just look at the art engraving!

10. And so all's well that ends well! I tell you straight, old Charlie and Ben scooped about—oh, well, £17635496176 19 0¾ and bought diamond scooters, and sapphire socks, and sealskin teapots, and everything in the garden was lovely! And so, at the end of a perfect day, they cried: "Cheerio!" and they cried: "Hooray!" and well, that's all. But NEXT week—oh dear!

Please pass this copy on to your best chum when you have finished with it.

A new golden age: Tiger Tim dominated comics produced for younger children. *Tiger Tim's Tales* (*below*) was started in 1919 and a year later became *Tiger Tim's Weekly*. Mrs Bruin's boarding-school for the assorted menagerie who were Tim's chums was partnered in 1925 by the scholastic establishment of Mrs Hippo, catering for the Bruin Boys' sisters. The girls were led by Tiger Tilly, in the new, brightly coloured paper *Playbox*. In the early thirties Laurel and Hardy took over the front page of *Film Fun* and remained there for more than twenty years. The example overleaf is typical of George Wakefield's work, with its small dog, sketchily simplified backgrounds and unchanging angle of vision. The text under the pictures was unnecessary but always provided, perhaps as a sop to the carpers who were constantly alleging that comics encouraged illiteracy. Today the captions are interesting for their examples of dated slang.
Tartan curtain: *Golden*, started in 1937, continued the text caption. A short-lived paper, dying in the early part of the war, it was one of the last of the old-fashioned comics. Its front page, brilliantly printed in tangerine and black, was one of the finest examples of its kind. The same year the Dundee revolution began. The D.C.Thomson comics from Scotland were launched, including *Dandy* and *Beano*, and a new, more robust era began. Notorious for their reticence, Thomson's refused to allow *Beano* and *Dandy* to be reproduced in this book, but the front page of the Amalgamated Press's *Knockout* is a fair imitation of the style. Gone are all the tedious unread captions; the story is entirely in the balloons. This war-time issue was published after the comic had taken over the beloved *Magnet*, which published the Charles Hamilton saga of Billy Bunter and Greyfriars in story form.

DO NOT MISS FUNNY TOPSY AND TURVY SEE PAGE 12

No. 491. Vol. 15. EVERY FRIDAY July 14th, 1934.

BABY JUMBO'S BIG JUMP!

1. Dear Readers,—Well, here we are on the front page! We like it ever so much, and, of course, Baby Jumbo is simply delighted. "Hurrah!" she cried yesterday. "Now I can show the PLAYBOX readers how nicely I can jump!" "Well, don't jump on me, please!" said Polly.

2. And then Baby took a flying leap over the bed-rail. "Oh, how wonderful!" gasped Gertie. "You look just like a flying sausage, Baby!" "How do you do it?" I cried. "Have you been eating jumping-crackers for tea?" "Oh, no!" chuckled Baby. "A grasshopper taught me!"

3. But alas! Baby's wonderful jump came to a sad end, for she crashed on to the floor and broke all the boards!" Dear me! The floor looks a bit bent, doesn't it?" I gasped. "Oh, why did you fall down?" "Well, I couldn't fall up, could I?" yelled Baby.

4. But the next minute she vanished! "Good gracious! Has she gone off pop!" gasped Polly in dismay. "No, she has fallen through that hole," I said. "Oh dear, isn't it a big one?" "Yes, do you think Mrs. Hippo will notice it?" said Gertie.

5. Then we had another big surprise, for when we looked through that big hole we saw poor old Baby sitting in Mrs. Hippo's wash-tub. "Look! She has fallen into the kitchen!" gasped Betty. "Help me out of this tub, girls!" groaned Baby.

6. "Oh, no! You stop where you are, Baby!" said Mrs. Hippo sternly. "I think a good scrubbing will do you good!" "Ha, ha! Are you going to hang her on the line, Mrs. Hippo?" chuckled Polly. Yours merrily, TIGER TILLY.

THE PAPER WITH ALL THE FILM STARS.

No. 764. Vol. 15. Every Tuesday. September 8th, 1934.

LAUREL AND HARDY.

This Week: "HOLD HARD!"

THE FUNNIEST FELLOWS ON THE FILMS.

1. Stan Laurel was very hard up and he had ventured to ask Ollie Hardy if he could oblige him with a loan of ten bob. He wanted to take Ollie's girl out with the money. Very kind of him, wasn't it? But nothing doing. Stan was shot out by Ollie's best boot.

2. However, he was not discouraged and he hit on a very artful notion. When Ollie came along a little later, looking very posh indeed, he found Stan staggering under the weight of a pile of egg boxes which were wobbling badly. "Help me, Ollie!" cried Stan.

3. And Ollie fell for it. "Why, certainly I will!" said he. And he toddled forward and grabbed hold of one or two of those boxes with the idea of preventing them from falling as they threatened to do. That was just what Stan wanted. "Ha, ha!" he cackled gleefully.

4. For he'd got Ollie in a nice old tangle, and there was Molly coming along, too. Well, although Ollie had arranged to meet her he could hardly do so, lumbered up with those boxes as he was. So Stan obliged and took his place and off he toddled with the damsel.

5. Round the corner he steered Molly, and they seated themselves on the large portion of drainpipe they found. But meanwhile Ollie had managed to get away from those swaying boxes, after a bit of an argument with the shopkeeper. He came rushing wrathfully up.

6. And he arrived on the scene just in time to see Stan begging Molly to give him one little kiss. "Well, just one!" she lisped. Then Ollie jumped to it. Yes, he dived down and wriggled inside that large pipe. There was an opening half-way along the thing.

7. And he made good use of it. Yes, he popped up just when he wasn't expected. His face came between Stan and Molly, and the kinsequence was that Stan kissed his college chum instead of the charmer. And he didn't like that at all. ***(Continued on page 24.)***

8. Still, there it was, and Ollie had put it across him. But not for long. For when Molly got up and walked off with her nose in the air, Stan gave the pipe a push. "Now we've both been turned down!" he told Ollie. It was true enough. For the corpulent one shot forward with the pipe and kissed his facepiece heartily—biff!

9. It made him very cross, needless to say. And he lost no time in working his way out of that pipe. Then, seeing the paddy he was in, Stan decided it would be as well to skip out of it. So away he went at top speed, and Ollie was soon up and doing and chasing after him. "Dear, dear!" cried Stan. "He does look so cross!"

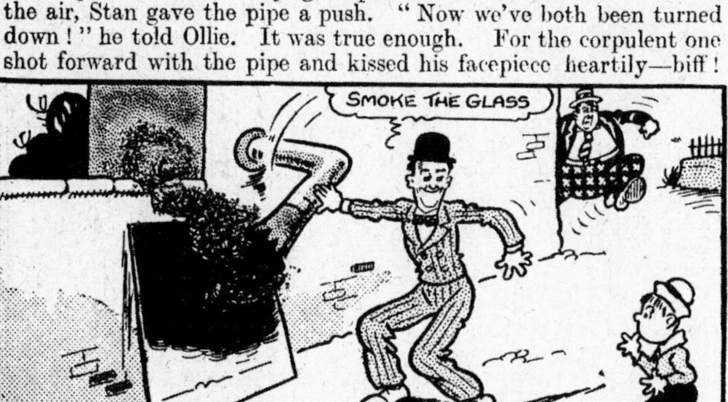

10. And he was pounding along the highway, wondering just what would happen when Ollie caught him, when he spotted the sheet of glass and the pipe that was chuffing merrily away, sending thick black smoke into the air. "What-ho!" he warbled. "That gives me the notion that does." So he turned that pipe downwards.

11. Whereupon the thick smoke went all over the sheet of glass and turned it black in a couple of split jiffies. So Stan lost no time in diving behind it, and he was well and truly hidden. Up dashed the wrathful Ollie in top gear, anxious to get at Stan. But he dashed right past old Stan without rumbling just whereabouts he was.

12. "Hurrah!" gurgled Stan. "It's worked. I've diddled him!" So, feeling very pleased with himself, forth he came from behind that slice of blackened glass. "Ha, ha!" he sang out. "Put it across you that time, Ollie." Hearing his voice, Ollie pulled up, and when he saw Stan he said a few very fierce things.

13. "Well, that wins it, that does!" he gasped. "So that's where he got to, is it?" And away went Stan, chuckling merrily, and after him whizzed Ollie. "I'll have you yet!" he howled. "See if I don't!" So Stan made for the park and, seeing the fountain, toddled across the plank and perched himself on it.

14. "Can't catch me now!" he chortled. "Ho, that's what you think, is it?" yelled Ollie. "You wait and see, my lad! I'll be with you in a brace of shakes and then—look out for yourself!" So he dashed across the plank. But it was more than it could do to stand his fairy weight. So Ollie went in and got a proper ducking.

15. Hard luck, eh? But that wasn't all. Stan lost no time in getting away while he had the chance, seeing Molly standing by. Yes, he tripped lightly across that plank which Ollie was balancing on his hair-parting. And he got safely to terra firma, greeted Molly, and steered her to the nearest ice-cream foundry. So Ollie got left.

INTRODUCE "FILM FUN" TO YOUR CHUM. GIVE HIM THIS COPY WHEN YOU HAVE FINISHED WITH IT.

Printed in Great Britain and published every Tuesday by the Proprietors, The Amalgamated Press, Ltd., The Fleetway House, Farringdon Street, London, E.C.4. Registered for transmission by Canadian Magazine Post. Subscription rates: Inland and abroad, 11s. per annum; 5s. 6d. for six months. Sole Agents for Australia and New Zealand: Messrs. Gordon & Gotch, Ltd., and for South Africa: Central News Agency, Ltd. —Saturday, September 8th, 1934. LS

No. 1.] LIEUTENANT DARING AND JOLLY ROGER, THE BOLD SEA ROVERS [OCTOBER 23rd, 1937.

FETCH!

?

I'M OFF!

OO!
POLICE

MY STOLEN UMBRELLA!

The trick that went wrong came right.

1. Meet Lieutenant Daring and Jolly Roger, our cruisers and amusers. Daring's tall, Roger's small. One day our gallant pair took Jill, the Admiral's daughter, for a picnic on wild Woolloomooloo Island.

2. They landed and were laying the cloth for tea when they heard the bushes rustling. Ho, ho, it was Hop-In, the Chinese pirate, pushing his nose in where it wasn't wanted. "Who asked you to the party?" cried Roger.

3. "After him, Roger!" cried Daring, leading the way, closely followed by the jolly one. "He means to do us a mischief, the saucy old spy!" "He'll look more like a mince-spy if I catch him!" cried Roger.

4. But next moment up popped Hop-In's half-brother, Hop-Out, and he carried off the Admiral's daughter, intending to kidnap her for a cash ransom. "Help, help!" cried Jill, her eyes flashing an S O S.

5. "We've been tricked, diddled, and done!" cried Jolly Roger as our bold sea rovers came dashing back to the rescue. But they arrived just in time to be too late! Hop-Out was afloat and they were ashore.

6. Yes, Hop-Out had pushed Jill into our lads' boat and then pushed off. "Aha! This is where you rise to the occasion, Roger!" cried Lieutenant Daring. "Yes, this is where we spring our surprise on Chinky."

7. Then, using the springy sapling as a catapult, he sent Roger soaring seawards. "Whoops! You can't get me, I'm down and you're out!" cried the sailor boy as he landed. "We're up to your tricks and ours too."

8. So having wiped his boots on the bandit, he tied him in knots and pulled for the shore. "You'd be a credit to the Flying Corps, Roger!" said Daring. "Now we'll finish our picnic with a tip top tea for three."

V FOR VICTORY! — "K.O." FOR BEST FUN!
3D
KNOCK-OUT
THE "MAGNET" COMIC
No. 139. October 25th, 1941.
EVERY WEDNESDAY.

DEED-A-DAY DANNY
FIND A TARGET FOR THE LITTLE BOY'S ARROWS
signed Scoutmaster

WOW!
TWANG

IF YOU'RE NOT CAREFUL YOU'LL HIT MY NICE NEW CAR WITH ONE OF THOSE ARROWS!
GOOD DEED!
I WISH I HAD A TARGET
SNAP

DON'T GO AWAY— I'LL BE RIGHT BACK!
?

I'M GLAD I THOUGHT OF THIS! IT'S THE VERY THING!
BIG GUN TARGET

THE TARGET'S GONE SIR— OH, THERE IT IS—IT'S MOVED!
FIRE!
TRY AND HIT IT THIS YEAR LADS
LONG RANGE GUN

BANG IN DISTANCE
GOOD BOY, DANNY! HE CAN'T HIT MY CAR NOW!
JOY
BIG GUN TARGET

?
CRASH
WHEE-EE
BIG GUN TARGET

BAW AW!
TWANG TWANG TWANG
NEVER MIND DANNY HERES A NICE SOFT CUSHION FOR YOU!

Wireless chuckles: *Radio Fun*, another of Amalgamated Press's replies to the Dundee attack, was the *Film Fun* idea in the style of *Dandy*. Popular characters from radio shows were featured. Issy Bonn was a noted Jewish comedian, famous not only on B.B.C. radio programmes but in the music halls, which in the mid-forties were still doing business. Today he is a variety promoter. Much of the dialogue in these comics, particularly that of Tommy Handley, sounds surrealistic to modern ears. A knowledge of the original radio programmes, with all their repetitious catch-phrases, was presupposed. The Petula Clark strip appeared in 1945 when she was a B.B.C. child star.

Last laugh: in the 1950s the old comics quietly faded away. In one after another 'important news' was announced to their readers, who would then find that they were expected to buy a different paper from the following week. Overleaf, the front page of the last *Chips* shows the farewell appearance of Weary Willie and Tired Tim after fifty-seven years of service in the cause of laughter. *Opposite*, the front page of the new *Eagle*, in four-colour gravure, presages the space-age comic. Childhood tastes had undergone radical changes since the days of Breezy Ben.

ISSY BONN INTRODUCES HIS FAMOUS FINKELFEFFER FAMILY

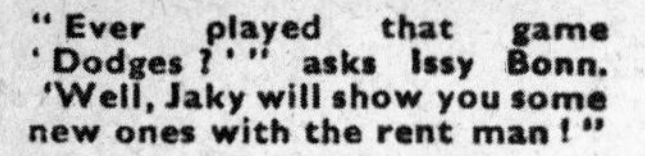

" Ever played that game 'Dodges ?' " asks Issy Bonn. 'Well, Jaky will show you some new ones with the rent man ! "

PETULA CLARK — Radio's Merry Mimic

EAGLE – THE NEW NATIONAL STRIP CARTOON WEEKLY

DAN DARE
PILOT OF THE FUTURE
THE HEADQUARTERS OF THE INTERPLANET SPACE FLEET SOME YEARS IN THE FUTURE

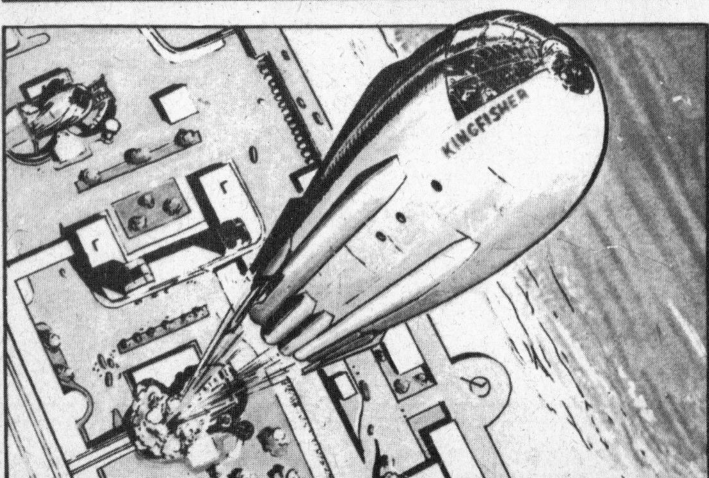

The Editor Has Important News For You Inside!

3d. EVERY WEDNESDAY

No. 2,997.

September 12th, 1953.

WEARY WILLIE AND TIRED TIM

HERE'S A JOB FOR YOU TWO. TAKE THIS PHOTOGRAPH OF MR MUMP, THE MILLIONAIRE ALONG TO SKINNEM HALL FOR ME.
OKAY, GUV'NOR!

1. Mr. Murgatroyd Mump, the millionaire mouse-trap maker, lives at Skinnem Hall in the county of Diddlumshire, and his new photograph is being taken by our two heroes, Willie and Tim.

HE'S A JOLLY-LOOKING CHAP. I SHOULD THINK HE'S VERY GENEROUS WITH HIS MONEY!
YOU'RE RIGHT, WILLIE! HE MIGHT HAVE A COUPLE OF WELL-PAID JOBS FOR US!

2. On the way, they take a look at the aforesaid mouse-trap millionaire's features. "He's got a catchy expression," wails Willie. "A nice kind smiling sort of a face, if I may so say, Tim."

THAT'S MY REAL FACE! YOU HAD IT THE WRONG WAY UP! I'M THE MOST MISERABLE MILLIONAIRE IN THE WORLD!

3. But their hopes of a soft well-paid job at Skinnem Hall fade rapidly when Mr. Mump appears and turns the portrait over to match his woeful features. "I never laugh," he croaks.

4. It seems that he hasn't smiled since the days of long ago. "I'm so miserable!" he wails. Now the job of cheering up this old lump of gloom doesn't look very promising, but they try it.

5. Then it seems that joke-books aren't much of a joke to Mr. Mump. "What—no funny bits?" asks Willie. "How about that screaming story of a chicken crossing the cross-roads, sir?"

6. Mr. Mump declines firmly, so Tim decides to try him with a few laughter pieces by radio. But here again the millionaire short-circuits the bright wheeze, and the wireless-set goes dead!

7. It's Willie's turn again, and he performs some clever and comical capers which bring a groan from Mr. Mump. "Not amusing!" moans the millionaire. "I'm feeling worse now."

8. Tim steps forward with some whispered words of good advice. "Pack up that stuff, pal," he says. "He'll soon be crying into the carpet. Why not act the goat properly, Willie?"

9. Willie thinks this is a bright brainwave, and he really does start acting the goat, as you will observe. "I'll play my part well and use my head to good effect—all goats do!" he chortles.

10. Tim gets butted right out of Skinnem Hall and the next thing he knows is that he is doing a marvellous header down the old well. "Well, well!" says Mump. "Well, well and well!"

11. And before he can stop it, his face splits into a large smile, and for the first time in fifty years he chortles at the sight of our Willie eating the grass on the front lawn. Ha, ha!

12. "You're the funniest customers I've ever seen," he roars. "You can stay here for just as long as you like, and the very best of luck to you both." Which is what we all say, isn't it?

TV takes over: in the fifties television began to influence the comics. *TV Fun* in 1953 was started for a growing nation of young viewers. Eventually programmes such as *The Flintstones* and *Thunderbirds* (*below*) would have comic papers devoted to them.

Backward look: the International Publishing Corporation became the largest comic publisher, having taken over many of the other houses which produced them, including Amalgamated Press, Odhams, and Hulton Press. *The Big One*, with its huge page size (more than four times that reproduced overleaf) was started to carry reprints of some of the vast backlog of already published material over many years. But tastes change imperceptibly – in spite of its size the paper was not a success.

Marvel-lous: the English comic today faces a take-over in style from the American comic books. *Fantastic*, launched early in 1967, consists almost entirely of reprints of the celebrated Marvel Comics, a development begun by its companion papers, *Smash! Wham!* and *Pow!* Followers of the old comics are saddened by this trend. But for *Dandy* and *Beano* and a handful of other papers, the indigenous product is virtually finished. Meanwhile, the new comics, reprinted in black-and-white, are pallid compared with their American originals.

JACK WARNER STARS IN A GREAT PICTURE-STORY: "THE HOUSE WITH RED SHUTTERS!" IN THIS ISSUE.

T.V. FUN
3D.
EVERY MONDAY!

Jean Carson

It's me, playmates – ARTHUR ASKEY

ARTHUR ASKEY REPORTING FOR WORK, MR FOREMAN!
SO YOU'RE THE NEW PAINTER, EH?

I'VE GOT THE VERY JOB FOR YOU, LITTLE MAN – YOU'RE JUST THE SIZE!

YOU CAN PAINT ALL THE SKIRTING BOARDS!
IT'S ALL RIGHT, PLAYMATES, HE'S ONLY TRYING TO TAKE THE MICKY OUT OF ME!

ANYWAY, I ALWAYS BELIEVE IN STARTING AT THE BOTTOM!
PAINT

I'VE FINISHED THAT JOB, WHAT'S NEXT?
THAT WAS QUICK!

I'VE BEEN PROMOTED, CHUM! I'M GOING UP IN THE WORLD!
OH! WHAT'S YOUR NEW JOB?

PAINTING CEILINGS!

DO YOU WONDER HOW I GOT THIS JOB, PLAYMATES? WELL, I TOLD THE EMPLOYMENT BUREAU I WAS FOND OF PUNTING AND SPECULATING –

– THEY THOUGHT I SAID "PAINTING AND DECORATING"!

OW! THAT'S DONE IT! I DIDN'T NOTICE THAT POT ON MY LADDER!

I'LL GET THE SACK! I'VE JUST SPILT SOME PAINT!
OF COURSE YOU WON'T! WHERE DID YOU SPILL IT?

ON THE FOREMAN!

The BIG ONE
FOR BOYS AND GIRLS
EVERY MONDAY
30th JANUARY, 1965
6D

SMILER

HA-HA-HA! - GOING TO A FANCY DRESS BALL, SMILER?

OF COURSE NOT, DAD! I'M GOING FOR A WALK AND IT'S (BRR!) COLD OUT-SIDE!
HOT WATER BOTTLE

TUT-TUT, SMILER, I'M ASHAMED OF YOU! COME ON, UNWRAP YOURSELF AND I'LL TAKE YOU FOR A NICE BRISK WALK!

NOTHING LIKE A TRAMP THROUGH THE SNOW, EH, MY BOY?
NO, DAD, (BRR!) THANK GOODNESS!

ER, BOTHER! MY SHOELACE IS UNDONE! YOU WALK ON AHEAD AND I'LL CATCH YOU UP!
OKAY, DAD!

HEE-HEE! THAT FOOLED HIM! NOW TO MAKE SOME SNOWBALLS AND I'LL SOON HAVE YOUNG SMILER WARMED UP!

(BRR!) DAD'S A LONG TIME OVERTAKING ME...(BRR!) WISH I'D BROUGHT MY HOT-WATER BOTTLE!

WHIZZ!
SPLOOSH!
UGH!

HA-HA-HA! GETTING WARMER, SMILER?
WHIZZ!!!

(PHEW!) HA-HA-HA! - COME BACK, SMILER, I'VE STILL GOT A COUPLE LEFT!

HO-HO-HO! THAT WILL TEACH HIM NOT TO BE AFRAID OF A SPOT OF COLD!

MEANTIME
HUH, I SUPPOSE DAD THINKS HE'S FUNNY... WELL, THIS JOKE IS GOING TO BE ON HIM!!!

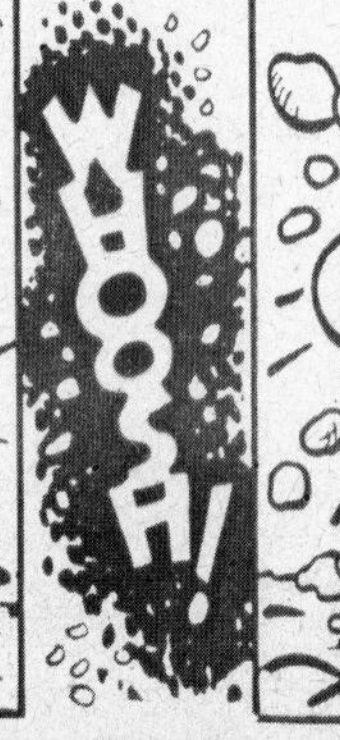
WHOOSH!

?

AT-CHOO!
JOLLY GOOD BOOK THIS, DAD, - ALL ABOUT ESKIMOS AND THE FROZEN NORTH!

FANTASTIC

A POWER COMIC

No. 7 1 APRIL 1967 EVERY MONDAY NINEPENCE

NEVER HAS MIGHTY
IRON-MAN
FACED SO DEADLY A FOE
AS
"KALA, QUEEN OF THE NETHERWORLD!"

EITHER BETRAY YOUR WORLD, IRON MAN, OR I WILL SLAY YOUR FRIENDS! THE CHOICE IS YOURS!

IF I SURRENDER, EARTH IS DOOMED! BUT IF I FIGHT HER, MY FRIENDS WILL DIE! WHAT CAN I DO??

YOU DAREN'T MISS THE MISSING LINK

The American Revolution - in Comics

The American Revolution – in Comics. *On with the Yellow Kid – the Press war – the first true strips – George McManus – Krazy Kat, greatest strip of all – birth of New York's* Daily News *– Dagwood and Blondie – Captain Patterson's influence – Milton Caniff – Walt Kelly – essential Americanness of strips – vital function.*

The United States has a knack for borrowing ideas from the Old World and improving them beyond recognition.

The first true American comic appeared in 1892, long after European prototypes. It was called Little Bears and Tigers and was composed of humorous animal drawings by James Swinnerton. It ran in William Randolph Hearst's *San Francisco Examiner*. The United States comic industry, which today claims more than a hundred million readers in America alone, did not begin in earnest until 1896, six years after Harmsworth in London had set *Comic Cuts* and *Chips* on their long careers.

Hearst's bitter rival, Joseph Pulitzer, had bought, in 1893, a Hoe four-colour rotary press for the Sunday supplement of the *New York World*, but its attempts to print famous works of art were disastrous and it was switched to reproducing big panel drawings. One colour was consistently elusive – yellow. The foreman in the engraving room, Charles Saalburgh, invented a tallow drying process. He needed a space to demonstrate it. He chose an ugly, night-shirted, gap-toothed child in a big cartoon drawn by Richard Outcault, who had originally been hired by the *World*'s brilliant Sunday editor, Morrill Goddard, to do popular scientific drawings. The night-shirt was given a bright yellow hue and on Sunday, 16 February 1896, in a three-quarter-page cartoon called 'The Great Dog Show in M'Googan Avenue', the Yellow Kid made his first explosive appearance.

The unpleasant urchin was a landmark in cartoon history. His night-shirt was used as a placard for words within the drawing, an innovation in American cartooning. The Yellow Kid's guttersnipe impudence endeared him to thousands of *World* readers, many of whom must have lived in similar slum environments to the M'Googan Avenue and the Hogan's Alley of Outcault's creation.

The meaning of the success was not lost on Mr Hearst. In October of the same year he started a comic supplement in his paper, the *New York Journal*, describing it as 'eight pages of iridescent polychromous effulgence that makes the rainbow look like a piece of lead pipe'. His scoop was the Yellow Kid himself, snatched from under Pulitzer's nose. Indignantly, Pulitzer bought Outcault back at a higher price. Then Hearst outbid him. At this point Pulitzer gave in, and hired George Luks to draw the Yellow Kid for his paper. This extended pantomime, accompanied by the phoney ballyhoo of the Press war, gave birth to a new phrase, 'yellow journalism'.

The Yellow Kid did not last long but he had started something. Outcault left Hearst in 1897 and went to the *New York Herald* where he drew a strip in frames, with balloons, called Li'l Mose. In 1902 Mose was replaced by a little boy in a velvet suit, whose taste for violent mischief totally belied his appearance. He was called Buster Brown and had as his companion a tough bulldog called Tige. Buster was Outcault's Yellow Kid up-graded to better social surroundings. The American language received the name Buster as a mode of address for the obstreperous, and the trademark of Buster Brown for countless merchandising items, which still include the products of a shoe company and a garment manufacturer.

Meanwhile, soon after Outcault's departure from the *Journal*, a new strip, drawn by Rudolph Dirks, appeared. It was The Katzenjammer Kids, owing its inspiration to Wilhelm Busch's Max and Moritz. Hans and Fritz, their Mama and the Captain are among the most durable of cartoon characters. Today they are drawn by Joe Musial for King Features. In 1912 Dirks was involved in a lawsuit which resulted in the loss of his rights to the title The Katzenjammer Kids, but not to the characters themselves. Ever since there have been two versions, Dirks renaming his The Captain and the Kids.

Another of the most prominent early names in American newspaper strips is that of Frederick Burr Opper, who was hired by Hearst in 1899. His great creations were Happy Hooligan, the tin-can crowned 'fall guy' whose shabby appearance went with a limitless good nature; And Her Name was Maud (a mule with a back kick like a steam-hammer); and Alphonse and Gaston, a Gallic pair whose names became synonymous with absurdly overdone courtesy (probably the inspiration for the war-time radio show ITMA's 'After you Claude' 'No, after you, Cecil' routine).

The first strip to run across the top of an ordinary editorial page was, according to the cartoonist-historian Coulton Waugh, A. Piker Clerk by Clare Briggs, which appeared in the *Chicago American* in 1904. It was the invention of Moses Koenigsberg, then editor of the *American*. He later founded Newspaper Feature Service Inc. (first of the modern large syndicates to supply the many hundreds of American dailies simultaneously with the same material) and in 1915 King Features ('Koenig' anglicized).

But the first daily strip was the creation of Bud Fisher, a Chicago sports cartoonist who moved west to San Francisco. Augustus Mutt, a punter constantly seeking his big killing, first appeared on the sports pages of the *San Francisco Chronicle* in 1907. A few weeks later, when it had taken hold, the strip was bought by Hearst for the *Examiner*. In March 1908, in the curious environment of an insane asylum, there occurred in the strip, an historic encounter to be equated with that of Stanley and Livingstone. 'This is gonna be a scream,' says Mutt as he meets a little man in a silk hat called Jeffries. Mutt and Jeff is one of the great gag strips of all time. It still appears today, drawn by Al Smith who joined Fisher in 1932.

Another powerful figure of the early comics was George McManus who, like so many successful cartoonists, was lured by Hearst from Pulitzer's *New*

York World. After many pioneering strips in varying styles, he worked a successful formula with The Newlyweds, a precursor of Blondie (suburban couple – the man a good-natured bungler, the wife beautiful and always in control of the situation). In 1913 he started a strip whose hero was an Irish immigrant working man who had come into a fortune. His terrifying wife, Maggie, took to parvenu ways with fantastic zeal; but Jiggs himself yearned to escape from the chandeliered mansion to corned beef and cabbage at Dinty Moore's. Bringing Up Father is yet another old strip that survives in spite of the death of its creator in 1954. Its continued popularity rests on repetition of the comforting notion that wealth alone is not happiness. McManus, who looked remarkably like Jiggs, put into his creation a sharp, clean line, always precise in the definition of Maggie's fine figure and incredibly hideous face, of Jiggs's mop of hair and tilted cigar butt. Even today there is a period feeling in the strip; Maggie's expensive dresses may be up to the moment, but Jiggs is still in the spats and wing-collar of more than half a century ago.

There are two media for the American newspaper strip. The daily strip appears in black and white six days of the week, four frames in a row, occasionally grouped as a square. The Sunday strip is in colour and can consist of a dozen or more frames to occupy up to a whole page of a comic supplement. Certain frames may be discarded to allow for flexibility in arrangement. Some strips might appear only on Sundays, others never on Sundays. Sometimes a different artist works on the Sunday page. All these conventions were established when the comics were still in their infancy.

The first comics were gag strips, complete in themselves, usually with a pay-off in the last frame. The serial strip, in which a suspense situation was left in the air for continuation the following day, appeared about 1910. One of the first was Harry Hershfield's Desperate Desmond, which was heavily burlesqued melodrama inspired by the movie serials of the day. The direct result was Abie the Agent, the first repository of in-jokes in strip history. Probably today the Abie strip would be ethnically impossible for its central character was a troubled, warm-hearted Jewish businessman who wandered through a villainous world solving his difficulties with the characteristic ingenuity of his race.

Another creation of the period is regarded by most strip cartoonists as the highest achievement of the profession. It was George Herriman's Krazy Kat. Herriman died in 1944 and such was its uniqueness that King Features let Krazy Kat die with his creator. No other artist could have matched the genius of the original. Krazy Kat evolved in 1910 from an earlier Herriman strip called the Dingbat Family. There was but one basic plot situation that underwent countless permutations over almost a quarter of a century. Krazy Kat loved Ignatz Mouse. But Ignatz despised poor Krazy and at every opportunity hurled a brick at him. The adoring cat discounted his bruises, grateful that Ignatz should notice him. The stern policeman, Offissa Pupp, unrequited lover of Krazy, acted as protector and locked the mouse in jail, only for release to hurl his brick the following day.

The gender of Krazy was indeterminate as were the surrealistic locations of the strip. The background would undergo startling transformations from frame to frame within the same sequence. Herriman, obsessed with the desert scenery in Arizona, transplanted this mysterious landscape into his strip. Against this fanciful background his characters, representing universal qualities, acted their stylized parts. No matter how often the brick 'bean-creased' the Kat it was Ignatz who was always the loser. For Ignatz was trapped by his own lack of imagination. The cynic, the anarchist, the scoffer – he was totally defeated by the Kat's love – an all-conquering force that could be deterred by nothing and no one. The language was no less surrealistic than the landscape, and was thick with poetry, strange spellings and puns.

Krazy Kat was elevated to art by no less respectable a critic than Gilbert Seldes in his book *The Seven Lively Arts*, and was subsequently taken up by intellectuals. The strip, with its Don Quixote feeling, its beautifully composed words, its poetic soul, could survive it all. Said Seldes: 'It is rich with something we have too little of – fantasy. It is wise with pitying irony; it has delicacy, sensitiveness and an unearthly beauty.'

Krazy Kat brought to the comic-strip industry the much-prized virtue of artistic respectability. The birth of the *New York Daily News* in 1919 was to bring it business. Started by Captain Patterson and Colonel McCormick, who had been publishing the *Chicago Tribune* since 1914, the *News* was inspired by the formidable success in England of the first Lord Rothermere's *Daily Mirror*, which had a circulation soaring up to the million. The *Daily News* copied the London paper's tabloid format.

Initially, it carried one strip, The Gumps, which almost overnight started the cartoon syndication business. Requests from small newspapers all over America came in. The *Tribune* and the *News* subsequently formed a famous syndicate. It was Patterson who was the force behind the strip development of the two newspapers. In the next few years he introduced several new titles, assessing the mood of the public against his own tastes. So shrewd was his judgement that most of them still survive.

Among them was Gasoline Alley by Frank King, initially a panel cartoon which turned into a daily strip chronicle of small-town life, its special quality being the realistic ageing of its cast to correspond with their natural lives. The baby boy, Skeezix, left on the doorstep of the Wallets in 1921, was old enough to go off and fight for his country in 1942.

Another was Little Orphan Annie, by Harold Gray, remarkable for the right-wing editorializing which has probably earned it the record number of cancellations from subscribing newspapers. Annie, unlike the Gasoline Alley folks, does not age. Forty-three years of orphanhood still leave her staring blank-eyed at the wicked world. Her protector, Daddy Warbucks – 'just about the most powerful man on Earth' – is a fearsome tycoon figure who has made his millions from armaments and who looks like Eisenhower. There is a Calvinistic streak in the morality of the strip with its philosophy that only the strongly virtuous people can enjoy the benefits of law, order, and happiness.

The event of 1930 was the appearance of a new strip in the *New York*

American. It was to become the most popular strip ever. By the mid fifties Blondie by Chic Young was appearing in 1,300 papers. At first, Dagwood Bumstead was heir to millions and Blondie his easy-on-the-eye but otherwise totally unsuitable fiancée. His father threatened to cut him off if he went on with the marriage. They married, were cut off, moved to their eternal suburbia and Dagwood got his job with Mr Dithers.

It was the best thing that could have happened to them. For they provided the public with a very familiar and readily identifiable situation – the marriage battlefield – but hammed-up almost to absurdity. Stephen Becker in his excellent book *Comic Art in America* points out how everyone in the Blondie strip overacts – Dithers is the most harassed boss in the world, a brush salesman at the door sells as if his life and sanity depend on it, even the Bumstead dogs perpetually play to the gallery.

Another popular strip, Chester Gould's Dick Tracy, started in 1931 after years of Prohibition gangsterism, also relies on exaggeration. The name for the square-jawed cop was suggested by Captain Patterson, a typical example of his skilful intuition. From the start Tracy used guns and the blood flowed, breaking two self-imposed taboos of the strip world. But violence is acceptable in the context of Gould's unrealistic style – flat and two-dimensional with an aggressive use of solid blacks – and after the initial protests had subsided the strip became immensely popular.

The villains that Tracy is pitted against number some of the most hideous grotesques ever conceived. Yet they have a strange attraction for their readers. In 1944 a dim-witted little gunman called Flattop (the top of his head was completely level) tussled for several weeks with Tracy before ending up impaled on a spike several fathoms deep. Half a dozen telegrams reached Gould claiming the body; then for weeks there followed a deluge of floral tributes, letters of condolence, and sympathy cards. Gould now sends Tracy into space to hunt out astrocrooks. 'I try to anticipate things,' he says. The Dick Tracy two-way wrist radio is now reality. Gould is a fierce defender of the law and studies police methods assiduously. His Sunday page always carries a crime-stopping hint. Recently he startled some of his readers by urging them to fingerprint their domestics.

Patterson was also responsible for bringing a young artist called Milton Caniff forward for public attention. He had been working on a fantasy adventure strip for A.P. called Dickie Dare. Patterson needed an adventure strip and invited him to draw one for the *New York Daily News*. It was to have an Oriental background and to feature a rugged hero, Pat Ryan, a boy, Terry Lee, and for laughs a comic Chinese underling. The villains were the pirates of the China coast led by a slit-eyed *femme fatale*, the Dragon Lady herself. Caniff had never been to China, so he read every book he could lay his hands on and combed the New York Public Library for reference information. It was the beginning of his well-merited reputation for painstaking thoroughness and inordinate labour to get the details accurate. Terry and the Pirates began appearing in late 1934, and for its first three years followed a straightforward course of exotic adventure.

In 1937 Japan launched a large-scale invasion of the Chinese mainland and gradually Caniff began to bring the war into the strip. Although America was neutral the Japanese were shown as being in the wrong. Incredibly, Japanese newspapers continued to run the strip until the events at Pearl Harbor in 1941 cut them off from further supplies.

By now Terry had grown up and Ryan faded out of the strip. He was replaced by 'Flip' Corkin, based on an old friend, an Air Force colonel called Philip G. Cochran. Colonel Corkin, a professional airman, was in charge of Terry's flight training. The Sunday page that followed the award of his wings in 1942 was read into the Congressional Record. It was a characteristic example of Caniff's fine draughtsmanship matched with excellently written dialogue. During the war years the indefatigable artist drew a special gag strip for the Service papers, featuring a typical curvy Caniff siren, Miss Lace, who warmed G.I. hearts from Reykjavik to Rangoon.

At the end of the war Milton Caniff took a decision which was unprecedented in the history of comic-strip cartoons. He decided to abandon his Terry and the Pirates feature and cross to the rival Field Enterprise to start an entirely new strip. No artist had dropped a strip at the top of its success to start another from scratch. No artist, for that matter, had been given two years and *carte-blanche* to produce what he liked. Therein lay Caniff's reasons – for although Terry had been his invention the copyright belonged to the *News–Tribune* Syndicate. He was to own the new strip he was to create down to the tips of its hero's lightly polished toecaps.

In January 1947 George Wunder took over Terry in a creditable imitation of the Caniff style. Meanwhile, Steve Canyon, ex-Transport Command captain, career flier and ready-for-anything, made his début. Canyon is a realistic hero, with the weakness and vulnerabilities of the real man. He went back into the Air Force during the Korean War. Today he is a colonel in handsome middle age with a trouble-shooting assignment that takes him all over the world. He is a red-blooded character and in his time has tussled with many shapely feminine figures, invariably bearing outrageous names like Herself Muldoon, Madame Lynx, Princess Snowflower and his own adoring ward, Poteet Canyon. What makes the strip really outstanding is the quality of its research and information.

The strip is seen in the Pentagon as a propaganda voice for the Air Force and Caniff frequently represents official arguments in a way everyone can understand; consequently, it comes under occasional fire for being 'militarist'. But Caniff is adamant that he doesn't take sides in presenting United States policy. As he sees it Canyon, like Caniff, is a professional getting on with his job. After thirty-five years of continuous strip-drawing there is no sign of flabbiness in the style, no flagging of the massive energy of Milton Caniff, who is highly popular among fellow-cartoonists.

Al Capp now makes more than half a million dollars a year from his anarchistic burlesque cartoon, Li'l Abner. He started his career as assistant to Ham Fisher, who drew Joe Palooka, a strip with a boxing background. Capp began Li'l Abner in 1934, initially as a series of humorous episodes in hill-billy country. Then his distinctive wit began to flower. Broad slapstick was coupled with Swiftian satire. American values were questioned and frequently demolished. Southern senators, captains of industry, bureaucrats and planners, militarists and the work of fellow-cartoonists have all been crucified within the strip.

Much of Li'l Abner has been absorbed into American folk-lore: Sadie Hawkins Day, when the girls chase and catch their men, Kickapoo Joy Juice with its magic therapeutic powers, and the Schmoo, a boneless happy animal that exists only for the pleasure of being eaten, followed by the Kigmy which exists only for people to vent their anger on and thus not hurt each other.

The gallery of Capp characters is a rich one, from his shy direct hero and his blonde wife Daisy Mae, through the pipe-smoking Mammy Yokum to such villains as Jack S. Phogbound and General Bullmoose and sirens like Stupefyin' Jones who stops men dead in their tracks so that they can't move. Recently Capp has shifted his sights from the right to the left with the appearance of characters like Joanie Phoanie, a globe-trotting protest singer. 'My mail is now much more obscene,' he claims.

Satire is not always happily translated into the strip format and is hard to sustain. Walt Kelly, however, has mastered the art. For six early years he was an animator in the Disney Studios; he has reached a thorough understanding of the cartoon medium. His little character, Pogo, who is a knowing possum, first appeared in strip form in 1948 in the short-lived *New York Star*. Fortunately, within the six-month life of the newspaper the strip had got off the ground. The Dell Publishing Company brought out a Pogo book drawn before it became a newspaper strip. It took time to get the strip back into the Press, the syndicates distrusting its kind of humour. But by 1954 it was appearing in 425 papers. Moreover, Kelly had not restricted himself to the newspaper page and Simon and Schuster regularly published books containing specially drawn sequences.

The setting is Okefenokee Swamp in Georgia, peopled with Pogo's anthropomorphic friends such as Albert the Alligator, Dr Howland Owl, and Porkypine. The many kinds of animal in the swamp are all capable of symbolizing any part of Walt Kelly's satirical allegory. He does not regard the strip as overtly political; yet it has often anticipated moods long before they became widespread. For instance, he revealed the true colours of Senator McCarthy some time before the editorial pages could bring themselves to do the same thing. Recently the Birch Society came under fire as Kelly's Jack Acid Society. He is constantly exposing the idiocy of political behaviour.

The detail of a Pogo strip is delightful. An old-fashioned character like the Deacon has his balloon filled with Gothic text, while Phineas T. Bridgeport, a huckstering showman type, has his filled with circus lettering. There is great attention to the language of the strip and Kelly has a fine ear for dialect and accent, giving the words colour and imagination. Often the characters will launch into verse. A gentle liberal, Kelly has the quality that Herriman had, of telling us the truth about ourselves with fantasy.

Charles Schulz is also in direct line with the creator of Krazy Kat. Instead of animals he uses children, the remarkable collection of playmates led by Charlie Brown in the Peanuts strip. The children have the characters of grown-ups – the formidable Lucy, a potential matriarchal ogress; the insecure Linus, inseparable from his blanket; the assured intellectual Schroeder, his young life already dedicated to Beethoven; the insatiably dirty Pigpen and Charlie himself, the confident leader so often deflated by one tiny fumble, whose moods – elation, despair, frustration – are absolute.

There is one animal, a dog called Snoopy. No ordinary dog this, but a canine philosopher who can lie on the roof of his kennel quoting Gertrude Stein or living out his famous fantasy where he is the fearless First World War aviator scouring the skies in search of the Red Baron. The strip started in 1950 and now appears in 700 papers. Schulz, a lay-preacher with four children and twenty-eight acres of Californian dairyland, is also America's highest-paid popular psychologist.

There must be many omissions in a short survey of more than seventy years of American strip cartoons. In that time, a man's lifetime, there have been many great cartoonists and many important strips. To some it will appear unjust not to deal in detail with Billy DeBeck's Barney Google or Frank Willard's Moon Mullins. Hal Foster's starkly dramatic Tarzan and the later impeccably drawn Prince Valiant must be mentioned. And Alex Raymond, who created Jungle Jim, Flash Gordon, and Rip Kirby, and was master of the inked-in shadow, a style so accurately continued after his death by John Prentice. Alfred Andriola, who began as Milton Caniff's assistant, drew Charlie Chan, then in 1943 started his still-flourishing white-haired detective, Kerry Drake, on the trail. The carefully drawn Mary Worth strip grew out of the Depression's Apple Mary. And there is Mort Walker's magnificently hopeless soldier, Beetle Bailey, in line of descent, but different from, George Baker's Sad Sack. And Crockett Johnson's Barnaby, a satirical strip from the brave newspaper *PM* which came too many years ahead of its time to survive. Lee Falk's Mandrake, still making magic after thirty-three years. Segar's Popeye, whose statue stands in Crystal City, Texas, heart of the spinach-growing country. And the great Rube Goldberg, father of Boob McNutt. He is virtually a living history of the comics from their infancy.

The American comic is as much part of the fundamental American scene as pumpkin pie, the Fourth of July, and the World Series. The comic is not permanent art, but part of the weight of ephemeral communication entering American homes each day. As such, it reveals to those of a later age, who take the trouble to untie the yellowed bundles and spread flat the brittle pages, the attitudes, prejudices, taboos, fads, talk – in fact, the life of the time in which it was produced. If more than half the population of a great country can spend a few minutes each day catching up on the latest 'funnies' then the comics represent one of the most effective forces of contact within that society. The comics are escape-hatches to laughter or fantasy or adventure, the momentary relief from the tedious subway journey or the day's decision-making. As such, their function is vital, their benefit unimpeachable – or so the Newspaper Comics Council would like us to think.

Comic Section

Enter the Yellow Kid: readers of the *New York World* on Sunday, 16 February 1896, were greeted with this large cartoon. Drawn by R.F. Outcault, it was called *The Great Dog Show in M'Googan Avenue*. At its centre, a hideous night-shirted child, his single garment coated in a jaundiced ochre. The Yellow Kid was the beginning of American comics. He started a cut-throat circulation war, its main contenders Joseph Pulitzer, proprietor of the *World*, and William Randolph Hearst of the *American*. He gave currency to the expression 'yellow journalism'. On the right is a page from a *World* Sunday supplement detailing the humorous attractions offered in the first years of the comics. The Yellow Kid was given pride of place, in spite of the fact that by then Outcault had abandoned the character and was working on the *New York Herald*, producing Li'l Mose. In 1902 he started a new character, Buster Brown, another mischievous small boy, only with a Park Avenue rather than a slum background. Hearst bought Outcault for the *American*. The first bathtub joke is from a 1905 *Herald*, the second after Outcault had moved across to Hearst.

Early entrants: other characters of the early American comics (on the pages following) were Foxy Grandpa, drawn by Charles Schultze or 'Bunny' and two magnificent creations of Frederick Burr Opper – Maud, the unpredictable mule, and Happy Hooligan, an engaging and amiable poverty-stricken victim of fate.

4 THE WORLD: SUNDAY, DECEMBER 9, 1900.

GRAND CONGRESS of A Galaxy of Wit & Humor

BY WAY OF CELEBRATION.

ORDINARILY, combining the best creations of the greatest comic artists would be about the same thing as putting lambs, lions, cats and dogs into a cage and asking them all to please be quiet. Some of them would be quiet, because there would be nothing left of them. Then the survivors would fight it out for the supremacy, and there would be mighty little sleep in the neighborhood.

But to-day the Sunday World accomplishes a hitherto impossible feat, made possible only by the joy which the comic artists feel in the increase of its Funny Side to eight pages. They are willing to dwell in harmony here, as you see them, and for this reason we are able to present the greatest comic creations of the last decade, the things that have made you not only laugh once, but watch for them week after week. In them, from the Brownies to the latest invention, you see what you have laughed at for years. That the Sunday World has been responsible for many of them—in fact, the great majority—you will admit after you have looked at them. Under the able directorship of Hon. George W. Peck the Funny Side will doubtless furnish you with many more humorous surprises.

J. K. BRYANS' CLEVER SILHOUETTES FROM THE WORLD FUNNY SIDE.
J. K. BRYANS' Silhouette Man
GEE! I'M SO BUSY I HAVN'T GOT TIME TO DO ANYT'ING OR ANY BODY
R. F. Outcault
THE MAN FROM BROOKLYN, (Bargain day at the Stores.) One of the best things by T. E. Powers that has appeared in the N.Y. WORLD
T. E. POWERS
"THE YELLOW KID," THE MOST POPULAR HUMOROUS CREATION OF THE CENTURY. THE YELLOW KID WAS FIRST PRODUCED IN THE "WORLD" IN 1895," by R. F. OUTCAULT.
R. F. OUTCAULT. THE YELLOW KID MAN
The FLUFFYDUFF SISTERS, Created in the Sunday World, 1900 by BRYANS
W. F. MARRINER
THE ROLY POLYS, ONE OF THE WORLD'S GREATEST SUCCESSES. First Presented in 1898.
PAUL WEST, CREATOR OF THE ROLY POLYS
TYPES OF KIDS Drawn by Marriner in the Sunday World. Their quaintness has made him famous
PLATT'S FAREWELL TO CROKER
ONE OF THE GREAT CARTOONS OF C. G. BUSH, THAT APPEAR IN THE N.Y. WORLD.
CHAS. G. BUSH. THE WORLD'S NOTED CARTOONIST
W. W. DENSLOW, the FATHER Goose Man
"FATHER GOOSE," W. W. Denslow's Popular Creation, as he appeared in the SUNDAY WORLD

BUSTER BROWN AND TIGE AND A KITTEN &c.
No. Steen
Cadogan Square
To Buddy Tucker London
My dear Son
I received your wireless from the steamer and your letter from New York. I am glad you are in such good hands and that you are having such a good time. Now that you are in America I want you to hunt up your uncle, my brother. His name is Mr. Smith and he lives in America. he is quite rich I understand and might assist you. Tell him you are his nephew. Think happy and keep a good true conscience. Dont get discouraged for as you think so you will be Your loving mater.
BUSTER I'M GOING TO GO AND FIND ME UNCLE
GOOD LUCK OLD CHAP
COME BACK WHENEVER YOU LIKE BUDDY
HELLO PUSSY! WHERE DID YOU COME FROM? DONT BE AFRAID - I WONT HURT YOU
WELL HOLY SMOKE WHAT DO YOU THINK OF THAT?
WHY YOU SASSY LITTLE THING — YOU MAKE ME LAUGH
HEY
PULL OUT THOSE PINS
IT'S LUCKY I WAS'N'T IN THE TUB
R. F. Outcault
TIGE WHAT IN THE WORLD ARE YOU DOING TO POOR PUSSY?
POOR PUSSY, 'GEE'
(COPYRIGHT, 1905, BY THE NEW YORK HERALD CO.)

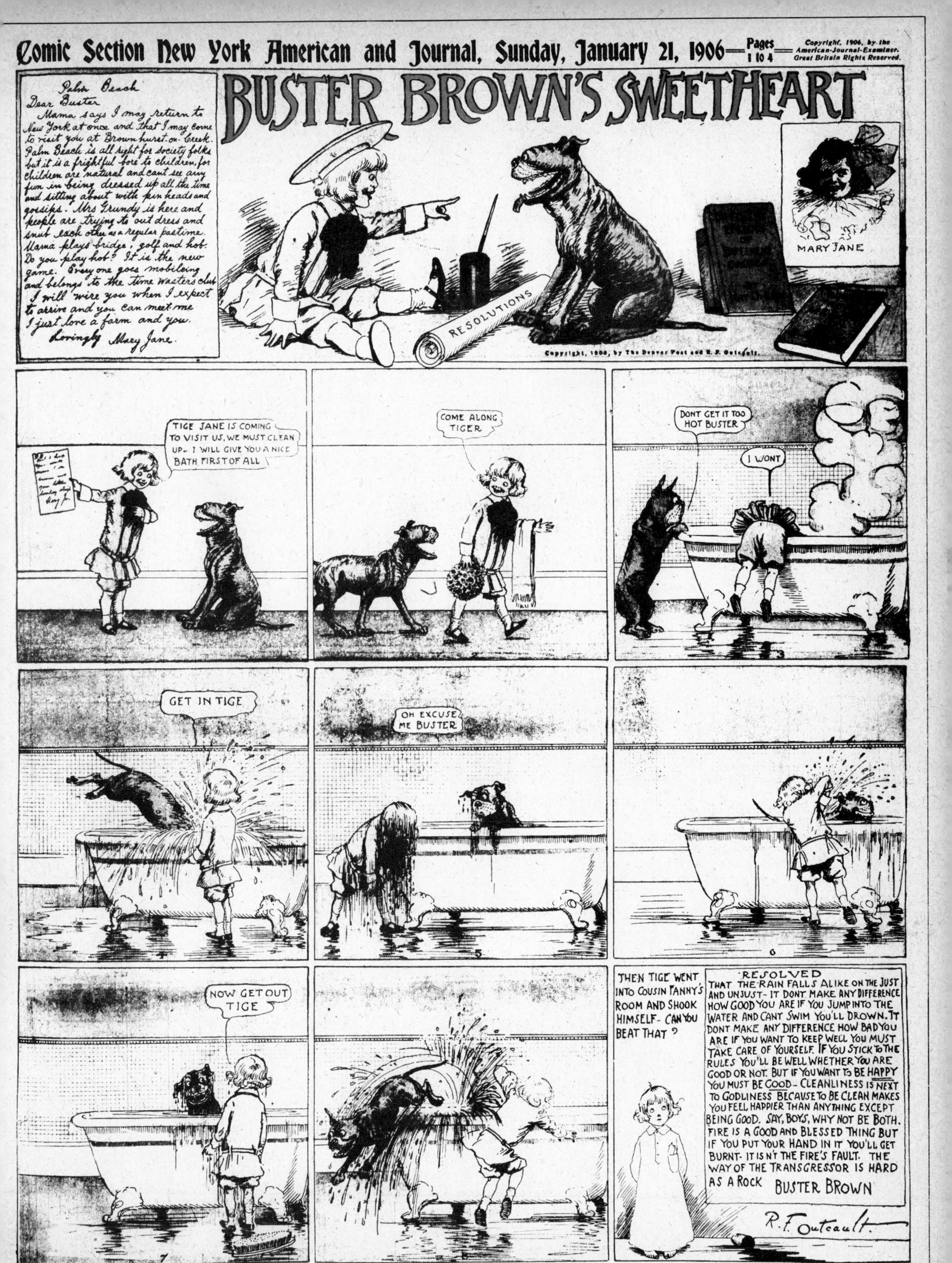
Comic Section New York American and Journal, Sunday, January 21, 1906—Pages 1 to 4
Copyright, 1906, by the American-Journal-Examiner. Great Britain Rights Reserved.
BUSTER BROWN'S SWEETHEART
Palm Beach
Dear Buster
Mama says I may return to New York at once and that I may come to visit you at Brown hurst-on-Creek. Palm Beach is all right for society folks but it is a frightful bore to children, for children are natural and cant see any fun in being dressed up all the time and sitting about with pin heads and gossips. Mrs Grundy is here and people are trying to out dress and snub each other as a regular pastime. Mama plays bridge, golf and bob. Do you play bob? It is the new game. Every one goes mobileing and belongs to the time wasters club
I will wire you when I expect to arrive and you can meet me I just love a farm and you.
Lovingly Mary Jane.
RESOLUTIONS
MARY JANE
Copyright, 1906, by The Denver Post and R. F. Outcault.
TIGE JANE IS COMING TO VISIT US, WE MUST CLEAN UP- I WILL GIVE YOU A NICE BATH FIRST OF ALL
COME ALONG TIGER
DONT GET IT TOO HOT BUSTER
I WONT
GET IN TIGE
OH EXCUSE ME BUSTER
NOW GET OUT TIGE
THEN TIGE WENT INTO COUSIN FANNY'S ROOM AND SHOOK HIMSELF- CAN YOU BEAT THAT?
RESOLVED
THAT THE RAIN FALLS ALIKE ON THE JUST AND UNJUST- IT DONT MAKE ANY DIFFERENCE HOW GOOD YOU ARE IF YOU JUMP INTO THE WATER AND CANT SWIM YOU'LL DROWN. IT DONT MAKE ANY DIFFERENCE HOW BAD YOU ARE IF YOU WANT TO KEEP WELL YOU MUST TAKE CARE OF YOURSELF. IF YOU STICK TO THE RULES YOU'LL BE WELL WHETHER YOU ARE GOOD OR NOT. BUT IF YOU WANT TO BE HAPPY YOU MUST BE GOOD- CLEANLINESS IS NEXT TO GODLINESS BECAUSE TO BE CLEAN MAKES YOU FEEL HAPPIER THAN ANYTHING EXCEPT BEING GOOD. SAY, BOYS, WHY NOT BE BOTH. FIRE IS A GOOD AND BLESSED THING BUT IF YOU PUT YOUR HAND IN IT YOU'LL GET BURNT- IT ISN'T THE FIRE'S FAULT. THE WAY OF THE TRANSGRESSOR IS HARD AS A ROCK BUSTER BROWN
R. F. Outcault.

FOXY GRANDPA.

He Steals a March on the Boys.

Come out, gran'-pa, and play war with us.

Now, you're the Boer, gran'-pa; we built this nice fort for you.

I guess I'll have to steal a march on those boys.

We're ready, gran'-pa.

Here we come---hurrah!!

Well, boys, I guess we've had enough war, so I'll have to run in now.

HAPPY HOOLIGAN HAD A DREAM ABOUT THE LEANING TOWER OF PISA

And Her Name Was Maud!

Heil Hans und Fritz! Rudolph Dirks created The Katzenjammer Kids in 1897 after Hearst, who also owned the *New York Journal*, had seen Wilhelm Busch's Max and Moritz in Germany. The Katzenjammers were not mere copies, but new characters with a distinct immigrant personality and dialogue in pidgin German. Dirks rested the strip in 1898 so that he could serve in the Spanish-American War. In 1912 he wanted another rest in order to go to Europe. Told that he would have to supply a year's worth of strips in advance he left, attempting to send his work in from far-off places. Then the *World* offered him a job which he accepted. The *Journal* sued, and won the case. An appeal resulted in a compromise. The title of the strip was to remain *Journal* property, but Dirks could draw it for someone else under an alternative title. Ever since there have been two versions of the strip. Dirks's version became known as The Captain and the Kids, while The Katzenjammer Kids was drawn by H.H. Knerr and today by Joe Musial. In the early days of strips there was often interchange of characters. In the Alphonse, Gaston and Leon cartoon overleaf the Katzenjammers made a guest appearance and the strip bears the signatures of both Opper and Dirks.

Dream world: Winsor McCay was another of the great early artists. His most famous creation was Little Nemo, a rich, decorative dream fantasy. The example overleaf is a Sunday page of 1906.

World

NEW YORK, SUNDAY, MARCH 24, 1929.

HAVE YOU A LITTLE CARTOONIST IN YOUR HOME?

THE CAPTAIN AND THE KIDS

Trade Mark, 1929, Reg. U. S. Pat. Off.

By R. Dirks

Originator of the Katzenjammer Kids

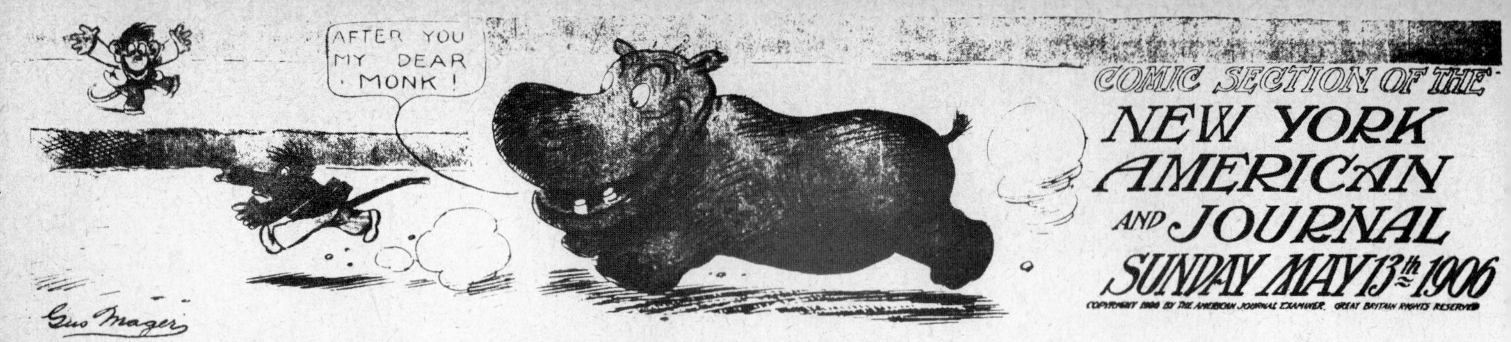

Dear Old Alphonse, Gaston and Leon!

They Turn Up

(COPYRIGHT, 1906, BY THE NEW YORK HERALD CO.)
LITTLE NEMO IN SLUMBER LAND
PSHAW!! THAT'S MEAN!
YOUR MAJESTY! LITTLE NEMO SIMPLY CAN NOT GET USED TO SLUMBERLAND. HE AWOKE TONIGHT JUST AS HE APPROACHED THE FOURTH GATE. WE HOPE TO MAKE GREAT PROGRESS WITH HIM FROM NOW ON. HOWEVER, SORROWFULLY YOURS!
NOW, NEMO, YOU WILL SOON BE READY TO START FOR THE FOURTH GATE. AREN'T YOU HAPPY?
YES. BUT WHY MUST I BE TURNED INTO A GIANT. HAVE I GOT TO FIGHT A BATTLE WITH SOME ONE TO GET IN?
NO. THE FOURTH GATE IS GUARDED BY BIG GIANTS. BRAINLESS FELLOWS WHO MUST BE APPROACHED VERY CAUTIOUSLY.
WELL, GOOD-BYE! YOU HAVE DONE SPLENDIDLY. GOOD BYE! TO YOU ALL!
SUC-CESS TO YOU!
BEST WISHES NEMO!
TA TA! NEMO! TA TA!
THEN I DONT HAVE TO FIGHT, DO I? ARE THESE GIANTS CROSS? MEAN, I MEAN.
NO. IF THEY SEE YOU ARE A GIANT THEY WILL BE MORE APT TO BE VERY KIND. ARE YOU AFRAID?
NO. I'M NOT AFRAID. I FEEL LIKE I COULD LICK A HUNDRED GIANTS NAW! I'M NOT AFRAID OF ANY BODY.
THATS JUST WHY YOU HAVE BEEN CHANGED INTO A GIANT, SO YOU WILL BE BRAVE.
WHEN WE PASS THROUGH THIS FOREST WE SHALL COME TO THE LANDS END AND THE FOURTH GATE. NOW, DON'T WAKE UP.
LITTLE NEMO HE LOOKS QUITE HUSKY TO ME
YOU MEAN BIG NEMO, DONT YOU?
GUARDS OF THE FOURTH GATE! IN THE NAME OF HER MOST GRACIOUS MAJESTY THE PRINCESS OF SLUMBERLAND, I COMMAND YOU TO ARISE! AND ALLOW TO PASS, HER NEW PLAYMATE, LITTLE NEMO.
QUIT PROWLING AROUND IN THEPE NEMO. YOU HEAR? AND GO TO SLEEP!

Classic team: Mutt met Jeff in 1908; they are still going strong. The artist was Bud Fisher, a former sports cartoonist, and he started the famous strip on the west coast, in a San Francisco newspaper. The middle example shows Fisher himself. Mutt, it will be seen, had no qualms in treating his small friend unscrupulously, but sometimes Jeff came out on top. The strip was continued after Fisher's death by Al Smith who had worked with him since 1932.

Monstrous marriage: George McManus, one of the most prolific of the early strip cartoonists, started Bringing Up Father in 1913. The saga of a wealthy working man, forced into top-hat and spats by his determinedly *nouveau riche* wife, has milked laughter for over half a century. The top example is from 1913, the lower from 1929. McManus died in 1954 but Jiggs and Maggie continue their conflict with unabated vigour, as the 1966 example overleaf shows.

Jeff Ought to Cheat Somebody and Trade His Head for a Brussels Sprout* ☘ *By "Bud" Fisher

Bringing Up Father

Registered U. S. Patent Office

BRINGING  FATHER

The greatest: Krazy Kat represents the comic strip at its zenith. It was the creation of George Herriman, who had been working in strip cartoons for about ten years before he started this one. It lasted for nearly thirty-five years. For all that time one basic situation persisted – the love triangle of Kat for Ignatz Mouse and Offissa Pupp the policeman for Kat. Ignatz loved nobody, and spent most of his time hurling bricks at Krazy, who took them as a sign of returned affection. Offissa Pupp as determinedly locked Ignatz in his jail. The settings underwent violent transformations as though a stagehand was playing around with the backdrops. The dialogue was written in a unique style, part poetry, part Joycean pun, part convoluted grammar. Rarely did Herriman follow a conventional layout, sometimes his frames would be irregular, sometimes non-existent. Almost a recluse, he lived in Hollywood and on one occasion is alleged to have refused a raise on the grounds that he was worth only what he he was already getting. He died in 1944; so idiosyncratic was the strip that King Features wisely let Krazy Kat die with him. The first two examples are from 1922, the third from a Sunday page of 1938.

Krazy Kat

By Herriman

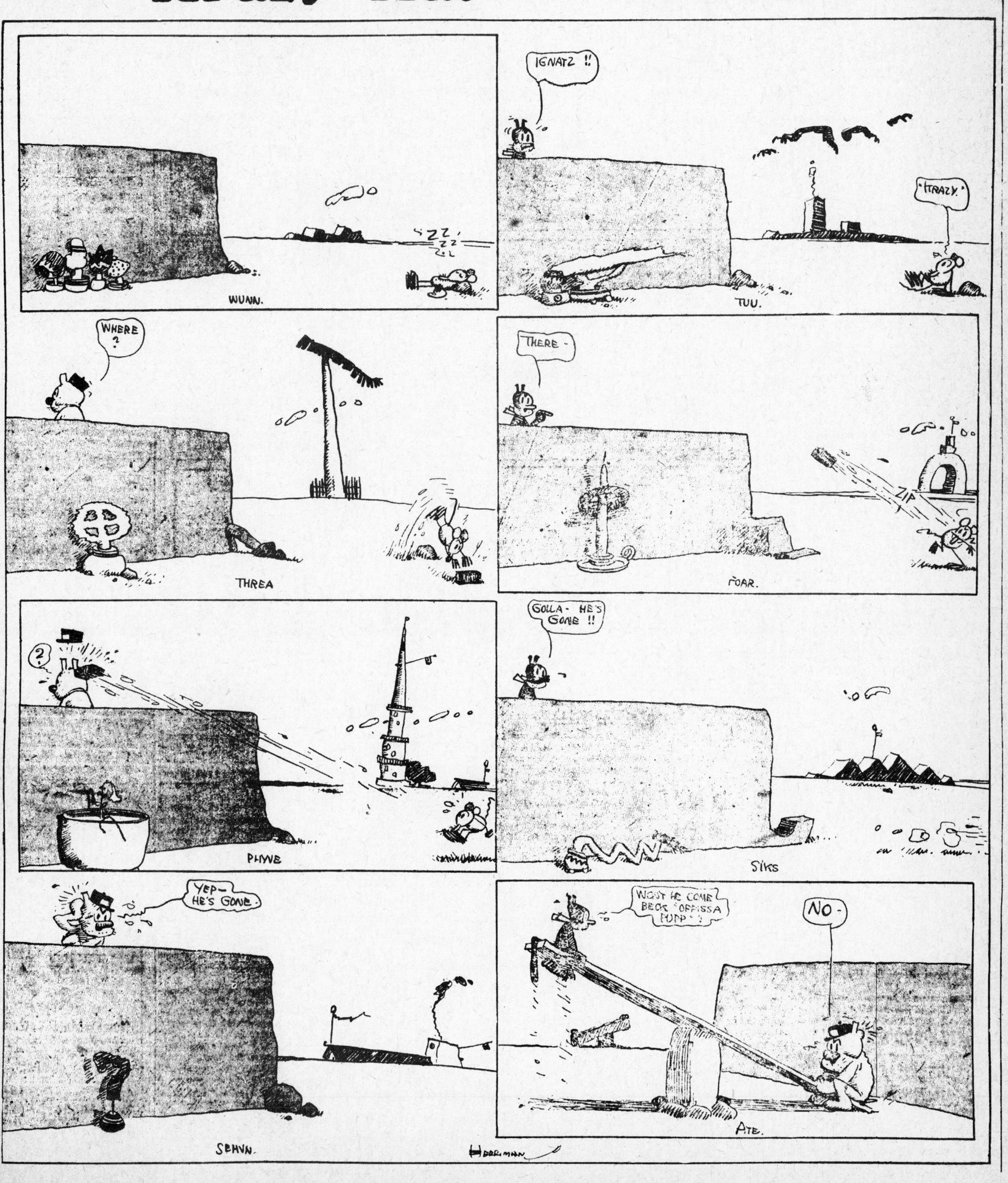

Krazy Kat

By Herriman

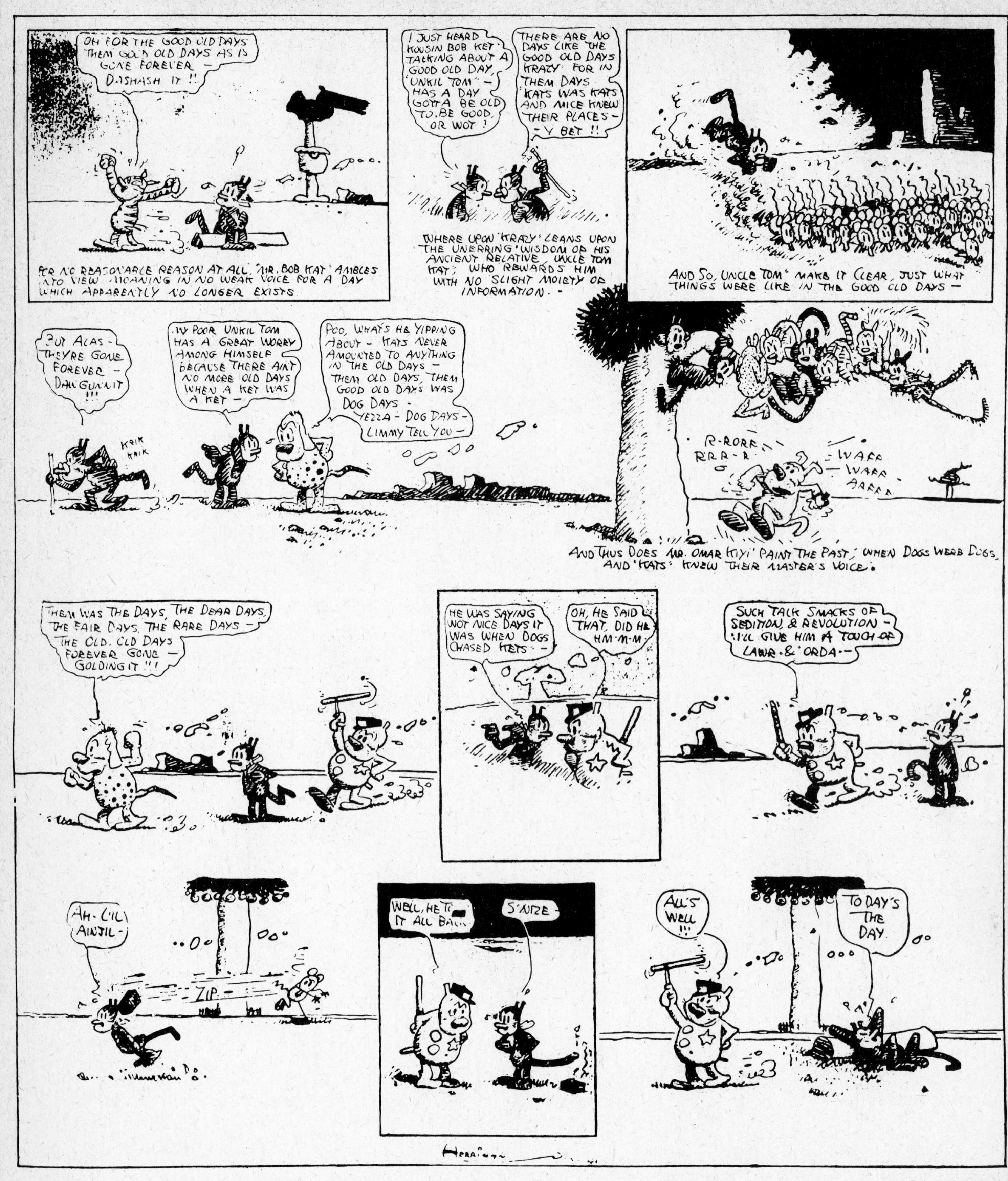

"KRAZY KAT"
Registered U.S. Patent Office
HE COMES, THE OFFENSIVE IFF - ALL ALOAD WITH SIN AND SHAME. HOWEVER, WHEN I GET THROUGH SHUCKING HIM DOWN, HE'LL BE HITTING THE TRAIL LIGHT.
PAUSE, MOUSIE, PAUSE, HALT YOURSELF A MOMENT - THE LAW BIDS YOU.
AH- BUT, KOPPIE DEAR - I CAN ILL-SPARE THAT MOMENT OF PAUSE - I AM ENROAD TO GIVE VISIT TO MY DEAR PAL KRAZY.
HAVE DONE WITH GAMMER - SPRING THAT VALISE BAG APART, AND SHED THE BRICK WITHIN - T'WILL LIGHTEN YOUR CARGO AND GIVE EASE TO YOUR LOCOMOTION.
OH, LODDY ME - I JUST KNEW THAT I WASN'T SMART ENOUGH TO SMUGG THAT BRICK APAST YOU - - - - I JUST KNEW IT, YOU KEEN, KEWT, KUNNING KOP -
INSUPPORTABLE NONENTITY - I LOVE TO HATE HIM -
GIVE THAT SWEET KAT MY FONDEST FELICITATIONS - AND THINGS BEING AS THEY ARE, I GIVE YOU PROMISE OF A SAFE RETURN THIS WAY - - - AND, AS WE SAY IN PIRREE, OH REEWAW.
THAT MOUSE PAID KELLY A DIME FOR IT - I WILL SELL IT BACK TO KELLY FOR A NICKEL - - ONE OF US IS A VERY ASTUTE BUSINESS PERSON.
BESIDES BEING A FAIR BAKER OF BRICKS, KELLY, I'D SAY YOU WERE ALSO A BONNIE ECONOMIST -
GETTING A TEN-CENT ARTICLE FOR A NICKEL IS A GOOD BARGAIN - AYE, A GOOD BARGAIN.
HOW COME YOU DID N'T BRING IN THE OTHER BRICK - - - EH ? I SOLD HIM TWO Y'KNOW
PARDON MY SEEMING UNGALLANTRY, MY DEAR KRAZY - - FOR NOT GIVING YOU A HAND WITH THAT BAG - BUT I AWAIT THE COMING OF A CERTAIN PARTY AND MY ATTENTION MUST NOT BE DIVERTED - - - IT'S DUTY.
DUN'T MINE ME, OFFISSA PUPP - I'M ARE GIVING THE BEG AN' THE SITIWATION ALL THE HEND WOT IS NEZZEZIZERRA - - TENX.
Copr. 1938, King Features Syndicate, Inc., World rights reserved
2-13
HERRIMAN

Another partnership : Barney Google was created by Billy DeBeck in 1919. He was one of nature's victims – the man everyone picked on. Like Jeff he was diminutive in stature, at least after the strip had been running a couple of years. In 1922 a grateful stable-owner gave him a race-horse; the episode is shown below. The horse was covered down to his ankles in a patched blanket, and apparently preferred to race with this encumbrance, which did not affect his performance. Barney Google enriched the language with many phrases; perhaps the most well known were 'heebie-jeebies' and 'yard bird'. Later in his career he met up with Snuffy Smith and his folk, in hill-billy country. The strip, now drawn by Fred Lasswell, is still going.

Comic array : a typical daily comics page from a 1919 *New York American*. Only Bringing Up Father is in anything like the standard modern three- or four-frame format. Barney Google has yet to lose several inches in height and Krazy Kat is having a Spanish pun session. Mr Jack by Jimmy Swinnerton is a late example of the work of a father of the comic strip. In 1892 he had drawn an animal series in the *San Francisco Examiner*, another Hearst paper, called Little Bears and Tigers. Strictly speaking they were not strips but humorous drawings. Nevertheless they had a regular audience four years before Outcault's Yellow Kid made a splash in New York.

BARNEY GOOGLE By Billy DeBeck

NEW YORK AMERICAN—A Paper for People Who Think—FRIDAY, DECEMBER 19, 1919
Bringing Up Father By George McManus
NOW-HOW DAUGHTER IS IMPROVING ON THE PIANO-ISN'T THAT BEAUTIFUL?
WELL-IF YOU CALL THAT MUSIC-I DON'T KNOW WHAT MUSIC IS-
© 1919 BY INT'L FEATURE SERVICE, INC.
OF COURSE YOU DON'T-HIGH CLASS MUSIC WOULDN'T APPEAL TO YOU-I MUST GO IN AND SEE WHAT OPERA SHE WAS PLAYING-
WHERE IS DAUGHTER-WASN'T SHE PLAYING THE PIANO?
NO MUM-
!
I WUZ JUST WIPIN' OFF THE KEYS LIKE THIS'
12-19
Say, Pop By C.M. Payne
The Story Was Too Much for the Boy.
I EXPECTED TO SEE YOUR FATHER IN REGARD TO SOME PRINTS I AM SELLING.
YUH JUST MISSED SEEING POP
BY THE SALE OF THESE PRINTS WE EXPECT TO PRESENT EACH PATAGONIAN CHILD WITH A TIN WHISTLE
JUST THINK OF THE POOR LITTLE PATAGONIANS NEVER KNOWING THE JOY OF A TIN WHISTLE
POP HADN'T YUH BETTER COME OUT AN' BUY A PITCHER FROM THA LADY ?
COPYRIGHT 1919 BY KING FEATURES SYNDICATE INC
12-19 Payne
Penny Ante WITH A STORY TELLER. By Jean Knott
SAY, IF WE'RE GONNA PLAY POKER LET'S DO IT I DIDN'T COME HERE TO LISSEN TO A CABARET
THIS IS POSITIVELY MY LAST ONE AL, LEMME TELL IT, JOE HASN'T HEARD IT YET
HEY EDDIE. HE'S GONNA TELL THAT ONE ABOUT THE MAN GOING TO HEAVEN AGAIN!
I BET A BLUE CHIP IS ANYBODY GONNA CALL IT?
HA! HA!! LET HIM TELL THIS ONE AL, ITS A BEAR
'SALL RIGHT AL, YOU DON'T HAVE TO LISSEN 'IF Y' DON'T WANT TO
WE OUGHTA PUT A MUZZLE ON THIS BIRD
Knott 12-19
Let the Wedding Bells Ring Out
FROM NOW ON I'M GONNA BE BOSS IN MY HOUSE
WE GOTTA ASSERT OUR SELVES, THAT'S ALL
YOU BET, THAT GOES FOR ME TOO
JUST WOT I'VE ALWAYS SAID
WILLIAM!
JOHN!
COMING
YES'M
12-19
Mr. Jack By Jimmy Swinnerton
1.
2. "YOU ARE SO VERY WONDERFUL! I KNOW A BEAUTIFUL POEM THAT DESCRIBES YOU!"
3. "MAY I CALL ON YOU FOR TEA AND READ IT?"
"WHY YES"
4.
5. "THESE ARE MY LITTLE BROTHERS THEY JUST ADORE HEARIN POETRY TOO!"
© 1919 by Int'l Feature Service, Inc.
12-19 SWINNERTON
Barney Google By Billy De Beck
I WONDER WHAT TIME IT IS?
SAY—I WANT MY ROOM CHANGED-EVERY MORNING THE SUN WAKES ME UP AT SEVEN OCLOCK-
IF YOU DON'T LIKE IT MOVE OUT!
I'LL SHOW THAT GUY-I AIN'T GOIN TO GET UP EVERY MORNING AT SEVEN WHEN I DON'T HAVE TO BE DOWN TO WORK TILL NINE I'LL PAINT THE WINDOW
OH BOY THAT WAS SOME SLEEP-I FEEL LIKE GOIN' TO WORK THIS MORNING
MANAGER
YOU'RE FIRED FOR NOT SHOWING UP FOR TWO DAYS!!
COPYRIGHT, 1919, BY KING FEATURES SYNDICATE INC.
12-19 DE BECK
Krazy Kat By Herriman
THAT'S DON EGON DE LOS FRIJOLES BLANCOS-FROM MEXICO-
OH-HO, A BANDIT. HEH?
YEP, A JOLLY BANDIT-
GOSH, AND WHY IS DON EGON A BANDIT?
HE DUNT LIKE THE GOVAMINT OF HIS COUNTRY-
BUT MEXICO HAS A NICE GOVERNMENT IS'NT IT A CONSTITUTION LIKE OURS?
YES, BUT IT'S A VERY RUN DOWN CONSTITUTION-
OH
AND THESE BENDITS IS RUNNING IT DOWN MORE YET-
HERE'S A BRICK THAT WILL RUN DOWN YOUR CONSTITUTION-
AY, CHIKITA QUE SI, AI CHIKITA QUE NO-OH-
ZIP
HERRIMAN

THE WORLD: SUNDAY, NOVEMBER 19, 1922.
MAIN STREET
BY GUS MAGER
MEATS
BIJOU MOVIE THEATRE
PAY HERE
O. SWEET CANDY EMPORIUM
CONFECTIONERY
BAKERY
BUTCHER
CHOICE MEATS
TAR
SAY GABB, DID YOU HEAR THAT OWEN TICK AND HIS WIFE HAVE GOT THE OUT-DOOR BUG? THEY'RE GOING TO LIVE IN A TENT, OUT ON PURDY'S LOT!!
BAH! I S'POSE THAT'S WHAT TICK TOLD YOU HIMSELF! BUT HERE'S THE REAL STORY–KEEP IT TO YOURSELF------
GENTLEMEN, AS ELMER, HERE, SAYS – THIS MR. AND MRS. TICK OWES EVERY MAN JACK OF US BUSINESS MEN MONEY! THEY'VE STUCK EVERYONE IN TOWN – BUYING NOTHING BUT THE BEST – RIGHT AND LEFT – AND NEVER PAYING UP THEIR BILLS – AN' I SAY WE SHUTS DOWN ON 'EM – THEIR CREDIT IS SHOT FULL O' HOLES IN THIS TOWN!
YOU SAID A MOUTHFUL BUTCH!
NEXT TIME SHE COMES INTO MY SHOP SHE PAYS UP – OR NO MEAT!! ARE YOU WILLING TO DO THE SAME ?!?
WE'RE WITH YOU – ONE FOR ALL AND ALL FOR ONE' – AMEN!
WHO IS IT, DEAR? UNCLE BEN? HANDLE HIM WITH KID GLOVES – REMEMBER HE HAS OODLES OF MONEY – WE DON'T WANT HIM TO FORGET US IN HIS WILL!
HELLO – THIS YOU, UNCLE BEN? YOU'RE AT THE STATION? FINE! WE'LL BRING OUR CAR RIGHT DOWN AND GET YOU!!
MARY, RUN TO THE BUTCHER'S AND GET TWO QUARTS OF MUSHROOMS AND FIVE POUNDS, CHOICEST CUT, OF PORTERHOUSE STEAK. TELL HIM TO PUT IT ON THE BILL!
COME ON DEAR – UNCLE BEN MUSN'T BE KEPT WAITING!
PARDON ME, MR. TICK, BUT AS YOUR LAST THREE PAYMENTS ON YOUR CAR HAVE LAPSED, I'VE BEEN SENT TO TAKE IT BACK!
NO MEAT, MRS. TICK – THE BUTCHER WON'T TRUST NO MORE!
YES, AND I MIGHT AS WELL TELL YOU, MRS. TICK, THAT I'M TIRED OF WAITING FOR MY LAST TWO MONTHS' PAY – I'M QUITTING THIS POSITION!
THE DOORBELL! DON'T OPEN! I BET IT'S THAT FURNITURE CREDIT MAN AGAIN FOR HIS INSTALLMENT – I ALWAYS MAKE BELIEVE I'M OUT! COME UPSTAIRS, DEAR, – WE CAN PEEK OUT THE WINDOW!
Copr. 1922 (N. Y. World) By Press Pub. Co.
WHY HELLO! IT'S ONLY UNCLE BEN! HOW'D YOU GET HERE UNCLE?
THE DRIVER OF THAT VAN OFFERED ME A LIFT – TOLD HIM WHO I WAS LOOKING FOR – HE SAID HE WAS ON HIS WAY HERE HIMSELF!
FURNITURE VAN
11-19-22
BUT LISTEN –
OUR ORDERS WAS TER GIT THIS FURNITURE – IF YOU'VE GOT ANYTHING TER SAY, BETTER CALL UP THE BOSS!!
JUST GO TO THE PALACE HOTEL, UNCLE BEN, AND CHARGE IT TO US!!
LAST WILL AND TESTAMENT OF BENJAMIN BONDS.
I hereby bequeath to ~~Cassie Tick~~ Owen Tick
ME FOR THE TRAIN BACK HOME AND I WON'T FORGET I'M OUT A ROUND TRIP FARE, EITHER!!!
FURNITURE VAN
Gus Mager

Small-town world: with the twenties the strips entered a new period of cosiness and familiarity. The domestic life of the average American was a fit subject for cartoons. It could be treated with high humour as in Gus Mager's Main Street (*left*) or with gentle seriousness as in Gasoline Alley. Started initially as a single panel, Gasoline Alley evolved into a long-term family bible in which characters grew up, married, had children, died. The 1920 strip (*top*) shows Walt Wallet at the wheel. Cars were originally the cartoon's pivot of interest, at a time when the Model T was beginning to transform the old pattern of life. In 1921 Wallet found a baby boy on his doorstep. He was called Skeezix and he grew up with Uncle Walt and Aunt Phyllis. In 1941 he faced the draft, with his fiancée doing war work in the big city (*centre*), and in 1967 he had a small gloom on the onset of middle age. Skeezix is America's Everyman. The artist who began it was Frank King, born and bred in Wisconsin. Just as the Midwest is the heartland of America, so his strip represents the comforting values of daily small-town life – although efforts are made not to over-sentimentalize it. Gasoline Alley is not afraid to meet social problems. But the strip's basic mission is to find reassurance in ordinary everyday events. The formula hasn't failed.

GASOLINE ALLEY — HELPFUL FELLOW-MOTORISTS.

GASOLINE ALLEY—JUST A SUGGESTION, YOU KNOW

Perpetual waif: Harold Gray's Little Orphan Annie started in 1924. The upper illustration represents a moment of some import, when a month after the start her part-time guardian, the powerful millionaire armaments king, lets it be known he wants to be called 'Daddy' Warbucks. The strip has been used by its creator for the furtherance of right-wing views and from time to time has been dropped by newspapers unwilling to be involved in the ensuing controversy. The lower illustration is a modern Sunday page, with Annie bravely carrying on after forty-three years of orphanhood. When her dog Sandy went missing Harold Gray was deluged with letters and pleas for his safe return, including a telegram from Henry Ford.

LITTLE ORPHAN ANNIE–AND THE SHOCK ALMOST KILLED ANNIE

Roaring twenties: Smitty, drawn by Walter Berndt, perfectly hit the mood of the pre-Depression era. He is a juvenile smart operator, determined to hit the bigtime eventually. Unfortunately for him, he is still, after all these years, only in his teens. Harold Teen by Carl Ed regularly needed a vocabularial refit to stay up to date with the latest slang. Harold was the late adolescent, rapidly growing aware of the problems of adulthood and still making a brave showing at college-boy razzamatazz. Mutt and Jeff at the foot of the page occasionally met real people and topical subject-matter. In this 1929 strip they are in the White House, Mutt in a menial position and Jeff in bed with Herbert Hoover.

SMITTY—WILL HE GET IT?

HAROLD TEEN—THE SAGE AND THE SHEIK

MUTT AND JEFF—It Seems to Be a Gift With Jeff - By BUD FISHER

Girls on the scene: the working girl was one of the twenties strip heroines. Two of the most famous were Tillie the Toiler by Russ Westhover, which first appeared in 1921, and Winnie Winkle by Martin Branner. Tillie was courted by the ugly little fellow in the 1930 strip below. In 1959 when the series ended Mac finally won his girl. Betty Boop by Max Fleischer (*next page*) was a success in animated film cartoons. In her strip guise she acted as a movie queen. The most famous of all strip heroines is undoubtedly Blondie, the creation of Murat (Chic) Young. In 1930 she began life as the brick-dropping, vivacious fiancée of Dagwood Bumstead, heir to his father's massive fortune. Bumstead senior disapproved and cut him off when they married. After that the newlyweds settled in to the familiar suburban pattern – Dagwood working for Mr Dithers, Blondie keeping house. George McManus had pioneered this particular *genre* of strip years earlier, with The Newlyweds, and there is in Chic Young's work more than a hint of McManus influence. But Blondie is a brilliant and consistent creation. The strip has been syndicated in more papers than any other in cartoon history. The top strip is the very first, appearing on 15 September 1930. The lower ones are of 1945, 1950, and 1967 and show how consistent the style remains. Blondie represents for many people in other countries the quintessential American wife – for good or otherwise.

"Tillie the Toiler" Works Every Day—in the Daily American

WINNIE WINKLE
THE BREADWINNER
VOTES

YOU'RE NOT GOING TO HANG AROUND THE STREETS WITH LOAFERS! YOU'RE GOING TO VISIT THE HIBROWS WITH ME!!
WOW! I TELL YA I GOTTA SELL THIS MAG'ZINE!! I'M WAY BEHIND ALL TH' OTHER GUYS AN' I GOTTA KETCH UP!! I DO' WANNA GO VISITIN'!!

AH, MISS WINKLE - JUST IN TIME TO ATTEND A MEETING OF OUR LITERARY CLUB!!
HOW DELIGHTFUL MRS. HIBROW!
A FELLER MIGHT JES' AS WELL LAY DOWN AN' DIE AS HAVE A BIG SISTER - NOW I'LL NEVER KETCH UP TO TH' REST OF TH' GANG!

I DIDN'T KNOW MRS. HIBROW WAS HAVING A LITERARY MEETING OR I'D NEVER HAVE ALLOWED YOU TO BRING THAT CHEAP MAGAZINE OF YOURS ALONG!! FOR HEAVEN'S SAKE DON'T LET ANYONE HERE SEE IT OR I'LL BE DISGRACED!!!
I S'POSE YOU'D LIKE ME TO BURN IT UP OR SUMP'N!??

LADIES, IT IS THE PURPOSE OF THIS CLUB TO UPLIFT AND ELEVATE LITERATURE ABOVE THE SO-CALLED POPULAR MAGAZINE VARIETY!!
APPLESAUSE!! WINNIE OUGHT'A GET SHOT FOR HANGIN' OUT WITH A BUNCH O' TOMATOES LIKE THEM!

OH - UH - WHAT A CUTE LITTLE BOY!! WHAT ARE YOU DOING OUT HERE - TRYING TO GET IN TO THE LITERARY MEETING?
NOT ON YER LIFE!! I'M TRYIN' TO SELL TH' SWELLEST BOOK IN TH' WORLD - TH' HOKUM MAG'ZINE! ONEY 25 CENTS FOR A WHOLE YEAR! TAKE A LOOK AT IT!!

WELL IT'S NOT EXACTLY HIGHBROW BUT HERE'S A FINE RECIPE ON "HOW TO MAKE SAUSAGE CUSTARD" - I'LL TAKE A SUBSCRIPTION BUT DON'T TELL ANY OF THE LADIES INSIDE!!!
JES' GIMME YER NAME AN' ADDRESS AN' A QUARTER AN' I WON'T OPEN MY HEAD!!

IT'S NOT AN ELEVATING MAGAZINE, BUT HERE'S AN ARTICLE ON HOW TO EMBROIDER "BURLAP DOILIES"! I'LL SUBSCRIBE, BUT FOR HEAVEN'S SAKE DON'T BREATHE IT TO A SOUL!!!
ONEY COSTS A QUARTER A YEAR! Y'CAN'T BEAT THAT FOR A BARGAIN!!!

IT'S RATHER A COMMON BOOK BUT I MUST CONFESS TO A WEAKNESS FOR LOVE STORIES - TEE-HEE -- AND THERE ARE SEVERAL HERE - UH - I'LL TAKE A SUBSCRIPTION, BUT MUM'S THE WORD!!!
25 CENTS A YEAR - THA'S ALL IT COSTS!

IT'S A VULGAR MAGAZINE BUT HERE'S AN ARTICLE DENTS OUT OF ROLLING SUBSCRIBE TO THIS, BUT YOU NEEDN'T TELL ANY OF THE OTHER LADIES!!
AIN'T IT SWELL, HUH?? AN' ONEY A QUARTER A YEAR!!

OH BOY, THEM HIGHBROW LADIES SURE DID FALL FOR THAT HOKUM MAG'ZINE! WELL I GOT NINE NEW S'CRIPTIONS - THAT OUGHT'A HOLD TH' GANG FOR AWHILE.!!!

I'M GLAD YOU BEHAVED YOURSELF PERRY!! IF THE LADIES OF THE LITERARY CLUB HAD SEEN YOUR MAGAZINE, I'D HAVE DIED FOR SHAME!!

YOU'SE GUYS DON'T MIX IN TH' RIGHT KIND OF SASSIETY!
STANDING IN THE VOTE CONTEST
PERRY - 10 Subscriptions - 15.000 VOTES
SPUD - 8 " - 14.000 "
SPIKE - 7 " - 13.500 "
CHINK - 5 " - 12.500 "
BRANNER

BETTY BOOP
-BY-
MAX FLEISCHER-

THIS PICTURE GIVES YOU A SWELL CHANCE TO SHOW OFF YOUR JEWELS-HURRY UP AND GET THEM-THE CAR IS WAITING!
OKAY! I HAVE THEM HIDDEN SOME PLACE UPSTAIRS!

HM-M! NOW LETS SEE-WHERE DID I HIDE THOSE JEWELS??

WHAT TH'- SHE MUST BE TAKING THE HOUSE APART!
BAM
SLAM
WAM
CRASH-

NOPE! THEY'RE NOT IN HERE EITHER- THEY WOULDN'T BE!

OOPS! NOTHING BEHIND THIS BRICK BUT A COUPLE OF LOTTERY TICKETS!

THIS IS GETTING SERIOUS-LOOKS LIKE WHEN I HIDE A THING IT STAYS HIDDEN!

'S'MATTER? YOU'RE HOLDING UP THE PARADE!
CALL IN THE "G-MEN" I'M AFRAID MY JEWELS HAVE BEEN S-STOLEN!

DON'T BE SILLY! YOU'VE PROBABLY JUST HID THEM ON YOURSELF!
NO I VE LOOKED IN EVERY HIDING-PLACE I COULD THINK OF-

AND I'VE LOOKED IN EVERY DRESSER DRAWER BUT THE **BOTTOM ONE**!
WELL WHY THE SAM HILL DON'T YOU LOOK IN **THAT DRAWER**!

BECAUSE THAT'S THE LAST DRAWER TO SEARCH -

-AND IF I LOOK IN THAT DRAWER AND FIND THEY'RE NOT THERE-**OW**! I'LL JUST PASS OUT!
???
© 1935, King Features Syndicate, Inc., Great Britain

2
PLAY MONEY
2

PLAY MONEY
2

2
PLAY MONEY
2

BLONDIE Registered U. S. Patent Office. By Chic Young

Now for action: in January 1929 a new kind of comic strip began. Tarzan was a strip version of an already successful character created in another form – the adventure novel. The first book, *Tarzan of the Apes*, by Edgar Rice Burroughs was given to a young artist called Harold Foster. At first the story was set in text below each frame. When the strip started it was the only action adventure in the field and consequently had a hard time to establish the *genre*. When it finally caught on it became a wild success and established Foster's reputation. Eventually Rex Maxon took the strip over. Foster also relinquished the Sunday page to Burne Hogarth, and an example is shown opposite. Foster created another new strip idea – a reconstruction of life in Arthurian Britain. Prince Valiant is a carefully researched, exquisitely drawn adventure with a literate text below the pictures instead of balloons. In appearance and subject-matter it is unique. There have been attempts to imitate it but none of the copiers have come anywhere near Harold Foster's painstaking style. The two sequences are 1938 and 1966 respectively and the single frame recalls the first appearance of the Prince, then aged six, in February 1937.

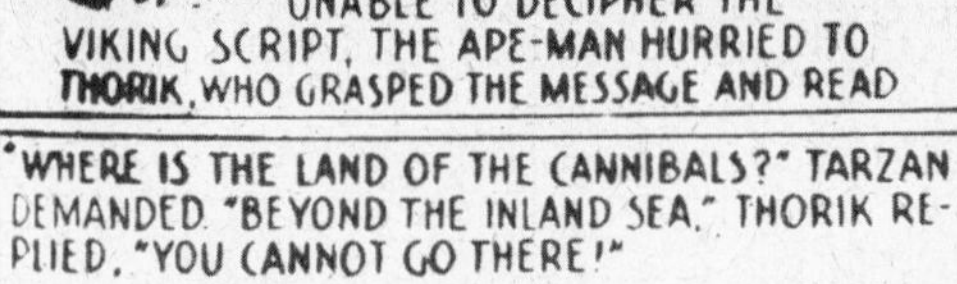

UNABLE TO DECIPHER THE VIKING SCRIPT, THE APE-MAN HURRIED TO THORIK, WHO GRASPED THE MESSAGE AND READ
"WHERE IS THE LAND OF THE CANNIBALS?" TARZAN DEMANDED. "BEYOND THE INLAND SEA," THORIK REPLIED. "YOU CANNOT GO THERE!"

"I CANNOT BEAR THE SHAME OF THORIK'S DECEIT. I GO AMONG THE CANNIBALS!" THORIK PALED AS HE CONTINUED

"IF THERE IS ANYONE WHO LOVES ME ENOUGH TO SAVE ME, I SHALL BE HAPPY. OTHERWISE, DEATH WILL END MY SUFFERING!"

"WHY?" "THEY DEVOUR ALL WHO CROSS THEIR BOUNDARIES," SAID THE VIKING; "NO ONE CAN SAVE SIGREDA NOW."

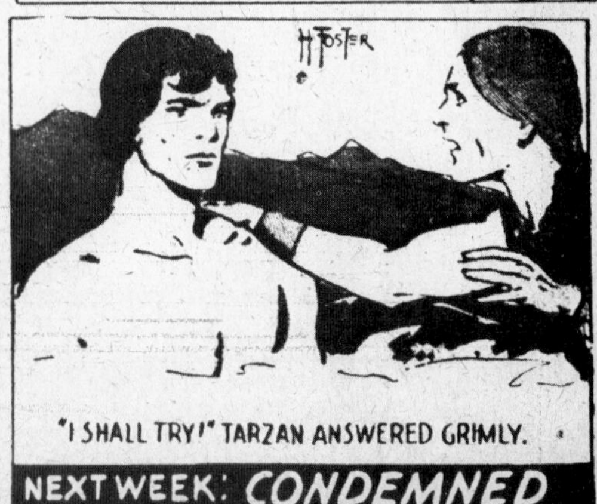

H FOSTER
"I SHALL TRY!" TARZAN ANSWERED GRIMLY.
NEXT WEEK: CONDEMNED

Tarzan

by EDGAR RICE BURROUGHS

EXPECTING TO SEE THE ELUSIVE TARZAN MOUNTED ON THE CAMEL, THE DESERT TRIBESMEN MADE READY TO FIRE.

BUT WHEN THE BEAST EMERGED FROM BEHIND THE TENT, TARZAN WAS MISSING.

THE MUSKETEERS WERE ASTONISHED; "HE'S TRICKED US!" THEY SHOUTED.

THEN THEY CAUGHT A GLIMPSE OF THE APE-MAN HANGING TO THE CAMEL ON THE FAR SIDE OF THE HUMP.

"WE CAN'T GET HIM WITHOUT SHOOTING MEHARA, THE CAMEL," THEY CRIED IN DISMAY.

"MEHARA IS OLD AND SLOW," THE SHEIK REMINDED; "AND ON THE OTHER CAMELS WE'LL SOON OVERTAKE HER."

THE DESERT WARRIORS HURRIED TO THE GRAZING HERD AND MOUNTED QUICKLY.

SOON THEY WERE IN HOT PURSUIT OF THEIR QUARRY.

THE RACE HAD HARDLY BEGUN WHEN TARZAN REALIZED HE WAS DOOMED TO LOSE.

Distr. by United Feature Syndicate, Inc.
558-11-16-41
UNDER THE APE-MAN'S URGING, OLD MEHARA DID HER BEST, BUT SHE WAS NO MATCH FOR HER SWIFTER AND YOUNGER MATES.

HOGARTH
TARZAN CROUCHED ON THE NECK OF THE BEAST, SO THAT THE HUMP PROTECTED HIM FROM THE EXPERT MARKSMEN. BUT NOW ONE OF THE PURSUERS SWEPT AROUND AT AN ANGLE TO GET A CLEAR SHOT!
NEXT WEEK: DEADLY BULLETS

Prince Valiant

IN THE DAYS OF KING ARTHUR BY HAROLD R FOSTER

SYNOPSIS:
WEARING A HORRIBLE MASK, PRINCE VAL HAS FRIGHTENED ALL THE OUTLAWS FROM THE CASTLE EXCEPT TWO. THESE HARDY RUFFIANS CHASE THE UNARMED PRINCE TO THE ROOF WHERE THEY ARE TRICKED TO THEIR DOOM BY A PIECE OF ROPE.
1
AS THE LAST OUTLAW HURTLES TO THE YARD BELOW VAL CRASHES WITH STUNNING FORCE AGAINST THE WALL.

AFTER A TREMENDOUS STRUGGLE THE HALF-CONSCIOUS YOUTH GAINS THE ROOF.
2

3
FINDING AN IRON BAR, VAL SMASHES THE LOCKED DOORS AND ENTERS THE NOW-DESERTED CASTLE.

AFTER A WEARY SEARCH HE DISCOVERS THE KEYS TO THE DUNGEONS.
4
53 2-12-38

5
AND THE YOUNG PRINCE IS ABLE TO LIBERATE ILENE'S FATHER, THE THANE OF BRANWYN WHO HAS BEEN IMPRISONED SINCE THE OGRE'S CAPTURE OF THE CASTLE.

6
THE DUNGEON CELLS ALSO GIVE UP THE REST OF THE THANE'S FAMILY AND RETAINERS.

VAL'S FIRST THOUGHT IS FOR THE MAID, ILENE, AND HE TELLS THE THANE OF THE HERMITAGE WHERE SHE IS WAITING.
7

8
THREE DAYS OF HARDSHIP WITH NEITHER FOOD NOR SLEEP HAVE TAKEN THEIR TOLL AND, HIS WORK DONE, THE YOUTHFUL PRINCE COLLAPSES.

H-L FOSTER
9
THE TENDER HEART OF ILENE BEATS WILDLY WHEN THE MESSENGER ARRIVES WITH THE NEWS OF VAL'S HEROIC DEEDS AND SHE HASTENS TO RETURN.
NEXT WEEK · CUPID USES AN AXE

Prince Valiant
IN THE DAYS OF KING ARTHUR
WRITTEN AND ILLUSTRATED BY HAROLD R FOSTER
Our Story: TRUE TO HIS PROMISE, OWEN, THE TROUBADOR, TAKES PRINCE VALIANT TO THE STREAM TO TEACH HIM HOW TO TAKE SALMON ON A FEATHERED HOOK. THE INNKEEPER'S DAUGHTER INSISTS ON CARRYING THE RODS AND LUNCH HAMPER.

EACH HAS HIS OWN PRIVATE THOUGHTS: "CAN THIS HAPPY YOUTH BE THE MISSING HEIR TO THE THRONE OF DINMORE?" DESPITE HIS PLAIN GARMENTS AND SIMPLE WAYS HIS BEARING IS THAT OF A GENTLEMAN BORN.

OWEN MEASURES HIS COMPANION: "NO ORDINARY WARRIOR IS HE. GOLD ARM BANDS AND NECKLACE, JEWELS IN THE HILT OF HIS GREAT SWORD, AND HIS CREST, THE CRIMSON STALLION. WHERE HAS HE HEARD OF THAT CREST? HE IS OBVIOUSLY A FELLOW OF THE ROUND TABLE."

"STRIP ENOUGH LINE TO REACH ACROSS THE RIVER," INSTRUCTS OWEN. "THE ROD IS AS A BOW, THE HEAVY LINE THE ARROW. THROW AND THE HEAVY LINE WILL TAKE OUT THE SLACK." VAL IS SO INTERESTED IN LEARNING TO CAST THAT HE ALMOST FORGETS THERE ARE SALMON THERE.

HE TRIES TO HALT THE LEAPING RUN BY HOLDING THE LINE AND IS REWARDED WITH SEVERELY BURNED FINGERS. TWO MORE SALMON ARE LOST ERE HE LEARNS TO PLAY THEM.

VAL IS MOST ENTHUSIASTIC AND WANTS TO KNOW WHAT WOOD IS BEST FOR A ROD, HOW TO BRAID A LINE AND WHIP ON THE GUIDES, ETC.
HAL FOSTER
558
12-18

AFTER DINNER THEY ARE DISCUSSING TACKLE WHEN OWEN SAYS: "I WILL TELL YOU SOMETHING IF YOU GIVE YOUR KNIGHTLY WORD TO KEEP IT A SECRET."
"OF COURSE," VAL PROMISES.
WITH A SLY GRIN OWEN ANSWERS: "I AM PRINCE HARWICK, HEIR TO THE DINMORE THRONE."
"AND," VAL SAYS, "I WAS SENT TO FIND YOU AND BRING YOU BACK. BUT YOU HAVE MY OATH; YOUR SECRET IS SAFE."
NEXT WEEK– Harwick's Story

More adventure: Alex Raymond graduated from a strip called Secret Agent X-9, which had a story line provided by Dashiell Hammett, to Flash Gordon, which began in 1936. It was the Prince Valiant of outer space – crisp and clean in style with skilful use of shadow, narrative captions, and the regular 'next week' announcement, in the true Harold Foster manner. Alex Raymond, after his war service, started Rip Kirby, the pipe-smoking, bespectacled, bookish detective, faithfully served by his butler, Desmond. American detectives rarely have butlers. In 1956 Raymond was killed in a car crash and the strip was taken over by John Prentice with scarcely a falter.

Flash Gordon

Asiatic villainy: Milton Caniff is another fine draughtsman and one of the most prolific and successful of all cartoonists. He first drew strips during his schooldays in Dayton, Ohio, and some appeared in the local paper. He worked for a while in a studio with Noel Sickles who influenced his style greatly. Sickles later drew Scorchy Smith. Caniff's first regular strip was Dickie Dare (*below*) which was started in 1932. The adventures of a lad transported into the past were drawn with a fine eye for detail and drama. The silhouette effects are characteristically Caniff. The big break came in 1934 with the start of Terry and the Pirates. Here was Oriental adventure – a boy and a young man battling villains off the exotic China coast. The strip shown appeared in the *New York Daily News* on 24 October 1934. The boy, Terry Lee, grew up and when Japan attacked China the strip grew up, too. The war became the strip's background and Terry learned to fly against the enemy. The 1942 Sunday page in which Colonel 'Flip' Corkin, a character based on one of Caniff's friends, delivered advice to the fledgeling pilot, was read into the Congressional Record, a unique honour for a comic strip. While slogging away at turning out the fine Terry strips, Caniff also produced a 'special' for Service newspapers such as *Stars and Stripes*, under the title 'Male Call'. Miss Lace (*foot of next page*) was the G.I.s favourite girl-friend and as the two examples show had a sympathetic concern for homesick servicemen in lonely stations. Caniff dropped a bombshell towards the end of the war with the announcement that he was going to quit the *News-Tribune* Syndicate and create an entirely new strip for a rival concern. It was unprecedented for a cartoonist to abandon a successful strip at the height of its career. Caniff was anxious to enhance the status of cartoonists – the new strip was to be his own property, not the Syndicate's. In early 1947 Terry passed into the hands of a new artist, George Wunder (a recent example of the Wunder version is illustrated) and Steve Canyon, Caniff's new character, made his entrance.

TERRY AND THE PIRATES—ON THE PAYROLL

Reg. U. S. Pat. Off.
Copyright, 1943 by News Syndicate Co. Inc.
TERRY AND THE PIRATES
by MILTON CANIFF
LET'S TAKE A WALK, TERRY...
YES, SIR, COLONEL CORKIN!

I'M GOING TO MAKE A SPEECH—AND IT'LL BE THE LAST ONE OF ITS KIND IN CAPTIVITY—SO DON'T GET A SHORT CIRCUIT BETWEEN THE EARS...
NO, SIR

WELL, YOU MADE IT... YOU'RE A FLIGHT OFFICER IN THE AIR FORCES OF THE ARMY OF THE UNITED STATES... THOSE WINGS ARE LIKE A NEON LIGHT ON YOUR CHEST... I'M NOT GOING TO WAVE THE FLAG AT YOU—BUT SOME THINGS YOU MUST NEVER FORGET

...EVERY COUNTRY HAS HAD A HAND IN THE DEVELOPMENT OF THE AIRPLANE—BUT, AFTER ALL THE WRIGHT BROTHERS WERE A COUPLE OF DAYTON, OHIO, BOYS—AND KITTY HAWK IS STRICTLY IN NORTH CAROLINA... THE HALLMARK OF THE UNITED STATES IS ON EVERY AIRCRAFT

...SO YOU FIND YOURSELF IN A POSITION TO DEFEND THE COUNTRY THAT GAVE YOU THE WEAPON WITH WHICH TO DO IT... BUT IT WASN'T JUST YOU WHO EARNED THOSE WINGS... A GHOSTLY ECHELON OF GOOD GUYS FLEW THEIR HEARTS OUT IN OLD KITES TO GIVE YOU THE KNOW-HOW...

...AND SOME SMART SLIDE RULE JOKERS SWEAT IT OUT OVER DRAWING BOARDS TO GIVE YOU A MACHINE THAT WILL KEEP YOU UP THERE SHOOTING I RECOMMENDED YOU FOR FIGHTER AIRCRAFT AND I WANT YOU TO BE COCKY AND SMART AND PROUD OF BEING A BUZZ-BOY..

...BUT DON'T FORGET THAT EVERY BULLET YOU SHOOT, EVERY GALLON OF GAS AND OIL YOU BURN WAS BROUGHT HERE BY TRANSPORT PILOTS WHO FLEW IT IN OVER THE WORST TERRAIN IN THE WORLD! YOU MAY GET THE GLORY—BUT THEY PUT THE LIFT IN YOUR BALLOON!...

...AND DON'T LET ME EVER CATCH YOU BEING HIGH-BICYCLE WITH THE ENLISTED MEN IN YOUR GROUND CREW! WITHOUT THEM YOU'D NEVER GET TEN FEET OFF THE GROUND! EVERY GREASE MONKEY IN THAT GANG IS RIGHT BESIDE YOU IN THE COCKPIT—AND THEIR HANDS ARE ON THAT STICK, JUST THE SAME AS YOURS...

...YOU'LL GET ANGRY AS THE DEVIL AT THE ARMY AND ITS SO-CALLED RED TAPE... BUT BE PATIENT WITH IT... SOMEHOW THE OLD EAGLE HAS MANAGED TO END UP IN POSSESSION OF THE BALL IN EVERY WAR SINCE 1776—SO JUST HUMOR IT ALONG...
14th AIR FORC
U S F

OKAY, SPORT, END OF SPEECH... WHEN YOU GET UP IN THAT "WILD BLUE YONDER" THE SONG TALKS ABOUT—REMEMBER, THERE ARE A LOT OF GOOD GUYS MISSING FROM MESS TABLES IN THE SOUTH PACIFIC, ALASKA, AFRICA, BRITAIN, ASIA AND BACK HOME WHO ARE SORTA COUNTING ON YOU TO TAKE IT FROM HERE! GOOD NIGHT, KID!

10-17
This way to TOKIO!
Next stop U.S.A.

Male Call by Milton Caniff, creator of "Terry and the Pirates" **There's A War On, Don't Be A 'No Show'**

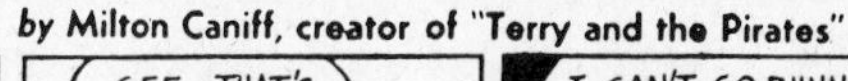

Male Call by Milton Caniff, Creator of "Terry and the Pirates" **Stand By To Repel Side Boys**

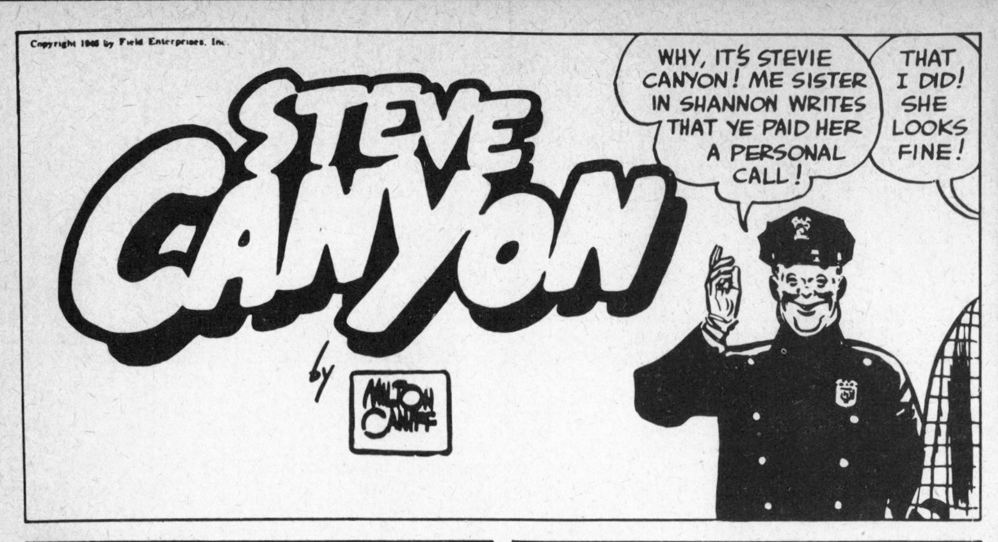
STEVE CANYON
by MILTON CANIFF
WHY, IT'S STEVIE CANYON! ME SISTER IN SHANNON WRITES THAT YE PAID HER A PERSONAL CALL!
THAT I DID! SHE LOOKS FINE!

GLAD TO SEE YOU BACK, MR. CANYON! MY BOY GOT THE SOUVENIR YOU SENT FROM EGYPT!
GOOD!

CHECKING IN, SARGE!
CAPTAIN CANYON! I REALLY SWEAT YOU OUT THIS LAST TRIP! HEY! I HAVE A FINANCIAL STATEMENT FOR YOU...YOU'LL NEVER REGRET HAVING BACKED ME ON THIS DEAL!...

WANT A FLOWER FOR YOUR BUTTONHOLE, MR. CANYON?
NOT TODAY, POSIE — BUT YOU AND YOUR MOM ARE ABOUT DUE TO SEE A MOVIE ON ME...

GOING UP?
THIS CAR, MR. CANYON! —AND FOR YOU WE DON'T WAIT TILL IT'S FULL! RIGHT, IRMA?
R-R-RAJAH!

OH... HERE IS MR. CANYON, NOW...
HORIZONS Unlimited

IT'S A MR. DAYZEE, SECRETARY TO COPPER CALHOON, THE BIG SHE-WOLF OF THE STOCK MARKET...
HMM—THEY CALL HER "THE COPPERHEAD" I WONDER IF SHE HOWLS OR HISSES?

MR. CANYON?... MISS COPPER CALHOON WISHES TO ENGAGE YOUR PROFESSIONAL SERVICES! PLEASE COME TO MISS CALHOON'S APARTMENT AT ONCE...
...BUT WHAT IF I DON'T WANT TO PLACE MY SERVICES AT THE COMMAND OF MISS COPPER CALHOON?

MIS-TER CANYON! PEOPLE DO NOT REFUSE WHEN SUMMONED BY COPPER CALHOON!
AND ALL THIS TIME I THOUGHT I WAS A PEOPLE! GOOD MORROW, MR. DOOZIE!

WHY, MR. DIZZY, WHAT YOU SAID!..AND ME SO YOUNG AND IMPRESSIONABLE! ...THE CLICK YOU HEAR WILL MEAN YOU'RE SOLOING!
WELL, IT WOULD HAVE BEEN NICE TO HAVE MONEY TO PAY THIS OFFICE RENT BUT I GUESS IT'S BAD FORM TO GET INTO REGULAR HABITS LIKE THAT...

COPPER! YOU HEARD ON THE EXTENSION WHAT STEVE CANYON SAID!.. I HAVE NEVER BEEN SO---
I WANT THAT MAN!! ...GET HIM!
1-19

New hero: opposite is the first Steve Canyon Sunday page, appearing on 19 January 1947. Canyon was an ex-Transport Command flier, a restless traveller, anxious that peacetime should not seem a dull anti-climax after his war years. He need not have worried – villainy and espionage were rife, and a long list of *femmes fatales*, a Caniff speciality, awaited his attentions. During the Korean War Canyon re-enlisted and has since worked his way up to full colonel. In virile middle age Canyon has no desk job. He is a roving trouble-shooter, liable to turn up wherever the Air Force needs him. The 1966 page below is a typical episode, reflecting the detailed military research, the exciting visual arrangement, and the combination of fanciful plot and sensible tactical solutions. Caniff's hero has a canyon in Arizona named after him.

Crime-stopper: Chester Gould's Dick Tracy is one of America's favourite strips. A product of the late Prohibition era, it broke countless taboos by showing murder, violence, and foul crime in detail. However, the chunky, flat style gave the strip an almost surrealistic quality which mitigated the gore to some extent. The tough cop Tracy has battled against an incredible array of freakish villains, Haf-and-Haf being a good example. Some of Tracy's gadgets like his two-way wrist radio have passed from fiction to reality. The compositions are meticulous and Dick Tracy has provided Pop artists with a constant subject.

DICK TRACY
by

SCENE: THE FRONT ENTRANCE TO THE HOME OF DICK TRACY AND JUNIOR TIME: NIGHT.
AH — THIS IS THE PLACE.

HEY, TRACY! DID YOU HEAR THAT? THE DOOR BELL!
RING
RING

WHO'S THERE?
THERE'S NOBODY THERE! BUT LOOK! WHAT'S THAT LYING ON THE STEP?

WE'LL INVESTIGATE, KID.
OH-BOY!

IT'S A PACKAGE OF SOME KIND... WITH MY NAME ON IT!
LOOK OUT! BE CAREFUL OF IT! WE DON'T KNOW WHAT IT CONTAINS!
Junior Tracy

WHAT IN BLAZES..! IT'S--A-A PUPPY.
A PUPPY? FOR ME? A LITTLE SCOTCH TERRIER! WHO SENT IT?

THERE'S NO NAME INSIDE, JUNIOR!
OH BOY! JUST LOOK AT HIM, TRACY!

WHAT A SWELL PUP. BUT WHO WOULD BE LEAVING A SCOTTIE ON MY DOOR-STEP?
GOSH - HE'S A CUTE RASCAL! HM! WHO IN THE WORLD COULD HAVE SENT IT? HM..MM-? MM?

TAKING THE LID OFF THE CARDBOARD BOX THAT THE PUPPY CAME IN-TRACY HURRIES TO HIS LABORATORY, REMOVES A CERTAIN PIECE OF PAPER FROM HIS POCKET, PLACES THE TWO PIECES OF PAPER UNDER A MICROSCOPE AND MAKES A COMPARISON.....
I WAS RIGHT! IT'S FROM HER!

WHAT IF IT DID TAKE THE LAST DOLLAR I HAD! I'LL GET ALONG SOMEWAY AND AT LEAST I FEEL I'VE DONE SOMETHING TOWARD MAKING HIS LIFE HAPPIER.

NOW I CAN RETURN WEST. I'LL GET BACK THERE SOMEHOW. MAYBE I CAN GET A JOB IN THE "COFFEE POT". AFTER ALL, I'M ONLY A HASH SLINGER-THAT'S ALL. AND MY BOY...HE WILL NEVER KNOW.

"THE NATION THAT CONTROLS MAGNETISM WILL CONTROL THE UNIVERSE."

CRIMESTOPPERS TEXTBOOK
BEWARE!
BEWARE OF THE FOREST PRESERVE! DON'T LET "WINTER BEAUTY" BECOME WINTER HORROR.
Dick Tracy

AFTER THEIR FIRST CHRISTMAS SPENT IN MOON VALLEY, THE TRACY FAMILY'S SPEEDY RETURN TO EARTH WAS A THRILLING CLIMAX.

MILE HIGH ANTENNA

FROM MOON VALLEY TO OUR SPACE PORT, EXACTLY 52 MINUTES.
THANKS FOR THE RIDE, DIET SMITH, AND A HAPPY NEW YEAR.

TESS, IT'S NICE TO GO AWAY, BUT IT'S ALWAYS NICEST TO RETURN.

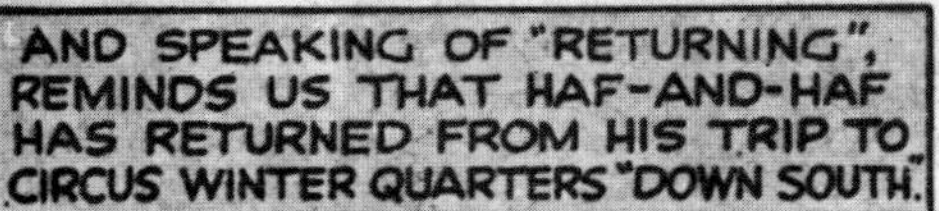

AND SPEAKING OF "RETURNING", REMINDS US THAT HAF-AND-HAF HAS RETURNED FROM HIS TRIP TO CIRCUS WINTER QUARTERS "DOWN SOUTH".

— WHY, EVERYTHING DOWN THERE'S FINE.

JUST FINE.
OH, I KNOW YOU WENT DOWN THERE TO SEE ZELDA!

I'M ONLY YOUR WIFE, BUT I KNOW YOU CAN'T FORGET YOUR OLD CIRCUS FRIEND, ZELDA!
The GREAT ZELDA HIGH DIVER

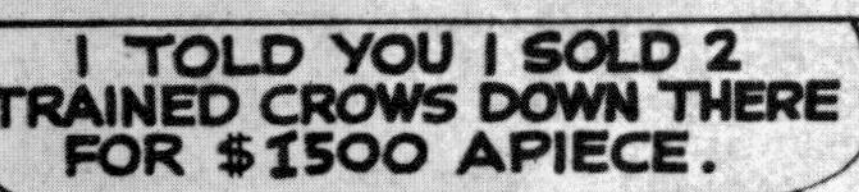

I TOLD YOU I SOLD 2 TRAINED CROWS DOWN THERE FOR $1500 APIECE.

THIS WAS A BUSINESS TRIP.
OH, SURE! BLONDE HAIRS ALL OVER YOUR COLLAR! ZELDA'S BLONDE HAIR!

WE'RE THROUGH, HAF-AND-HAF! THE CROWS AND I ARE LEAVING.
STOP IT— DON'T YOU DARE—

AS HAF-AND-HAF'S WIFE PULLS THE LEVER, A HATCH ON THE ROOF OPENS.

MY ENTIRE INVENTORY! WHY, YOU-★-!
CHESTER GOULD
1-1-67

Bucolic satire: Al Capp's Li'l Abner has, since the mid thirties, poked fun at nearly all the holy cows of American life and got away with it. The simple folk of Dogpatch, the mountain community in deepest Wherever, have provided a hilarious microcosm of the lunacy of the world at large. The good-hearted Abner, seen above in a 1935 encounter with Daisy Mae, represents the naïve, but well-intentioned universal American. Capp's brilliantly free-wheeling imagination has gone a long way towards initiating institutions like Sadie Hawkins Day, when the girls chase the men, and the mythical and mysterious country of Lower Slobbovia. In 1957 the attack turned on another strip, Mary Worth, the serious solver of social problems, who in Capp's strip became Mary Worm, America's favourite busybody (*opposite*). The Mary Worth cartoonists retaliated by inserting a disagreeable, drunken strip cartoonist called Hal Rapp, into their strip.

Li'l Abner Abner, after receiving a letter from his Aunt Bessie, is going to New York. He is overjoyed, but not so his sweetheart, Daisy Mae. What will she do while he is gone? **By Al Capp**

LI'L ABNER by AL CAPP

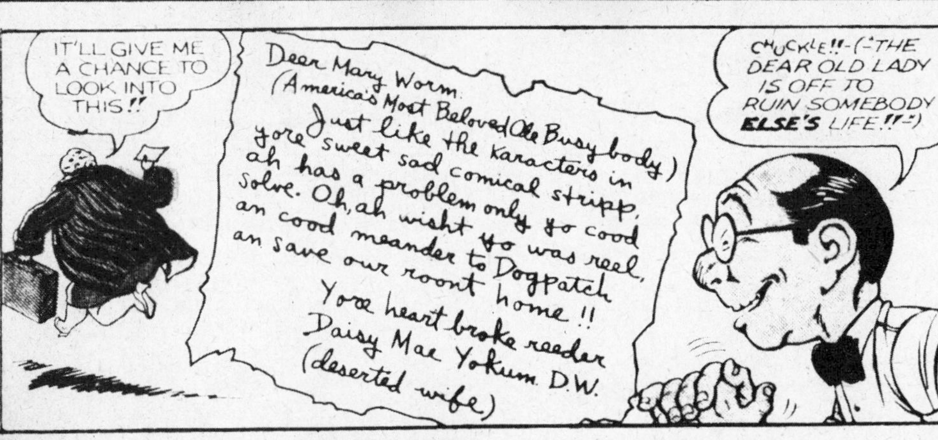

Barnaby. **By Crockett Johnson**

Small boy trio: Crockett Johnson's Barnaby, the story of a small boy with a fairy godfather, was a gentle satirical strip in the brave but short-lived New York evening paper, *PM*. Skippy was the creation of Percy Crosby, drawn in a more literal style than most strips, and enjoying its greatest success in the thirties. Henry was the mute, mouthless creation of Carl Anderson, who began drawing the strip in 1935 when he was already seventy. Although drawn by John Liney since 1942, it still bears today the signature of a man who died almost twenty years ago.

HENRY
By
CARL ANDERSON
OOO-OUCH!
8 18
CARL ANDERSON

Forties miscellany: Elzie Segar's Popeye grew out of the Thimble Theatre of the thirties. Before the war the strip was popular throughout the world. Mussolini banned American strips with this one exception. Popeye made spinach desirable – a statue of him stands in Crystal City, Texas, heart of the spinach-growing region, and his friend J. Wellington Wimpy has his name immortalized in a chain of European hamburger houses. The Sad Sack was the military creation of George Baker. Many of its fans were G.I. readers of *Yank*. 'The Proposition' appeared in 1943. On the right is a typical comics page from a 1943 *New York Daily Mirror*, with a string of leading runners: the liberal boxer, Joe Palooka, in service dress; an early Kerry Drake strip; Barney Baxter, an air strip; Henry, drawn by John Liney; Li'l Abner and Mickey Finn. Over the page is a 1944 comics page from the *Journal-American*, a display of many popular strips, packed tight because of newsprint restrictions. At the lower left-hand side is one of the last Krazy Kat cartoons to appear, part of the small, posthumous backlog of Herriman's work still appearing after his death a few weeks before. The vogue for superheroes caught on in the Press and in the forties Superman, Batman, and Wonder Woman were among those who shared a double life between comic books and newspapers. The Superman page is from a *New York Sunday Mirror* colour comic section of 1947.

YANK The Army Weekly • FEBRUARY 13

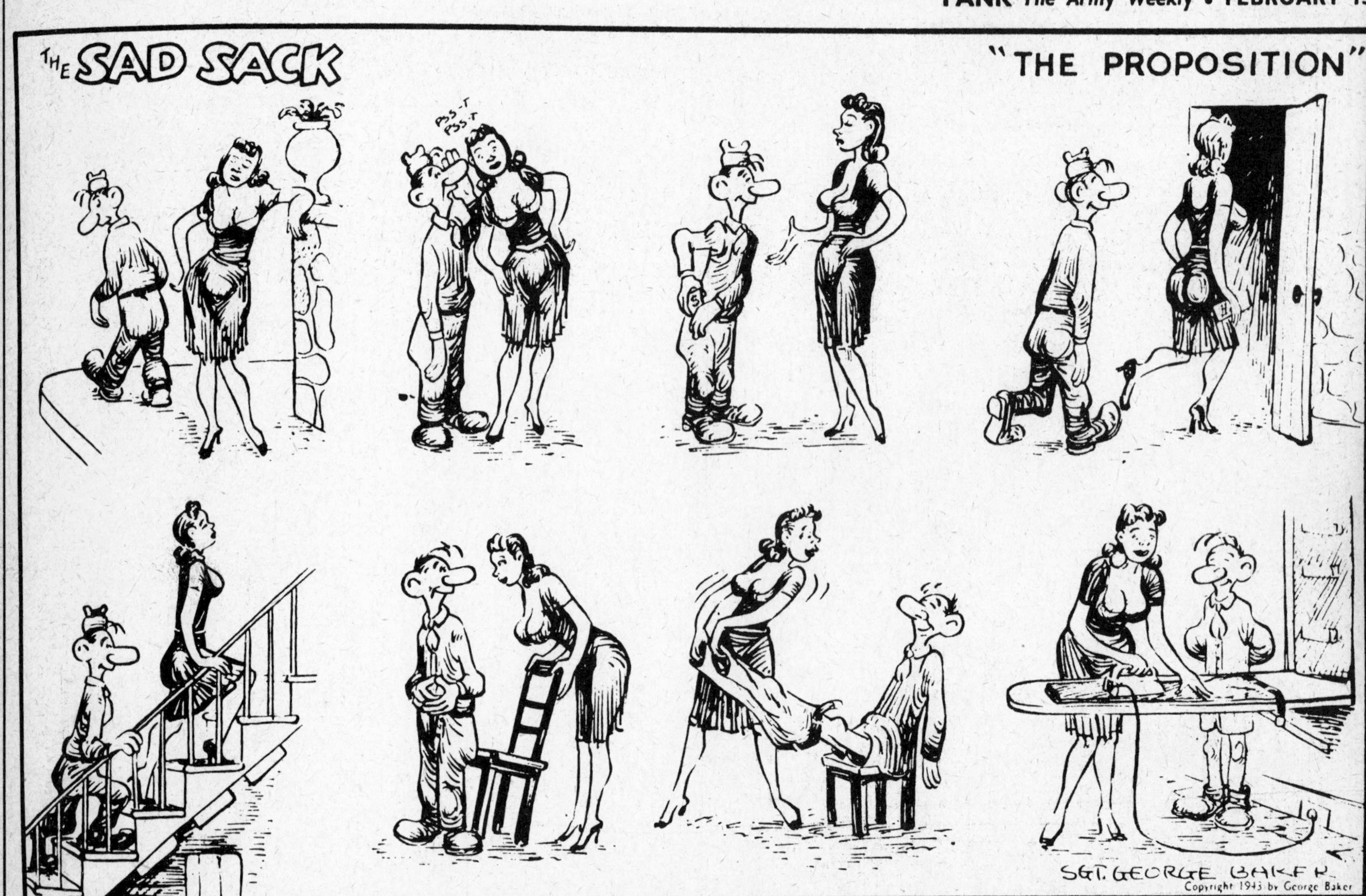

JOE PALOOKA
(A full page of Joe Palooka appears in the Comic Section of the Sunday MIRROR)
By Ham Fisher
LOOK AT THEM POIFUMES— WISH I HAD SOMEBUDDY T'BUY 'EM FER.
THEY'D COST A FORTUNE BACK IN THE STATES.
ALI HAIBIE
PARFUME
C'MON.
WHATCHA GONNA DO?
I'LL TAKE A BOTTLE OF THAT AN' ONE OF THOSE.
HEY- THAT'LL BE A WHOLE MONTH'S PAY. WHO YA BUYIN' 'EM FER?
I'M GONNA TAKE 'EM BACK WITH ME FER--- UH--- SOMEBUDDY.
THINK YER KIDDIN' ME?
KERRY DRAKE
(A full page of Kerry Drake appears in the Comic Section of the SUNDAY MIRROR
By Alfred Andriola
I JUST REMEMBERED, RILEY- THAT OLD GUY ASKED YA FOR A RIFLE! SPOSIN' YA GET IT FOR ME!
S-SURE, "FINGERS"! I KEEP IT IN THIS CLOSET!
OKAY! NOW PUT UP YOUR HANDS!
BE YER AGE! YA KNOW IT AIN'T LOADED! I CHECKED IT LAST NIGHT WHILE YOU WERE SLEEPIN'!
NOW TAKE THAT DEAD POOCH OUT AN' BURY HIM- AN' IF YA GET ANY IDEAS ABOUT RUNNIN' AWAY, REMEMBER- YOUR WIFE IS HERE WITH ME!
BARNEY BAXTER
Old Eagle-Eye
By Frank Miller
BARNEY! A FLOCK OF MESSER-SCHMITTS ARE ON OUR TAIL!!--- GIMME THEM TWO PISTOLS YOU SNAGGED FROM TH' HEINIES--- THAR'S NO AMMUNITION ON BOARD!!
!
WHILE GUS RACES FOR AN OPEN PORT, BARNEY MANEUVERS FOR TIME----
IT SEEMS LIKE A FUTILE GESTURE--- BUT, LOOK! GUS' EAGLE EYE HAS PICKED ONE OFF!!
NEXT!! ---HEH-HEH!
BANG!
(See America's funniest youngster, Henry
in the SUNDAY MIRROR 16 page
By Carl Anderson
PUBLIC SCHOOL
IF 3 APPLES WERE CUT INTO 4 PIECES - HOW MANY PIECES WOULD YOU HAVE ?
LI'L ABNER
He Goes Agin'
By Al Capp
OH - SOB - AH CAINT FORCE YO' BY LAW T' KISS ME. IT HAINT SPORTIN'
THASS RIGHT- IT HAINT. BUT IT'S LEGAL- SO (GULP) LE'S GO!
YO' (GULP) GOTTA RIGHT T'EXPEC' ME T'ACK LIKE A ROOTIN'-TOOTIN HUSBIN. YO' DONE KETCHED ME IN TH' RACE - FAIR AN' SQUARE.
THASS JEST - SOB - IT!- AH DIDN'T KETCH YO! AH JEST STARTED IN TH' RACE AN' WHEN IT GOT ALL DARK AN' RAINY -AH SASHAYED HYAR -AN' WAITED-
-WHILE SHE TOOK MAH PLACE AN' KETCHED YO' - NAME OF PATRICIA HALLROOM. SHE HAD A SARTIN' POWER OVER YO'.- SHE ONCE KISSED YO' IN A DARK ROOM - AN' ANYONE WHO'S EVAH KISSED BY HER--
CHASES HER LIKE A FEEND ANYTIME THEY SEES HER AGIN -
STOP!! LI'L ABNER-STOP!!
MICKEY FINN
Food for Thought
By Lank Leonard
OWNEY! WHAT IN THE WORLD HAS BROUGHT YOU HERE?
WHY, PHIL! WELL, WELL — THIS IS CERTAINLY A SURPRISE!
WHAT'S HAPPENED? HAVE YOU AND FANNY SPLIT UP?
OH, NO! I JUST—
LISTEN! IF THIS IS A FAMILY RE-UNION, IT'LL HAVE TO WAIT UNTIL LUNCH TIME! GET BACK TO YOUR MACHINE, PHIL!
IS HE THE BROTHER THAT YOU ONCE TOLD ME WAS SUCH A SMART GAMBLER?
THE SAME ONE, DEVANNY! GOOD OLD OWNEY!
THEN YOU'D BETTER NOT LET HIM KNOW THAT YOU'RE CLEANIN' UP ON THE HORSES! HE MIGHT START TAKIN' BETS FROM THE BOYS, HIMSELF!
BY GOLLY — I NEVER THOUGHT OF THAT!

"That umpire isn't taking any chances after making the decision that started the riot yesterday!"

"Does your countree have other sailors, maybe, yes?"

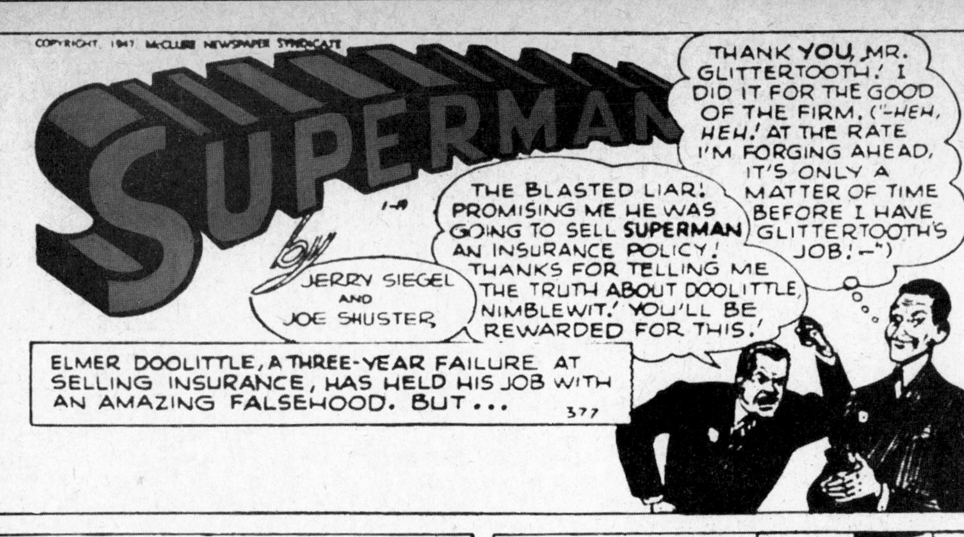
COPYRIGHT, 1947, McCLURE NEWSPAPER SYNDICATE
SUPERMAN
by JERRY SIEGEL AND JOE SHUSTER
ELMER DOOLITTLE, A THREE-YEAR FAILURE AT SELLING INSURANCE, HAS HELD HIS JOB WITH AN AMAZING FALSEHOOD. BUT...
THE BLASTED LIAR! PROMISING ME HE WAS GOING TO SELL SUPERMAN AN INSURANCE POLICY! THANKS FOR TELLING ME THE TRUTH ABOUT DOOLITTLE, NIMBLEWIT! YOU'LL BE REWARDED FOR THIS!
THANK YOU, MR. GLITTERTOOTH! I DID IT FOR THE GOOD OF THE FIRM. ("-HEH, HEH! AT THE RATE I'M FORGING AHEAD, IT'S ONLY A MATTER OF TIME BEFORE I HAVE GLITTERTOOTH'S JOB!-")
377

MEANWHILE—CLARK KENT SIGHTS ELMER DOOLITTLE'S APPROACH.
("-POOR LITTLE GUY! HE SEEMS AWFULLY WORRIED ABOUT SOMETHING!-")

THAT MOMENT—AT A NEARBY UNIVERSITY...
THE SEISMOGRAPH! LOOK AT ITS INDICATOR!
VIBRATING LIKE MAD!

AN INSTANT LATER...
EARTHQUAKE!
???

SUDDENLY—BEFORE CLARK'S HORRIFIED EYES, THE EARTH CRACKS OPEN BENEATH DOOLITTLE!
HELP!
GOOD GRIEF!

A SWIFT SWITCH IN IDENTITIES!
THIS IS A JOB FOR SUPERMAN!

DOWN AFTER THE TOPPLING FIGURE SPEEDS THE MAN OF TOMORROW!
MUST CATCH HIM BEFORE HE'S DASHED TO DEATH!

CAUGHT HIM!

UP THE SIDE OF THE MIGHTY FISSURE SPEEDS THE COLORFULLY COSTUMED FIGURE.
THE GAP—CLOSING!

NO SOONER DOES THE MAN OF STEEL FLASH ABOVE THE GROUND, THAN THE FISSURE SNAPS SHUT!
NOT AN INSTANT TOO SOON!
S-SUPERMAN!

THE EARTHQUAKE HAVING SUBSIDED, SUPERMAN DEPOSITS DOOLITTLE SAFELY ON EARTH AND SPRINGS OFF. BUT THEN...
A STOWAWAY!
W-W-WOULD YOU P-P-PLEASE STOP SW-SWOOPING FOR A M-MINUTE, P-P-PLEASE? I'VE G-GOT S-SOMETHING TO ASK YOU!

Comic master: Walt Kelly's Pogo is one of the richest gifts to the comic-strip medium. The topmost of the three strips below is the first appearance of Pogo in the late forties. The other two represent the first hearing of the famous carol, 'Deck us all with Boston Charlie', a much more inspiring lyric than the more conventional 'Deck the Halls with Boughs of Holly'. Pogo is more than mere verbal slapstick, however. Within his settings, mainly of Okefenokee Swamp in Georgia, Kelly is able to satirize the failings of the modern world by means of allegory. The language of a Pogo page is inventive and intelligent – the Sunday page opposite gives an indication of the use Kelly makes of his speech balloons. One of his greatest successes was the inclusion of a monstrous character, Joe Malarkey, long before his real-life original, Senator McCarthy, had been discredited.

POGO
OL' BEAR IS WRITIN' STUFF BUT HE CAN'T READ.
WE'D MAKE A GOOD TEAM.

I CAN READ BUT I CAN'T WRITE.
CALL THAT READIN'? YOU GOT THE BOOK UPSIDE DOWN.

OF COURSE I CALL IT READIN'... LISTEN! "A IS FOR APPLE. B IS FOR BETULACEAE, A FAMILY OF TREES, MONOECIOUS, RARELY DIOECIOUS FLOWERS AND...."
OH, ROWR BAZZ FAZZ

WHAT'S HE WRITIN'?
HE DON'T KNOW... HE CAN'T READ. YOU GOTTA READ IT FOR HIM.
3-23
HALL SYNDICATE

GLADLY!

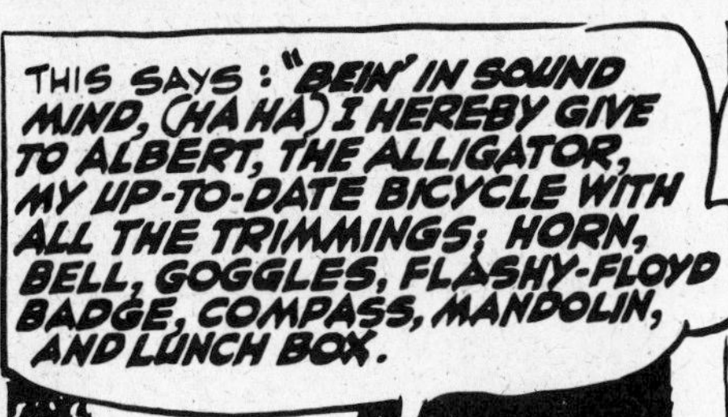
THIS SAYS: "BEIN' IN SOUND MIND, (HA HA) I HEREBY GIVE TO ALBERT, THE ALLIGATOR, MY UP-TO-DATE BICYCLE WITH ALL THE TRIMMINGS: HORN, BELL, GOGGLES, FLASHY-FLOYD BADGE, COMPASS, MANDOLIN, AND LUNCH BOX.

NO! NO! I COULDN'T OF WRIT THAT!
A CONTRACK IS A CONTRACK!

OH, PLEASE! PLEASE! IF YOU TAKE AWAY MY BICYCLE YOU'LL DESTROY THE SEEDS OF A FAMILY FORTUNE! MY LITTLE BOY WILL BE UNABLE TO GET A JOB DELIVERING LIVERWURST; MY WIFE WILL NO LONGER BE ABLE TO CARRY COAL; MY MOTHER WILL NEVER AGAIN BE KNOWN AS SPEEDY AT INDIANAPOLIS; SIS WILL HAVE TO GO BACK TO HAWKING BUNS ON FOOT.
HEH HEH

THE LAW IS THE LAW.. HEY, BOY, GIT AWAY!

I'LL BE YOUR SLAVE, I'LL COOK! WASH! CUT YOUR HAIR!
GIT AWAY! GO TO CHOIR PRACTICE!
THIS DON'T SAY WHAT YOU SAY!

IT SAYS: BY A OLD MOULMEIN PAGODA, LOOKIN' LAZY AT THE SEA.. HM.. NOT BAD.
WHOEVER PUT THAT DOWN COULDN'T WRITE GOOD ENOUGH TO MAKE THE GIRLS HOCKEY TEAM.
NOT ONLY AIN'T YOU NO CRITIC BUT I JUS' RECALLS I AIN'T GOT NO BICYCLE!

THE WIZARD OF ID by parker and hart

KNOW WHAT TOMORROW IS, DUCKY?

DOOMSDAY?

IT'S OUR SILVER WEDDING ANNIVERSARY!
SO?

SO... I WANT SOMETHING SILVER!

LOOK!... ONE LOUSY BULLET ISN'T GOING TO BREAK YOU!
12-18

Sixties satire: Johnny Hart's Wizard of Id and Mort Walker's Beetle Bailey are of the moment – sharp, hip, rich in psychological innuendo. Beetle Bailey was originally a college strip but Walker switched the scene to the Army with excellent results. Beetle, the eternal rookie, does not appear in this example, but the celebrated feud between the tough old sergeant and the gauche lieutenant does.

beetle bailey by mort walker

AH! I SEE THE CAPTAIN IS GOING TO A CONFERENCE TODAY

I'LL BE GONE FOR THE DAY, SARGE
YES, SIR. DON'T WORRY ABOUT A THING

I ONLY WORRY ABOUT ONE THING, BUT FORTUNATELY HE DOESN'T SEEM TO BE AROUND

WHO'S IN CHARGE HERE?
CAPTAIN SCABBARD, SIR, BUT HE'S OUT. I RUN THINGS WHEN HE'S NOT HERE

I BEG YOUR PARDON!

THAT'S JUST THE SORT OF THING I'VE COMPLAINED ABOUT! I HAPPEN TO BE NEXT IN LINE! I WANT THIS SORT OF THING STOPPED!

STOPPED! DO YOU HEAR!? STOPPED! STOPPED! STOPPED!

LOOK, WHAT I WANTED TO SEE ABOUT WAS...

Child cruelty: Peanuts is the most successful strip in the new idiom. Started in 1950, an early example is shown here at the top, it is about a world of children who intensify adult ideas. The second example features the bullying Lucy, a blue-rinsed gorgon in the making. In the lower strip the gentle dog, Snoopy, is seen living through one of his Red Baron fantasies in which he dreams of shooting down the infamous German aviator from his Sopwith Camel.

PEANUTS By Schulz

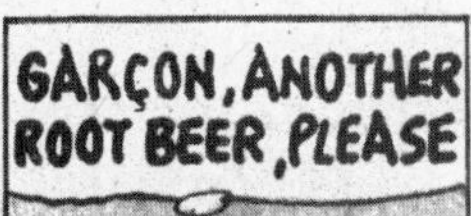

DISTURBANCE? WHO'S CREATING A DISTURBANCE?

I'M A PILOT WITH THE ALLIES! I'M GOING TO SAVE THE WORLD!

Whatever happened to the comic book?

Whatever Happened to the Comic Book?

So long off the mark – Famous Funnies *– Action Comics – Superman, first of the superheroes – Batman's beginnings – golden age for the comic book – Wonder Woman – the denunciators – the industry defends itself – the Marvel revival – the amazing Stan Lee – the great Will Eisner.*

In Britain, the penny dreadful – the nineteenth-century version of the horror comic – declined when *Comic Cuts* and similar periodicals started in the nineties.

Yet in America the comic-book industry is a flourishing ancillary section of the strip world. Its golden age is allegedly about a quarter of a century ago, when millions of G.I.s in far-flung theatres of war stayed in touch with hometown America by following the adventures of Captain Marvel and Superman.

As long ago as Outcault's day collections of newspaper cartoons, including the Yellow Kid, were occasionally issued in book form. In the years before the First World War several books containing reprints of daily strips were published by newspapers. The most famous of these was the appearance of Mutt and Jeff in 1911, the page size of eighteen inches by six providing a startlingly different shape from the modern comic book. It was printed from the original plates of the *Chicago American* and sold by coupon returns to the newspaper. It was an excellent circulation-booster and reached a sale of over 45,000 copies. Yet it appears to have been an isolated stunt, for the idea was not followed up.

Many years passed. Then in 1929 George Delacorte, owner of the Dell Publishing Company, brought out a tabloid-size collection, in four colours, of specially drawn strips. Called *The Funnies*, it looked like a newspaper supplement without the accompanying newspaper. It ran for only thirteen issues.

Other predecessors of the modern comic book were the *Big Little Books*, with a page size only three inches by two. Well-known newspaper strips appeared in this format, with one frame at a time on each right-hand spread, and facing typeset narrative on the left. These thick, miniature books were popular in the thirties, but yielded in time to the regular comic books.

As the corner was turned from the Depression the big consumer goods manufacturers sought new ways to sell their products. They started using reprints of strips in comic-book form as premiums in grocery stores; these were given away like trading stamps to customers buying specific products. Sometimes as many as a quarter of a million of such give-away books were printed. As an experiment one of them, *Famous Funnies*, was put on a news-stand with a ten-cent sticker on its cover. It sold out at once.

At this point George Delacorte again entered the scene. He put *Famous Funnies* on sale in big chain stores where casual shoppers might be tempted. There was still reluctance from the ever-cautious news-stand companies in spite of the pilot success. But, shortly after the *New York Daily News* printed an

advertisement attributing the Sunday circulation success to their comic section, The American News Company was prepared to sign a contract for the regular news-stand display of 250,000 copies of a version of *Famous Funnies*. The first issue of this new publication, the first comic book to be deliberately directed at the magazine- and newspaper-buying public, appeared in May 1934. It contained reprints of several famous newspaper strips including Mutt and Jeff, Toonerville Folks, Hairbreadth Harry, Nipper, Tailspin Tommy, and The Nebbs. The page size was virtually the same as that of today's comic books. Initially it lost money; but by the seventh issue it was making a modest $2,500 profit.

Then M.C. Gaines, another pioneering figure in the business, signed up the Skippy strip exclusively for one comic book; this was the first four-colour reprint to be devoted to the same character and to have a half-million print order. In 1935 Delacorte, now fully alive to the possibilities of the new medium, published *Popular Comics* for Gaines, carrying strips from the McClure Syndicate. The other syndicates followed: United Features brought out *Tip Top Comics*; Hearst's King Features leased out *King Comics* to another publisher.

Superman of Action Comics was the creation of Jerry Siegel who wrote the strip and Joe Schuster who drew it. He was the first of the comic-book heroes, setting a pattern for the future development of the *genre*. A striking feature of the new hero was his double identity. In one guise he could be an extraordinarily ordinary citizen, useless where action was needed. In the other he metamorphosed into a strangely garbed, sky-riding avenger, capable of invoking supernatural powers to defeat his – and the world's – enemies.

Superman, as a baby, was evacuated to Earth from the doomed planet Krypton, and brought up by an elderly couple, the Kents. As a toddler he would toss chests of drawers around to the astonished horror of doctors; as a youth he liked to leap across skyscrapers and pace streamlined expresses. His good-natured foster parents taught him to keep his enormous strength for mankind's benefit. Jules Feiffer, in his excellent book *The Great Comic Book Heroes*, makes the point that Superman, unlike his successors, puts on the disguise of Clark Kent, the weakling, bespectacled reporter – not the other way round. It is Superman who is the real character, Clark Kent the improbable one.

With his unlimited physical resources and capacity for spectacular action, Superman rapidly became one of the most popular characters of modern American mythology. His own magazine achieved a circulation of 1,400,000. He was put on radio and made into animated cartoons for the movies. In the war years, when many Americans found themselves fighting for their lives, Superman, to the chagrin of many an Army chaplain, stood as a symbol of a new patriotic faith – the hero supplanting the gangster of the previous generation.

He had his imitators. Captain Marvel was able to take on his supernatural powers by uttering a magic word – 'Shazam!'. Unfortunately for him, Superman's publishers launched a plagiarism suit, which ultimately they won.

Captain America, in starred and striped leotard, was a laboratory creation, a weakling injected with a secret virility serum. He was to have been first of a corps of super-agents but somehow a couple of Nazi spies got into the laboratory and shot the professor, leaving the hero on a limb. Nevertheless, he went on to make quite a good job of winning the war.

Batman, by Bob Kane, first appeared in the May 1939 issue of *Detective Comics* and in April 1940 in his own magazine. Like Superman, Batman was also syndicated as a newspaper strip. This was discontinued in 1946, but in the mid-sixties Batman and his youthful henchman, Robin, went back into the newspapers.

In 'real' life millionaire playboy Bruce Wayne – Batman – took up his strange calling after seeing his parents murdered when involved in a stick-up walking home from a movie. Since Wayne senior must have been possessed of immeasurable wealth (Batman has an expensive *ménage* to keep up and doesn't appear to earn any money) it is hard to understand what they were doing *walking* home from a movie. After many years of perfecting his physical strength and his skills as a scientist Bruce Wayne takes to the Bat disguise ('Criminals are a superstitious cowardly lot . . . . I must be able to strike terror into their hearts. I must be a creature of the night, black, terrible . . .').

Unlike so many of his caped colleagues Batman has no supernatural power. Everything he does is just possible – for someone in perfect physical condition and with a complete knowledge of science. His attitudes to the law are absurdly deferential and he often lets villains slip through his hands to knock hell out of him on a later occasion simply because he has not carried out the formalities necessary to make an arrest. ('Holy search warrant,' says a disgusted Robin.) The villains, like those pitted against Dick Tracy, are often freakish – the Penguin, the Joker, the Riddler, the Catwoman.

The vast comic-book industry of the early forties was seen by some people as the purveyor of opium to a nation of addicts. Fifteen million copies were sold each month, giving a total readership of over fifty million. The Flash, the Human Torch, the Sub-Mariner, the Hawkman were among the adventure characters enlisted in the mythical battle for victory against the Axis, and were already the targets for attack by critics who felt that American youth was becoming corrupted by the constant displays of excessive force from their cartoon heroes.

Wonder Woman, a kind of female Superman, was created in 1942 on the inspiration of a psychologist, one William Moulton Marston, who hoped to counteract the blood-curdling masculinity of the rest of the comic books. 'Wonder Woman,' said her creator, 'saves her worst enemies and reforms their characters.' Jules Feiffer wrote of her: ' . . . I could never get myself to believe that she was that good. For if she was as strong as they said, why wasn't she tougher looking? Why wasn't she bigger? Why was she so flat-chested? . . . Wonder Woman seemed like too much of a put-up job, a fixed comic strip – a product of group thinking rather than the individual inspiration that created Superman. It was obvious that a bunch of men got together in a smoke-filled room and brain-stormed themselves a Super Lady. But nobody's heart was in it.'

As the stuff of violent fantasy was rolling off the four-colour presses so also was a vast amount of humour and juvenile subjects. Walt Disney, at pains to produce matter innocuous to children, used comic books extensively. They were employed for the telling of stories from the Bible and for the presentation of literary masterpieces. Sections of the industry were already sensitive to the criticisms of educators, psychiatrists, churchmen, and women's organizations.

Perhaps the most vociferous of the denunciators of comic books was Dr Frederic Wertham, who until 1952 was Senior Psychiatrist for the New York City Department of Hospitals. After seven years spent studying the effects of comic books on children and adolescents he published in 1954 a book called *Seduction of the Innocent* which was to have a major influence on attitudes to and within the business.

Dr Wertham's thesis was that the comics were almost without exception bad for young people and that the increase in juvenile delinquency could be accounted for by the pernicious content of their reading material. His book was illustrated with a number of hair-raising examples of comic-book art – eyes being gouged out, faces stamped on, policemen shot down, women beaten up and, most sickening of all, a grisly nocturnal baseball game where the base lines were marked out with human intestines, lungs and liver indicated the bases, a heart the home plate, a human leg served as a bat, and the ball was a man's head.

However, although many shady publishing houses were undoubtedly putting out quantities of sordid rubbish, none of these examples came from the major comic-book series. But Dr Wertham in his text was able to find much that was wrong with the best-known and most popular comic characters. Batman and Robin were 'like a wish dream of two homosexuals living together'. Wonder Woman was 'the Lesbian counterpart of Batman'. Dr Wertham was alarmed by the tendency of children to regard the magic exploits of such superheroes as Superman, Captain Marvel, and the Green Lantern almost as religious miracles. For him, even Bugs Bunny revealed an example of racial violence.

Inevitably, there were calls for rigorous censorship. In England the so-called horror comics imported from the United States were outlawed. In America the industry fought hard to protect itself from self-appointed censors and at the same time attempted to put its own house in order. The fringe publishers moved to other fields. Apart from the Dell Publishing company, who claimed that all their comics were wholesome enough not to warrant voluntary curbs, the major comic-book publishers banded together and formed the Comics Code Authority with a self-imposed code of standards. Defenders of the old comics felt that the industry had gone too far and had damaged the products by too severe a cleaning-up. But if it had not done so compulsory sanctions would almost certainly have been imposed.

One of the more ticklish problems connected with the general mud-slinging of the early fifties was the dragging-in of the newspaper comics into the argument. Some of the critics, often non-readers of the strips, did not grasp the difference between comic books and newspaper strips; it was easy to lump 'the funnies' together generically and attack everything regardless. This attitude horrified the newspaper comic producers, who had always maintained reasonable standards for the very simple commercial reason that if a strip was to be syndicated in papers from coast-to-coast it could not afford to alienate its family readership.

The National Cartoonists Society, led by Walt Kelly (then its President), Milton Caniff and Joe Musial, drew up a statement which was probably the most important pronouncement ever made on behalf of the industry. It read:

'The National Cartoonists Society views as unwarranted any additional legislative action that is intended to censor printed material. The Society believes in local option. We believe that offensive material of any nature can be weeded from the mass of worthwhile publications by the exercise of existing city, state and federal laws.

'Further, we believe that the National Cartoonists Society constitutes a leadership in the cartoon field which has previously established popular trends. We therefore will restrict any action we take to continually improving our own material and thus influencing the coat-tail riders who follow any successful idea.

'We believe good material outsells bad. We believe people, even juveniles, are fundamentally decent. We believe, as parents and as one-time children ourselves, that most young people are instinctively attracted to that which is wholesome.

'Our belief in this sound commercial theory is only in addition to our belief in free expression and the noble traditions of our profession. Our history abounds in stalwarts of pen and pencil who have fought for freedom and the resultant growth of ideas. We cannot submit to the curb, the fence or the intimidating word. The United States of America must remain a land where the Government follows the man.'

The statement was drawn up by men who understood their public; this was why they were at the top of their profession. It is not surprising that they could produce a document which had something for everyone. The critics were routed by their well-argued, articulate manifesto; it convinced the public too, of the sincere notion of responsibility held by the majority of cartoonists and of the fact that black sheep were exceptional. Thanks largely to this effort, the comics were allowed to sort their own industry out for themselves.

In January 1955 the Newspaper Comics Council was formed, with the intention of marking differences between newspaper strips and comic books more vividly. It was to be a research organization, an information forum for both artists and publishers, and a medium for disseminating knowledge of the industry to the general public and promoting artistic recognition of the best comics. All of such endeavours, read its statement of aims and objects, would have 'the ultimate objectiveness of improving the content and format of newspaper comics and increasing the prestige of newspaper comics and interests therein among the reading public'. By publishing books, both for schools and bookstores, arranging lectures, and staging exhibitions, the Council has done a great deal of hard work to make the American public comic-conscious. As a result of a highly successful Cavalcade of Comics Exhibition, which attracted great crowds in 1966, the Smithsonian Institution in Washington, D.C. has asked them to prepare a permanent exhibit. So at last the comics will have a place in 'the nation's attic'.

The climate has greatly improved since the early fifties. Comics are blamed for crime no more or less than other media. Indeed, television is usually the whipping-boy today.

In the last few years, with the growth of Pop Art and other influences, there has been a great comic-book revival. In the vanguard of the new interest is the Marvel Comics group. It publishes the adventures of nine superheroes, including Captain America, the Human Torch, the Amazing Spider Man, the Mighty Thor, the Incredible Hulk, and the Thing. The amazing creative genius behind this grotesque gallery is Stan Lee (real name Stanley Lieber), a dynamo of creative energy in his early forties, who works in a small yellow-painted office overlooking Madison Avenue. It has an unclosed door and a queue of cartoonists, writers, inkers, and letterers waiting to see him.

After many mundane years of hard slogging the time came recently when Marvel Comics became part of the campus life of America. A college student quoted in *Esquire* said: 'We think of Marvel Comics as the twentieth-century mythology and [Stan Lee] as this generation's Homer.' Deluged with requests, the hard-working Mr Lee delights in addressing university audiences. He spends only two or three minutes at these sessions with a prepared talk; the rest is question and answer.

He sees the superhero fantasies as fulfilling the same function that myths, legends, tales of romance and fairy stories did for earlier generations. Most of the heroes are flawed in some way. The Amazing Spider Man, in his other identity, is an insecure, guilt-ridden teenager who has no luck with the girls. The Mighty Thor is a crippled doctor whose nurse despises him but is in love with the Thor side of him, unaware of his dual character. Marvel heroes have problems. Says Stan Lee: 'I like Shakespeare more than anything. Everything there is on such a grand scale – so heroic. I guess I'm corny at heart.' He dislikes most of the rival companies' products, particularly Superman and Wonder Woman which he finds dull.

One of the few comic-book series which Stan Lee does admire, because, as he says, it has style, is Will Eisner's creation, the Spirit, who was brought out of retirement by Harvey Comics in 1966. Unlike many of the other comic heroes who have to slip behind corners unobserved and climb frantically into their tights, cloaks and masks before they can become operational, the Spirit wears an ordinary suit and wide-brimmed hat, with the merest concession to a mask outlining his eyes. Fortunately, he does not constantly have to change back to something else – his former self is thought to be dead. In fact, the Spirit is very much alive but in a state of suspended animation, which is why he lives in a graveyard. The line is hard and decisive, with lots of shadows, strange angles, and elegantly intricate headings.

Humour is one of the ingredients used by Eisner in a very idiosyncratic manner. As Jules Feiffer has noted, many of the stories have a Jewish shape to them, being up-dated fables or cautionary tales; the spirit of the Spirit is basically Jewish. Perhaps this comic-book hero is nothing more than the Wandering Jew in a modern or futuristic guise.

The early forties provided the strip with its really great days. The revived Spirit has a narrower hat-brim and a better fitting suit, but the Eisner style is still there and unmistakable, if frequently imitated. Jules Feiffer says: 'Alone among comic book men, Eisner was a cartoonist other cartoonists swiped from.'

Comic Section

VOL. I. NO. I.
PRICE 5 CENTS
THE YELLOW KID
PASTE
SAY IF YOU SEE IT IN DE YELLER KID IT GOES SEE
HOWARD AINSLEE & Co. Publishers, NEW YORK.
R. F. Outcault
BY PERMISSION OF THE N.Y. JOURNAL.

The comic-book origins: the first comic books consisted of reprints of strips which had already been published in the newspapers. In this form the Yellow Kid appeared as a comic book nearly seventy years ago, when R.F. Outcault was drawing him in Hearst's *New York Journal* (*left*). It was not until more than thirty years later that comic books really got off the ground. The cover below is of the first magazine to be sold directly on news-stands. It contained reprints of many successful newspaper strips. The predecessors of *Famous Funnies* were either linked in newspaper promotions or were premiums in grocery stores. The new magazine appeared in 1934 as a very cautious venture, but a new era was born. Its modest success pointed the way to a host of competitors. Very soon comic magazines containing specially created strips were appearing in this medium – the first was *New Fun* in 1935. Five years later a circulation of fifteen million comic books a month was commonplace.

The new superheroes: Ancient Greece had Hercules, modern America has Superman. He was the invention of Jerry Siegel and Joe Schuster and first appeared in Action Comics magazine in June 1938. Circulation doubled. Newspaper syndication began six months later. The character possessed a magnificent array of characteristics guaranteed to appeal to the public. He was supernaturally strong. He could fly. He had X-ray vision. He had a dual identity, and could slip casually from his heroic self to an ordinary, unspectacular citizen without rousing undue suspicions. He was everyone's wish-fulfilment hero. His hold on the public imagination was tremendous and he was the prototype for nearly all the comic-book superheroes. American soldiers went off to fight the Nazis in World War II fortified by Superman adventures in their kitbags. Superman stood for hope – to such a degree that some army chaplains became worried. Superman was dangerously close to becoming a substitute for conventional religion. On the next two pages are Superman's origins, then follows a page from a modern adventure.

10 CENTS
No. 1
AUK
JON MAYES
Toonerville Folks · Mutt & Jeff · Hairbreadth Harry · S'matter Pop · Nipper
Dixie Duggan · The Bungle Family · Connie · Ben Webster · Tailspin Tommy
Pam · The Nebbs · Highlights of History · Amaze-a-Minute · Screen Oddities

SUPERMAN
by
JEROME SIEGEL and JOE SHUSTER
JUST BEFORE THE DOOMED PLANET, KRYPTON, EXPLODED TO FRAGMENTS, A SCIENTIST PLACED HIS INFANT SON WITHIN AN EXPERIMENTAL ROCKET-SHIP, LAUNCHING IT TOWARD EARTH!

WHEN THE VESSEL REACHED OUR PLANET, THE CHILD WAS FOUND BY AN ELDERLY COUPLE, THE KENTS.
LOOK, MARY! —IT'S A CHILD!
THE POOR THING! -- IT'S BEEN ABANDONED!

THE INFANT WAS TURNED OVER TO AN ORPHAN ASYLUM, WHERE IT ASTOUNDED THE ATTENDANTS WITH ITS FEATS OF STRENGTH.

WE -- WE COULDN'T GET THAT SWEET CHILD OUT OF OUR MIND.
WE'VE COME TO ADOPT HIM IF YOU'LL PERMIT US.
I BELIEVE IT CAN BE ARRANGED. (—WHEW! THANK GOODNESS THEY'RE TAKING HIM AWAY BEFORE HE WRECKS THE ASYLUM!-)

THE LOVE AND GUIDANCE OF HIS KINDLY FOSTER-PARENTS WAS TO BECOME AN IMPORTANT FACTOR IN THE SHAPING OF THE BOY'S FUTURE.
NOW LISTEN TO ME, CLARK! THIS GREAT STRENGTH OF YOURS --YOU'VE GOT TO HIDE IT FROM PEOPLE OR THEY'LL BE SCARED OF YOU!
BUT WHEN THE PROPER TIME COMES, YOU MUST USE IT TO ASSIST HUMANITY.

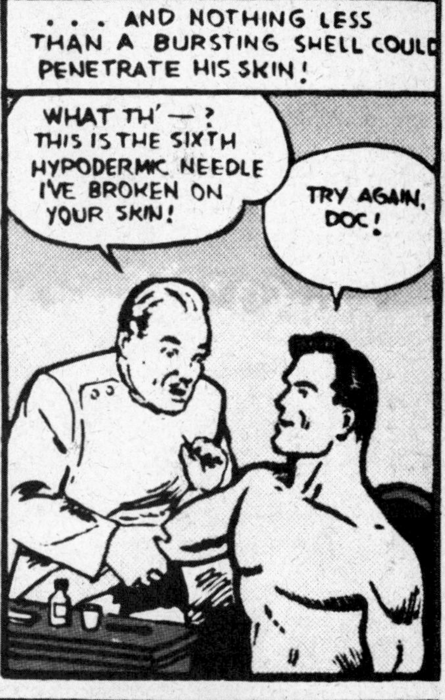

AS THE LAD GREW OLDER, HE LEARNED TO HIS DELIGHT THAT HE COULD HURDLE SKYSCRAPERS . . .

. . . LEAP AN EIGHTH OF A MILE . . .

. . . RAISE TREMENDOUS WEIGHTS . . .

. . . RUN FASTER THAN A STREAMLINE TRAIN --

. . . AND NOTHING LESS THAN A BURSTING SHELL COULD PENETRATE HIS SKIN!
WHAT TH' — ? THIS IS THE SIXTH HYPODERMIC NEEDLE I'VE BROKEN ON YOUR SKIN!
TRY AGAIN, DOC!

THE PASSING AWAY OF HIS FOSTER-PARENTS GREATLY GRIEVED CLARK KENT. BUT IT STRENGTHENED A DETERMINATION THAT HAD BEEN GROWING IN HIS MIND.

CLARK DECIDED HE MUST TURN HIS TITANIC STRENGTH INTO CHANNELS THAT WOULD BENEFIT MANKIND • AND SO WAS CREATED--

CHAMPION OF THE OPPRESSED, THE PHYSICAL MARVEL WHO HAD SWORN TO DEVOTE HIS EXISTENCE TO HELPING THOSE IN NEED!

SOON, IN THE NEWSROOM...
THIS COULD BE A BREAK FOR ME. I'M GOING HOME AND START THAT NOVEL I'VE BEEN MEANING TO WRITE FOR YEARS!
AND I'LL TOUR MY FAN CLUBS AROUND THE COUNTRY... I'LL LECTURE ABOUT ANTI-CRIME TECHNIQUES I LEARNED FROM SUPERMAN AND BATMAN!

BUT WHAT ABOUT ME? HMM... SINCE MY CLARK KENT CAREER IS AT A TEMPORARY STANDSTILL, THIS IS MY CHANCE TO TRY OUT A NEW SECRET IDENTITY... A ROLE I COULD ADOPT IF EVER I HAVE TO ABANDON MY CLARK KENT ROLE PERMANENTLY.
ON STRIKE

WHAT KIND OF ALTER-EGO SHOULD I SWITCH TO? LET'S SEE... BECOMING A POLICEMAN OR STATE TROOPER WOULD FIT IN WITH MY LAW ENFORCEMENT DUTIES AS SUPERMAN!

OR I MIGHT BECOME A DRIFTER... A PANHANDLER WHOM NO ONE WOULD EVER SUSPECT OF BEING THE MAN OF STEEL!

LOST IN THOUGHT, CLARK WANDERS TO A WATER-FRONT PARK, WHERE SUDDENLY...
A SQUAD CAR, PROBABLY CHASING A SPEEDSTER. BUT I'D BETTER CHECK...
WREEEEEE

THE MAN AT THE WHEEL OF THAT CAR... HE'S AN ESCAPED CONVICT! I'D BETTER SWITCH TO SUPERMAN!
2

Something for the girls: Wonder Woman was created by a psychologist in 1942 as an antidote to the predominantly masculine superheroes then abounding. It was thought that her feminine romantic instincts would temper the toughness of the other comic books. In fact, comic-book attackers have found her an even more sinister manifestation. She has been accused of lesbianism, fetishism, and sadism. As the modern example shows she is really just an ordinary goddess who wants to marry and settle down.

Batcult: Batman, the creation of Bob Kane, was partly in the Superman mould. His powers were, however, self-taught rather than supernatural. Batman is a brilliant scientist, a physical giant, a fantastic acrobat, and master of a long list of other skills. Comic book collectors – the kind of person who buys two copies of each magazine as it appears, one to read, the other to put inside an airtight polythene bag in mint condition for posterity and profit – have long been aware of Batman's appeal. No. 27 of *Detective Comics*, the issue in which he makes his first appearance, sells for around $125 if it comes on the market. Even Bob Kane himself no longer has copies of the early issues of his creation. The true enthusiast is unimpressed by the general revival of interest in Batman, largely as a result of the television series. Only in the comic books, his true medium, is he at his best, they feel. The 'camp' elements in Batman must be unintentional, not deliberately created. The newspaper strip is particularly guilty. His first appearance in 1939 is on pages 170–1 and a modern sample is on pages 172–3. Other heroes included Captain America, who was created by a secret serum, the formula for which was immediately lost. Two samples of his early days are on pages 174–5 and a recent adventure is shown on pages 176–7, demonstrating the force of the drawing style. Stan Lee, Marvel Comics' chief editor and Jack Kirby, its art director, allow themselves a personal mention at the top of the left-hand page.

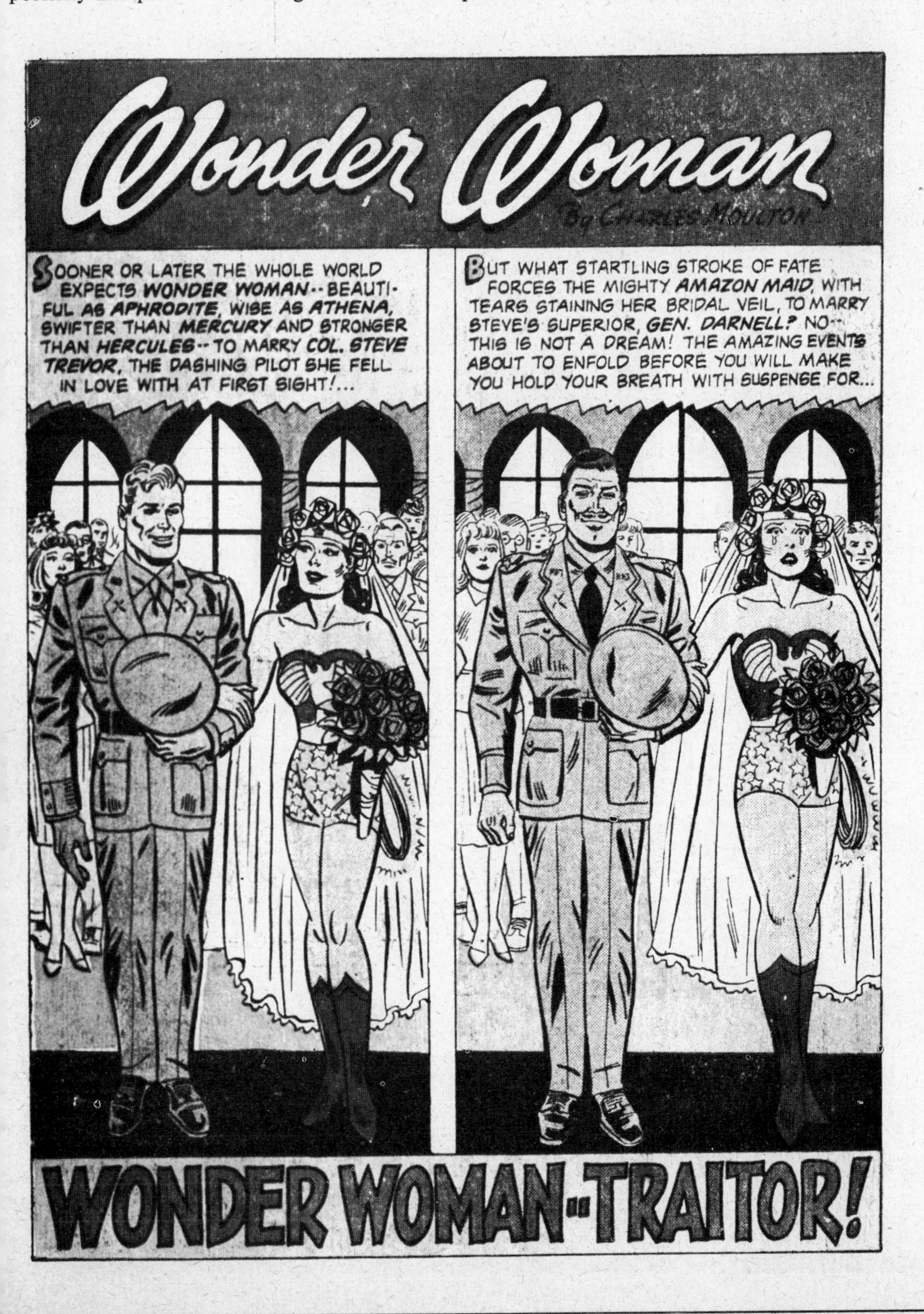

The LEGEND of the
BATMAN
BY BOB KANE
— WHO HE IS AND HOW HE CAME TO BE!
SOME FIFTEEN
AGO, THOMAS WAYNE,
WIFE AND HIS SON WERE
FROM A MOVIE...
W. WHAT IS THIS?
A STICKUP, BUDDY! I'LL TAKE THAT NECK LACE YOU'RE WEARIN' LADY!

LEAVE HER ALONE, YOU! OH......
YOU ASKED FOR IT!

THOMAS! YOU'VE KILLED HIM. HELP! POLICE.. HELP!
THIS'LL SHUT YOU UP!

THE BOY'S EYES ARE WIDE WITH TERROR AND SHOCK AS THE HORRIBLE SCENE IS SPREAD BEFORE HIM.
FATHER.. MOTHER!

.. DEAD! THEY'RE D..DEAD

DAYS LATER A CURIOUS AND STRANGE SCENE TAKES PLACE
AND I SWEAR BY THE SPIRITS OF MY PARENTS TO AVENGE THEIR DEATHS BY SPENDING THE REST OF MY LIFE WARRING ON ALL CRIMINALS.

AS THE YEARS PASS BRUCE WAYNE PREPARES HIMSELF FOR HIS CAREER. HE BECOMES A MASTER SCIENTIST.

TRAINS HIS BODY TO PHYSICAL PERFECTION UNTIL HE IS ABLE TO PERFORM AMAZING ATHLETIC FEATS.

DAD'S ESTATE LEFT ME WEALTHY. I AM READY.. BUT FIRST I MUST HAVE A DISGUISE.

CRIMINALS ARE A SUPERSTITIOUS COWARDLY LOT, SO MY DISGUISE MUST BE ABLE TO STRIKE TERROR INTO THEIR HEARTS. I MUST BE A CREATURE OF THE NIGHT, BLACK, TERRIBLE.. A A..

- AS IF IN ANSWER, A HUGE BAT FLIES IN THE OPEN WINDOW!
A BAT! THAT'S IT! IT'S AN OMEN.. I SHALL BECOME A BAT!

AND THUS IS BORN THIS WEIRD FIGURE OF THE DARK.. THIS AVENGER OF EVIL. 'THE BATMAN'

"My body hit the top of a display case and slid along it as if it were slippery ice!
I rammed into the hoodlums on either side of the counter with the speed of a bowling ball..."
STRR--IKE!
POW!
SOK!

You can have as many of these socks as you want--free of charge!
ZAPP!

"I finished up feet-first, taking everyone before me..!
Quite a "feat," huh?
WHUNNK!

CONTINUED ON 2ND PAGE FOLLOWING.

HALF-CRAZED WITH FEAR AND PAIN-- THE SPY STUMBLES INTO THE LABORATORY EQUIPMENT IN A FRANTIC EFFORT TO ESCAPE THE TERRIFIC BEATING!
HE BECOMES ENMESHED IN POWERFUL COILS OF WIRE WHICH, LIKE BANDS OF DEATH...CAUSE A MILLION VOLTS OF ELECTRICITY TO BURN OUT HIS LIFE!
NOTHING LEFT OF HIM BUT CHARRED ASHES... A FATE HE WELL DESERVED!

ALTHOUGH THE WONDER SERUM HAS BEEN DESTROYED--ITS FIRST CREATION...CAPTAIN AMERICA, BECOMES A POWERFUL FORCE IN THE BATTLE AGAINST SPIES AND SABOTEURS!
CAPTAIN AMERICA CAPTURES SPY RING!
CAPTAIN AMERICA NABS SPY!
CAPTAIN AMERICA PREVENTS DAM EXPLOSION
CAPTAIN AMERICA... NATION'S No.1 SPY BUSTER!
WHO IS CAPTAIN AMERICA?
BOY-- HOW I'D LIKE TO MEET THAT GUY! I WISH I COULD BE LIKE HIM!
MAYBE YOU CAN, BUCKY...MAYBE YOU CAN!
CAPTAIN AMERICA NABS SPY

WHO IS CAPTAIN AMERICA? A WHOLE NATION THRILLS TO HIS DARING EXPLOITS! HIS NAME BECOMES A SYMBOL OF COURAGE TO MILLIONS OF AMERICANS...AND A BY-WORD OF TERROR IN THE SHADOW-WORLD OF SPIES!
AT CAMP LEHIGH, OF THE UNITED STATES ARMY, BUCKY BARNES, MASCOT OF THE REGIMENT, APPROCHES PRIVATE STEVE ROGERS...
OH...STEVE... STEVE! LOOKIT THIS...CAPTAIN AMERICA'S DONE IT AGAIN!

TALBOT'S YOUR HUNCHBACK KILLER, BROGAN! HE'S A FANATICAL NAZI AND A JEALOUS FOOL NOW HE'LL PAY FOR BEING BOTH!
YOU'LL FIND BARLOFF UNCONSCIOUS ON THE CASTLE TOWER! HE WAS THE ONE WHO SCALED THE CASTLE WALL TO TRY TO CAPTURE TALBOT!
SIGN THAT CONFESSION, TALBOT! YOU GOT A BIG SCENE TO PLAY IN COURT!
GOIN' BACK TO CAMP, CAP?
YEP! THE SARGE IS PROBABLY PINING AWAY FOR US!
BACK IN CAMP, PRIVATE ROGERS AND BUCKY BUY A NEWSPAPER TO READ OF CAPTAIN AMERICA'S LATEST EXPLOIT!
THIS BIRD SURE GETS A LOAD OF PUBLICITY!
YEAH, HE'S JUST AN OVER-RATED BUM!
CAPTAIN AMERICA NABS MOVIE MURDERER
SO, CAPTAIN AMERICA'S AN OVER-RATED BUM, IS HE? IF YOU MUGS HAD HALF HIS BRAINS, YOU'D BE GETTING SOMEWHERE IN THIS MAN'S ARMY!
YES, SARGE!
TOO TRUE, SARGE!
THE END
17.

THE WISE MAN KNOWETH WHEN TO SPEAK, AND WHEN TO SHUTETH UP! SLY STAN KNOWS THAT NO WORDS OF HIS CAN DO JUSTICE TO JOLLY JACK'S GREAT ACTION SCENES... AND SO...
SEE WHAT WE MEAN, FRANTIC ONE?
8.

HAD ENOUGH, BATROC?
IT EES BEYOND BELIEF! YOU 'AVE FOUGHT ZEE MOST SKILLED BATTLER OF ALL TO ZEE STANDSTILL!
NEVAIR HAS SUCH A THING 'APPENED BEFORE!
LOOK OUT! BEHIND YOU---!

ZEE MEN FROM HYDRA... SHOOTING AT YOU!
BUT, ZEY PROMISED ME--- ZEY WOULD NOT INTERFERE!
PAKA-THANNG!
NOM DU CHIEN! BATROC FEELS ZEE TERRIBLE ANGER!

WATCH IT! HE'S GONNA LEAP AT-- UNNHH!
WOK!
MEN WIZOUT HONAIR DESERVE NO MERCY!

YOU ARE TOO POWERFUL...TOO UNCONTROLLABLE.. THEREFORE, YOU ARE A THREAT TO HYDRA!
WE SHALL DISPOSE OF CAPTAIN AMERICA IN OUR OWN WAY--- NOW!--AND OF YOU, TOO!
HAIL HYDRA!
BATROC-- DUCK!

HE--HAS THROWN HIS ACCURSED SHIELD--!
IT'S COMING RIGHT AT US...NO WAY TO STOP IT!
SACRE BLEU! SUCH SPEED... SUCH POWAIR!

FTLANNGG!
ZEY WEEL NOT THREATEN ANYONE AGAIN ZIS DAY!
NOW TALK, MISTER! WHERE'S THE GIRL...BEFORE THE OTHERS REACH HER!
9

Snap-brimmed superhero: Will Eisner's Spirit stands out among the hooded, caped, masked, and spangled gallery of comic-book figures. Apart from the minuscule mask his appearance is normal. He works mainly as a detective using intuition and deduction to solve mysteries and prevent injustice. The style is decorative and assured. Below is a typical vintage heading and on the right a page from a 1944 adventure. In 1966 in the new comic-book boom Harvey Comics revived the Spirit. Eisner's style is as potent as ever; there is still a mocking, satirical note in his work as the two-page excerpt overleaf demonstrates. The Spirit is one of the most satisfying of all comic-book creations, with a completely unique style.

DO YOU REALLY THINK, ELLEN, YOU'RE SUITED TO A STAGE CAREER?
DADDY PUT YOU UP TO THIS! AND YOU'RE BOTH SELFISH!

IF YOU THINK I'M SO FOOLISH TO ACT -- WHY BOTHER WITH ME?
MR. BRISCOE CALLED US ON STAGE, MISS DOLAN!

WE'LL START THE SECOND ACT! JUST BEFORE THE ENTRANCE OF JOHN, AS LORD RALLES IN HIS CRAZY MOOD!
I SPEAK FIRST -- THEY SAY HIS VIOLENCE IS MURDEROUS!

AND NOBODY TO HELP -- HERE HE IS NOW!
A DAGGER, LADY JENNIFER? HOW CONVENIENT!

LET US SEE THE COLOR OF FALSE BLOOD!

DON'T STRIKE HER!
YOU INTERFERING FOOL!

THAT'S ONLY A FAKE DAGGER -- IT WOULDN'T HAVE HURT CLARA!
NO?

IT'S A REAL DAGGER -- AND SHARP ENOUGH FOR MURDER!
THUD

SPIRIT LAB
SPIRIT, YOU'RE BEHIND THE TIMES. EVERY MODERN CRIME FIGHTER HAS SCIENTIFIC DEVICES HE USES TO FIGHT CROOKS. JAMES BOND...HAS BOMBS... OUR MAN FINK HAS CIGAR LIGHTER...YOU, THE COOLEST OF THEM ALL HAVE NOTHING.
Will Eisner

NOW... I HAVE DEVISED FOR YOU THE GREATEST COLLECTION OF DEVICES KNOWN TO MODERN SCIENCE!

FIRST... YOUR HAT. NOTICE IT'S PLIABLE BUT BULLETPROOF!
BANG

INSIDE THE SWEATBAND WE HAVE A TRANSMITTER RECEIVER OF UNLIMITED RANGE, WITH OPTIONAL EXTRA-SENSORY WAVE LENGTH.

MICRO-MODULAR X-RAY UNIT... EXTRACTS POWER FROM BODY HEAT
THE MASK PROVIDES YOU WITH X-RAY VISION AND LETS YOU SEE AT A DISTANCE OF 100 YARDS THROUGH THICK STEEL, WOOD OR STONE...
+500° FARENHEIT
−100° FARENHEIT
THESE GLOVES ARE WOVEN OF A THERMAL BARRIER MATERIAL WITH SUPER INSULATING QUALITIES.
TIE
AND A TIE THAT CAN BE USED AS A ROPE OR CHAIN... IT IS LACED WITH A TITANIUM-CERAMIC WIRE... VERY STRONG.
5000 LB.
1.

NOW... WITH THESE YOU WOULD BE ...INVINCIBLE!

YES SIR!
BY GOLLY I FEEL INVINCIBLE IN THESE CLOTHES!

IN FACT... I THINK YOU DON'T DESERVE THESE THINGS.. AFTER ALL WHY SHOULD YOU GET THE FRUITS OF MY GENIUS...

SPIRIT, I'M TAKING OVER!

I, HANS KNAGLE VON SHMERTZ WILL HENCEFORTH BE THE SPIRIT!

HELLO THIS IS LONDON CALLING

HEADQUARTERS
MR. KOTCHITURIAN, WOULD YOU BE INTERESTED IN SOME INVINCIBLE DEVICES FOR THE MEN FROM UNK!

Miraculous Marvel: the comic books endured a long period of opprobrium following the uproar over the horror comics which formed a minority proportion of the output in the early fifties. A self-regulating body was set up to vet all art-work, text, and even advertisements appearing in the comic books, and to issue seals of approval to appear on the covers of publications that passed the intensive scrutiny. Marvel Comics in 1961 started sending up the comic medium with the most outrageously exaggerated and un-conventional stories, laced with odd snatches of liberal philosophizing. The Fantastic Four, a quartet of assorted superheroes, including the muscular Invisible Girl, and in spite of hi repulsive appearance, the amiable Thing battled against an even more bizarre barrage o mutants. Circulation boomed. Captain America reappeared. The Amazing Spider Man and th Mighty Thor joined the party. Another teenag four are the X-men, whose members are the Iceman, the Angel, Marvel Girl, and the Beast, all of whom are seen below taking a ride on the subway. Now Marvel Comics' collection o superheroes form a highly successful section o the industry. Many of the stories have a Homeric ring and have as much appeal for college students as high school drop-outs.

THE WORLD'S GREATEST COMIC MAGAZINE!
APPROVED BY THE COMICS CODE AUTHORITY
Fantastic Four
MARVEL COMICS GROUP
12¢ IND.
63 JUNE
"BLASTAAR, THE LIVING BOMB-BURST!"

TALES OF SUSPENSE featuring
APPROVED BY THE COMICS CODE AUTHORITY
IRON MAN AND CAPTAIN AMERICA
MARVEL COMICS GROUP
10d
89 MAY
"THE MONSTROUS MENACE OF..
THE NEW MYSTERIOUS MELTER!"

THE MIGHTY THOR
APPROVED BY THE COMICS CODE AUTHORITY
MARVEL COMICS GROUP
10d
140 MAY
THE GROWING MAN

the AMAZING SPIDER-MAN
APPROVED BY THE COMICS CODE AUTHORITY
MARVEL COMICS GROUP
12¢ IND.
47 APR
WOULD'JA BELIEVE--- KRAVEN THE HUNTER!

THE AMAZING SPIDER-MAN!
"THE WINGS OF THE VULTURE!"
NOW THAT MY PETER PARKER DUDS ARE SAFELY STASHED AWAY, IT'S WEB-SWINGIN' TIME AGAIN!
IF KRAVEN, THE HUNTER IS STILL IN THE CITY, I'VE GOT TO KEEP SEARCHING TILL I FIND HIM!
CAN'T LET THAT TIN-HORN TARZAN GO THROUGH LIFE THINKING HE'S BEATEN ME!* EVEN A STARRY-EYED SPIDER-MAN HAS HIS PRIDE!
BUT, IF THIS COLD SPELL DOESN'T BREAK UP SOON, I'M LIABLE TO BE THE ONLY WEB-CRAWLER IN TOWN WEARING A MUFFLER... AND MITTENS!
THESE LONG-UNDERWEAR RAGS ARE GREAT FOR THE SUPER-HERO IMAGE.. BUT A FELLA CAN FREEZE TO DEATH IN WEATHER LIKE THIS!
AND, AS IF THE COLD ISN'T BAD ENOUGH, THE HEAVY SNOWFALL IS MUFFLING MY SPIDEY SENSE, MAKING IT TOUGHER THAN EVER TO LATCH ONTO KRAVEN!
BUT, I CAN'T QUIT NOW! I'VE GOT A FEELING THAT THE DEADLIEST FIGHT OF MY LIFE WILL SOON BE COMING UP!
AN AWESOME AGGREGATION OF AIRBORNE THRILLS BY: SMILIN' STAN LEE and JAZZY JOHNNY ROMITA
LEARNEDLY LETTERED BY: WHAMMY SAMMY ROSEN
* IF YOU DIDN'T READ ALL ABOUT IT LAST ISH, WE'RE BEGINNING TO LOSE PATIENCE WITH YOU! ... STERN STAN!

NO! I CAN'T CHICKEN OUT AT A TIME LIKE THIS!
I'VE FOUGHT THE VULTURE BEFORE... I KNOW HIS STYLE!
EVEN IF THIS IS A NEW JOKER WEARING THOSE CRUMMY WINGS, IT'S STILL SPIDER-MAN'S JOB!
WHATEVER ELSE I MAY BE, I'M NO QUITTER!
SLAM!

BESIDES, A LITTLE WEB-SWINGING MAY MAKE ME FEEL BETTER! IT COULD BE A TONIC TO A FELLA LIKE ME!
I CAN'T LET A COMMON COLD PUT ME OUT OF ACTION--!

...OTHERWISE, NEXT TIME AROUND, I'M LIABLE TO CRY UNCLE IF I DEVELOP SOME DANDRUFF... OR A CASE OF CHAPPED LIPS!
I MIGHT EVEN BECOME THE ONLY SUPER-HERO IN TOWN WHO WON'T FIGHT BECAUSE HE'S GOT ACNE!
IF ONLY I COULD JUST STOP SHIVERING!

ACCORDING TO THE NEWS BULLETINS, THAT FLYING FREAK HASN'T EVEN BEEN BOTHERING TO HIDE!
SO, WITH A LITTLE LUCK, IT SHOULDN'T TAKE ME TOO LONG TO TRACK HIM DOWN!
ANYWAY, I'VE GOT TO KEEP MOVING.. UNLESS I WANNA FREEZE OUT HERE!
SAY--- I THINK I'M ACTUALLY BEGINNING TO FEEL A LITTLE BETTER!
UNLESS IT'S JUST THAT I'M GETTING NUMB FROM THE COLD!

AND, AS OUR SOLILOQUIZING STALWART MAKES THE ROOF-TOP SCENE---
THE VULTURE!
I THOUGHT I HAD SEEN SOMETHING HOVERING OUTSIDE THE WINDOW BEFORE--!
HOLD IT, MAC! YOU'VE GONE FAR ENOUGH!
THOSE NEGOTIABLE BONDS YOU STUFFED IN THAT BRIEFCASE ARE JUST WHAT I NEED TO ROUND OUT MY COLLECTION!
11.

THE MIGHTY
THOR
APPROVED BY THE COMICS CODE AUTHORITY
MARVEL COMICS GROUP
12¢ IND.
139 APR
"TO DIE LIKE A GOD!"

NO SOONER HAS THE GUTTERAL COMMAND ESCAPED GEIRRODUR'S LIPS, THAN A MYSTIC VIBRATION SEEMS TO FILL THE UNDERGROUND CAVERN, LIFTING THE TWO LONE ASGARDIANS ABOVE THE HEADS OF THEIR SAVAGE FOES--!
WE ARE IN THE GRIP OF SOME STRANGE ENCHANTMENT!!
'TIS THE WORKINGS OF A POWER BEYOND ANY TROLL!!
NOW HOVER WE HERE.. UNABLE TO DE-SCEND!
ZZZZZZZZZZ

THE FORCE THAT HOLDS US HERE MAKES US HELP-LESS TARGETS FOR THE ENEMY'S JAVELINS!!
FTOK!
TO MY SIDE, VALIANT ONE! NO HARM SHALL COME TO THEE WHILE THOR DOTH LIVE!
THAK!

GODDESS... SHIELD THY FACE!!
WE SHALL TAKE SHELTER BEYOND THE WALL--- FOR YON WALL SHALL EXIST NO MORE--!!
BY THE THOUSAND THREATS OF RAGNAROK--

THOR HAST SPOKEN!
BUHROOOM!
11.

‘You mean they have newspaper strips in Britain?’

'You mean they have Newspaper Strips in Britain?'

American disbelief – late arrival of strips in British newspapers – the pioneering Daily Mirror – *Jane – Andy Capp – few American strips in Britain – Flook, developed into satire – serious competition from the* Daily Express – *Bristow, cumulative hilarity – a future for the funnies.*

Unlike the United States, Great Britain has a national Press. A small group of large circulation newspapers can appear each morning with very little difference in content between the editions on sale in Penzance and those in Inverness. This means that the provincial daily is a very poor relation to the flashy giants of Fleet Street, merely providing a supplementary dose of local matters to flavour the national and global fodder served up in the London papers.

The decline of the once-powerful British provincial Press was accelerated in the fifties by the growth of television, particularly the commercial channels, which were able to cream off much of the regional advertising. Today, after a thin decade or two, the provincial papers are among the first to turn to new methods such as computerized typesetting, offset printing and multiple 'slip' editions, and as the national distributive system gets more and more clogged it could be that the local Press will undergo a revival.

In America distance, geography, and the character of metropolitan conurbations have made it more practical for cities to create their own papers. Apart from the *Christian Science Monitor* and the *Wall Street Journal*, the American Press today is entirely provincial, individual newspapers generally having much smaller circulations than are familiar in Great Britain. But on the basis of a daily Press totalling more than 1,700 papers, the big feature syndicates have plenty of customers. So comic strips in America are usually devised, produced, and edited not by individual newspapers but by syndicates.

In Britain the reverse is the case, although newspapers do maintain syndication departments for selling the strips to lesser English papers and to Europe.

The strips were late coming to British newspapers. Lord Northcliffe, who started *Comic Cuts* and *Chips* in 1890, is the acknowledged founder of the popular Press in Britain; he launched the *Daily Mail* in 1896 ('a penny newspaper for one halfpenny'). The first issue is devoid of anything resembling a strip, or even a cartoon. Its innovations were way behind what was being done at the same time by Hearst and Pulitzer in America where, even at that early date, Sunday supplements were being printed in colour and cartoons were thriving.

The *Daily Mail* got round to bringing out the first British newspaper strip in 1915. This was Teddy Tail, a children's cartoon which ran until recent times, although its format changed considerably through the years. In 1919 the *Daily*

Mirror, then owned by Northcliffe's brother, the first Viscount Rothermere, started another children's strip – Pip, Squeak and Wilfred. It ran until the war, when paper shortage and lack of space pushed it out. In 1947 it was revived and continued until 1955. The artist responsible for the strip which featured the dog Pip, the penguin Squeak, and Wilfred, a rabbit, was A. B. Payne, one of the artists to succeed Tom Browne in drawing Weary Willie and Tired Tim for *Chips*. Payne stayed with Pip, Squeak and Wilfred until the end.

The outstanding record for newspaper strip cartoons in Britain is that of the *Daily Mirror*, which has constantly initiated and run more than any other paper. Even in its infancy the *Mirror* was featuring the work of W. K. Hazelden; not strips strictly speaking, these were finely drawn topical panel cartoons in a style comparable with that of Clare Briggs in America. Certainly the *Mirror* was the first newspaper in Fleet Street to accept that the comic strip could have as much appeal for adults as for children.

In November 1920 the *Daily Express* started a children's strip called Rupert, the adventures of a young bear, always dressed in a sweater and checked trousers. The creator of the strip was Mary Tourtel, who retired in 1935. Since then – and it still appears, two frames a day – its artist has been Alfred Bestall, and now his successors maintain the style with astonishing precision.

In May 1921 J. Millar Watt started a strip in the *Daily Sketch* called Pop. This was a daily gag about a corpulent, lovable old knucklehead with occasional interruptions from his lean, bristling military friend, the Colonel. The strip enjoyed the privilege of being exported to America, an early case of coals to Newcastle in strip terms. Watt had an interesting technique which fascinated American cartoonists. Often he would not limit the action to the areas between the edges of the frames but spread it across all four frames so that the effect was like looking on the scene through several window-panes. The gag occasionally occurred in the third frame, leaving the fourth for a character to undergo a 'slow burn'. In 1948 the strip was taken over by Gordon Hogg, who drew it until its recent end.

In the London evening newspaper *The Star*, J. K. Horrabin started, in 1922, a gag strip with an office background. Designed to appeal to home-going typists on the Underground, Dot and Carrie ran for the rest of *The Star*'s life. In 1960 *The Star* merged with the *Evening News* and its parent paper, the *News Chronicle*, with the *Daily Mail*. From 1919 Horrabin had drawn for the *News Chronicle* a children's cartoon, Happy, Japhet, and the Noah family; like Teddy Tail in the *Mail*, Pip, Squeak and Wilfred in the *Mirror*, and Rupert in the *Express*, it formed the basis for a juvenile readership club. Young *Chronicle* readers could join the Arkubs and possess a special badge. A talented and versatile cartoonist, Horrabin died shortly after the disappearance of the two newspapers.

The event of greatest significance in the history of the British strip probably occurred on 5 December 1932, in the pages of the *Mirror*. It was the first episode of Jane's Journal – or the Diary of a Bright Young Thing. Its pyjama'd young heroine received a telegram telling her to prepare to meet Count Fritz from Germany who couldn't speak English. She struggled into her latest backless

ANDY CAPP

creation from Paris; the last frame showed the arrival of Fritz – a dachshund who was to share her subsequent adventures.

Until the war these adventures were trivial stuff. But with the sudden expansion of the Armed Forces it was found that her popularity count was soaring. Jane became the favourite pin-up of the British Army. Great ingenuity was needed to find different reasons for her to lose items of clothing. The story is told in Hugh Cudlipp's book, *Publish and be Damned!*, of how an American Forces newspaper linked cause and effect: one day Jane appeared completely nude and within a week one British division had pushed the enemy back six miles and another had launched a major attack.

Jane was the invention of Norman Pett; after the war Mike Hubbard took over from him and Jane was revamped for the new times. Her day ended in 1959, when she drifted into the sunset in the arms of Georgie, her lover of long standing. Jane had an amazing innocence and aplomb, even when losing her skirt in a public place. Life was a series of embarrassing adventures coped with in a stiff-upper-lipped, British way which Americans found incredibly sexy. Attempts to find a successor to Jane seemed doomed to fail. Patti, a rebellious Northern teenager, didn't last. Then for a few months in 1961 Jane – Daughter of Jane appeared on the scene. She was a noisier, brasher, switched-on sixties girl; she too couldn't stay the course. Like Betty Grable or Betty Hutton, Jane belonged completely and inescapably to her period.

Before the war the *Mirror*, under the encouragement of Guy Bartholomew, stood almost alone in running strips. By the late thirties the *Express* was running a daily gag strip called Colonel Up and Mr Down, and the *Mail* had the Nipper. But the *Mirror* in 1936 carried Jane, King Sweepea (from the King Features syndicate), Ruggles, Beelzebub Jones, Buck Ryan, Belinda Blue Eyes, Pip, Squeak and Wilfred, and Just Jake.

Buck Ryan, a thick-ear detective story, had begun in 1937, one of the first strips in Britain with a continuous plot. He lasted until 1962 when he finished in a clinch with Twilight, his former adversary turned girl-friend. Ruggles, the creation of Stephen Dowling, started out in 1935 as an ordinary domestic strip, later turning into a kind of cartoon Citizen's Advice Bureau. Its informative descriptions of the workings of local government and social services were considerably more assimilable than the usual advice columns.

Stephen Dowling's other impressive creation was Garth. The hero is a reincarnated Greek god who, with the help of the scientist, Professor Lumiere, flits from present to past or future in order to champion human freedom against the tyranny of science. He is the British Superman, less flashy in his action and richer in his compassion.

Belinda Blue Eyes was a perpetual waif, a British counterpart to the transatlantic Little Orphan Annie. Over the years she grew slowly. By 1959 when the strip ended she had just about reached the stage when she needed a bra.

Of the vintage *Mirror* strips only Garth remains. The rest were killed off by the passage of time, many during a purge in the early sixties. The daily circulation of Britain's most popular newspaper continues to soar over the five million mark, and it now carries fewer strips than it did ten years ago. Its most notable cartoon addition is Andy Capp, who has been with the paper for just over ten years. Andy is rough and boorish, a wife-beating drunkard. His cloth cap is clamped firmly on his head and a dangling cigarette butt defies gravity on his lower lip, even in bed or in the tin bath which he can occasionally be persuaded to use in front of the living-room fire.

Andy is held in enormous affection by his readers. He still lives in a man's world. He is a symbol of a vanished species; as suburban privets grow higher and washing machines throb in more and more English kitchens, Andy Capp becomes increasingly a nostalgic figure, a memory of the days when working men could spend all their wages on booze, kick their wives around, never lift a finger to help with the housework, and be independent and unfettered by apron-strings.

Reg Smythe, the creator of Andy Capp, comes from north-east England and the backgrounds are those of the Tyne–Tees area where the memories of hunger marches, closed dockyards, unemployment, and tunnel-back housing give a touch of poignancy to Andy's appalling behaviour.

In America, where the male is said to have declined to an even more sub-servient relationship, Andy Capp is immensely popular. In spite of its Englishness the strip is carried by papers as exotic as the *Arizona Republic*, the *Denver Post*, the *Houston Chronicle* – far and away the most successful that Britain has exported. Usually Americans are not in tune with British humour and regard most Fleet Street strips as very dull stuff.

The same attitudes occur in reverse: although the language is shared the comics are not. Many non-English-speaking countries carry more American strips in their papers than Britain. Very few samples of the great wealth of American comics are nationally syndicated in British newspapers. Blondie and Peanuts appear in the *Daily Sketch*, Rip Kirby in the *Daily Mail*, Batman in the *Sun*; there the list ends.

A Fleet Street cartoon editor says that American strips are not popular with the British public, that they are designed for lower intelligence levels in the United States, and that as, unlike home-grown products, they have no resale value to other papers, they take up the scanty space allocated for strip cartoons unprofitably. The last is probably the truest explanation. It is a tragedy that no paper in Britain can run a strip as wise as Pogo, as well constructed as Steve Canyon, as adventurous as Kerry Drake.

Attempts have been made to popularize American strips. Mutt and Jeff first appeared in Britain in 1923. The *Sunday Pictorial* kept Popeye going for many years, and after the war had a brief affair with Li'l Abner. In the early post-war circulation battle when strips were called in to join the fight, the *Express* used Steve Canyon and Dick Tracy. Both, however, disappeared when native products became available. The Briton who wants to keep an eye on the American strip scene has to buy the European edition of the *New York Herald Tribune—Washington Post*.

Rip Kirby in the *Mail* is the only foreign survivor of that post-war battle, when the easing of newsprint rationing made more space available. The *Mail*'s other strips are stoutly British. Quite unique and the most brilliant is Flook. Drawn by Wally Fawkes, a jazz musician, it began in 1949 as the adventures of a small boy called Rufus (originally the title of the strip) who meets a strange bear-like animal, with a short trunk instead of a nose. The trunk possesses the magical ability to change its owner into different objects at will. The early days of the strip were passed in a kind of fanciful whimsy. For a while the story line was provided by Compton Mackenzie. But since 1958 the strip has been written by George Melly, who in Flook has managed to combine anarchism with a brilliant ear for the dialogue of our times. Should a public relations man or TV commentator or a politician speak within the strip then their words will carry the phrases, nuances, and inflexions of their kind, given a splendidly satirical twist.

Under Melly, Flook spends less of his time turning into odd objects. He has a more serious purpose – to knock the stuffing out of pompous British institutions. Characteristically, he is loved for his iconoclastic spirit. When in a recent episode the Royal Yacht Squadron at Cowes was unmercifully lampooned, the Squadron requested the entire series of originals for their clubhouse.

The inspiration for a Flook story invariably comes from the news section of the paper. When Harold Wilson was fulminating against Rhodesia, Mr Muckybrass, the plain man's P.M. in Flook, was imposing sanctions on the Isle of Wight. The gallery of supporting characters is a rich one. It includes Scoop, a modish young man who is always hooked on the fad of the moment; Bodger, a villainous, pock-marked tearaway, and his monumentally ugly sister Lucretia, a witch who in one hilarious episode was somehow persuaded to become a deb; and Moses Maggot, a shrivelled embodiment of all that is evil.

Carol Day started in 1956. Drawn with subtlety by the late David Wright, the strip is an old-fashioned romantic adventure serial for moderns, the model-girl heroine passing from man to man in a perpetual amorous whirlwind, its glamour marred only by the crippling truth that she is forever a virgin. Such is the general interest in her moral welfare that the newspaper dare not let it be otherwise; only on the day that she marries – which when it comes will spell the end of the strip – can the vigilance be relaxed. Until then, no matter with whom she consorts – playboys, *divorcés*, eccentrics, elderly roués – Carol must stay out of bed. The creator of the strip died in 1967; other artists have attempted to continue it.

The third star in the *Mail*'s collection is Fred Basset, now syndicated in American dailies. A doggy strip, this, about a Basset hound; like Peanuts' Snoopy, he has the mind of a human but not the voice. He is a family dog with a sense of humour, who gets pleasure from his war of nerves on the postman, satisfaction from his master's inability to pick the right cards at bridge, and expresses weary resignation at his mistress's constant inability to drive.

The *Express* has given the *Mail* serious and successful competition in comic strips. Its current balance consists of Jeff Hawke by Sydney Jordan, a science-fiction serial set in the not-too-distant future with the hero simultaneously facing the bureaucratic machinery of Whitehall and alien creatures from another existence and another time-scale without losing too much sleep; Gun Law, a reliable, unexceptional but solidly drawn Western; James Bond, a series until now of adaptations from the original Fleming stories and thus marred by familiarity and unsuitability for the strip format; Choochie and Twink, a whimsy strip which in 1966 replaced the lamented Four D. Jones, a strange cowboy who went around with a hoop through which he could crawl to escape the particular dimension he was in (in order not to milk the stunt dry the hoop seemed to spend ninety-five per cent of the time lost); and the Gambols, a domestic strip about an archetypal suburban couple – querulous, childless, selfish, lazy, and immensely popular with readers.

In 1962 the James Bond strip was subjected to a strange demonstration of the extraordinary mental processes of the late Lord Beaverbrook. Lord Thomson's *Sunday Times* launched its colour magazine with a long Fleming short story featuring James Bond. Beaverbrook held newspaper rights for the novels but apparently not the short stories. Though *Thunderball* had just begun in the strip it was ordered to finish forthwith. Readers one morning were astonished to find three-quarters of an extremely complicated plot dismissed in the space of four frames. The Bond strip stayed out of the *Express* until shortly after Lord Beaverbrook's death in 1964, when it was restored.

The London *Evening Standard*, also within the Beaverbrook group carries three remarkable strips. Modesty Blaise, drawn by Jim Holdaway from Peter O'Donnell's stories, is a Bond-type spy adventure. But the difference is that the central character is a superbly-equipped girl, able to fight, maim, and kill with expertise similar to that of her masculine counterparts. She represents the most successful incursion of a female character into the male escapist fantasy type of strip.

Billy the Bee, by Harry Smith, is an anthropomorphic serial in which the insect world is seen as another version of our own, with the same sort of royalty, politicians, and officials, in many cases based on very obvious genuine prototypes.

Bristow by Frank Dickens is a daily gag strip set in an office; its ingenuity borders on masterpiece. Bristow of Buying is a lowly clerk with overbearing bosses and incurable optimism. His dull life in the vast amorphous Chester-Perry Organization is enlivened by the plop of the house magazine on to his desk or the prospect of a visit from Miss Pretty of the Kleenaphone service. Epitomizing as he does all little men in routine jobs, Bristow's unquenchable spirit points the way to salvation from the humdrum dreariness of everyday life.

Newspaper strips may not be as plentiful in Britain as they are in America, but those that are produced are of a reasonable standard. Whereas formerly it was treated with suspicion or derision by editors the strip is now an accepted section of the British Press. Even the *Guardian* carries a daily strip cartoon serial and it can only be a matter of time before the walls of Printing House Square itself will fall.

In the popular Press in Britain the next revolution will be in colour, especially as commercial colour TV will be going after the advertising. The problem will then be to find material for the pages of colour that newspapers will be expected to produce. It could well be that the strips will come to the rescue and that Britain at last, after seventy years of waiting, could have 'the funnies' in the American style.

Comic Section

Early English: one of the first newspaper strips in Britain was Dot and Carrie in *The Star*. Illustrated is its first appearance in 1922, introducing the characters who were to stay in business until shortly before the death of the artist, J. K. Horrabin, in 1962. Today's counterpart of the office strip is probably Bristow in the *Evening Standard*. Pip, Squeak and Wilfred in the *Daily Mirror*, besides being one of the earliest British newspaper strips, achieved the status of a craze, during the craze-mad twenties. Wilfred the rabbit, who joined the dog Pip and the penguin Squeak after the latter pair had got off to their start in May 1919, was the strip's most popular character and the Wilfredian League of Gugnuncs, with its nationwide membership, raised thousands of pounds for charity.

Jane, the one and only: she is probably the most legendary of all British newspaper cartoon characters. Andy Capp may have surpassed her commercially but it is Jane who occupied the more permanent place in the imagination. Her first appearance in 1932 (*top right*) was reasonably discreet. The middle two strips are of Jane at the peak of her career, the self-same 1943 strips of which the U.S. Army newspaper *Round-up* wrote: 'Well, sirs, you can go home now . . . Jane peeled a week ago. The British 36th Division immediately gained six miles and the British attacked in the Arakan. Maybe we Americans ought to have Jane, too'. Jane's fade-out into a blissful 1959 sunset is below.

1. Wilfred waved to the car mascot—
2. —smiled on the Wilfred "dolly"—
3. —chortled at the walking-sticks—
4. —saluted the "Wilfred" troop of scouts—
5. —marvelled at the "Wilfred" trees, but—
6. —flew in terror from the poulterers!

JANE'S JOURNAL—Or the Diary of a Bright Young Thing - - - ENTER THE COUNT

Frame game: J. Millar Watt's Pop started in the *Daily Sketch* in 1921; the first strip is immediately below. In time the character lost his hair, gained a larger paunch, and moved against a more stylishly executed background. Many of Pop's jokes became classics – such as the one about the rainbow. The use of frames dividing the pictures was interesting – the action often overlapped from one to the next. The artist was also adept at reaching the punch line by the third frame, leaving the fourth serving luxuriously to show the reaction. The two strips at the foot of each page were drawn by Gordon Hogg in 1959. He had taken the strip over in 1948 when J. Millar Watt retired. The other strips on these two pages are of 1935 vintage.

ISN'T THAT LOVELY?

YES! WHATS IT ADVERTISING ?

HE'S JUST THREE AND

HE'S BEEN WALKING SINCE HE WAS SIX MONTHS OLD!

DEAR ME! HE MUST BE TIRED!

WHAT DID THE DOCTOR SAY ?
F45

I HAVEN'T GOT WHAT YOU THOUGHT I'D GOT

THEN YOU'LL HAVE TO MAKE DO WITH WHAT HE SAYS YOU'VE GOT!

Mainly for children: J.K.Horrabin, the cartoonist of Dot and Carrie, started the saga of the Noah family in the *News Chronicle* in 1919. In it a toy-like man and woman with a bespectacled small boy, Japhet, kept a suburban house containing an arkload of animals, Happy the little bear (*below*) being one of the most prominent. Another celebrated small bear was Rupert (*bottom*) who began his adventures in the *Daily Express* in 1920 and is still going strong as the 1967 extract shows. His originator was a woman, Mary Tourtel, who retired from the scene in 1935. Her creation continues with a strange timelessness – there is never anything in a Rupert cartoon to date, for even the occasional modern intrusions such as aircraft are so basic and stylized they belong to no particular period. With only a year or two before his half-century Rupert continues as an unruffled permanent feature of the English scene.

Genuine Old Salt

Rupert and the Jumping Men—30

A moment later the tiny airplane has landed and Rupert runs forward as an old friend gets out of it. "Why, surely you're the Golliwog that runs errands for Santa Claus, aren't you?" he cries. "Yes, I am, but who are you?" asks Golly. "You look like Rupert of Nutwood but you're four sizes too small!" "Yes, I *am* Rupert," says the little bear. "I couldn't get in here while I was my right size." And he tells why he came and how the jumping men are squabbling with one another about their moves.

Rupert and the Jumping Men--31

The Golliwog is evidently in a hurry and he marches off to the factory just as the manager appears again. "Hi, what are you up to?" says Golly. "Santa Claus is stocking up for his Christmas journeys and he hasn't yet received a single game of Halma or Ludo or Tiddleywinks or . . ." "But I've just told you about the quarrelling counters and the jumping men," Rupert interrupts. "I told them what their squabbling means to other people, but they're so angry they won't listen to me!"

Rupert and the Jumping Men—32

When he hears where all the quarrelling pieces are the Golliwog turns and storms away towards the big board where the Counters and the Halma men and the Chess pawns are now dashing and leaping about more furiously than ever. "Oh dear, I'm *sure* they've all gone mad!" says Rupert. "How can anybody stop them? They don't even know what they want, nor how to get it if they did." "Don't worry, I'll stop 'em!" says Golly grimly. Approaching the board he gives a long, loud shout.

Rupert and the Jumping Men—33

At the voice of the Golliwog the pandemonium on the board grows less and when he shouts again there is complete silence. Seeing who is before them the jumping men begin to tremble and four of them shuffle forward and wait. "Who started all this nonsense of one game being jealous of another game?" Golly sounds very angry. "Why couldn't you listen when Rupert told you the trouble you were causing? What will all the children think? What will Santa Claus say?"

Homeward entertainment: strips are in evening as well as morning papers. Here are three developed by the London *Evening Standard*. Bristow by Frank Dickens may sometimes baffle the casual, unfamiliar reader. It achieves its effect by a cumulative attack on the senses – the ceaseless milking of a situation day after day until every possibility has been covered. Bristow, like many great clowns, is essentially a pathetic figure, a little man determined to make the best of a dull life by resolute cheerfulness at all costs. Billy the Bee is an allegorical adventure strip, occasionally satirizing recognizable government figures disguised as inhabitants of its strip world. Modesty Blaise is a vogueish spy thriller strip in the James Bond mould with a girl as its central character, able to fight and kill in the manner of her male counterpart. Willie Garvin is her loyal and platonic (where she is concerned) supporter. She enjoys a certain amount of syndication in North America.

British superman: Garth, the nearest to an English superhero, was the invention of Stephen Dowling. A typical display of his god-like physique is shown in the top strip. Below is Buck Ryan, one of the first continuous adventure serials to be developed in Britain. The first Buck Ryan strip of 1937 appears over the last, twenty-five years later. During that time the detective hero, of a more rugged character than most, had bounced around the underworld like a renegade table-tennis ball. Ruggles (*top right*) was another Stephen Dowling invention. It started out as straightforward domestic strip but later took on a serious social duty with responsible citizen Ruggles explaining the inner workings of bureaucratic machinery. Arthur Ferrier was an artist skilled in drawing shapely girls and two of his 1938 creations for the *Daily Mirror*'s stablemate, the *Sunday Pictorial*, are shown below.

BUCK RYAN

NEW DETECTIVE STORY

BUCK RYAN

The Ruggles by Blik

TOMORROW
MR RUGGLES SEES THE SOLICITOR!

OUR NEW *Strip-Cartoon* SECTION

A SCHOOL FOR TRAINING WOMEN SPIES HAS BEEN DISCOVERED. EXAMINATIONS SHOULD BE INTERESTING.

OUR DUMB BLONDE

Mirror images: before the war the cartoon strips were scattered throughout the *Daily Mirror*. War-time newsprint restrictions brought them down in size and for convenience they were grouped together on one page, with the exception of Jane. This is a typical war-time *Mirror* strip display, from July 1943. Popeye, syndicated from King Features, is the sole non-*Mirror* strip. At the bottom of the page is the third Garth strip to appear, where the hero washed ashore on a raft, feebly mouths his name, before being whisked off to meet Professor Lumiere and to begin their famous partnership.

BUCK RYAN

BEELZEBUB JONES

BELINDA

POPEYE

RUGGLES

GARTH

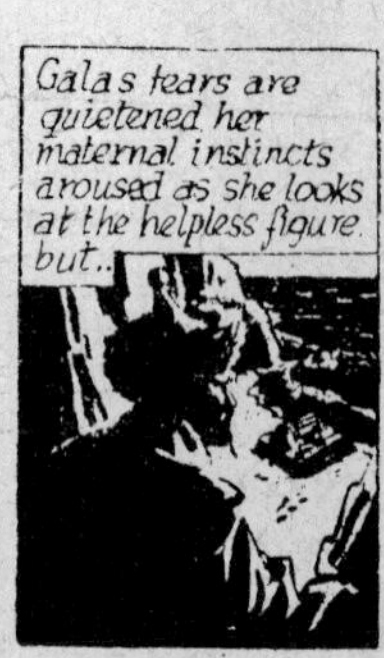

BUCK RYAN

THE LARKS

BELINDA

THE FLUTTERS

GARTH

ROMEO BROWN

Last fling: the single page persisted in the *Daily Mirror* even when the number of pages was restored to the pre-war level. This 1959 page was shortly before the twilight of the six-strip display, for a draconian purge was to carry away many of the long-standing favourites. Belinda appears for the last time on this page. Buck Ryan was nearing the end of his long run. The strip at the foot of the page, Romeo Brown, ended in 1962. Its artist, Jim Holdaway, moved to the *Evening Standard* and started Modesty Blaise.

Popular psychology: occasionally the *Daily Mirror* has gone outside normal comic-strip subjects and used the format for the presentation of feature ideas. Dreams started in 1946 and was wildly successful, appearing in an early post-war era of psychological cinema like Hitchcock's *Spellbound*, and the new age of psychiatry. Keeping Up With the Jones also fitted the mood of the time – the Macmillan period of optimism and spare cash waiting to be invested. When the post-1959 election euphoria subsided the interest in the strip abated and it was stopped.

New girls: Patti and Jane – Daughter of Jane were unsuccessful replacements for the greatest *Mirror* girl of them all. Neither had the charm nor the innocence that had made the original Jane so popular with the previous generation. Since Patti of 1959 and Jane, junior, 1961, the *Daily Mirror* has made no further attempts to find a girl heroine.

Capp in hand: the biggest post-war figure in the British comic-strip world is the *Mirror*'s Andy Capp, by Reg Smythe. The boorish, drunken, lazy, insolent, wife-beating but essentially loveable lout has endeared himself to readers on both sides of the Atlantic. Although his background is Tyneside in north-east England he is often billed in American newspapers as a Cockney. He is the last repository of masculine freedom before women finally take over.

HAVE YOU EVER DREAMED THAT—
YOUR HANDS WERE COVERED WITH WARTS—

AND THAT YOU WERE UNDRESSED IN PUBLIC?
E.2

—THIS DREAM MEANS:

This is the dream of someone who is too much concerned with physical appearances and with minor bodily symptoms. All your anxiety has gone into your skin-sensitiveness. You are rather like the schoolboy with the spotty face; every spot seems to him the size of an apple.

Being undressed in public indicates how much you are concerned with superficial appearances. All your anxiety is finding its way into a supersensitiveness which is getting you nowhere.

This is the anxiety dream of the self-centred individual. It indicates that your life is too lonely; it is revolving too much about yourself. You must really get out among people.

KEEPING UP WITH THE JONESES
MEET NEWLY-WEDS JOE AND PRUE HOPE. THEY'VE GOT JOBS, THEY'VE ALSO GOT AMBITIONS... BUT THEY COULD DO WITH MORE CASH!
BRRR! WHY SHOULD WE FREEZE TO DEATH ON THIS SCOOTER, JOE? THE JONESES FROM UPSTAIRS HAVE A CAR!
MAYBE HE'S GOT A BETTER JOB THAN ME, PRUE!

MAYBE—BUT I BET BETWEEN US WE DON'T MAKE MUCH LESS THAN HE DOES
ANYWAY, BETTY TOLD ME THEY GOT IT OUT OF INVESTMENTS

I KNOW, EASY MONEY—MY OLD MAN WAS ALWAYS GOING TO WIN A FORTUNE ON THE DOGS!
IT'S NOT LIKE THAT, JOE. YOU OUGHT TO TALK TO BILL JONES...

JANE . . . Daughter of Jane

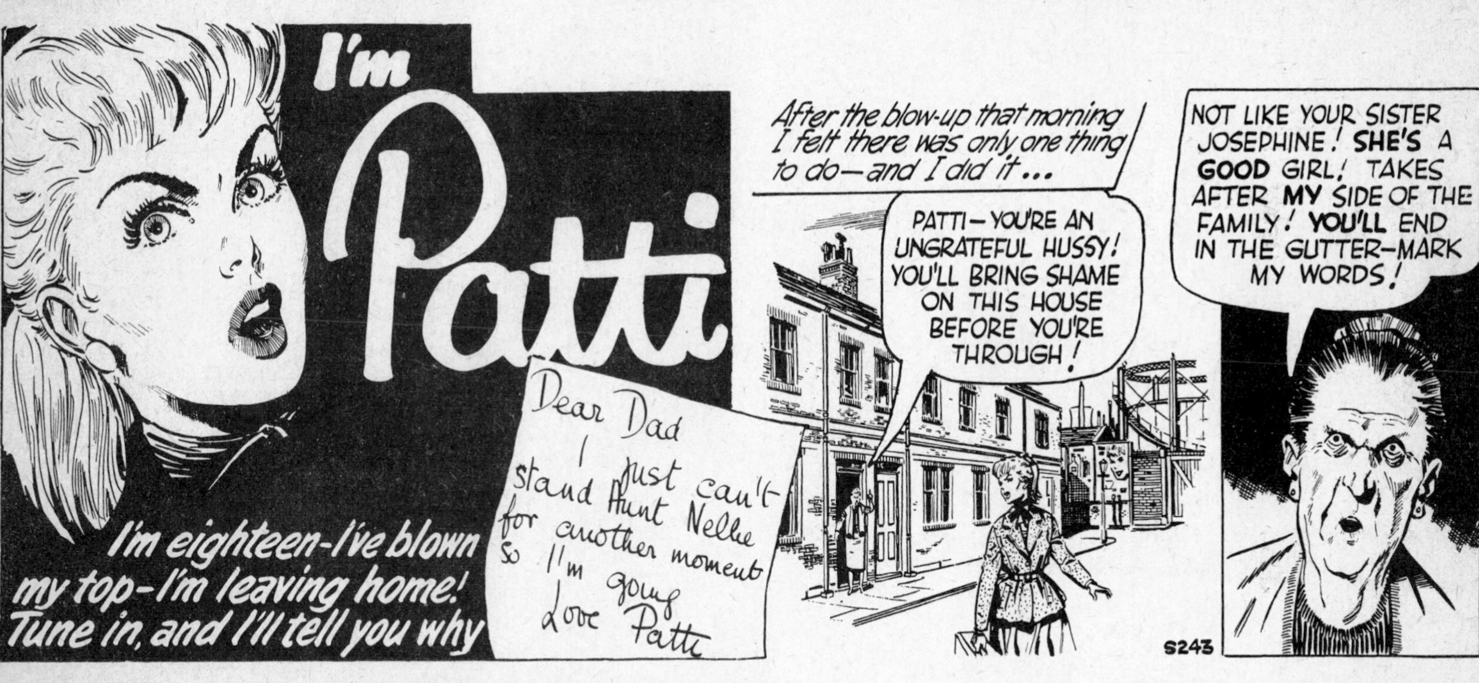

Whimsy into satire: when the Flook strip began in the *Daily Mail* in 1949 its style was gentler, more fanciful than now. Flook was a strange animal with a magic snout who materialized one night in a dream of Rufus, the small boy. Over the years the strip, drawn by Wally Fawkes (Trog), grew a cutting edge. Today, with the story line and dialogue by George Melly, it is Britain's foremost satirical strip. The example, from a recent episode in which the Isle of Wight made a unilateral declaration of independence, features the Duke of Edinburgh and Uffa Fox, the yachtsman. The strip's strength is in the combination of the brilliant ear for contemporary speech possessed by Melly and Trog's accurate portrayal of standard figures.

100
THIS OUGHT TO CHEER THE OLD BOY UP

COME ON, CYRIL, EAT THIS AND LET'S BURY THE HATCHET

IF I BURY IT, IT'LL BE IN THAT FLOOK'S HEAD!
Trog

YOU OUGHT TO BE ASHAMED OF YOURSELF, YOU OLD MISERY

101
COME OVER HERE, FLOOK, AND I'LL SHOW YOU HOW TO MAKE CONCRETE

THIS'LL TEACH YOU TO MAKE A FOOL OF ME!

HELP! RUFUS!!
Trog

RUFUS!

102

FLOOK! I'M SURPRISED AT YOUR CUPIDITY!
Trog

I DON'T THINK WE'LL BE HAVING ANY MORE TROUBLE FROM CYRIL

103
ALL RIGHT, MEN, TIME TO KNOCK OFF

HAVE YOU TWO GOT ANY-WHERE TO SLEEP?
NO SIR, BUT WE'LL BE ALL RIGHT

WELL, I'VE GOT A SPARE ROOM AT HOME. YOU'D BETTER COME BACK WITH ME
THAT'S VERY KIND OF YOU, SIR.
Trog

GOOD NIGHT. DON'T BE LATE IN THE MORNING

Morbid model: Carol Day, a superbly drawn *Daily Mail* strip by David Wright, started in 1956. The heroine flits through a series of curious adventures, sometimes with macabre undertones. This example from an early adventure published in 1957 has a hint of the obsessive interest in death which pervades the strip. The artist died in 1967.

American export: since 1946 the *Daily Mail* has carried the Rip Kirby strip, started in America by Alex Raymond, one of the greatest cartoonists. The two 1954 vintage extracts, drawn by Raymond two years before his fatal car crash, give a good demonstration of his loose but controlled style. Today the strip is drawn by John Prentice in much the same manner.

THEN YOU REALLY THINK YOU CAN OPEN HASKIN'S SAFE, DESMOND?
IF DISHPAN HANDS RETAIN EARLIER SKILLS, SIR.
Copr. 1954, King Features Syndicate, Inc., World rights reserved.

GOSH, MR. KIRBY, IT SURE CARRIES A FELLOW BACK TO SEE DESMOND LIKE THAT.
YES, CRUSHER. SOMETIMES I'M GLAD HE DIDN'T REFORM TOO EARLY IN LIFE.

OPEN, SESAME! THERE YOU ARE, SIR...
GOOD!

HMM. HASKIN'S SAFE IS CLEANED EXCEPT FOR A FEW BILLS AND THIS LITTLE REVOLVER...
Copr. 1954, King Features Syndicate, Inc., World rights reserved.

ODD... THIS THING'S LOADED WITH BLANKS AND ONE HAS BEEN FIRED. LOTS OF FINGERPRINTS ON IT, TOO.
BUT WILL THAT HELP US, MR. KIRBY?

I'LL SOON FIND OUT, DESMOND. YOU AND CRUSHER GO BACK TO THE HOTEL... I'M VISITING THE LOCAL FINGERPRINT BUREAU...

IT'S THE MANGLER! HE'S EARLY...
LET'S GRAB 'IM, OURSELVES...
LOANS

I'VE BROUGHT THE ROCKS. YOU'D BETTER BE READY FOR ME THIS TIME!
I HAVE THE MONEY... WHERE IS YOUR MERCHANDISE?

AS CRIMPER AND SMILEY CLOSE IN ON THE MANGLER, A KNIFE CLICKS OPEN...

2967
HIS SENSES AS SHARP AS THOSE OF THE JUNGLE BEASTS HE HUNTED, THE MANGLER HEARS THE CLICK OF AN OPENING KNIFE BLADE...

LOANS
THERE HE GOES! I'M TOO LATE...

WITH KIRBY IN CLOSE PURSUIT, THE MANGLER VAULTS INTO HIS CAR AND IS OFF WITH A ROAR...
HBC 219
2968

THE CHASE SOON FINDS MANHUNTER AND PREY ON A LONELY STRETCH OF SEACOAST...

UNTIL THE MANGLER FAILS TO NEGOTIATE A CURVE.

FRED BASSET
by GRAHAM

Not to worry, dear. Even though there's only four of the patrol left practically down to their last bullet, and surrounded by hundreds of Sioux, all will be well...

1124

Dog days: Fred Basset, one of the *Daily Mail*'s strips, enjoys wide syndication throughout the world, including the United States and Canada. The humour is that of frustration. Fred is often more knowing than his human master and mistress of their failings. But communication is impossible. He has to put up with his doggy speechlessness. Consequently, the hero's daily words are always in the form of 'thinks' balloons. Tiffany Jones (*below*) is a relatively new strip, appearing in the *Daily Sketch*, another newspaper in the *Mail* group, all of which share the same cartoon editor. It is created by two women and its elegant style is an inheritance of Pat Tourret's experience as a fashion artist.

TIFFANY JONES
by Pat Tourret & Jenny Butterworth
AH, MA CHERE TIFFANY! WHAT DELIGHT TO SEE YOU! FIFINE—YOU WILL SHOW HER WHERE SHE WILL SLEEP?
OF COURSE, ROGER!
N 20

IT IS VERY LARGE—YOU WILL NOT BE FRIGHTENED HERE BY YOURSELF?
FRIGHTENED? NO—OF COURSE NOT!
ON THE OTHER HAND—I DON'T THINK I'M GOING TO FEEL PARTICULARLY RELAXED, EITHER!

TIFFANY JONES
by Pat Tourret & Jenny Butterworth
EARLY MORNING AT THE CHATEAU...
MMM! GORGEOUS MORNING! THERE'S A REAL SMELL OF SPRING IN THE AIR!
N 21

AND IT LOOKS AS IF SPRING IS CAUSING ROGER VALENSKI'S FANCY TO LIGHTLY TURN TO THOUGHTS OF LOVE, AS THE OLD SAYING GOES!

BUT THAT'S NOT FIFINE WITH HIM... THAT'S GERDA—GUY MORGAN'S WIFE!

TIFFANY JONES
by Pat Tourret & Jenny Butterworth
BON JOUR, TIFFANY! I SEE YOU ARE ALSO AN EARLY RISER. COME DOWN AND LET ME SHOW YOU THE GROUNDS...
NOT JUST NOW, THANK YOU—SOME OTHER TIME...
N22

SO GERDA'S STAYING HERE, TOO—AND WITHOUT GUY—I KNOW HE'S IN NEW YORK DOING THAT 'WHIRL' FASHION FEATURE...
AND IT LOOKS AS THOUGH WHILE THE CAT'S AWAY THE MICE ARE PLAYING...AND HOW!

Express gallery: The *Daily Express*, where once Steve Canyon and Dick Tracy had a space, has cultivated its own strips with proficiency. Four D. Jones by Maddocks, now unhappily terminated, was a fantasy about a strange little cowboy able via a magic hoop to wander at will through time and space, with occasional surrealistic consequences. The Gambols, a man-and-wife creation by Mr and Mrs Barry Appleby, is syndicated widely abroad. James Bond is a straightforward adaptation of the Ian Fleming books, in this example *Dr No*. The strip was in abeyance for the two years preceding Lord Beaverbrook's death in 1964. It returned with a different artist. Gun Law is an accomplished treatment of familiar Western characters made popular on TV, and drawn with a stylish flair by Harry Bishop. Sydney Jordan's Jeff Hawke is the most original of the *Express* strips; it is in a science-fiction idiom which blends realism with fantasy in a sometimes disturbing manner.

THE GAMBOLS . . . . by Barry Appleby

THE GAMBOLS . . . . by Barry Appleby

JAMES BOND
by IAN FLEMING
Drawing by John McLusky
200
I LEFT THE DYING OCTOPUS AND SUDDENLY ABOVE MY HEAD I SPOTTED THE KEEL OF MR. BIG'S YACHT SECATUR

I FIXED A LIMPET MINE TO THE SECATUR AS A BARRACUDA FLASHED BY. ITS JAW HALF OPEN

SUDDENLY I WAS SURROUNDED BY BARRACUDAS DRIVEN MAD. SOMEONE ABOVE WAS SPRAYING THE SURFACE OF THE SEA WITH OFFAL

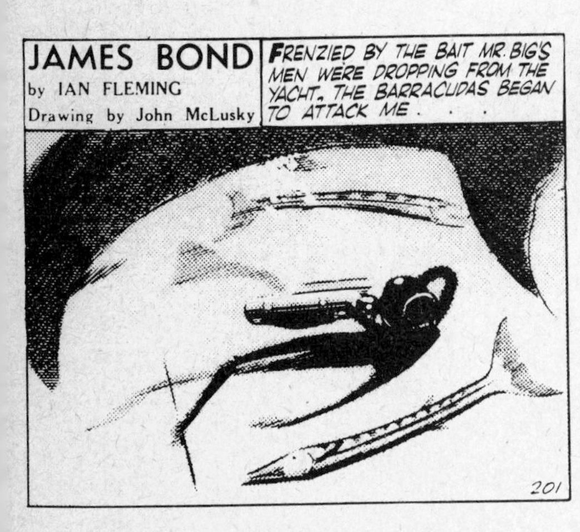

JAMES BOND
by IAN FLEMING
Drawing by John McLusky
FRENZIED BY THE BAIT MR. BIG'S MEN WERE DROPPING FROM THE YACHT. THE BARRACUDAS BEGAN TO ATTACK ME . . .

ONE RIPPED MY RUBBER SUIT OPEN. I SHOT IT WITH MY HARPOON GUN – THEN IT JERKED AWAY CARRYING BOTH GUN AND LINE . . .
201

I TOOK REFUGE IN AN UNDERWATER CAVERN . . .

Gun Law
BY HARRY BISHOP
YUP, MISTER TIMMS, LIGHTHEARTED LIL IS AN EXPERT. SHE WOULDA MADE SHORT WORK O' THAT NEW CHUBB SAFE YOU GOT THERE!
I DON'T BELIEVE IT, THIS CANNOT BE—

— MY BEST BUGGY, AN' THE FINEST HOSSES IN TOWN, NOT T'MENTION THAT DANGED CARTLOAD O' FLOWERS!
OF COURSE, TIMMS, THERE'S THE MATTER O' THE REWARD—
— AS YOU'RE THE ONE WHO'S RECOVERED THE STOLEN MONEY FOR THE PINKERTON BOYS, HERE, YOU'RE ENTITLED TO A TEN PERCENT CUT O'ONE HUNDRED THOUSAND DOLLARS!
2867

Jeff Hawke
BY SYDNEY JORDAN
CHALCEDON'S ENERGY-PENCIL SWEEPS ACROSS THE SWITCH-BOARD LINKING MOTORS AND BATTLECRUISER CONTROLROOM...

THEN HE SHORT-CIRCUITS THE MAIN MOTOR LEADS—
PREPARE FOR BLAST-OFF!

H 3020

Comics and the cultural overflow

Comics and the Cultural Overflow *Development of the strips – strips into movies – movies influenced by strips – Pop Art and what it owes to comics – strips on the stage – strips in strange media –* Playboy *and* Private Eye *– perilous future for American strip – what will happen to the British Press – always a place for comics.*

The comic strip is a gregarious creature. It is unhappy on its own: it needs the company of other editorial matter to look its best. Since it is hard, too, for any one strip to satisfy all tastes, a single strip will rarely flourish. In a group, however, comic strips have all the variety, experience, and interest of a roomful of assorted people.

Cartoon editors of newspapers have to aim for 'balance' in their selection of comic efforts appearing in their pages, for many readers do not study every strip but look for particular favourites among several. And in order to survive, the strips have to keep up with public taste; many die when their readership ratings reveal a sustained depreciation.

In America, where many 'middle-aged' strips have become national institutions, the differences over the years are subtle. But they are there, minute indices of social change. Every strip, too, is a barometer of attitudes at its period of inception.

The early days in America were those of broad slapstick – Buster Brown, the Katzenjammers, Alphonse and Gaston, Happy Hooligan – and these had their British counterparts in Weary Willie and Tired Tim, and Tom the Ticket-of-Leave Man in *Comic Cuts*.

The twenties brought a quieter, more domestic type of humour – Gasoline Alley, Out Our Way, Winnie Winkle, Tillie the Toiler, Betty Boop – together with the first of the eternal heart-tugging serials such as Little Orphan Annie.

The thirties produced many adventure strips – Buck Rogers and Flash Gordon were heroes of the future, Prince Valiant of the past, and Dick Tracy, Terry, Mandrake the Magician, and Superman belonged to the troubled present.

The forties and early fifties brought the neo-realist strips, such as Kerry Drake, Steve Canyon, Rex Morgan, Judge Parker, and Juliet Jones.

The most important recent trend has been the development of the strip which gets more laughs from wit than slapstick, a field led by Walt Kelly's Pogo and Charles Schulz's Peanuts and which includes Johnny Hart's The Wizard of Id, Miss Peach, Beek and Meek, Beetle Bailey and the work of Jules Feiffer.

The development of the strip has always been interdependent with other forms of communication. It has its parallels in the eighteenth century, when the great period of English political satire accompanied a high level of political awareness and the growth of the novel, and in Victorian times when pictorial narrative was modified and enlarged by the burgeoning new art of photography.

Today, familiarity with films and television enables the public to accept methods of strip presentation which would have been incomprehensible at the beginning of the century. Strips such as Steve Canyon make extensive use of techniques learned in the cinema – the alternation of close, medium, and long shots, sudden changes of angle of vision, quick cutting from one sequence to another, dramatic foreground lighting. An arsenal of acceptable visual devices is available to the cartoonist and their use has brought a new freshness to the strip narrative form.

Conversely, the cinema borrowed from the strips. Success is often translated into another medium, and the film industry, with its constant hunger for material, has turned to well-known comic strips on many occasions. Blondie in the late thirties and forties was brought to the screen in several films starring Penny Singleton, with Arthur Lake as a lifelike Dagwood. Prince Valiant was translated into Technicolor and CinemaScope in the mid-fifties. Tillie the Toiler was filmed in the twenties and again in the forties. Tarzan has been on the screen as long as he has been in a strip. Flash Gordon, impersonated by Buster Crabbe, was a hero in cinema serials as well as in strips. More recently, Modesty Blaise, the British strip heroine, came to life on the screen, impersonated by the Italian actress Monica Vitti, in Joseph Losey's agreeable contribution to the spy *genre*.

Certainly the most notable serial character, at least in current mythology, is Batman. In 1942 he took to the screen in order to rid America of the menace of the Japanese fifth column. In 1965, when the cult of 'camp' was in its finest hour, this old serial was revived and shown in continuous sequence – all fifteen episodes in one astounding four and a half hour programme. The modern audiences were amazed and amused. A new widescreen colour film was released in 1966, in glossy but soulless competition with the zest of the old version.

A Batman television series was started, intended as a jocular revival of comic-book camp. But it quickly became such high-rating channel fodder for juvenile addicts, and spawned so many imitations, that American TV in the winter of 1967 appeared to consist of little else but live action and animated cartoon comic-book heroes, all in living colour. Saturday morning on nearly all channels is the top time for cartoons, most of them crudely made and quickly put together to cash in on a seasonal craze already doomed for dismissal from next season's network schedules.

The animated film cartoon is of course a cousin of long standing to the comic strip. Much of Walt Disney's massive output has been featured in both media; not only were Mickey Mouse and Donald Duck popular strips but the full-length cartoon feature films were often rendered into comic form for serial publication. Segar's Popeye was turned into a screen cartoon series, made in Florida by Max Fleischer, who had earlier made a film-star of the bow-mouthed glamour girl of the strips, Betty Boop. The animated film's first screen cartoon to achieve any sort of commercial success was dreamed up by an artist from the comic-strip world, Winsor McCay, creator of Little Nemo. This was Gertie the Dinosaur who appeared in 1909, nearly twenty years before Mickey Mouse made his début on the screen.

BBC
CONTRACT
ITV
Contract
HERO

Today, continuing the dual media tradition, the output of the Hanna–Barbera Studios, which includes several favourites such as Yogi Bear, Huckleberry Hound, and the Flintstones, appears both in print and on film. Associated with the animated cartoon is the puppet film. The foremost practitioners in the English-speaking world are Gerry and Sylvia Anderson, who have devised several series of futuristic adventures, *Supercar*, *Stingray*, *Fireball X-15*, and *Thunderbirds*. Those have also appeared as children's strips.

The serious cinema has taken inspiration from the strips largely as a result of the work of the French 'new wave' directors, who have sought new forms of narrative technique and have shown a persistent fondness for popular Americana. In his film version of Ray Bradbury's science-fiction story, *Fahrenheit 451*, François Truffaut visualized a future where, with the banning of all printed words, the only literature available for the general population would be in the form of wordless comic strips.

His compatriot, Jean-Luc Godard, has made several films whose iconography has been influenced by strip cartoons – for example, *Alphaville* with its pulp-cum-science-fictional subject-matter and *Une Femme Mariée* with its 'narrative frame' technique. Godard, a film director whose antennae are well tuned to the media of communication, sees the narrative strip as a modern vehicle for putting across the heroic legend. The strip exists alongside pulp fiction, women's magazines, advertising, and Hollywood B-pictures as a framework for projecting the Godard vision of the world.

In Britain the work of the expatriate American director Dick Lester has also been influenced by cartoon styles, particularly in *The Knack* and the two Beatles films, *A Hard Day's Night* and *Help!* where many of his visual gags are pure comic strip.

But the area where the strips have made the most impression is the much-discussed movement known as Pop Art. The term was invented in 1954 by a critic, Lawrence Alloway, who defined it as art based on the products of mass media, broadened to include advertising, packaging, film posters and stills, pin-table facias, neon signs, foundation garments, cars – and the comic strip.

As far as strips are concerned Pop Art's high priest is Roy Lichtenstein. Born in New York in 1923 and formerly an abstract expressionist, he turned to painting enormous blow-ups of frames from mediocre comic strips; the new scale monumentalized their banality so that ephemerality was both inflated and fossilized. By subtle alterations to the originals – the thickening up of a line, the heightening of a detail – Lichtenstein makes an ordinary crude piece of cartoon artwork assume the pretensions of grand design, thus intensifying the emptiness of its attitudes and its essential superficiality. He uses bad art to make good art, a trick that might have been copied from Shakespeare.

Lichtenstein is also fascinated by the technical details of comic-strip artwork. He carefully mimics the Benday tints, the dotted screens which provide the tones in a strip. A series of works consists simply of a magnified brush-stroke, drawn in the cartoon idiom, superimposed on a magnified Benday dot pattern. With titles like 'Big Painting' or 'Abstract Expressionist Brushstroke' they reduce the intense subjectivity of the action painting to the trashy formalization of routine commercial artwork.

In the art season of 1963–4 Pop Art really took root and proved to be the fashion fad of the year. Predictably, fanatic interest has now declined as other movements have taken over and the mainstream has diversified and filtered in different directions. But Pop Art cannot now ever really die out. For as the communications media grow more hysterical and all-pervading so will their influence on art. The artist cannot account for his society by turning his back on it.

It is worth remembering that radio too has long been a platform for the strips, whether for straightforward soap-opera serials in the manner of the B.B.C.'s Dick Barton, or simply as a round-up of the day's newspaper strips, read out balloon-by-balloon as a service to the blind and hospital-bound. This type of presentation originated in the thirties when New York's Mayor La Guardia, in a burst of electioneering paternalism, read the funnies to a population deprived of newspapers by a strike.

Ever since 1923, when Krazy Kat was turned into a ballet, the New York theatre has sought ways of adapting strips. In 1956 Norman Panama and Melvin Frank were able to make a substantial Broadway musical out of Li'l Abner; its plot was concerned both with government intentions to use Dogpatch, 'the most useless place in the U.S.A.', as a testing-ground for atomic weapons, and Li'l Abner's hazardous courtship of Daisy Mae, which was ultimately sanctified by the Matrimonial Stomp in the presence of Marryin' Sam. This was also filmed, not so successfully in spite of the remarkable physical resemblance of many of the actors to the original characters. In 1966 a musical derived from Superman briefly flitted across the Broadway boards. More recently a musical built from the Peanuts characters has been successfully staged.

The comic strip has also been exploited as a weapon of overt persuasion. It is popular in advertising, but for some reason has always been more favoured in the public interest sector of the business. British teenage magazines run strips on the perils of smoking; in America Blondie has been called to the aid of mental hygiene and Steve Canyon to the littered state of New York's subway. Public service propaganda is liked within the industry as it is thought to encourage a universal image of responsibility and respectability. The Newspaper Comics Council regards one of its tasks as being the selection of causes on whose behalf this kind of public relations exercise can be promoted for the benefit of the industry's morale.

Commercial advertising is, however, not without its strips. For example, in Britain Horlicks used continuities for nearly thirty years to advertise their product, and in America the strip character Little Lulu became inseparably associated with Kleenex.

Today there is a tendency for comics to wander into unfamiliar media. *Evergreen Review*, a periodical for campus intellectuals in America, started running Barbarella, which it picked up from France. The strip, invented by Jean-Claude Forest, a thirty-seven-year-old Parisian, first appeared in the French magazine *V* in 1962. His heroine is a combination of Jane and Modesty Blaise, projected into the future and interplanetary space. Like Jane she has the same difficulty in retaining her clothes; like Modesty she is mistress of every situation. A fantasy for grown-ups with liberal doses of eroticism, Barbarella was favourably received by *Evergreen*'s readers. In 1966, taking a temporary rest, she was replaced by an even more chimerical heroine, Phoebe Zeitgeist.

The pages of *Playboy*, Hugh Hefner's expensive and glossy monthly magazine for men, which enjoys a massive circulation, have since October 1962 offered welcome space to a strip adventure. Its heroine, Little Annie Fanny, is a super-nubile *voluptueuse*, who, predictably, has serious problems staying dressed. The strip is a satirical lampoon, owing its conception to *Mad* magazine, which pioneered the use of spoof strips in the early fifties. Satire and slapstick generally meet in a head-on collision.

Annie's artwork is superb. She is drawn in full colour, with shaded tones like a magazine illustration, and rendered in four-colour separations for reproduction on the glossy art paper of the magazine, which uses colour printing of a very high standard. As a consequence of its technical sophistication, several artists have to work on the strip, but its chief begetters are Harvey Kurtzmann, writer and editor, and Will Elder, artist. Annie's satirical targets might include the Ku Klux Klan, the Peace Corps, James Bond, Madison Avenue, the Beatles, and television. Through a nightmare world of TV hucksters and C.I.A. men, beauty queens and astronauts, Annie moves with a magnificent wide-eyed innocence.

In Britain there is no real counterpart. But it is worth mentioning the Barry Mackenzie strip in *Private Eye* as an example of magazine satire. MacKenzie, like his creator Barry Humphries, is an Australian and the humour is based on a raw cobber's view of British institutions. Somehow the slouch-hatted hero is always getting entangled with heiresses from the more stuffy families, to whom he is then pleased to demonstrate the delights of consuming 'tubes of Foster's' and then 'chundering'. The dialogue is often unprintable outside *Private Eye*, the drawing style crude to the point of insult. Yet Barry MacKenzie has a spirit and attack that is completely lacking elsewhere in British strip cartoon humour, with the exception of Wally Fawkes' Flook.

What is the future of the comic strip? In America the industry has been gripped by pessimism. To a large extent, this has been part of a *malaise* that has infected the Press as a whole. With the loss of many New York newspapers in the past year or two and the rapid death of the hybrid *World Journal Tribune*, the national showcase has shrunk. Exposure of a strip in a New York newspaper has always been an important factor in gaining additional syndication appearances. Undoubtedly, within the next decade many of the strips that have been familiar for two or three generations will disappear. This will not be because their creators have retired – for some, like Bringing Up Father, have already reached into the third generation of artists – but because the pattern of newspaper communication itself is due for a massive shake-up.

For a long time the industry has resisted technological change but it is becoming increasingly difficult to hold out. For example, facsimile transmission, already used in Japan, could make an American national daily possible.

In Britain, too, drastic changes must befall the newspaper industry. The evidence suggests that the quality newspapers will be in a position to gain, but that the popular Press will get increasingly into trouble. *The Observer*, the *Sunday Times*, and *The Times* are now vastly different newspapers from only ten years ago. Bifurcation, even quadrifurcation, into sections, the introduction of colour magazines, massive increases in size – these are all things that have happened since the beginning of the sixties. These papers, once the ultra-conservative stronghold of the literate British Press, are now the torchbearers of a newspaper revolution; the others will be dragged along with it or perish in the Fleet Street gutters.

Certainly there will be a race for colour. It is already a technical possibility, withheld to see who will plunge first. As colour television in Britain grows a head of steam so will the necessity for newspaper competition.

When colour does come the editors of popular newspapers will quickly become aware of the limitations as well as the advantages. Advertisers will demand colour space. Graphics, a once neglected section of newspaper make-up, have already lifted editorial design. Their real opportunity will come with colour. Colour photographs are not enough by themselves to support a visual revolution. There will be a chance for the comic strips to blaze out, to bring to the Press in Britain what William Randolph Hearst described seventy years ago as an 'iridescent polychromous effulgence that makes the rainbow look like a lead pipe'.

Looking even further ahead, the time should one day arrive when every home will have its own machine to produce a newspaper, beamed in through television or telephone circuits, and when the only publications left on the news-stands will be magazines and paperbacks.

The future is in fact full of exciting possibilities for the visual arts. The time could come – the signs are already apparent – when the traditional over-dominance of the printed word in European culture will collapse. With ever-increasing exposure to visual stimuli and a heightening appreciation of them, the devaluation of pictures, moving or still, to low-grade pulp for the masses on the one hand and an art so esoteric that only an elect few can understand it on the other, can be reversed.

With their colour and humour, their ingenuity and style, and above all their rich variety of fantasy, the comic strips will have a place in the brave new world.

Picture Section

Film strips: Hollywood has often turned to the comic strips for material to fill the movie screens. Tillie the Toiler, Russ Westover's office-girl comic-strip heroine, has twice been filmed. Below, the silent version made in the twenties with Marion Davies, mistress of the newspaper tycoon William Randolph Hearst. Left, the 1942 Tillie, played by Kay Harris.
Bumstead saga: Chic Young's Blondie provided the basis for a long series of films during the forties, the golden age of the B-picture. They always filled the bottom-half of a double bill with predictable, harmless entertainment, with life in the Bumstead household faithfully translated to celluloid. Right, Arthur Lake and Penny Singleton in a typical situation.

Dynamic duo: more films made from comic-strip characters – Batman was first filmed in 1942 with Lewis Wilson playing the part, and Douglas Croft as Robin. At that time it was a fifteen-episode serial. In 1966 the new Batman, Adam West, already prominent on television, appeared in a cinema film (*below*) with assorted villains and Robin. He was glossier and sleeker than his 1942 predecessor (*left*). Harold Foster's Prince Valiant was turned into a widescreen adventure in 1954, with Robert Wagner (*right centre*) playing the title role. A popular serial of the late thirties and early forties was Flash Gordon (*bottom right*) played by Buster Crabbe, seen in a spot of futuristic bother with Carole Hughes. In 1966 Joseph Losey directed Monica Vitti (*bottom left*) as Modesty Blaise, Peter O'Donnell's fierce heroine.

Strip influence: some film-makers have shown the possibilities of cartoon strip effects in cinematic terms. An example is Orson Welles in his *Citizen Kane*, made in 1941 when its young director was a Hollywood prodigy. His use of angles for dramatic effect, overlapping dialogue, sudden cutting from one scene to another, inset effects with one scene superimposed on another, and the opening sequence with its advancing succession of shots of an old mansion, echoed the work of the comic-strip artist and created a new library of film clichés. The film-makers who have been most influenced by the strips are a group of young French directors. They include Alain Resnais, a strip collector, whose *L'Année Dernière à Marienbad* and *Muriel* are rich in strip effects, such as the whiting out of backgrounds to throw the foreground characters into relief, and Jean-Luc Godard, who has constructed a succession of films in the manner of the strip, with titles announcing each phase of the action. His *Alphaville* (*right*) features Eddie Constantine as a tough agent in a future that was recognizable as well as fantastic, photographed by Raoul Coutard in a deliberate Dick Tracy-ish flat, bleached-out manner. François Truffaut in *Fahrenheit 451*, his version of Ray Bradbury's story of a future where the printed word is banned, had wordless comic strips as the only reading matter. His hero, Oskar Werner, with Julie Christie, is looking at such a publication.

OST NO BILLS.

On stage: Krazy Kat was turned into a ballet in 1922 by Adolph Bolm who played the lead (*left*). The settings were reasonable representations of Herriman's style. Offissa Pupp and Ignatz appear in the other scene from the production. In 1956 a musical based on Li'l Abner opened for a long Broadway run (*left centre*). Peter Palmer played Capp's hero and Edith Adams was Daisy Mae. Two years later it was turned into a Hollywood musical. In 1966 Superman (*bottom left*) was also staged on Broadway, but unlike Li'l Abner its run was short.

Strips bring business: there is a big overlap into other enterprising fields. The advertisement is for the superheroes and other strip characters turned into fifteen-minute animated cartoons for television. Other uses for strip characters in profitable ancillary roles have been for merchandising all kinds of clothes, especially tee-shirts, children's play outfits, toys (the Bat-mobile was a favourite), table games, soft drinks and food items. Superman and Batman have given their names to hundreds of products, all paying royalties. Even pop songs can be derived from the strips. Early in 1967 the Royal Guardsmen had a hit with 'Snoopy *vs* the Red Baron'. A few weeks later they issued a sequel, 'Return of the Red Baron'. Meanwhile a Peanuts musical opened off Broadway to applause and favourable notices. And a Californian church has Charlie Brown cartoons on the pulpit. Says the minister: 'There is something of him in each of us.'

Public duty strips: as a propaganda medium the strips have an effectiveness of their own. In America every year a number of public service causes are given the backing of the industry. Below is a 1950 example of Dagwood and Blondie supporting a campaign for mental hygiene. On the right a trio of subway car cards featuring Steve Canyon were used a few years ago in a drive to make New Yorkers litter-conscious. Among the chief agencies for promoting this aspect of the work of the strip cartoon is the Newspaper Comics Council, a body set up by the industry in 1955.

STEVE CANYON
MILTON CANIFF
Daily and Sunday N.Y. MIRROR
NICE TO BE BACK IN NEW YORK...
LOCAL
Newspaper Comics Council
HMM...
MAYBE THIS IS THE WAY THEY LIKE IT!
LOCAL

TEACHER'S LESSON

A UNIVERSITY PLACE FOR MARION WHITE – IT SEEMED POSSIBLE, WITH EXTRA COACHING WILLINGLY OFFERED BY AUDREY ALLEN, HER SCIENCE TEACHER. IT EVEN SEEMED PROBABLE– UNTIL RECENTLY...

Miss Allen, are you sure two grammes of copper sulphate is right? It doesn't seem...
Questions, questions, questions! You'll never get anywhere like that, Marion!

I've been looking over your test results, Marion. You seem to have gone very wrong. We may have to reconsider entering you for the exam.
But I... yes, Miss Orley. I'm sorry.

It's not Marion's fault at all. I've muddled her because I've just been too tired to explain things properly...and now I've ruined her chances.
No, she's still got a chance– if you can pull yourself together. See the school doctor tomorrow. Perhaps he can help.

SO FIRST THING NEXT DAY...

You're in good health– organically. But your sleep sounds all wrong. Going to bed early won't help, you know, if you're not getting the right depth of sleep. Better have a cup of hot Horlicks every night. That'll help give you the proper sleep you need to deal with that all-day tiredness.

SOON SOUND HORLICKS SLEEP WAS RESTORING AUDREY'S NATURAL VITALITY

RESEARCH
LABORATORY
Marvellous! That's made everything much clearer. How did you get us into the research labs?
Just pestered them till they gave in!

A FEW MONTHS LATER

A Scholarship–even better than we expected! Congratulations, Marion.
THINKS
Thank you, Horlicks!
It was all Miss Allen really– thank you, Miss Allen.

IT'S DIFFICULT TO GIVE YOUR BEST TO ANY TASK WHEN YOU'RE TIRED AND RUN-DOWN. THEN, LIKE AUDREY, YOU CAN FAIL PEOPLE WHO RELY ON YOU. HORLICKS HELPED HER TO GET BACK ON FORM... IT COULD HELP YOU AND YOUR FAMILY TOO.

HORLICKS

CHILDREN? TRY CHOCOLATE HORLICKS!

Strip commercials: advertising has used strip cartoons for many years as a method of selling its client's products. In Britain one of the longest-lived campaigns using continuity strips was for the popular malted drink, Horlicks. From the early thirties until 1962 with a war-time interruption the J. Walter Thompson agency in London produced hundreds of these advertisements always following the rigid formula: problem, advice, solution, success. They became probably the most parodied advertisements in the history of British advertising. Another use comics can be put to in advertising is to employ familiar faces for making the sell. An example is the Continental Insurance advertisement by Doyle Dane Bernbach, New York which uses Superman in a testimonial capacity.

Pop cop: Chester Gould's great strip Dick Tracy with its solid, crisp shapes, has a magnetic attraction for Pop artists. Right, a collage called *Tricky Cad*, by Jess Collins, made up from disconnected frames from an assortment of Dick Tracy adventures.

Yell "help"
and watch how fast your
mild-mannered Continental
Insurance agent turns into
Superman.
Ordinarily, he's just a quiet guy in a dark suit who comes around once in a while to talk insurance.
Shy. Retiring. Not one of your pushy types.
But suddenly, emergency strikes.
Burglars in your bedroom. Garage fire bubbling the paint on your new Cadillac. Hurricane Zena heading straight for your chicken farm.
You call for help.
In a flash, he becomes the Man of Steel and flies to your side. To protect your rights, and fight your battles, and give you counsel as long as you need it.
Your Continental agent acts as your champion for one very good reason. You're his bread and butter.
He figures the more he helps you, the more *kinds* of insurance you'll buy from him.
And we figure the more we help him help you, the more of your insurance he'll place with us. (He has his choice of many companies, you know.)
That's why we handle his clients' claims intelligently, fairly, and with a minimum of red tape and delay. (This little gimmick is the thing that helped us get so big.)
If you think you might need the services of a Superman some day, get to know your mild-mannered Continental agent now.
He's listed in the Yellow Pages under Continental. (In some areas, under America Fore Loyalty Group.)
He wants your business.
How else is he going to pay for all those suits he keeps leaving in phone booths?
The Continental Insurance Companies
The Continental Insurance Co. · Firemen's of Newark
Seaboard Fire and Marine · National-Ben Franklin
Fidelity-Phenix · Fidelity and Casualty · Milwaukee Insurance
Niagara Fire · Commercial of Newark · The Yorkshire
Home Offices: 80 Maiden Lane, N.Y. 38, N.Y.;
10 Park Place, Newark 2, N.J.

TELEPHONE
©1964 NAT. PER. PUB. INC.

TRICKY CAD - - - - - CASE VII
—SLIPPING OUT! GOT IT! GHOST! IT!
OH?
LONG EMERGENCY, PLEASE.
M! N. O!
I'LL SAY I'LL ENJOY IT! WONDERING IF IT PROVES INCIDENTALLY SUFFICIENTLY EASILY THIS TIME TOMORROW.
RATHER READY!
WHINEMEAL—
FORTUNATELY YOU KNOW WHERE HER STORY IS STAYING OFF COURSE! I SUGGEST, SENOR CIRCULAR, JUST YOU TAKE HER IRONY!!
WE'RE FLYING EMPTY-ONE-WAY.
ABANDON FLIPS THE—??
IDENTIFY ANSWERING HUH? SPLIT—CAN YOU READ ME? HUH? —I WONDER— SH?
UH-UH— IS THAT THAT?
I KNOW WHAT THOSE MEAN.
R-RIP
RIP
AND— JUST—
(SNIFF, SNIFF) IT? ROPE?
REALLY, SOMEBODY, WHY? TUT-TUT! YOUR SENSE OF SOMETHING IN IT— TRUTH! OH-H-IT!
WHAT DO YOU MEAN?
HA, HA, HA, AH, IT! HA!
WE'LL RISK ONE SHOT.
?
MEAN AS WELL AS MAINLAND, THE RESPONSE STILL RAGES. LOCATED STABILITY— ABANDONED IN ITS POWER AHA, YES, A BASEMENT.
IT'S RISING— EVERY THANKS, IT'S RISING!
I NOT ONLY KNOW WHO PERFECTED MY MIRACULOUSLY MAKING MORE EVIDENCE TO PROVE BEGINNING, BUT—I MUST NOT CATCH NOBODY!
THREE LONGERS LATER ON THE COUNT OF THREE.
—APPARENTLY SEEMS ABSOLUTELY DEVOID OF TEMPORARILY—EXCEPT FOR THE UNDOUBTEDLY, MISS, AND COCKS'VE FLOWN AWAY—
I LOSE IT, GOD!
BUMP
ONE! FREED! STOP!
I'M HERE TO TAKE ONE MORE YESTERDAY
CR-RAK
TRICKY, OLD CAD, AS SOON AS WE'VE REGAINED OUR SIGNIFICANCE, SUPPOSE WE GO TOPSIDE AND LEAVE NO REMNANTS OF OUGHT STILL RAGING. MANANANANA

Pop explosion: Roy Lichtenstein's *Whaam!* was bought at the end of 1966 for the Tate Gallery in London. As an illustration of the influence of strips on painting it is a magnificent example. Lichtenstein has used the comic strip as his inspiration perhaps more than any other painter in the 'pop' *genre*. By analysing, enlarging, and simplifying the cartoonist's work he has been able to interpret the formalities of its design and show the rhythmic patterns imposed on the composition by the dots of the Benday screen. *Whaam!* is a large, almost overpowering painting. A reproduction little bigger than a real strip cartoon cannot possibly simulate the effect of the real canvas. It demonstrates some of the conventions of the strip with the skill of a connoisseur showing off the finer points of his collection. The words of narrative over the attacking aircraft have the mixture of quasi-technical language and litotes expected of fighter pilots. The impact in the next frame depicts the customary starburst with the visual onamatopoeia of the word W-H-A-A-M! superimposed, an impact that is both fatal and final. Lichtenstein is the observer and codifier of the comic strip who has discovered for us that within its apparently humble shape there lies an exhilarating array of magnificent design forms.

WHAAM!

JUDAS, MEANWHILE SEES JESUS CONDEMNED TO DEATH–HE REPENTS OF HIS BETRAYAL AND WANTS TO RETURN THE THIRTY PIECES OF SILVER...
I HAVE SINNED IN BETRAYING AN INNOCENT MAN!
WHAT'S THAT TO US?–THAT'S YOUR BUSINESS. YOU TOOK THE MONEY!

REMORSEFULLY, JUDAS THROWS DOWN THE MONEY BEFORE THEM IN THE TEMPLE
THERE, TAKE BACK THAT DIRTY MONEY, I CAN'T STAND HAVING IT!

WHAT WILL WE DO WITH THIS MONEY?
IT'S NOT LAWFUL TO PUT IT IN THE TEMPLE TREASURY!
LET'S BUY A CEMETERY TO BURY THE POOR!

CRAZED BY HIS AWFUL CRIME, JUDAS HANGS HIMSELF–A FIELD FOR BURIAL WAS BOUGHT WITH THE MONEY HE RETURNED THEREBY FULFILLING AN OLD TESTAMENT PROPHECY–"AND THEY TOOK THE THIRTY PIECES OF SILVER, THE PRICE OF HIM THAT WAS VALUED, WHOM THEY, OF THE CHILDREN OF ISRAEL DID VALUE–AND GAVE THEM FOR THE POTTER'S FIELD–JEREMIAH (ALSO SEE ZECHARIAH 11:12-13)

AS JESUS IS LED ALONG TO BE CRUCIFIED BY THE ROMAN SOLDIERS, HE IS REQUIRED TO CARRY HIS CROSS.
WITH ALL THE PUNISHMENT HE HAS ALREADY RECEIVED, HE CAN NEVER CARRY THAT CROSS ALONE!
HERE YOU, SIMON OF CYRENIA, YOU CARRY HIS CROSS!

EVEN IN HIS GREAT HOUR OF TRIAL, JESUS THINKS OF THE MULTITUDE, AS THEY WEEP FOR HIM....
MY SIGHTLESS CHILD HE CURED–GOD MUST SAVE HIM!
HE HEALED MY SON LAME FROM BIRTH!
DAUGHTERS OF JERUSALEM, WEEP NOT FOR ME, BUT FOR YOURSELVES AND FOR YOUR CHILDREN!

Matthew 27:3-10, 27:32, Mark 15:21, Luke 23:26-30, John 19:17

Picture-learning: no one is seriously proposing that a cartoon strip version of the Bible is going to replace the real thing, and the minority of educators who have deplored this treatment have missed the point. Research has shown that the visual memory, far from being a barrier to assimilation, can heighten awareness and consolidate learning processes. The Bible strip simplifies and visualizes the written word – children facing a blockage when they come to reading the text can be made familiar in advance with the action and moral of Biblical narrative. In fact, the Bible adapts to the medium with startling success, particularly the Old Testament, where the prophets perform like superheroes, driving back the Red Sea and blowing down the

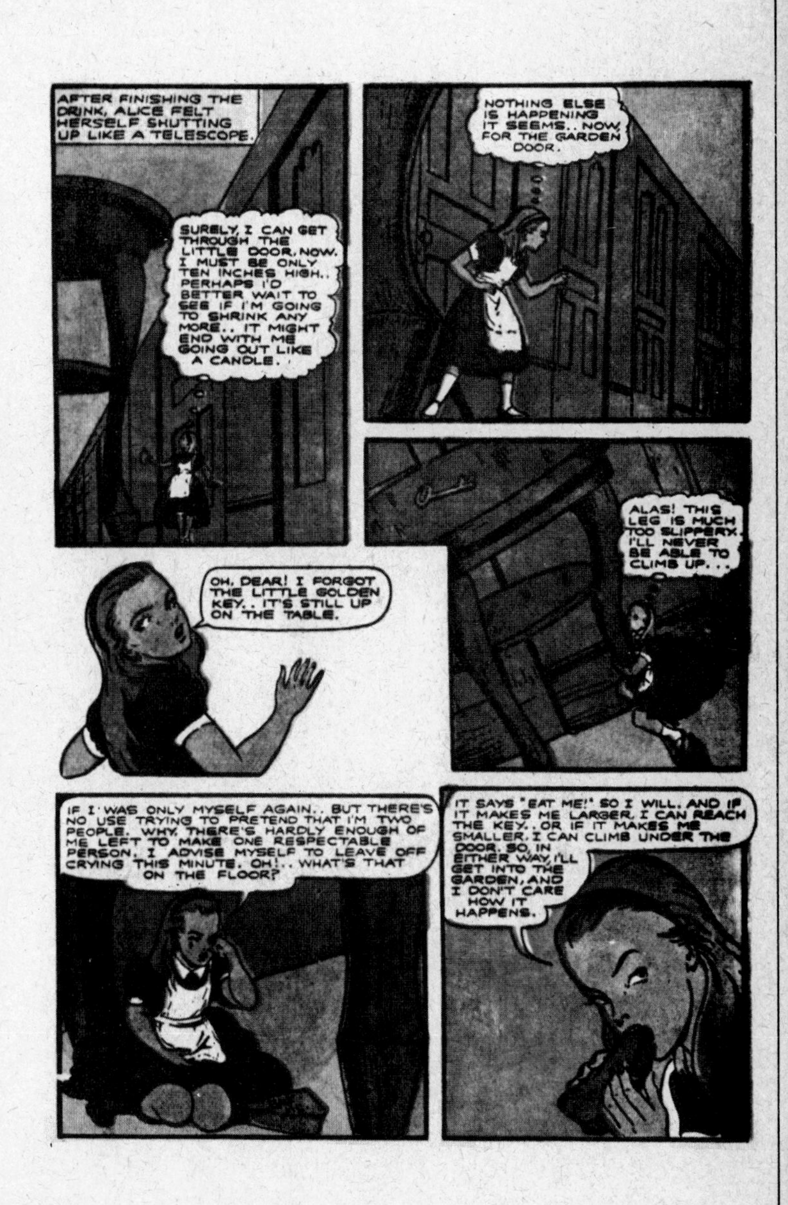

walls of Jericho. This example shows part of the treatment given to the death of Christ. Each page bears the reference to the place of origin in the Gospels. Classics Illustrated has made a success of comic-book versions of literary masterpieces. Two pages from *Alice in Wonderland* appear above. Again, the comic books are not intended as replacements of the originals. Children who might have been put off by grey type read the strips and have their appetites whetted. If an adaptation has succeeded the plot will retain its shape and the action will rivet the child who, if his curiosity is to be satisfied, will seek out the book itself and meet it as a friend rather than a cold stranger.

Strange bedfellows: *Evergreen*, an American literary and social review, has run with success the French comic strip for adults, Barbarella (*below*). An erotic fantasy, she is a kind of Jane for intellectuals. This is by no means the first strip cartoon to appear in what at first would seem unfamiliar media. The old-established humorous magazines such as *Punch* and the *New Yorker* often publish cartoons in strip form, although rarely featuring the same characters. An exception was Otto Soglow's Little King who appeared first in the *New Yorker* before moving to more popular pastures. Two examples on the right show the work of great humorous cartoonists on both sides of the Atlantic during the twenties, who from time to time used the strip form. At the top, a typical John Held cartoon of 1927 from the old *Life* magazine. Its title is 'A John Held Girl crossing her legs'. Below, a joke of the same period drawn by the British humorist, W. Heath Robinson. In recent times the cartoons of Jules Feiffer, originally only seen in a coterie New York paper, *The Village Voice*, has appeared in newspapers such as the *Observer* and the *Sunday Telegraph* which do not normally consider strip cartoons. Even in America, Feiffer's syndicated work, because of its unique use of the strip medium as a vehicle of social comment, is usually placed in a completely different section of the paper from the regular comic strips.

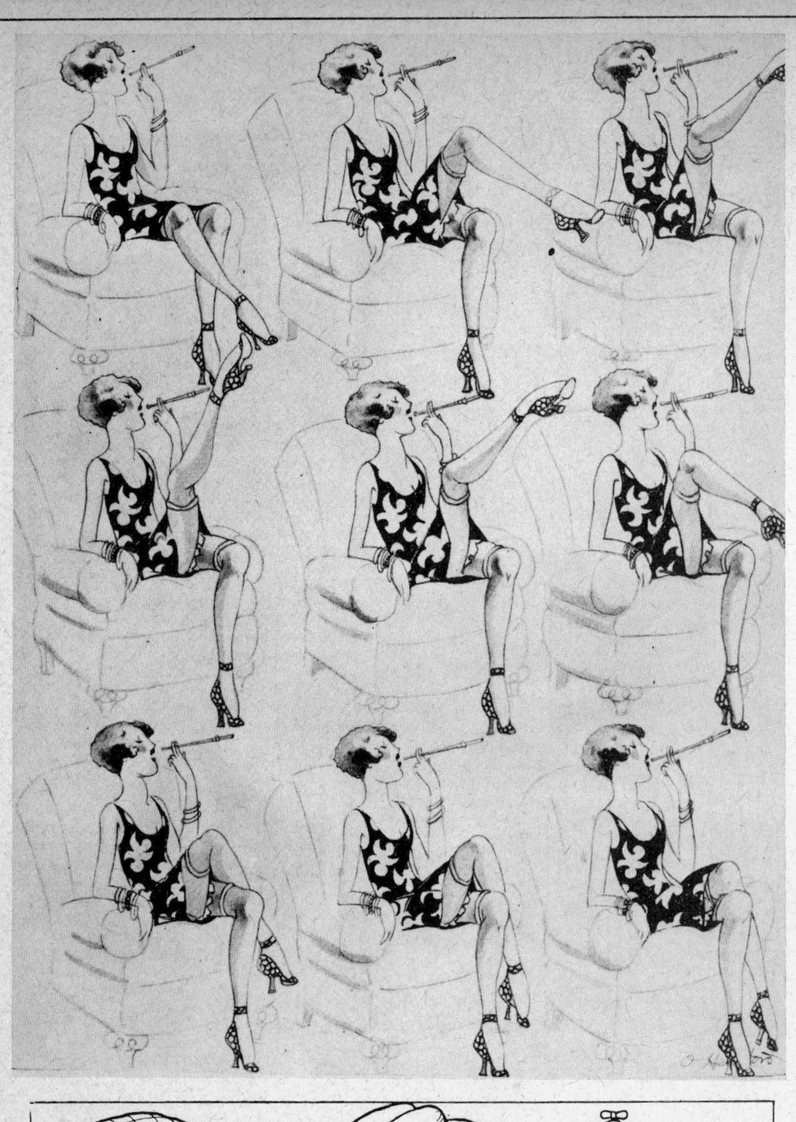

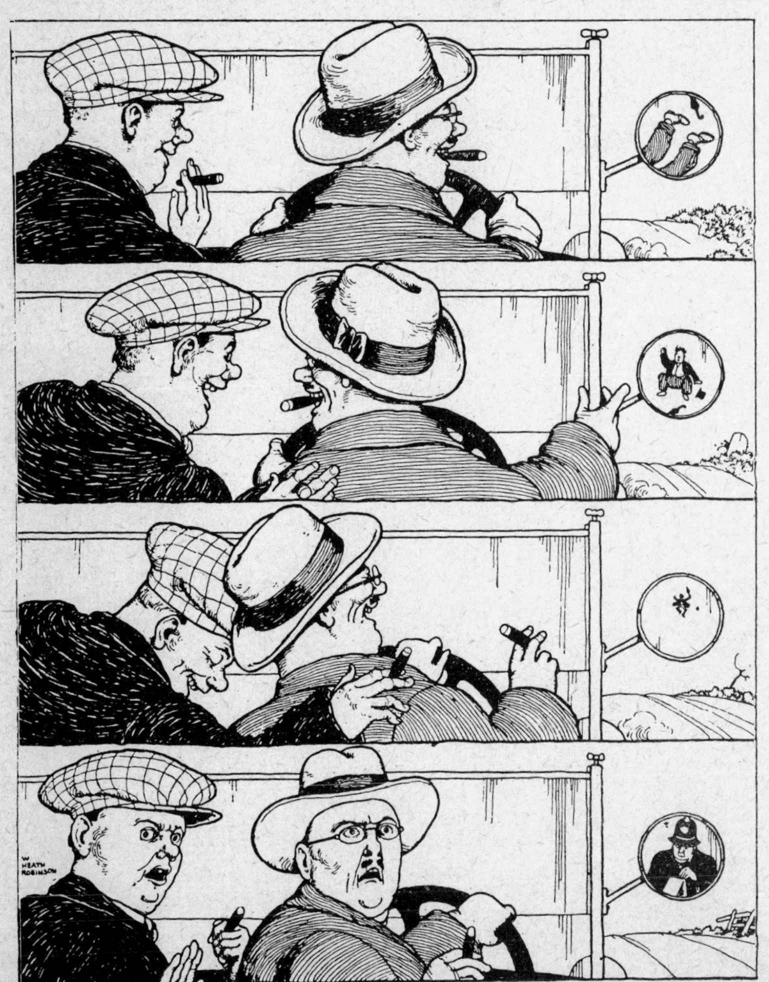
W. HEATH ROBINSON

I'VE QUIT GOING OUT.
WHAT IS THIS YOU'VE QUIT GOING OUT BIT? HOW CAN YOU QUIT GOING OUT?
1.
I'VE JUST QUIT, THAT'S ALL. IT'S DISHONEST AND I'M THROUGH. THE HELL WITH IT!
DISHONEST? WHAT DO YOU MEAN DISHONEST?
2.
ALRIGHT. A WEEK AGO I'M ASLEEP IN BED- TWO IN THE MORNING- AND THE PHONE RINGS- THE SEXIEST VOICE I'VE EVER HEARD!
3.
SHE SAYS HER NAME IS DARLENE AND SHE JUST FLEW IN FROM THE COAST AND SHE'S A FRIEND OF A FRIEND AND SHE HAS NO PLACE TO STAY AND CAN I PUT HER UP FOR THE NIGHT.
4.
ALRIGHT. I KNOW SOMETHING MUST BE WRONG - BUT I TELL HER TO COME OVER. AN HOUR LATER SHE ARRIVES. THE MOST BEAUTIFUL GIRL I HAVE EVER SEEN! AND IN SHE COMES WITH TWO BOTTLES OF BRANDY AND A DOZEN EGGS.
5.
SHE WHIPS UP THE MOST FABULOUS BREAKFAST I'VE EVER TASTED. WE SIT AND TALK FOR HOURS. SHE'S READ ALL THE BOOKS I'VE READ- LOVES ALL THE MUSIC I LOVE - THE BRIGHT-EST, MOST SEN-SITIVE GIRL I'VE EVER KNOWN!
6.
ALONG TOWARD DAWN WE BEGIN TO NUZZLE A LITTLE. I BUILD A FIRE. SUDDENLY WE'RE GRABBING EACH OTHER! WARM? YOU WOULDN'T BELIEVE IT! AFFECTIONATE? YOU HAVE NO CONCEPTION!
7.
IT WAS THE LOVELIEST, PUREST EXPERIENCE I EVER HOPE TO HAVE - A FANTASY COME TRUE- ME WITH THE MOST BEAUTIFUL, DELIGHTFUL GIRL IN THE WORLD- AND SHE LOVES ME! SHE LOVES ME!
8.
AND ALL THAT TIME DO YOU KNOW WHAT I WAS THINKING?
WHAT?
9.
"WAIT TILL I TELL THE FELLAS."
10.

Acknowledgements

Many people helped in the production of this book: among them artists, editors, collectors, researchers. We are deeply indebted to them all. Those who gave special assistance in America include the following: Milton Caniff, Walt Kelly, Alfred Andriola, Bob Dunn, Joe Musial; Mrs Avonne E. Keller of the Newspaper Comics Council; Sylvan Byck of King Features Syndicate; Chip Goodman and Stan Lee of Marvel Comics Group; officials of the New York Public Library and the New York Historical Society; Miss Evelyn Irons and Mrs Mildred Temple of the *Sunday Times* New York office and Miss Carla Davidson of American Heritage who carried out much research. In Britain the following people gave valuable advice and help: Bill Herbert and Julian Phipps, cartoon editors of the *Daily Mirror* and the *Daily Mail* group respectively; Colin Thomas of Fleetway Publications; Eric Fayne, editor of the *Collectors' Digest*; Ray Wergan of Transworld Feature Syndicate Inc; Alf Wallace of Odhams Press; Conrad Frost of the Thomson Organisation; Miss Doris Bryen who gave her usual excellent advice on picture research; Vicky Owens, general researcher; Harry Willock, Bob Smithers, Rick Goodale, John Aldridge and David Barnes who assisted in the design of the book; Miss Jackie Addison who did vast amounts of typing; Mrs Susan Raven who made valuable text suggestions and Miss Susanne Puddefoot who researched pictures, dug out caption information, read proofs and as wife of the writer of this book had to live with comics.

Illustration Acknowledgements

Picture Section 1
18 Radio Times Hulton Picture Library: Editions du Chene
19 British Museum 20 British Museum 21 Mansell Collection
22 Mansell Collection: Radio Times Hulton Picture Library
23 Radio Times Hulton Picture Library 24 British Museum: Leonardo drawing by Gracious Permission of Her Majesty the Queen 25 Penguin Books
26–32 British Museum 33 Mansell Collection 34–5 Hans Schmoller
36–41 British Museum

Comic Section 2
52 Author's collection 53–4 British Museum 55–7 Fleetway Publications Ltd
58 British Museum 59–63 Eric Fayne 64–8 Fleetway Publications Ltd
69 Eric Fayne 70–1 Fleetway Publications Ltd 72–3 Eric Fayne
74–83 Fleetway Publications Ltd 84 Odhams Press Ltd
85 Fleetway Publications Ltd 86 Century 21 Publishing Ltd (from TV Century 21) 87–8 Fleetway Publications Ltd 89 Odhams Press Ltd

Comic Section 3
102 Author's collection 103 New-York Historical Society, Bella Landauer Collection 104–10 New York Public Library 111 Permission given by Ray Winsor Moniz, grandson of Winsor McCay 112 Bell-McClure Syndicate
113–19 © King Features Syndicate Inc 1967 120 New York Public Library
121 News Syndicate Co Inc 122 *Chicago Tribune* 123 *Chicago Tribune*: Bell-McClure Syndicate 124 © King Features Syndicate Inc 1967
125 *Chicago Tribune* 126–7 © King Features Syndicate 1967
128–9 United Feature Syndicate 130–2 © King Features Syndicate 1967
133 AP Newsfeatures: News Syndicate Co Inc 134–5 News Syndicate Inc
136–7 Publishers Newspaper Syndicate and Milton Caniff 138–9 *Chicago Tribune* 140–1 News Syndicate Co Inc 142 Crockett Johnson: Skippy © King Features Syndicate 1967 143–4 © King Features Syndicate 1967
144 Bell-McClure Syndicate 145 The McNaught Syndicate Inc: © King Features Syndicate: Publishers Newspaper Syndicate: News Syndicate Co Inc
146 © King Features Syndicate 1967 147 National Periodical Publications Inc
148–9 Walt Kelly 150 Johnny Hart and Publishers Newspaper Syndicate: King Features Syndicate 151 United Features Syndicate

Comic Section 4
164 New-York Historical Society, Bella Landauer Collection
165–73 National Periodical Publications Inc 174–7 Marvel Comics Group
178–81 Will Eisner and Harvey Comics Inc 182–7 Marvel Comics Group

Comic Section 5
200 Associated Newspapers Ltd: Daily Mirror Ltd 201 Daily Mirror Newspapers Ltd 202–3 Associated Newspapers Ltd 204 Associated Newspapers Ltd: Beaverbrook Newspapers Ltd 205 Beaverbrook Newspapers Ltd, *Evening Standard* and Frank Dickens, Jim Holdaway, Peter O'Donnell, Harry Smith 206–11 Daily Mirror Newspapers Ltd 212–14 Associated Newspapers Ltd 215 King Features Syndicate 216–17 Associated Newspapers Ltd 218 Beaverbrook Newspapers Ltd, *Daily Express* and Peter Maddocks, Barry Appleby, John McClusky, Ian Fleming Estate, Harry Bishop, Sydney Jordan, Purnell and Sons Ltd

Picture Section 6
232–5 Museum of Modern Art, NY: Twentieth Century Fox: Culver
236–7 National Film Archive: Universal 238 Crawford Theatre Collection, Yale University Library: Friedman-Abeles Inc 239 United Features Syndicate: CBS Inc 240–1 Newspaper Comics Council 242 Horlicks Ltd, J. Walter Thompson Company Ltd 243 Continental Insurance, Doyle Dane Bernbach Inc: Los Angeles County Museum 244–5 Tate Gallery 246 M.C. Gaines Inc
247 *Classics Illustrated* 248 La Terrain Vague 249 Henry T. Rockwell: Collins Publishers

Index